# WAVE AFTER WAVE
## Sarah Ansbacher

CASA MOCHA BOOKS

This novel is dedicated to the memory of
Jeannette Schleimer, my beloved mother,
who encouraged my writing attempts from the beginning.
I wish you could have read this one.

# CHAPTER 1

**10 November 1938**
**Vienna, Austria**

The sound of breaking glass shattered the predawn quiet. Somewhere in the distance, shards cascaded onto the street to incongruous laughter.

'What was that?' Lilly reached across to her husband's side of the bed to find it empty, the covers flung back in haste. Her bare arms bristled against an unexpected rush of cold air. Salo stood beside the window, craning his neck to peer out.

Another smash. Louder and closer than before.

'Salo, what's happening?' Lilly said, her heart pounding.

'I'm not sure. It sounds like there's a crowd working their way along the street, smashing shop windows.'

Lilly leapt from the bed to join him. 'We should call the police.'

'It wouldn't surprise me if some of them are the police.'

'They aren't targeting shops at random, are they?'

Salo shook his head. 'I think they know exactly which ones to target.' An unfamiliar tension had crept into his calm, even tones.

A heavy thud against a shopfront caused Lilly to flinch. From the window of a nearby apartment, a woman screamed.

'What about our shop?' Lilly tried to control her rising panic.

At ground level, three floors below their apartment, was her father's leather goods and luggage shop, first established by her late grandfather and now managed by Salo.

'There is nothing we can do. We'll have to stay put until they've gone and pray they don't cause too much damage.'

'I wish we could leave this place!' Lilly retreated from the window, hugging herself.

'We will. Soon.'

'When? How much longer is it going to take?' she said. 'We've been trying for over six months already. So have Papa and Mama, and none of us is any closer to securing visas. There is not a single country we haven't tried. I don't mind where we go. I just want to get out!'

Salo placed a steadying hand on Lilly's shoulder. In the dim light, his dark eyes looked even more brooding than usual. 'So do I, my love. I wish I had the means to have already secured visas and travel passes for us all.'

Lilly let out a slow, shaky breath. She brushed a stray lock from his forehead and ran her fingers through his thick, black hair. 'I'm not angry with you. Just afraid and so sick of this situation.'

'I know. The past few months have been especially hard for you.' He placed his hand on her stomach.

'Vienna is no longer our home. We have no future here.'

'It won't be for much longer. Others have received visas, and we will too. Just a little more patience. We'll find a place where we'll be safe from these hooligans harassing us ... where we don't have to worry about anyone breaking the windows of our shop. We'll start over. A new life.' Lilly rested her head on his shoulder. 'Please don't despair. We mustn't give up hope.'

A van roared past their building. Salo returned to the window. 'Looks like the police have arrived.'

Lilly shielded herself behind Salo and looked out. The mob had advanced closer. In the glow of the overhead amber street lights, Lilly made out at least twelve youths swinging metal bars and axes. The police van stopped just short of them and three officers with swastika armbands exited. They all but ignored the youths, as if oblivious to their wanton trail of destruction. Instead, they crossed the road and forced their entry into an apartment building opposite.

'What on earth is going on?' Lilly said.

The mob had reached the clothing shop four doors away, continuing their vandalism unhindered. Two mannequins sailed out the door and came to rest on the road in a tangle of broken limbs.

From the building across the street, a wooden chair hurtled out of a first-floor window, cracking as it hit the pavement. Quilts and pillows followed. A cloud of feathers billowed in the wind like snow.

Minutes later, the officers led two men from the building, deaf to the pleas and cries of three women at the entrance.

At this sinister turn, Lilly looked to Salo for reassurance, but she found her fear reflected in his face.

'Let's try to outrun them,' he said. 'Quick!'

Lilly fumbled in her wardrobe and tugged a woollen grey dress from its hanger. An overcoat landed on her shoulders.

'No time!' Salo said, already wearing a coat over his baggy pyjamas, and a leather bag over his coat. Lilly shrugged her overcoat on top of her strappy nightdress.

In the hallway, they slipped their shoes onto their bare feet and wound their way down the stone staircase. They reached the bottom just as the sound of pounding feet came to a standstill outside their building. Salo motioned to Lilly. They crept backwards, one cautious step at a time. The shop's shutters clanged with what could only be blows from the men outside. Lilly's heart beat faster at the unrelenting reverberation. The padlock clattered to the ground, and the shutter squealed in protest, as the mob forced it open. A moment of silence, then a thunderous crash. A torrent of glass rained down. The mob whooped as they set about ransacking the shop and destroying the family's livelihood.

'We'll try to slip out when they move on,' Salo whispered.

At a powerful knock on the front door, they froze. The knocking continued, insistent, and the command that accompanied it was unmistakable: '*Juden raus! Juden raus!*' Jews out.

Salo grabbed her hand. They charged up the stairs two at a time to the first floor. 'Let's try Frau Graf,' he said, already knocking. 'She might help us.' They waited for their friendly neighbour to open her door. She had remained on good terms with Lilly and Salo even after the Anschluss, when the Nazis annexed Austria, even though she knew they were Jewish.

At ground level, the police could be heard above the crowd, ramming their way through the front entrance to hunt for Jews. Frau Graf still wasn't answering.

Lilly wondered whether the Blumenkranz family whose home was next along the corridor had already fled or found refuge.

'What about Frau Sauer?' Lilly said. Just the evening before, the older woman had come up to their apartment and asked to use their telephone. They raced up the stairs to the second floor and pounded on the door. No response.

The front door to the building was flung open.

Out of desperation, they tried the other doors, neighbours with whom they had little acquaintance. All remained closed. The occupants did not answer.

'*Juden raus! Juden raus!*' Footsteps stomped up the stairs, and a baton clinked and clanked against the wrought-iron railings. On the first floor, the men hammered on the Blumenkranz family's door.

A tumult of splintering wood, smashing crockery and screams rose through the stairwell.

By the third floor, Lilly and Salo had exhausted their options. The only one they hadn't tried was Frau Helga Wagner, their immediate neighbour. They didn't dare. Her stern husband was a member of the Nazi party, their seventeen-year-old son a Hitler youth, and their daughter's husband an eager new recruit in the SA who strutted around the neighbourhood in his uniform at every opportunity.

'We'll have to barricade ourselves in our apartment.' Salo fumbled with the key, struggling to insert it into the lock.

The Wagner's door opened a crack and Helga's face appeared, her white blonde hair pulled into her habitual tight bun that emphasised her stern features. She trapped them in a piercing glare and the hope Lilly had been clutching inside herself drained away. She felt only dread as she braced herself for the inevitable shout that would announce their presence to the men climbing the stairs. Instead, Helga put a finger to her lips and beckoned them into her home.

The baton struck the railings, resuming its journey to the second floor.

Lilly turned to Salo for an answer. His eyes widened with the same surprise she felt. He glanced from the stairs to their apartment, from Lilly to Helga, uncertain which way lay safety.

'Come!' Helga hissed.

She all but dragged them across her threshold, bolted the door, and drove them into a bedroom.

'The wardrobe.'

Lilly and Salo climbed in as instructed and pressed together in the tight space beneath a rack of clothes. Helga threw a pile of musty bed sheets on top of them.

'Be quiet and don't move.'

Helga shut the wardrobe and turned a key.

Lilly inhaled sharply, her chest heaving as she sought air. Salo reached for her and placed his tremulous arm around her shoulders.

'*Mizmor l'Dovid*,' he whispered into her ear, reciting the words of a psalm. 'The Lord is my shepherd; I shall not want.' His voice comforted her in the darkness. 'Though I walk through the valley of the shadow of death, I will fear no evil, for You are with me ...' Mid-verse, he fell silent.

From the recesses of the wardrobe, urgent knocking on Helga's door transmitted as a muffle. Lilly strained to hear the faint mumble of voices. Trickles of sweat rolled down her back, dampening the lining inside her heavy coat. Her leg cramped. She clenched her teeth against the pain, but remained still.

Was Helga setting up an elaborate trap, or was she actually shielding them? Her welcome, even as brusque as it had been, was distinctly out of character. Eight months ago, on the day of the Anschluss, Helga's husband had been the first on the street to hang a swastika flag out of their apartment window. And two days later, Helga had been a bystander to that humiliating incident – Lilly cringed to think of it.

She had been returning home from the bakery when she noticed a peculiar sight: a crowd clustered on the street outside their shop, roaring with laughter. Mocking, sinister laughter. She rose onto her toes, trying to see over the sea of heads. Without thinking, she edged her way towards the centre, where the sickening spectacle presented itself.

Four Nazi Brownshirts stood over five men in smart business suits on their hands and knees. They were scrubbing the pavement with small brushes and what appeared to be buckets of caustic lye. The victim of their efforts was white graffiti in protest of the Anschluss that had appeared the day before. Lilly's chest tightened as she understood that all of the men on the ground were Jewish. Then it registered that her beloved Salo was among them and she had to clamp her hand over her mouth to keep herself from crying his name. There too was her brother, Eugen. They'd been hauled out from the shop, respectable businessmen humiliated before their neighbours and customers. They kept their heads bent in concentration, their hands red-raw from the chemicals.

'Go faster, Jews!' said a Brownshirt whose belly bulged out of his uniform. 'Stop dawdling. Scrub harder!'

Salo glanced up for an instant, as if he sensed Lilly's presence. His eyes looked defeated to Lilly, as they focused sadly on her – and then darted to the side, warning her to leave.

The paunchy Brownshirt advanced on Salo, his boot a fraction away from Salo's face. 'It's not break time. Get back to work, you lazy Jew!'

In the blur of faces, Lilly spotted Helga's despicable son, Gunther, in his Hitler Youth uniform, head thrown back, mouth wide open, guffawing. Helga stood beside him, lips pursed, staring at Lilly.

Lilly inched her way out of the crowd, their jeers ringing in her ears and her face aflame.

She paced the apartment until her husband and brother returned. She fought tears as she rinsed and bandaged their burning hands. Salo's eyes remained downcast, his jaw tense. Eugen yelled in rage and declared their life in Vienna over. Two weeks later, when he left for Eretz Israel, British-controlled Mandatory Palestine, as part of a group organised by the pioneering youth movement, *Hechalutz*, Lilly discovered just how serious he'd been.

Salo and Lilly had begun making their own plans to emigrate, but Lily couldn't bear to leave her parents behind. Salo had agreed, despite the priority being given to younger people. Getting visas for the four of them was proving impossible. The British had imposed strict immigration quotas. The United States had placed their names on the waiting list for immigration, but had said they would not receive their visas until 1940 at the earliest. That was two years away. For the past six months, they had spent several hours of most days waiting in queues outside every single international embassy, in turn. They'd discovered that every other country had apparently tightened its immigration policies too.

In the seven months since she had last seen her brother, Eugen had settled on a kibbutz near the Sea of Galilee, adapting to life as a farmer. Meanwhile, Lilly and Salo found themselves hiding in the wardrobe of a Nazi, terrified for their safety.

Helga's apartment was eerily quiet. The sound of their breathing, the ticking of Salo's watch, loud in her ears. Seconds passed by like hours.

Then, footsteps. Across the wooden floor.

The door creaked open and Helga yanked away the sheets. 'You can come out now.'

First Salo, and then Lilly emerged, blinking against the light. She glanced past Helga, scanning the empty hallway beyond.

'You're safe for the meantime,' she said in answer to Lilly's unspoken question.

'Thank you,' Salo said. 'We really appreciate how you helped us. If not for you—'

Helga dismissed his gratitude with a wave of her hand. 'Now you must leave. My husband and son will be home in a short while and I can't risk them finding you here.'

'Of course,' Salo said.

Helga studied them. 'Best go back to your apartment and put on some proper clothes. Find somewhere else to stay, at least for the next few days. The SA may still come back later to arrest you.'

'Why are they making these arrests?' Salo asked.

'Vom Rath died of his wounds last night. Didn't you know?' Helga said.

Three days earlier, Herschel Grynszpan, a seventeen-year-old Jew living in France, had shot the Paris-based Nazi diplomat Ernst vom Rath as a protest against the expulsion of his parents from Germany. His family were among seventeen thousand Jews of Polish origin banished from Germany who were now languishing in no-man's-land, between the borders of Germany and Poland. Stuck outside in the rain and cold, without food or proper shelter, because Poland had refused them entry.

'Yes, I heard the news,' Salo said. 'But why attack us for the actions of one irresponsible youth? It has nothing to do with us. We wouldn't condone such behaviour; we don't! We have always been law-abiding citizens.'

'*Ach*, so naive.' Helga sniffed. 'Grynszpan is a Jew. The German government holds all of you Jews responsible for what he did. They're arresting the Jewish men, all the ones they can find. It's the excuse they needed.'

'If you believe we're all at fault, why did you help us?' Lilly asked.

'Because I don't believe that. I hate what is happening to our country and to my family.' Lilly thought she caught a glimpse of Helga's torment, nearly concealed by her hard expression. 'The Nazis have my husband, son, and son-in-law in thrall. It's like a cult. A poison that has blinded them. It has become impossible to have a rational discussion and I'm afraid to say too much. They are so brainwashed I doubt they'd hesitate to betray a member of their own family, not even me, as a traitor. Do you remember the morning the Brownshirts hauled your husband and brother from the shop for the *Reibpartie*?' She turned to Lilly.

Scrubbing party. Trust the Nazis to coin a ridiculous term for their humiliating ritual. 'As if I could forget.'

'I was in the crowd.'

'I know. I saw you.'

'My husband forced me to stand there alongside my son and watch. He wanted me to be seen supporting his colleagues. I was furious at this ... their cruelty. I felt guilty for standing by and watching your suffering.' Helga twisted her hands together. 'I was brought up a Christian and always got on with my Jewish neighbours. They were hard-working and friendly. We were respectful towards each other. I've never had a reason to dislike them. This is my own atonement and my own quiet rebellion.'

'Thank you for what you did.'

'Please don't mention a word to anyone, and don't take offence if I ignore you next time I see you.'

Lilly nodded and reached for the door handle.

'Wait!' Helga hurried to the console table where she scribbled a quick note in the margin of the week's *Der Stürmer* newspaper. Tearing off the scrap, she pressed it into Lilly's hands. 'This is my number. If I can help you further, please call me. If someone else answers, give your name as Frau Hoff and say that you need some clothes altered. No one will be suspicious – that is my work. I will know it is you and will call back with a time. We can meet in the entrance hall at the Nordbahnhof railway station. Wait for me there.'

'I didn't realise you were a seamstress. I also sew,' Lilly said.

'In another world, we might have been good friends.' Helga gave a wistful smile. 'My advice, leave the country as soon as you can. If I could leave, I would, but I am trapped in my circumstances.'

'We are trying. We are waiting for visas. Then we need to sell the shop and the apartment.'

'From what my husband says, they will confiscate your shop. It will be Aryanised. Perhaps your apartment too. My husband has his eye on it for my daughter and her husband. I could try to persuade him to make an offer before anyone else from the party takes it. His offer will be well below the market price, but at least you'll get something for it.'

'The apartment belongs to my parents. He'd need to speak to them.' Even as Lilly said the words, the notion that Helga's Nazi husband would talk to her father about the purchase of their apartment seemed absurd. Surreal.

'I wish there were more I could do.' She checked the hallway. 'It's clear. Be careful, and God be with you.'

Back in their own apartment, Lilly and Salo quickly dressed and stuffed a change of clothes each into a small bag. Lilly tried to telephone her parents.

'The line is engaged,' she said. 'I hope they are all right.'

'We'll just have to go straight there and find out. Hopefully, the trouble hasn't reached that far. Perhaps your father will drive us into the countryside and find a quiet place where we can stay for a while until the situation has calmed,' Salo said. 'One more thing. Fetch your jewellery and any other valuables. I'll hide them in case they ransack the apartment while we're away.'

Lilly brought her jewellery box, their silver candlesticks and Kiddush cup and brought them to Salo, who waited in the kitchen. 'Perhaps best not to take your ring either.'

She twisted off her wedding band and added it to her box.

'Watch me carefully,' he said.

Lilly knew that following the Anschluss, Salo had created a hiding space below the kitchen drawers, but she had never accessed it. He pulled out the bottom drawer, and using a butter knife, unscrewed a false panel at the base. Then he lifted the floorboards below to reveal a hollow where he placed the items.

'I want you to know ... Inside, there is also some emergency money and a percentage of the shop's takings from the past few months. Your father knows about it. Will you remember how to access it?'

'But Salo, we'll be together. You can open it when we get back.'

'We will. All the same, you should know how to open it. Just in case.' He replaced the floorboard and the false panel, and closed the drawer. He brushed himself down as he stood and took her hand. 'Let's go.'

# CHAPTER 2

The pavement was a sea of broken glass, strewn with the wreckage of ransacked shops. On any other morning, school children, shoppers, and the many people scurrying to work would have filled the streets. But on this overcast day, an unnatural stillness shrouded their neighbourhood of Leopoldstadt, the predominantly Jewish Second District of Vienna.

Lilly and Salo stepped around a suitcase that blocked their path, and, from the corner of her eye, Lilly caught sight of the devastation in their shop. The thugs had overturned the shop counter, ripped every display shelf from the wall, and sliced gashes through the fine leather suitcases. The cash register was nowhere to be seen.

'Don't stare or react,' Salo murmured. He put his hand on the small of her back to urge her onwards. 'Let's try to catch a tram and get away from here.' Usually, they enjoyed the twenty-minute walk across the neighbourhood to her parents' home. They liked the fresh air and the quality time together. But not today.

The grinding shards beneath their feet announced their presence, and Lilly felt conspicuous even though she wore a beret that hid her dark, wavy hair and Salo had pulled his fedora low over his eyes. They couldn't really hide that they were Jewish.

Salo focused straight ahead. 'Stay calm and keep walking.'

Their path was a trail of devastation. Once-elegant display windows appeared to have been gouged out of the sandstone buildings, looking like faces without eyes, blinded by the city's citizens, marred by mindless hate.

Ahead, past the next street crossing, a cluster of passengers waiting at the tram stop frantically waved their identification papers at a swastika-clad officer who examined each in turn, picked out an older man and dragged him to a waiting car. Lilly recognised him as a friend of her father by his distinct limp: the result of an injury sustained during the Great War, when he had served with distinction in the Austro-Hungarian Army.

Salo made a seamless about-turn to avoid the tram stop, and they detoured right into the next side street. Less than halfway down the block, he hesitated. Another gang was vandalising the fabric shop at the next corner. Bolts of pale blue silk and bridal lace unravelled out of the door and onto the pavement.

Lilly and Salo backtracked and picked up their pace.

'*Juden*!' a youth shouted. A battery of boots pounded the ground in their direction.

The couple broke into a run, Salo glancing at his wife nervously. At the junction with the main street, they darted across the road in front of an approaching tram, its bell ringing in warning. They reached the other side mere seconds before it crossed their path.

The trundling carriages offered them the briefest of covers. Salo tugged the handle of an apartment entrance, but the lock wouldn't yield. To the left, a porte-cochère that served two buildings opened to an inner courtyard. Out of desperation, they slipped through its archway and pressed themselves against the wall behind the column.

'Where did those dirty Jews go?' shouted a youth, as the menacing division rushed past.

'Who cares? Let's get back to work. The Brownshirts will track them down soon enough.'

Their trail of laughter faded into the distance.

Salo stepped forward from their hiding place and studied Lilly with a worried look. He beckoned to her. 'Are you all right?'

None of this was all right. These were the familiar streets of her once peaceful neighbourhood. She had grown up here. From the age of six, she had walked to school, played with friends, and shopped on these streets, never giving her safety a second thought. Now, a myriad of threats lurked around every corner. A strange tremor vibrated through Lilly's feet. Not from her shaking legs, she realised after a moment, but from the ground itself. She felt a force in her chest. The dull rush of an explosion in her ears.

'What was that?'

'I don't know.' Salo glanced from side to side. Then his eyes were drawn upwards to the clouds of smoke that wafted across the sky. From his wary expression, Lilly realised he suspected its source. So did she. It had to be a Jewish-owned building.

'Let's try another route,' he said. 'We must get to your parents.'

They hurried through the gate at the far end of the courtyard, which let them out on a parallel road. Salo shepherded Lilly on a zigzag route through the side streets of the Second District. An acrid tang hovered in the air and fire engine bells clanged from several directions.

Not far from Lilly's parents, near the entrance to a small synagogue, they encountered a blazing pyre. Like a scene from some demonic medieval rite, a gleeful crowd watched the undulating flames devour a pile of prayer books and Torah scrolls.

Lilly stared at the fire, unable to look away, until Salo pulled her hand and diverted around yet another corner.

'There's nothing we can do,' he said. 'Nothing.' His voice cracked.

They started running again and didn't stop until they reached her parents' apartment. The quiet residential street of her childhood was unaffected by the chaos on the other side of the neighbourhood.

Inside the foyer, Lilly dropped her head towards her knees, tried to breathe deeply, and pressed a stitch at her side. The black and white chequered tiles swam before her eyes.

'We're ... safe ... now,' said Salo, between breaths.

She leaned against Salo and he offered his arm for support as they climbed the stairs to the first floor. He rang the bell once and then let them in with his own key.

'*Gott sei Dank*!' Lilly's mother rushed to the door and drew them into a tight embrace. Lilly inhaled the comforting rose scent of her Mama's perfume. 'We've been so worried about you. Papa has been trying to reach you on the telephone for hours. There are terrible reports.' Mama stepped back and looked at her. 'You're so pale. What's wrong? Are you hurt?'

In the safe haven of her parents' home, Lilly suddenly felt light-headed. The full weight of their ordeal hit her. She couldn't even summon the energy to speak. Salo eased her onto the divan in the living room.

Lilly overheard him say, 'She's not been harmed. A fright though ... Perhaps sweet tea?'

Then her father's solid voice filled the room. '*Boruch Hashem*! I am so relieved to see you.' He leaned over to kiss her on the forehead, and Salo stood to hug his father-in-law.

Mama bustled in from the kitchen with a click of heels and a swish of her blue dress. She set the tray of refreshments on the coffee table. Salo began relating the story of how Helga had hidden them, and Mama started pouring cups of coffee and doling out homemade biscuits. She served them on the delicate china that she had used for as long as Lilly could remember: soft pink buds framed by a golden oval that itself was surrounded by a band of eggshell blue, and gold edging around the rim.

'Unbelievable!' Mama said, stirring three sugar cubes into the tea intended for Lilly. 'Out of all the neighbours, the Nazi's wife was the one who hid you.'

'I dread to think what might have happened otherwise,' Salo said.

Mama kneeled beside Lilly, bringing her soft hand to Lilly's cheek. 'Drink this. It will help.'

Lilly sat up and took the cup in her trembling hands, using both to hold it steady. The warm tea eased down her throat like a balm and she was comforted, just as she'd always felt better when Mama had made her sweet tea as a child.

'I suppose you haven't eaten.' Mama handed Lilly a biscuit. 'Have one. It will give you some energy, and the ginger in them will help too.' She offered a reassuring smile. Even today, she had taken care to paint her lips in a red that matched her manicure.

'There's something else I have to tell you,' Salo quieted his tone, attempting to soothe his father-in-law even before he shared the bad news. 'There was a mob ... ransacking the Jewish shops, smashing all the windows.'

'And what about our shop?' Papa leaned forward in his chair and straightened his jacket. Although he was semi-retired and mainly worked from home on the orders and accounts, he still wore a formal suit daily, complete with tie and a white handkerchief in his top pocket.

Salo shook his head. 'From what I saw as we rushed out of the building ... They almost gutted it. I'm sorry. I wish I could have stopped them, but I couldn't see a way.'

Papa looked past Salo, staring into the distance. He held one hand in the other to keep them both from shaking, and straightened his shoulders. Containing his dismay, he said, 'I'm glad you didn't. You aren't to blame for any of this.' He released his grip on his hands to pat Salo's shoulder. 'The most important thing is that you weren't hurt. Let's hope the situation calms down soon so we can clear up the mess and reopen.'

Salo paused. 'I wish I didn't have to say it, but that may not be possible. From what Helga said, the Nazi authorities will want to confiscate the shop and Aryanise it.'

Papa let out a troubled sigh. His late father had started that business from scratch. It was their livelihood. 'I had hoped we'd be able to sell the shop as an ongoing business to help us get a fresh start when we emigrate.' He shook his head, still trying to absorb the news. 'I heard some other terrible news. Apparently, they have set fire to several shuls, and even blown some up.' He removed his handkerchief, dabbed his forehead, and blew his nose. 'The Schiffschul has been left in a smouldering ruin.'

Just nine months earlier, Lilly and Salo had married in that synagogue.

'We heard the fire engines and saw … other fires.' Salo wiped his reddening eyes. 'Helga also advised us to leave Vienna for a short while. She says they are making mass arrests of Jewish men around the city. It's not safe to stay. I think that the four of us should take your car, and drive into the countryside to find secluded lodgings for a few days?'

'I think it's a good idea. Besides, I'm not sure we have an alternative,' Papa said. 'Let me just put some papers together and we'll go.'

'But what will we do about Tante Rebecca?' Mama and her sister were very close. 'When I spoke to her earlier, she told me that she and Hannah are holed up in their apartment, while the disturbances rage on the street outside. They are terrified. We can't just up and leave them here!'

Lilly spoke up. 'I don't think we have a choice, Mama. We can't all fit in the car, even if we squish together. It's too dangerous for Salo and Papa to remain in Vienna. They'll be arrested on sight.' Lilly thought for a moment. 'When we've found a safer place to stay, we can tell Tante Rebecca and Hannah where we are and maybe they can join us?'

Mama's lips trembled. 'How has it come to this? How have we become second-class citizens? Less than second-class citizens. We have no rights. Do you know that the other week, they hung a *Der Stürmer* poster outside the Wiener Opera House? "To be Jewish is to be criminal," it said. And now we're being hunted down like criminals. No, like animals.' She stood up and stacked the cups and plates on the tray. 'I'm sick and tired of this. We cannot go to the cinema, sit in a café, or walk in a park. Not even sit on a public bench, never mind do the shopping. Everywhere I go, I see signs in shop windows saying Jews aren't welcome. And last week, when I was buying milk, a stranger accosted me and shouted, "Go back to Palestine!" Eugen was right. Our life in Vienna is over. I wish we were already there with him.'

Papa put his arm around Mama, carefully avoiding the china. '*Meine Liebe*, I know, it's too much already. We'll only be gone for a few days and when we return, we'll redouble our efforts to get visas and we'll join Eugen.'

Less than ten minutes later, Lilly's parents had packed a bag and were ready to go. Mama had regained her composure. She had donned her fur-collared coat dress and matching hat, as if ready for a luxury weekend away, and paused at the hall mirror to touch up her lipstick.

They filed out of the apartment. Papa was locking the door when they heard a heavy stomp of boots cut through the foyer of the building, one floor below.

Salo was the first to realise what was coming. He placed his hand over his father-in-law's and turned the key to unlock the door again. 'Back inside!' Salo said. 'Back. Back.'

The family crept inside without so much as a shoe tap on the floor. Papa closed the door quietly too, but he wasn't quick enough. The force of the opposing weight on the other side of the door overwhelmed him. Four Nazi Brownshirts stormed into the apartment, reeking of alcohol.

'Going somewhere, Jew?' said one, fixing his bloodshot eyes on Lilly's father.

Papa took a step back, rendered speechless.

'We're here to make an official search for weapons,' he said. He appeared to be their ringleader and wore his lank, straw-like hair in a side parting. A pathetic imitation of his idol, the Führer.

'We don't have any weapons.' Mama's voice quavered.

'We'll be the judge of that,' a heavyset Brownshirt said. He raised his baton above Mama. She stooped and shielded her head. He swung the baton in a backward arc and hit the mirror. She swallowed a shriek.

The intruders shoved the family aside and took charge of the apartment. Crockery smashed in the kitchen, a mirror splintered in the bathroom, wardrobe doors slammed, and Lilly heard what she was sure were hangers clattering onto the parquet in her parents' bedroom.

In the living room, the ringleader and the heavyset Brownshirt set to work. They flung books across the room and hurled Mama's prized porcelain vases to the floor. The ringleader unsheathed a knife and sliced through the well-stuffed divan where Lilly had been lying just minutes before. Mama's eyes bulged, and she placed a hand over her mouth to help keep herself quiet. Lilly felt like she was standing outside of herself. It couldn't be real. Papa stood dazed, his head turning from right to left and back again in the living room, as they ransacked his beloved library.

'Out of my way, Jew!' The ringleader jabbed his hand into Papa's ribs. He was still holding the knife in his other hand.

Mama screamed.

Salo and Lilly stepped forward and each took Papa by an arm. 'Best stay out of their way,' she whispered. 'We'll clean up later.'

'What are you saying to him, Jew-whore?' the heavyset one said.

'Nothing. I—' The back of his hand struck her cheek with a sharp slap. A whimper escaped from her mouth.

'Get out of my sight!' The man raised his hand once more, and lunged towards Lilly with a roar.

She hunched over her body protectively, tucked her head to her chest, and covered her head with her hands. Salo stepped in front of Lilly to shield her. 'Please don't hurt my wife.' Even when addressing this beast of a man, her beloved Salo remained polite. But there was no appealing to his humanity.

The Brownshirt adopted a whiny voice. 'Please don't hurt my wife.' His nostrils flared, and he snarled, baring his teeth like a rabid dog. 'Jew-swine, don't tell me what to do!' He clenched a fist and aimed it at Salo's face. Salo staggered, lost his balance, and struck his head on the edge of the coffee table.

'Salo!' Lilly crouched beside him, fumbling in her pocket for her handkerchief, as blood gushed from his nose.

'I'll be fine,' he said. He gripped her hand and rose unsteadily to his feet.

The ringleader grabbed hold of Lilly by her shoulders. 'Out!' He propelled her towards the door.

'Please, leave her,' Mama said.

'You too,' the heavyset one said.

'Please,' Lilly said.

Deaf to her cries, the ringleader ejected Lilly from the apartment and forced her along the building corridor at a brisk pace. She half-slid, half-stumbled over her feet. Mama landed beside her, trying to stifle her sobs, and Lilly reached out to hold her mother, wanting to comfort them both.

'Get out! Downstairs. Now!' A sudden push from the heavy-set Brownshirt caught Lilly unaware. Too late, she realised the staircase was right behind her.

Lilly grabbed for the handrail, but it was out of reach. She tipped over the edge and for what seemed like an eternal second, her feet hovered in mid-air. Lilly's heart lurched in the face of the sharp drop. One foot found a tread. Arms flailing, she teetered, then connected with the railing. Terror sucked the breath from her lungs and she grabbed on. Still, she tumbled sideways, and everything spun into a blur. A final blow struck her side, and she slid down the stairs, winded and disorientated.

'Lilly, can you hear me?' Mama rushed down after Lilly, took her hand, and helped her sit up.

Another Brownshirt motioned for them to go. 'Outside,' he barked.

'Can you stand?' Mama said.

Lilly gave a low moan and allowed her mother to support her to a sitting position. She clutched her abdomen and wheezed.

'Move!'

With her mother's arm around her, Lilly hauled herself up, immediately doubled over, and then forced herself to remain standing. Holding onto each other, the two of them shuffled out of the building. Outside the neighbouring apartments stood wives, mothers and children. Their eyes, wide with dread, were fixed on an idling police van. Jewish men were being shoved inside. Some women were stunned into silence, others choked down anguished sobs. All were helpless to prevent the roundup of their loved ones.

'What will they do with us?'

'I don't know, *mein Schatz*,' Mama said. 'We have to stay strong. Stronger than we've ever been. Yes?'

Two Brownshirts marched out of the building with Lilly's father in tow, arms forced behind his back, yanked along by the heavyset one. Papa's face contorted in agony. 'Take care of each other. I love you,' he managed before they flung him into the vehicle, next to the rest. A few minutes later, their neighbour, Herr Weinberger, and his seventeen-year-old son, Ernst, were shoved into the van next to Papa.

Lilly turned her attention to the front door. Her stomach clenched with fear as she waited for the Brownshirts to bring out Salo. It felt like time had slowed. The packed police van drove off, its engine rumbling into the distance. But Salo still had not emerged. Lilly broke away from her mother, summoned her last reserves of energy, and scrambled up the stairs.

'Salo!' she shouted.

A sharp cramp brought Lilly to a standstill, holding on to the bannister. She breathed through the pain. And then tried to ignore the dampness between her legs and the trickle that followed. She clung to the railing and dragged herself the rest of the way.

The front door was ajar. Lilly inched her way into the wrecked apartment.

'Salo!' she screamed.

# CHAPTER 3

**3 September 1940**
**Vienna, Austria**

Lilly handled one item after another in her suitcase, double-checking that she had packed everything and that she wasn't forgetting anything else. She shut the lid, still unsure she had made the right decision. Was it more reckless to leave or to stay?

She circled her childhood bedroom, looked inside the wardrobe once more, scanned her bedside table, and opened the two drawers in the chest; the only ones that remained intact after the damage wrought by the Brownshirts.

This had been the bedroom of her youth, where she had once dreamed of a bright future with Salo, the home they would build together, the children they would raise together. Never could she have conceived of the turn their lives would take. Nearly two years had passed since that terror-filled day of the November Pogrom – *Kristallnacht* – when the Nazis had rounded up some six thousand Jews, and many hundreds more had been killed or disappeared. Distraught, traumatised, Lilly had remained at her parents' home. Not that she had had any choice. Helga's husband had seized their apartment for his own use without fear of recourse. Tante Rebecca and Hannah had moved in too, and there, sharing the room with her cousin, they comforted each other through their darkest hours.

Hannah, a year her junior, was more like a sister than a cousin. She and Lilly had grown up together. When Hannah was just five years old, her father had died of a sudden heart attack. From that time onwards, Lilly's family home was always open to Hannah and her mother. They had stayed over almost every Shabbos for years, though they always returned to their own place when the Sabbath was over. That changed after the November Pogrom, when the Brownshirts seized their apartment, confiscated their keys, and physically threw them out onto the street. Shaken, homeless, and near destitute, Tante Rebecca and Hannah fled to Lilly's parents' apartment for shelter. There they found Mama and Lilly – and devastation.

Chairs overturned, prayer books ripped to shreds, the floor blanketed in shattered china. Mama paced the room in a wild frenzy. Fear and panic had replaced her usual poise. Papa, her steadying anchor, was gone. Arrested, transported to a place unknown, with no assurance they would ever see him again. And as for Lilly ... She had tried to erase the memories, but they still haunted her. A vivid scar branded in her mind. It had taken the combined strength of Hannah, Tante Rebecca and Mama to wrench her away from her beloved's body. For a week, she lay in bed in a sedated haze, unable to speak.

Hannah became their rock. During those first days, when Mama waited at the police station to determine Papa's whereabouts, Hannah took charge. She sorted, she organised, she consoled.

Later, when the rest of the family was too afraid to leave the apartment, Hannah bleached her caramel hair a light shade of blonde, feigned confidence, and ventured out to shop for food.

On sleepless nights when Lilly paced the room, numb and broken, Hannah stayed up with her. When Lilly screamed out during recurring nightmares, Hannah was there to hold her and to reassure her.

Lilly was also Hannah's shoulder to cry on and her closest confidant, as she faced one disappointment after another.

In their lowest moments, they had clung to each other: in the aftermath of *Kristallnacht*; on the day war broke out and they feared for their fate; on the night they heard their neighbour had jumped from the roof and taken his own life. Facing deportation, he had tried to escape to Yugoslavia, only to be turned back when he reached the border. Lilly had then questioned whether her own life was still worth living. It was Hannah who hauled her from the depths and offered her a life preserver neither had expected.

Hannah had discovered a daring immigration plan for both of them, and charted a course for Lilly. Their separation was supposed to be brief. Subsequent delays and difficulties took their toll while Lilly waited for her turn to depart. It was a fraught, lonely time, when Lilly had too much opportunity to mull over her decision to leave, which gave rise to too many doubts. Now Lilly would finally follow Hannah and was looking forward to their reunion, despite her uncertainties.

Lilly opened her suitcase once more. Everything was there: the three new dresses she had sewn herself, her washbag, the leather-bound photo album her mother had given her as a gift. She hadn't yet dared look inside. Now, she opened it for the first time. On the first page, a family portrait taken on the occasion of her brother Eugen's bar mitzvah. How beautiful her mother looked in a fitted, long satin dress and how dapper her father in his tuxedo and bow tie. A picture from a family skiing trip to the Austrian Alps, together with Tante Rebecca and Hannah, when she was fourteen. Lilly with her best school friend, Serina, both aged sixteen and dressed in their school uniforms.

A wedding photograph.

Lilly stared at the young woman dressed in flowing silk. Her face radiated with love as she gazed at her new husband. It was like looking at a stranger. Lilly no longer recognised herself in that twenty-year-old bride. She belonged to another lifetime.

Despondency had replaced optimism, and Lilly felt far older than her twenty-three years.

Lilly snapped the album shut and buried it at the bottom of her case. She blinked back the sting in her eyes and crossed the room to the window. The sky was a cloudless blue and the early morning sun shone on the same tree-lined street where she, as a four-year-old, had held her parents' hands and squealed with delight when they had swung her in the air.

So many memories. This city. This neighbourhood. It was the only home she'd ever known. Her world wasn't large, but once it had been happy. Now they lived in a constant state of tension. Every knock at the door made their hearts miss a beat. Each time Lilly had to leave the apartment, she worried that she was taking her life in her hands.

Lilly and her family had first begun their attempts to leave Vienna more than two years earlier. She had continued Salo's efforts to get a visa, and stood in line together with hundreds of other equally desperate Jews, through the rain and snow of winter, and in the heat of summer without shade. They were willing to go somewhere, anywhere, that would have them.

At long last it was happening, but, thought Lilly, her departure wasn't supposed to be like this. On her own, leaving her parents behind. She felt no joy or excitement, just doubts and sorrow.

'Lilly, it's almost time.' Mama placed a shaky hand on her shoulder. Lilly turned from the window and faced her mother, taking in her sunken eyes, lined face, greying hair, the worn, patched dress. When had her elegant, vivacious mother aged so?

'I'll say goodbye to Papa.'

Lilly crept into her father's bedroom at the end of the corridor. He lay propped on two pillows, covered by a checked woollen blanket. His face remained expressionless and showed no acknowledgement of her presence. Papa had endured two months in Dachau concentration camp until the Nazis released him because he was over sixty, and he had never been the same since. He would not speak of what happened, but the haunted look in his eyes, the stoop in his shoulders, and his screaming nightmares testified to his suffering. In the months that followed, he had suffered two strokes, the second leaving him bedridden and unable to communicate.

'Papa,' Lilly said.

He continued to stare into the distance.

'I have to leave now.' She took his limp hand in hers and forced enthusiasm into her voice. 'Soon I'll see Eugen again. Isn't that wonderful?'

From his bedside table, she picked up the picture of her older brother in shorts and a short-sleeved shirt, a wide smile on his tanned face, an orchard behind him and a crate of oranges at his feet. She held it up to her father. 'I'll send Eugen your love.'

Lilly felt a featherlight squeeze against her fingers. From the corner of his eye, a tear escaped.

Lilly kissed his hand, then his forehead. 'I love you, Papa.'

She fled from the room and took several breaths to steady herself.

Mama and Tante Rebecca waited for her in the hallway. Lilly gathered her luggage and paused in front of the cracked mirror that divided her face in two. They'd never replaced it. She adjusted her red cloche hat and allowed herself to remember that Salo had always complimented her when she wore that hat. He said it suited her brown eyes and olive complexion. Next, she armoured herself with a dab of burgundy lipstick from the small nub left in her last tube. Another pair of eyes appeared beside her in her fractured reflection. 'Beautiful!' She could hear Salo's voice in her head. But the sad eyes were hers, both sets. There was no one else in the mirror.

A sudden knock made them all stiffen. Three knocks. Pause. Three knocks. Lilly relaxed and opened the door.

'Oh, thank goodness, I didn't miss you!' Helga scurried inside, lugging two large bags. She set one on the floor and unpacked the other on the console table. 'I got held up by a customer fussing about the hem of her skirt. She went on and on. I was afraid I wouldn't get here in time. I brought you a few more cans of food.'

'You are so kind,' Lilly said. 'I don't think I can fit much more in my bag.'

'Squeeze in whatever fits. You'll need it. Everything else is for your Mama and Tante Rebecca.'

Lilly crammed three more cans into her backpack, alongside several others and her mother's homemade Gugelhupf cake, and stuffed another four in her case.

'You should have enough groceries to last for a couple of weeks,' Helga said.

'I'm so grateful to you, as always,' Mama said.

Through all the hardships they had endured since the November Pogrom, Helga had proven to be a most unexpected source of help. The neighbour who had hidden Lilly and Salo in her wardrobe had come to their aid time and again.

'Have a safe journey and God be with you.' She drew Lilly into a hug. 'I'm sorry to see you go, but it's for the best. Your Mama will keep me updated on how you are getting on, and I promise I'll do my utmost to continue looking after your family.'

'Thank you, Helga,' she said. 'Thank you so much for everything.'

Helga opened the door a crack, made sure no one was watching, and slipped away.

'It's getting late,' her mother said. 'The taxi will be waiting.'

Tante Rebecca hugged and kissed her. 'Goodbye, my darling. Safe trip and I hope all goes well.' Tante Rebecca's tears were unchecked as she handed Lilly a sealed envelope. 'Send my love to Hannah. Take care of each other.'

'Look after yourself, too, and Mama.'

In the short taxi ride, neither spoke. Mama held Lilly's hand and every so often gave it a reassuring squeeze. There was nothing more to say. There was too much still to say.

On Wohlmut Strasse, hundreds of people streamed from all directions and converged outside the designated assembly point – a white stucco school building. The passengers, each with their permitted two small pieces of luggage and family members seeing them off, bid their loved ones tearful farewells.

Lilly and Mama stood and faced one another. 'I'm sorry, Mama. I wish I didn't have to leave you ...'

'Shhh.' Mama pressed a finger to Lilly's lips. 'You have nothing to apologise for. I couldn't wish for a better daughter. But you have to leave. I'll breathe easier once I know you're safe and away from here. Send Eugen and Allegra all our love. Hannah too. And please write as soon as you can.'

Mama placed her hands on Lilly's head and Lilly bowed as her mother blessed her, just as her parents had on every Shabbos for her entire life. She kissed Lilly on both cheeks. 'Make a new life for yourself. Don't look back.'

'I'll try.' Lilly's voice wavered. 'I love you, Mama.'

She hugged Lilly. 'I love you too, *mein Schatz*, very much.'

Lilly held onto Mama. She didn't want to let go. Her mother pulled away first. 'I shouldn't keep the taxi waiting.'

Lilly nodded. Her mother walked away, head bent, a discreet dab of her eyes with a handkerchief. The driver held open the passenger door. Mama turned and gave one last little wave before she climbed inside.

It wasn't too late, she realised. Lilly could change her mind and chase after Mama. As tempted as she was, she knew she wasn't going to do it. If she gave up this chance, there would be no other. To pay for this journey, she had sold almost everything she possessed.

Lilly raised her arm and waved back. The taxi drove away and turned the corner towards home. She stood alone on the pavement.

# CHAPTER 4

Lilly dragged her suitcase down a short flight of stairs into the gloomy school basement and edged her way through a throng of people. Georgian wired glass windows were high on the wall, just at pavement level outside. They allowed wisps of daylight to seep into the dank, concrete-floored space, enough to cast a dim glow.

She kept going until she reached the far corner, and then she shrank into its safety. Despite the warmth of the late summer day, the thick walls of the building resisted the sun's heat, and the basement air was frigid. Lilly hugged her Mama's coat dress against her, the elegant one with the fur collar that she had insisted Lilly take, right before they left for the taxi.

'You'll need it more than I will,' Mama had said. 'And you want to look smart when you travel.'

'It's still too warm for a coat and it will be even hotter when I arrive. I don't think I'll ever have a need for it.'

'You never know what may come in handy. It might get cold during the journey. Take the coat.'

Her mother had been right – as usual. Lilly self-consciously draped the coat over her shoulders, the delicate scent of Mama's perfume still lingering in the fabric. Then she lay down the sturdy leather case, a remnant from her father's shop, seated herself on top of it, and waited.

Surrounded by people, Lilly had never felt more alone. She knew no one. Men and women, young and old, rich and poor, traditional and secular, singles, couples, families with children, men with the shaven heads and haunted eyes that marked them as recent concentration camp internees. Jews. Refugees. Illegal immigrants. These were her fellow passengers. Together, they were about to embark on a perilous journey.

There was none of the excitement that usually preceded a trip. People spoke in low tones – if they spoke at all. The transport organisers had already warned them that there were no assurances that they would arrive safely at their intended destination, British-controlled Mandatory Palestine, the Promised Land. And even if they succeeded, there was no guarantee that the British would permit them to enter.

Lilly had planned to meet Hannah en route – her cousin would await her arrival along the way – but Lilly was no longer certain that would happen. So far, nothing had worked out as expected. Lilly drew up her knees and wrapped her arms around them. What if they didn't meet? Could she manage the fraught journey on her own? She was only there because of Hannah.

Since the Anschluss, Hannah and Tante Rebecca had also been trying to leave Vienna. Obstacles and heartache had beset each attempt. They had even obtained entry permits for England and would have left for those shores in September 1939 but then Britain closed its consulate in Vienna at the end of August 1939, in anticipation of the impending war (it broke out one week later). Hannah and Tante Rebecca had no way of picking up their visas. Daring Hannah had considered joining a group that was planning an escape across the border into Yugoslavia, but she backed out when their neighbour tragically killed himself after he had failed to escape via the same route. And then they'd heard other accounts of Jews being shot at the Yugoslavian border. Finally, in November 1939, Hannah learned of a new possibility of escape.

At the time, Lilly had noticed Hannah acting suspiciously over the course of a few days. She had left the apartment more than usual and had given only vague answers about where she was going. Lilly wondered whether her cousin had a secret new boyfriend and had been debating whether to ask her, when Hannah burst into their bedroom, flushed in the face. Lilly couldn't decide whether it was from guilt or excitement.

'We need to talk!' Hannah sat on her bed and tapped her foot until Lilly settled down on her own.

'I've found a way out,' she said.

'You're not thinking of escaping across the border again?' Lilly said.

'No, nothing like that. This is a proper emigration scheme.' She paused, making sure Lilly was listening to her. 'To Eretz Israel.'

Lilly, who had long since abandoned all thoughts of being able to leave, leaned in closer. 'Eretz Israel?'

Hannah's face softened into a gentle smile. 'Yes.'

'How?'

'They are organising a transport of Jews to sail by boat along the Danube to Romania, then by ship, through the Black Sea to the Mediterranean.'

'That's unbelievable.' Since the start of the war, it had become almost impossible to leave the country, especially as a Jew. 'And you said it is an official emigration scheme?'

'Yes! It's being organised by a man called Berthold Storfer through the Central Office of Jewish Emigration—'

'What?' Lilly jumped from the bed, the springs creaking with her movement. It sounded like it should be a helpful organisation, but Lilly had her doubts. In the summer after the Anschluss, a Nazi lackey named Adolf Eichmann had set up the office to supervise the emigration and expulsion of Jews from Vienna. 'Don't go. It's a trap.'

'I don't think so. They said they would give me an exit permit and documents to travel. Berthold Storfer, the organiser, is Jewish, and he's trying to help Jews leave Vienna.'

'Who is he? Do you know anything about this Berthold Storfer?'

For the first time, Hannah seemed less confident. 'I ... I'm not sure. He's a businessman, I think.'

'So it's not that you know him,' Lilly said. 'Do you know anyone who does?'

'No.'

Lilly paced. 'How do you know you can trust him? Who is to say he isn't a collaborator? What if they are planning to send everyone on this transport to a concentration camp like they did my father? And even if not, how can you be sure it's not fraudulent? There's a war on, for goodness' sake! You can't believe that they'll allow us to leave with the current restrictions.'

But Hannah was determined. 'You're right. I don't know for sure, but it seems legitimate. When I was in the office, many other people were also signing up for the transport. I recognised some from around the neighbourhood.'

'So that makes it all right then?'

'Do you have a better idea? I've exhausted every other option.' Hannah rose to face Lilly. 'Do you remember the threat Hitler made in his speech earlier this year? He said war would mean the annihilation of the Jewish race in Europe. And, look, now we're at war. Didn't we suffer enough with the November Pogrom?'

Lilly remained silent, her teeth toying with her lower lip.

'There is no other way to get out,' Hannah said. 'They have us trapped. With each passing day, we're in greater danger. Maybe I'm being ridiculous and melodramatic, but I am truly afraid. I don't think Hitler's words were empty threats. I believe there is worse to follow. I know this scheme is a risk, but it's one I'm willing to take. I have to do something.'

'Please don't, Hannah. I couldn't bear it if something were to happen to you.' Lilly put her head in her hands.

'The truth is ...' She spoke carefully. 'I signed up today.'

Lilly looked up, startled. 'How? I don't understand.' She caught her breath. 'Have you told your mama yet?'

'She was the one who persuaded me to do it. She said I should seize the chance. Right after the Anschluss, Mama hid some savings with her friend, Frau Schmidt. You remember her – she used to play bridge with Mama on Monday evenings. Frau Schmidt isn't Jewish, but she's a kind-hearted woman and a proud Austrian who detests the Nazis. So earlier this week, Mama got the money back from her and gave it to me to pay for my place.' Hannah sat down beside her. 'Lilly, I want you to come with me.'

'I ... I.' Hannah had caught Lilly off guard. Her mind raced with all the logical reasons for joining Hannah – and the reasons she couldn't. 'You know I can't leave my parents.' Her voice emerged as a whisper.

'Listen to me!' Hannah said, her voice urgent as she grasped Lilly's arm and looked her in the eye. 'I don't want to leave my mama, either. But we have no choice. We are in danger, and this is the only way. Your parents will give you their blessing.'

'I need to stay and help look after Papa,' Lilly said, but her voice lacked conviction and Hannah shook her head.

'My mama will be here to help. Please come with me.'

'I can't! I can't!' Lilly shifted her gaze down and balled her fists in frustration.

'Why not?'

How could she admit to Hannah what was keeping her in Vienna, despite the Nazis, despite everything? How could she make her understand? To go meant she would have to face the finality of her situation. And she still couldn't accept it. 'It would mean ... leaving ... Salo.'

It would mean she could no longer visit his grave. It would mean she could no longer talk to him, even if she could only hear his replies in her head.

'My beloved cousin.' Hannah hugged Lilly tight, as if trying to absorb her pain. 'Salo is gone.'

'But I can't abandon him here.'

'Staying here won't bring him back. But also, Lilly, if you could ask Salo, what do you think he'd say you should do?'

Lilly forced down the lump in her throat and looked Hannah in the face for a moment. 'He'd tell me to leave.'

'Yes, he would. This is your chance. You have to take it. If not for yourself, then do it for Salo.'

'Hannah, I'm scared.'

'So am I. But we'll be together. Let's take this chance to start a new life. We'll share an apartment. We'll find work, and then hopefully we'll save enough money to bring over your parents and my mama, too. Will you please think about it?'

Hannah made it sound possible. Lilly remained torn, but she managed a timid nod.

The next morning, when Hannah asked her if she'd reached a decision, Lilly replied she was still giving the matter further thought. She repeated the same answer every time Hannah asked. She wondered whether Hannah might tire of asking her, but she didn't. After three days, Hannah took a different approach; she raised the subject at supper, as soon as the whole family had sat down together.

'Hannah is right,' Mama said. 'You must take this opportunity. There is nothing for you here.'

'But how can I leave you and Papa?' Lilly looked across the room to her father. He sat in an armchair, wrapped in a blanket, staring ahead into the distance. Three months after Papa returned from Dachau, he had suffered that first stroke, paralysing his right side. Lilly and her mother had become his carers.

'I will look after him,' Mama said. 'I'll rest easier knowing that you're safe, and together with Hannah and Eugen.'

'And I will look after your mama,' said Tante Rebecca. 'Hannah, please check first thing tomorrow – we need you to reserve a spot for Lilly on the transport.'

Lilly opened her mouth to protest. 'But—'

'Lil-ly.'

She turned to stare at her father. She hadn't realised he was following the conversation.

He struggled to form his words. 'You ... m-must ... go.'

Mama nodded, her face etched with sadness. 'See, Lilly, even Papa agrees. If not for me, please listen to your papa.'

On a raw night in mid-December, shivering in icy rain, Tante Rebecca, Lilly and Mama bid a tearful farewell to Hannah at the station platform, beside the Reichsbrücke bridge, over the Danube, close to their home in the Second District. Hannah was to travel by train to Bratislava, Slovakia, where she would board a paddle boat and sail down the Danube. Despite Hannah's best efforts, the transport was full by the time she had inquired on Lilly's behalf. Hannah was leaving on her own.

She gave Lilly a final hug. 'They are supposed to be opening applications for the next transport any day now. Please keep checking and promise me you will sign up.'

'I will,' Lilly said, and she meant it.

'Promise?' Hannah was remembering Lilly's hesitations.

'I promise.'

'I'll be waiting for you.' Hannah took a deep breath and squared her shoulders as she boarded the train.

It was still frosty December when Lilly arrived with the first light at the Central Office for Jewish Emigration to register for the next convoy. A long queue had formed outside the grand Neo-Renaissance-style building; at least ninety people waited ahead of Lilly. It took no more than an hour for the line to double, and it continued to grow. Hundreds of desperate Viennese Jews grasping for a chance to leave their once beloved city.

They made for a conspicuous sight. Before long, two passing SA officers stopped to mock them. They found the sight of these once proud, now downtrodden, second-class citizens of Vienna a hilarity. One of the Brownshirts, whose prominent nose reminded Lilly of a bird's beak, accused a white-bearded Jewish man of obstructing his way and knocked off the old man's hat. The man bent to retrieve it and the Brownshirt aimed his foot at the man's behind. The elderly man collapsed on all fours. As he struggled to his feet, the second Brownshirt kicked him in the rear once more, and the two of them fell about laughing.

Lilly felt shame for the poor man. She wished she could run over and help him, but didn't dare. Instead, she stood as still as she could and kept her eyes on the ground. She detested herself for standing by and doing nothing. But she shrunk into herself anyway, as the two SA officers moved on down the line, still chuckling to themselves. The beak-nosed Brownshirt next picked on a handsome, well-built man in his twenties and ridiculed his ordinary-looking nose. The man stayed silent, his head lowered.

'Answer me when I speak to you, *Judenschwein*!' the Brownshirt said in a grating, nasal voice.

The man muttered a response.

'I didn't hear you. Speak up. What are you?'

'I am a *Judenschwein*.'

'Very good.' The man smiled at him, a cold, hard smile, and without hesitation, punched him in the face. The young man stifled a moan and clutched his nose to stem the gush of blood.

Lilly shut her eyes. A whimper escaped her throat. The sight brought her back to the gruesome day that destroyed her world.

'Shhh.' Someone took hold of her hand. Lilly opened her eyes again and found herself comforted by the gentle blue eyes of a grey-haired woman, her round figure swathed in muted grey wool. She had put herself at risk by moving back in the line to approach Lilly.

'Stay strong. Don't let them see you upset. Soon, we'll be out of here.'

Lilly nodded and regained her composure.

The woman patted Lilly's hand and moved to return to her place in line, her silk scarf with its vivid pattern of peacock feathers dancing over her shoulder as she made her way.

To Lilly's relief, the two SA men tired of their vicious entertainment and left. But the worry she had expressed to Hannah niggled.

What if this entire emigration plan was a trick? What if the officials didn't let them leave, but rounded them up instead? But what choice did she have? She knew she was no safer at home. Her father, taken from their street. Her Salo, killed in her parents' living room. She could so easily be next. Besides, she had to keep her word to Hannah – she'd promised her cousin that she would apply for the next transport. And so she was.

Resolute, Lilly shivered through the late morning and early afternoon, keeping to her place in line, and shuffling forward a few centimetres at a time, just like the people ahead of her. But when there were five people between her and the door, a man appeared from within the building and closed the main entrance.

'Come back tomorrow,' he said.

Lilly trudged home. She was disappointed, and numb from the cold. She would have liked to stop off on her way to warm up with a hot coffee, but she would not take the risk: they had barred Jews from entering coffeehouses.

The next morning, Lilly arrived even earlier at the Central Office for Jewish Emigration. This time, she'd armed herself with a vacuum flask of hot coffee and greater determination. Fifteen people had arrived before she had. She wondered whether they had spent the night there.

It was even colder than it had been the day before, and she was glad for her hot drink. Then snow began to fall. First, a dusting of flakes, but soon they were coming down thick and fast. Lilly turned up her collar and huddled into her coat. She watched the indent of her footsteps in the snow on the pavement as her place in the line advanced. Now there were only six people ahead of her.

'*Jude*!' said a grating voice.

Lilly looked up to find the beak-nosed Brownshirt right next to her, looming above.

'There's snow on my boots. Clean it off!'

At first, Lilly did not realise he meant her and she didn't move.

'What are you waiting for? I haven't got all day.' He pointed to his shoes, grabbed her by the scruff of her neck, and pushed her to the ground. Lilly cowered at his feet and silently wiped his boots with her gloved hands. Everyone in line witnessed her humiliation, but no one came to her defence. How could they have? The same way she had remained silent the day before when the Brownshirts attacked the elderly man and the younger man. The same way she couldn't protest when Salo and Eugen were on their hands and knees scrubbing the pavement ...

'Our life in Vienna is over!' Eugen had yelled. He had been right. So right. An unfamiliar rage burned inside Lilly. The Nazis were intent on crushing their spirits, stripping them of their dignity, rendering them helpless.

But she was not helpless. She could leave this place. She would.

When the Brownshirt yanked Lilly to her feet, she fixed her eyes on the snow-covered pavement, but she was shouting curses at him in her head.

'Well done.' He stroked her cheek with a leather-gloved hand and Lilly flinched. 'What a good *Mädchen*.'

Bastard. *Arschloch*.

Now she stared straight ahead, focused on the people before her. Nothing else. Just five more people to go. Four. Three.

'Two-thousand marks,' the administrator said.

Lilly gulped. 'Two-thousand marks?' Is that the price Hannah had paid? Why had it never occurred to Lilly to ask?

'That's the cost of the journey. If you can pay, you have a place. But we only have a limited amount, and as you see, demand is high. So if you want it, you need to sign up now and come back with the payment by noon tomorrow.'

Where would she find that kind of money? Her parents didn't have it, even if she had been willing to ask them for it. The shop was gone, their bank accounts frozen, and the family could only withdraw a pittance each month. Money had become a source of constant worry and they had to count every *Reichspfennig*. If not for the sale of the apartment to Helga's husband – well below the market price – and that small amount of money Salo had hidden, her parents would be destitute, and Lilly and her aunt and cousin along with them. The little money that they had left would have to sustain Mama and Papa and Tante Rebecca, for the foreseeable future.

Lilly had an idea. 'Could I please use your telephone?'

Lilly strode beneath the colonnade, hastened into the Nordbahnhof railway station, and stopped in her tracks. All at once, she was struck by the grandeur, loftiness – and the familiarity. Nearly two years had passed since she had last stood in this entrance hall.

She stepped haltingly across the polished white stone floor. With near reverence, she walked through the central nave, flanked by imposing marble columns. Lilly tilted her gaze upwards, tracing the Moorish-style arches. The swirling frescoes on the vaulted ceiling, with its gilded chandeliers. Nordbahnhof was every bit as palatial as she remembered it.

Lilly positioned herself at the far end of the hall, where she could observe the two sweeping staircases that ascended to the platforms. She leaned against a pillar, the cool stone against her back, and watched passengers travelling up and down the stairs. The low hum of their voices set off a forgotten rush of anticipation and reawakened her precious memories of this station. At eighteen, when Lilly first started going with Salo, she would often meet him here. Lost in the crowds, they found privacy. They would pretend they were saying goodbye before a train journey and could kiss without attracting attention. Their goodbyes were long. They missed many trains.

Their rendezvous point had been beside the railings that protected an imposing statue of the station's founder and financier. Rendered in white marble, the late Salomon Mayer Rothschild stood proud on his plinth, one foot forward, elegantly dressed in a buttoned waistcoat, long tailcoat, and requisite cravat. On one occasion, Salo had pointed up to the statue with a mischievous wink. 'Are you sure you wouldn't rather go out with that Salo, rather than with this penniless orphan here?'

'I'm very sure, Salomon.' Lilly said, addressing him by his full name, and she ran her hand through his thick waves. 'For a start, you've got better hair.'

Salo looked up at the balding man on the plinth and burst out laughing.

'Now, if we don't hurry, I'm going to miss my train,' she said. 'Shall we say goodbye?'

Lilly felt a sharp pang at the recollection. What she would give for one more long goodbye. One more kiss.

Not even the statue of Salomon Mayer Rothschild remained in the great hall. The Nazis had removed it after the annexation. They didn't want anyone remembering that the benefactor behind the magnificent station had been a very wealthy Jew

A light tap on the shoulder jolted Lilly out of her thoughts. Helga rested against a pillar facing away from Lilly. She reached back and, as if paying no attention to what she was doing, slipped a sealed brown envelope into Lilly's hand. Lilly felt the neat wad and stowed the envelope in her bag.

'How much did you get for it all?' Lilly whispered.

'Two thousand, three hundred,' Helga said. 'The ring is in there, though.'

'Thank you for doing this.'

Helga had rescued the box that Salo had hidden underneath the chest of drawers in their old apartment and sold every piece of Lilly's jewellery that had been in it. The gold necklace that was her parents present to her when she turned twelve, the string of pearls she'd inherited from her late grandmother, and the diamond drop earrings Salo had adorned her with on their wedding day. The only piece Lilly held onto was her wedding ring.

'I'm sorry you had to sell your precious things,' Helga said in a tight voice. In the months since they had become acquainted, Lilly had learned the woman's gruffness was a mask for her kindness.

'They were beautiful, but really, only things. What was most precious was already stolen from me a year ago.' She sighed. 'If the jewellery is the price I pay to get away from these ...' her voice wavered, and she scanned the station – Helga would understand what she couldn't bring herself to say aloud in public – 'then so be it.'

First one woman stood, then the other. With near imperceptible nods that acknowledged all they'd been through, they went their separate ways. Lilly hurried into a waiting taxi.

The car wove its way through the traffic-filled streets surrounding the station, then turned south onto Zirkusgasse, where the Türkischer Tempel once stood, the magnificent Turkish synagogue. Lilly had often attended Shabbos services there with her best friend, Serina, whose family was part of the Sefardi community. Lilly had considered it the most beautiful synagogue she'd ever seen. A wonder of the world, like its design inspiration, the Alhambra Palace in Granada, Spain.

Painted stucco and marble adorned the walls, arched windows welcomed the natural light, and, by night, dozens of golden hanging lanterns illuminated the interior. In an alcove at the front, which faced Jerusalem, the centrepiece shone: a golden-domed *aron hakodesh*, supported by marble pillars and framed with an intricate arch.

Seated beside Serina, her sister, Allegra, and their mother, Lilly would find herself transported by the haunting ethereal melodies, composed during Spain's Golden Age, sung to prayers first recited in ancient Israel. And as Lilly united her voice in harmony with the congregation and the chazzan, she would raise her eyes to the soaring hexagonal-domed roof that let shafts of sunlight enter the synagogue. The experience always held Lilly in awe.

The last time Lilly had entered the Turkish synagogue was in March 1938 for Serina's wedding. That evening, they had all basked in love: Eugen, her brother, who was seeing the bride's sister, Allegra; her cousin, Hannah, with Gerhard, the boyfriend she used to think was the *one*; Lilly and Salo, just married.

Less than two weeks later, the Anschluss changed everything. Almost immediately, Serina and her husband travelled to his relatives in England. Eugen and Allegra joined the *Hechalutz* group that left for Eretz Israel. Hannah's boyfriend moved to the United States with his family. And now, two years later. Salo was gone, Hannah was in transit, and Lilly was making her preparations to leave.

The once beautiful Türkischer Tempel lay in ruins, destroyed during the November Pogrom. As the taxi passed Zirkusgasse 22, a cat scampered over the pile of rubble: all that remained of the once breathtaking *aron hakodesh*, dome, arched windows, and lanterns inspired by the Alhambra.

It was in the original Alhambra Palace, almost four hundred and fifty years earlier, where King Ferdinand and Queen Isabella signed the Edict of Expulsion and sealed the fate of Spain's Jewish community. It seemed the spectral architects of the Inquisition had risen again, this time as Nazis, to torment the Jews under their rule.

Lilly's taxi reached the former Palais Albert Rothschild. Once, it had been home to a grandson of Salomon Mayer Rothschild – founder of the Nordbahnhof, whose statue had stood in the great hall where Lilly and Salo would meet. Like most Jewish-owned buildings, the Nazis had seized and Aryanised the Palais Albert Rothschild. Today, it housed the Central Office for Jewish Emigration, established by Adolf Eichmann, which Lilly hoped would provide her ticket out.

She stood in line, waiting for her turn once more, and gripped her bag, doing her best to ignore the jitters that had returned. When she reached the clerk, it was with relief and the deep breath of a final goodbye that she surrendered the money from the sale of her jewellery. Paperwork in her hands, her place on the transport secured, Lilly stepped back out into the cold and made her way home as quickly as she could manage without drawing attention to herself. Soon, she would be away from there and be glad for it.

'Soon' took far longer than expected. Fraught days of waiting became weeks, then months. In the meantime, her father suffered a second stroke, which left him bedridden and unable to speak. The doctors said it was only a matter of time. Lilly was loath to leave under these conditions. She nearly cancelled her place on the transport, but Mama and Tante Rebecca wouldn't hear of it, and insisted that she continue as planned.

Almost nine months later and here she was: part of the next convoy, sitting in the school's basement, racked by guilt, waiting for the arrival of the enigmatic Berthold Storfer, organiser of the convoy, representative of the Viennese Jewish community, with whom no one from said community seemed familiar, head of the committee for overseas transports. And answerable to the Nazi, Adolf Eichmann.

Lilly still couldn't be sure she wasn't in the middle of a conniving plot to betray them all, but was desperately gambling that the plan would save them. Would she end up stranded like Hannah, in an unfamiliar, uncomfortable place far from home?

Because nine months after Hannah's departure, she remained trapped in Bratislava.

# CHAPTER 5

**3 September 1940**
**Bratislava, Slovakia**

H annah was a bundle of nerves tied with a knot of guilt. At long last, she would reunite with Lilly.

Perhaps.

Then again, disaster seemed to follow Hannah like an unwanted companion. Bitter experience had taught her not to raise her expectations too high.

Hannah had left Vienna believing her journey would take three to four weeks: a train to Bratislava, a paddle boat down the Danube to the Black Sea port of Tulcea, Romania, and from there, a ship bound for Eretz Israel. But after nine months, she still hadn't left Bratislava. The unforeseen delays and trying conditions were taking a toll, though it hadn't all been bad.

When Hannah had said goodbye to her mama, Tante Amalia, and Lilly on the station platform, she begged her cousin to secure a place on the next transport. From the letters she'd received, Hannah knew Lilly had kept her promise. But what about Hannah's own promise? She had assured Lilly that they would stay together. The months since she'd left Vienna had taught her she couldn't guarantee her own future, let alone Lilly's.

On that dismal night in December 1939, pelted by icy rain, over-whelmed in the wake of parting from her mother and everything familiar, Hannah boarded a train, together with seventy strangers. All refugees, who had little else in common. The carriage smelled of wet wool and a forlorn mood hung thick in the air. Hannah slumped into the first available seat she found, halfway down the aisle. As the train pulled out of the station, she heard muted sobs accompanying the clickety-clack of the wheels on the track.

Hannah cracked the spine of her new book, a parting gift from Lilly: *Around the World in Eighty Days* by Jules Verne. Holding the leather-bound volume gave her a measure of comfort, but she couldn't concentrate on a single word.

Her eyes wandered from the woman with grey streaks in her auburn hair, who was sitting opposite and sniffling into a hand-kerchief, to the man in the grey homburg hat across the aisle who was staring at his hands. Three rows further along sat a woman of her own age in a carmine-red princess coat. The young woman hugged her rucksack close, and scanned the train compartment from end to end, and back again. Noticing Hannah, she made a point of turning up the corners of her mouth briefly. Her lips matched her coat. She beckoned to Hannah and patted the spare seat beside her, so Hannah stuffed Jules Verne into the rucksack and hauled her luggage down the aisle.

'I see you're travelling on your own, too. Would you like to sit with me? I'd be glad for some company.' She extended a slender hand. 'My name is Erika.'

'Lovely to meet you. I'm Hannah.'

'This feels strange, doesn't it?' she said, as soon as Hannah sat down. 'I wanted to leave Vienna for so long and now that I am, I wish I didn't have to.'

'Me too. Saying goodbye was harder than I expected.'

'Who did you leave behind?'

'My mother, aunt and uncle, and my cousin, Lilly, who is more like a sister to me. I'm hoping she'll follow and join me in a short while.'

'Has your father already left Vienna?'

'He died when I was five.'

'Oh.' Erika's cheeks coloured. 'I'm sorry.'

'It's all right. What about you? Do you still have family in Vienna?'

'My mother.' Erika hesitated. 'And my father. They arrested him in a round-up in October and sent him to Dachau. My mother won't leave without him, but she wanted me to go somewhere safer for the meantime. She's doing everything she can to get him released.'

'My uncle was arrested in the November Pogrom and held in Dachau. They released him after a couple of months.'

Erika's face brightened with a glimmer of hope. 'That's a relief to hear. Maybe my father will be released soon.'

Hannah didn't have the heart to tell Erika her uncle had come back a broken man. Nor did she have the energy to answer any more questions about the life she had left behind; instead, she feigned interest in the other passengers. Rebuffed, Erika stared out the window, focusing hard on the raindrops running down the pane, until her attention wavered. Then her gaze met Hannah's, and they smiled awkwardly at each other.

'Have you ever travelled overseas on your own before?' Erika asked, wanting to resume their conversation.

'Never.'

'Me neither. How old are you?'

'Twenty-one.'

'I turn twenty-one in a month.' Erika flicked a lock away from her face. She wore her shoulder-length brown hair in pin curls, styled like the actress Hedy Lamarr. 'What do you plan to do when we reach Eretz Israel?'

Hannah couldn't help fiddling with the brittle tips of her own peroxide-blonde hair while she shared her plan with her new friend. 'The first thing I need to do is find an apartment to share with my cousin Lilly, and then I'll need to get a job as fast as possible so I can pay the rent.'

'What do you do?'

'I used to work as a secretary for an architecture firm in Vienna until ...' Hannah shrugged. 'The usual story. The firm could no longer employ non-Aryans so they had to fire me. I'll probably have to look for a different kind of job to begin with since I can't speak much Hebrew and only basic English. Maybe I could work in a shop. What about you?'

'I had a similar experience.' She sympathised with a nod. 'I was studying to be a nurse until they expelled the Jewish students and wasn't able to finish my studies. But since then I've been volunteering at the Rothschild Hospital, and I've gained a great deal of experience. What I'd really love to do is continue my training. I've heard that there's an excellent school in Jerusalem, the Hadassah Nursing School.'

'That sounds like a wonderful plan,' Hannah said.

Erika beamed, displaying her dimples. She lowered her voice. 'Do you have a boyfriend?'

'Not at present.' Hannah squirmed in her seat. 'You?'

'I've been out a few times, but I never had a proper one. Maybe we'll find boyfriends on the way.' Erika looked hopeful.

'For the time being, I don't intend to look for one. Not until I'm settled in an apartment with my cousin and have a steady income.

I've been down that road already and I'd rather not make the same mistake twice.'

'Sounds as if you've had an upsetting experience.'

'You could say.'

'What happened?'

Hannah sighed. It wasn't that she minded opening up to Erika, but it came to her how much she missed Lilly, where there was no need for explanation. 'His name was Gerhard, and I was sure he was the one. He said he loved me and when we went out in town, he seemed so proud to have me by his side. We'd been seeing each other for a year and spoke about a future together. I was sure it was only a matter of time before he proposed. Then came the Anschluss and about two months later, with no warning, Gerhard announced he was moving to America with his family. He said he didn't want to leave me behind, but what choice did he have? He was twenty-six, not a child. Of course he had a choice, but back then, I didn't see it. Or maybe, I just didn't want to.' Hannah shook her head in disbelief to recall her naivete.

'Gerhard assured me it wouldn't be long until we were back together again. He knew my mother and I had applied for visas to the States – but it was such a long waiting list. Gerhard's family had some American relatives who helped them get their visas quicker. He promised me that once he arrived, he would do everything he could do to speed up our immigration process too. He said all the usual things, made all the typical promises. He said he'd miss me and he would write often. But weeks passed without a word. My mother and I should have tried to go elsewhere, but I realised that too late. I was waiting for Gerhard because I loved him and I believed him. I told myself there must be a good reason for his silence. Then, three months later, I received a letter from him saying he wanted to end our relationship. He thought it would be best for both of us, since

we didn't know when we would see each other again and he wished
me well.' Hannah threw up her hands. 'And that was it. He didn't
even mention trying to help with our visas.'

Erika winced, sucking air in through her teeth. 'You must have
been heartbroken.'

'Yes. I can't begin to tell you. I'm over him now, but I still feel
guilty. If only I hadn't waited. If only we'd started looking elsewhere
sooner. We immediately applied to all the other embassies as soon as
I got that letter, but we got nowhere. So my mother contacted my
uncle – my father's brother – who lives in England. He promised
to help, and he kept his word.' Hannah shut her eyes for a second
and exhaled. 'Last August, near the end of the month, the British
granted us entry permits and invited us to fetch our visas from their
consulate in Vienna. But when we got there, the gates were locked
and the staff were gone. The war was about to break out, so they
shut the consulate. There was no way to get our visas out of there. I
stood at the gates shouting and shouting in case anyone would hear
me. No one did. I'd have broken in to get them if that would have
worked.'

'How terrible!' Erika said. 'But it's not your fault, you do realise
that? You mustn't feel guilty. You didn't know how things would
turn out. I'm sure your mother doesn't hold you responsible.'

'She doesn't, but I feel awful that I've left her behind.'

'I'm in a similar situation. My family applied for permits to
America, and it was just about impossible for us, too. We then tried
...' she held up a hand and ticked them off her fingers. 'England,
Canada, Australia, New Zealand, Cuba, with no luck. Finally, we
got visas for Brazil. We had all the paperwork sorted and our tick-
ets were booked for the second week in September. And just ten
days before we were due to travel, it was war, and everything we'd
arranged fell through. And then the Nazis arrested my father, a

month later.' Erika patted Hannah's hand. 'It's not easy for any of us to leave our parents.'

'I'm so sorry for everything you've been through,' Hannah said.

'Perhaps our luck will change in the Promised Land.'

The train slowed and pulled into a deserted station. The flow of conversation ceased, and an unarticulated tension descended on the passengers. They had arrived in Bratislava.

Hannah and Erika joined the scramble of people disembarking the train. The station clock struck midnight just as Hannah stepped down onto the dark platform. The bitter cold shocked her at once.

A brawny man wearing a military cap, black uniform and knee-length boots was the only one waiting for them on the platform. A member of the Hlinka Guard, the Slovak fascist paramilitary unit, he stood with his legs astride and arms crossed, a formidable unwelcoming party. No sooner had they assembled than he started waving his arms and shouting incomprehensible orders at them in Slovak until they realised he was ordering them to follow him.

With no porters or any other help, the refugees carried their own luggage: backpacks and blankets were strapped to their backs, cases were in hand. Their footsteps clacked on the red-tiled floor of the modest concourse as the guard marched them through the station, down the steps, and back outside. The frigid air felt like needles on Hannah's skin.

On this bleak edge of the city, the streets were empty. The group passed rows of joyless apartment buildings.

'Where is he taking us?' Hannah said.

'Perhaps a hotel for the night, before we board the boat?' Erika said.

The intense cold coiled its way around Hannah. It penetrated her coat, seeped through the soles of her lace-up boots, numbed her face, and stung her fingers. She struggled to keep a grip on her suitcase.

They turned the corner onto a narrower road, hemmed in on both sides by the drab apartment blocks. Hannah lost her sense of time: they had been walking for five or ten minutes, but it felt like an hour, at least. She wanted to cry from the icy burn that permeated her hands and ears. How could an ice-cold wind burn so hot?

'I've n-never f-f-felt so cold in my life,' Erika said, her teeth chattering. 'I hope that, wherever we are going, there will be a hot drink, a bath, and a warm bed.'

The guard came to a stop outside an austere, five-storey building. Rows of windows spanned the flat facade. He ushered them up a low flight of stairs and into a bleak but well-heated foyer with greying walls and a stone-tiled floor. The warmth was a blessed relief, but the air hung heavy with the smell of stale cigarettes and body odour. Hannah's stomach churned. The guard directed the men to the basement and the women to the first floor. Upstairs, two more uniformed Hlinka men stood guard in the narrow hallway. The women streamed up the stairs and through a door on the right, Hannah and Erika among them. Until they reached the room's entrance. Erika's jaw dropped.

'*Um Gottes willen*!' Hannah said. 'This is where we are supposed to sleep?'

The room was already occupied. Women lay on torn, sagging mattresses packed close together with the occasional narrow aisle. There must have been seventy women. Yet the new arrivals were grabbing mattresses – in no better condition – from a pile next to the door.

'I suppose we ought to take one too,' Hannah said. Though it repulsed her to touch one of the stained mattresses, never mind sleep on it. All the same, they each took one and dragged them to a tiny square of empty space near the door.

'I'm going to search for the ladies' room,' Erika said. 'I'll be right back.'

She returned after half an hour, her face pulled in disgust.

'How are they?' Hannah asked.

'Long queues, two sinks and two showers to share between all of us. You don't want to imagine what they look like after one hundred women have used them.'

Hannah wrinkled her nose.

'It's awful. Don't even ask about the two toilets.' Erika shuddered. 'They're in such a state.'

'How are we going to stand it?'

'We'll have to. Somehow. At least it's only for the next day or two.'

'Don't be so sure,' a voice piped up.

The two of them turned to a long-limbed young woman with high cheekbones and wavy, chin-length brown hair, lying prone on the next mattress over, her head in a book and her eyes on Hannah and Erika.

'What do you mean?' Hannah asked.

'We arrived a week ago as a *Hechalutz* group from Prague and we still have no idea when we'll be leaving,' she said. 'But even before we left Prague, they started playing their tricks. Twice, they told us to come to the train station. We packed our bags, gathered with our group and said emotional goodbyes to our families. The Gestapo looked at us all and laughed. Then they said there was a delay and ordered everyone to go home. Then, just over a week ago, they called us back a third time. We stood on the platform, waiting in heavy snow, sure they'd send us home again. Imagine our surprise when they instructed us to board the train. It was supposed to be just a quick stop in Bratislava, but when we arrived there, Hlinka

guards brought us on to the Slobodarna. And when we're leaving
is anybody's guess.'

'What's Slobodarna?'

'That's the name of this hostel. It means liberty in Slovak. Ha ha!'
Her laugh rang hollow. 'Some liberty. They guard us twenty-four
hours a day. We're forbidden to leave the building and we're only
allowed out into the rear courtyard for short periods of exercise. At
first, we were sure our stay here would be brief. Then the guards
told us that winter had come early, and the Danube had frozen over.
For now, there's no real way to travel by boat down the river.'

'I wonder why they sent us here if they knew we can't travel any
further?' Erika said.

'I really couldn't tell you. I've begun to wonder whether the
entire scheme is a hoax.' The room plunged into darkness. She
groaned and shut her book. 'One good thing about your arrival: the
lights stayed on longer. Usually they go out by ten.' She wrapped
herself in a blanket and rolled over.

'Have we made a big mistake coming here?' Erika said in the
darkness. 'I wish I could go home.'

'So do I. But this is our only way out. We've come this far, we
can't turn back now. Besides, we wouldn't get very far with those
guards,' Hannah said.

'What do you think they're going to do to us?'

The silence lay heavy between them.

Hannah couldn't get comfortable. She couldn't stop thinking
about the possibility that her great escape was all a lie – and one
that would trap Lilly soon enough too. Her skin crawled thinking
about the mattress and the imaginary, or real, bugs that infested it.
She tried to ignore her need to use the facilities until she couldn't
anymore. Hannah gritted her teeth and fumbled her way in the
dark.

When she eased herself down to the mattress again, Erika propped herself up on one elbow. 'Have you slept at all?'

'Not a wink,' Hannah said.

'I can't sleep either.'

They kept each other company for the rest of the night, reminiscing about the lives they had left behind. At daybreak, their hundred roommates awoke. The room buzzed like a railway station. The young woman on the mattress beside them yawned, stretched, then turned to face them. 'How did you sleep?' She seemed softer than her prickly demeanour suggested the night before.

'We didn't,' Hannah replied.

'The first night is hard. You'll get used to it.'

'I doubt I ever could.'

'Somehow, you do. The tiredness overtakes you,' she said. 'I'm Janka, by the way.'

Hannah and Erika introduced themselves.

'I'm sorry I was abrupt last night. I was tired and fed up. Why don't you fetch your bowls and I'll take you to breakfast.'

On the ground floor, men and women from the various transport groups gathered in a stuffy communal room, the air clouded with cigarette smoke. Rows of rough wooden tables and benches lined the space.

'Good morning, Janka!' A dark-haired man in his mid-twenties waved at her from the other side of the room.

'Morning, Alexander!' She airily waved back.

Erika's eyes widened. 'Who is that?'

'Just my older brother, Alexander. Come, I'll introduce you.'

They wove their way between mingling groups to where Janka's brother stood in a cluster with several other young men. Straight-backed, he stood half a head taller than any of his companions. Janka greeted him with an affectionate hug, then gave another to a younger boy in a peak cap standing alongside him. He was almost as tall, though of a slighter build, and, Hannah noted, had the same long-lashed hazel eyes as Janka and her brother.

'Alexander, this is Hannah and Erika. They arrived with the transport from Vienna last night.'

He bowed his head in greeting. 'Nice to meet you both. And welcome to ... this,' he swept his arm in a semi-circle. 'Luxury, isn't it? Let's hope we won't be here much longer.'

'All we need is a boat,' said the boy in the cap.

'We are a committed and idealistic group. This is Isaak, by the way,' Alexander said, indicating the boy in the cap. 'He's also from Vienna originally.'

'Are you brothers?' Hannah said.

'Cousins.' Janka patted Isaak's shoulder. 'But he's more like our little brother.'

'Less of the little, if you please.' He winked. 'I'm taller than you and I'm nineteen.'

'You are? When was your birthday? How could we have missed that?'

'It was the day we arrived at the Slobodarna.'

'*Ach*! That explains it. But why didn't you remind us? I'm sorry anyway. We'll have a big party for your twentieth in Eretz to make up for it.'

He grinned. 'I'll hold you to that.'

Janka returned her attention to Hannah and Erika. 'Isaak lived with us and our parents for over a year. He'd escaped arrest by the Gestapo in Vienna and sneaked his way to Prague by smuggling on a train.'

'And then he joined our group for this journey,' Alexander said.

'Once we get to Eretz, I hope to reunite with my parents and brother,' Isaak said. 'They left from Vienna on a different transport over a week ago. I received a letter from them before we made our way to our own transport just before they left. By now, they must be at sea. Lucky them.'

Alexander waited patiently for his cousin to finish talking, but seemed eager to talk to them again. 'The rest of us are planning to join a kibbutz and become pioneers when we arrive in Eretz,' he said. 'What are your plans?'

'I'm hoping to work in nursing,' Erika said. 'But ... I might be interested in joining a kibbutz.'

This was the first Hannah had heard of it. She noticed Erika's huge brown eyes never left Alexander. His face was serious, but not unattractive. He held a certain charisma.

'You're a nurse?' he asked.

'Not quite.' She cast him a furtive glance. 'I still have to complete my studies and qualify. But I've also gained experience volunteering in the Jewish hospital in Vienna.'

'That's excellent. I'm sure it will be helpful to have an experienced, trainee nurse here.'

She smiled and was rewarded by a brief smile from him in return.

Alexander turned to Hannah. 'How about you?'

'I want to find work and an apartment to share with my cousin. She's trying to reserve a place on the next convoy.'

'Where are you planning to settle?' he persisted. 'Would you also consider a kibbutz?'

Hannah laughed. 'I don't think so. But I haven't given it too much thought yet. My priority is to get there first.'

'Yes, that is the most important thing.'

Janka shook her head in amusement and tapped her brother's arm. 'You'll have to continue the lecture later. We have to get breakfast before we miss our chance. We'll see you later.'

Hannah and Erika followed Janka, who stepped into the waiting line and started chatting with another woman from the Prague group.

'On second thoughts,' Erika whispered into Hannah's ear, 'Maybe staying here for a few days won't be so bad after all.'

'Which one?' Hannah asked.

'I'm still deciding.'

'It's Alexander, isn't it?'

Erika giggled. 'Perhaps.'


Janka was right about getting used to life at the Slobodarna. That night, Hannah covered the mattress with her coat, wrapped herself in her blanket, and let sheer exhaustion lead her into sleep. In the coming days, she adapted to the routine, the lack of privacy and crammed sleeping conditions in a stale, dusty room. She became used to the long queues for the washroom day and night and at mealtimes, and the guard's bellow announcing exercise time in the yard.

She also grew close with Janka and Erika. Janka, she discovered, shared her love of reading, and favourite writers: Franz Kafka, Heinrich Heine, Erich Maria Remarque – all authors recently banned by the Nazis. Hannah and Janka would swap books, first their own, then later those they borrowed from fellow bibliophiles in Janka's group, and discuss them for hours. Erica was warmhearted, and her general effervescence boosted Hannah's spirits. Somehow, Erika remained cheerful even under Slobodarna's conditions. Hannah suspected that her friend's secret crush on Alexander had something to do with it. It gave her something to look forward to each day, though their snatched conversations at mealtimes and passing encounters in the yard offered limited opportunities for a relationship.

Twice a day, the guards sent them out to exercise in the cramped, paved backyard, surrounded by high concrete walls. Hannah found it too cold to do much beyond shuffling around, as her hands and feet grew numb. Sometimes, the group from Prague would form a circle and dance the Hora. Erika liked to join them, especially if it meant she got to hold hands with Alexander, but Hannah looked on, shivering from the sidelines, unless Janka or Erika dragged her into the circle.

Every morning at the Slobodarna started with the same wish: Would that today be the day they heard news about their journey? Hannah and Erika had been in Bratislava for two weeks when news spread among the refugees and sent them into a tailspin of worry: their ship had sunk in a storm off the Black Sea. Their convoy was cancelled until further notice.

# CHAPTER 6

'Hannah, wake up. Let's go for breakfast.' Erika's voice echoed in the distance as if she was talking through a long tunnel. 'I know you're disappointed. We all are.' Her eyes closed, Hannah sensed Erika crouching beside her. 'But the news isn't as bad as we thought it was. Alexander says they haven't cancelled our transport, just postponed it until they can source a replacement ship. Don't despair. Please get up.'

'My ... head,' Hannah managed.

'What's wrong with your head?'

'Aches.'

Erika felt her forehead. '*Mein Gott!* You're burning with fever. Stay right where you are.'

Hannah must have drifted off, because the next thing she was aware of was a cold rag on her forehead and a cup to her lips. Sweet tea soothed her throat a few drops at a time. A buzzing sound hummed in her ears. She tried to swat away what she was sure were insects, but the buzz continued until she fell asleep once more.

More time passed, but Hannah had no sense of it. Then helping hands lifted her to her feet. Supported on both sides, she walked until she found herself standing on the rain-soaked pavement, in front of her old home, possessions strewn across the street, including a smashed photograph of her late father.

'Mama!' she cried.

'Shhh. It's all right.' It wasn't her mother's voice.

Hannah became aware that she was in a strange washroom. She shivered under a shower of cold water.

'Lilly?' she said.

'It's Erika. Janka is here too.'

Erika. Janka. She recognised those names.

'What is this place?' She was walking again. Such a distance. 'This isn't my home.'

'No, you're in the Slobodarna hostel.'

'Where ...' The words wouldn't form. It was an effort to speak.

They lay her down. She was so tired. She needed to sleep.

Darkness. Her throat was dry. The warm tea was welcome relief. Daylight.

'Hannah, you have a letter from Vienna.'

A letter.

Gerhard wanted to break up with her. She would never see him again.

'I'll never find someone to love me.'

'Don't cry, Hannah.' A woman stroked her cheek. 'You'll find someone who will love you.'

Drifting. Water. Drifting. Tea.

In the darkness, she shivered.

Footsteps. They were coming up the stairs.

'Don't hurt them!' Hannah said.

'It's all right, I'm here.'

'Is that Lilly?'

'It's Erika.'

Heat. A synagogue on fire. She was burning. Hannah tossed from side to side. She couldn't escape.

'Mama! Lilly!'

A hand squeezed hers.

Sleep. She sank into a restful sleep.


Hannah awoke. Daylight streamed in through the window. She was in a bed, in a poky, unfamiliar room, with three strangers. Erika was asleep on a hard wooden chair beside her. But where was she?

Erika changed position and stretched, when she noticed Hannah and sprang to her feet. 'You're awake.' Her face lit up with relief.

'Where am I?'

'You're in the infirmary of the Slobodarna. You were burning up and quite ill for a couple of days. You had us worried.' She pressed her hand to Hannah's forehead. 'I'm glad to see you awake and your fever seems to have broken. You're not the only one who's been unwell. This fever has been going around. Several others came down with the same symptoms.'

'I've been ill for two days?' Hannah was stunned to realise she had lost her sense of time and that she had been unaware of the activity happening around her. Then it came to her in snatches: the reassuring voice, the drinks that soothed her parched throat, the comforting hand in hers. 'And you looked after me for all that time?'

Erika gave a little nod. 'I put my nursing skills to use.' Hannah caught a fleeting expression of pride and saw a more serious side to her fun-loving friend. The woman was passionate about her chosen vocation and eager to serve. 'How are you feeling?'

Hannah tried to sit up, but found herself grabbing for the bed-frame. 'Dizzy,' she said.

Now Erika bustled about her ward like the nurse she would be one day, popping a thermometer into Hannah's mouth, opening the window for some fresh air. 'You need to build up your strength again. I'll fetch you something to eat.'

Voices drifted up from the backyard. It was exercise time. Hannah heard the Prague group singing in Hebrew as they danced the Hora. She felt the weakness in her limbs and wondered how long it would be before she was strong enough to walk.

Erika returned with a bowl of hot soup. She set it down on the wooden chair beside the bed and checked Hannah's temperature. Satisfied, she gently took Hannah by her shoulders to prop her against two rolled-up blankets and make her more comfortable. Another moment and Hannah had the bowl of soup and a spoon in her hands. She breathed deeply and had the sense that healing was in that bowl. The soup was thick, rich in flavour, and full of vegetables. Not like the usual watery soup served at the hostel.

'Wherever does this come from?' Hannah marvelled.

'A kind woman from the Bratislava Jewish community called Gisi Fleischmann brought us a cauldron of homemade soup,' Erika said. 'And I have something else that might make you feel a bit better.' She waved a letter in the air. 'From Vienna.'

Hannah spotted the familiar handwriting and felt a flutter of excitement. Erika took Hannah's empty bowl and handed her the letter. Hannah ripped open the envelope at once.

*Liebe Hannah,*

*I've kept my promise. Now waiting for further news. Will update when I can. I look forward to seeing you again. I will write you a proper letter soon, but I wanted to let you know as soon as possible and don't want to miss the post collection. I hope you are keeping well. Your mama and mine send their love.*

*Lilly*

Hannah understood the reason for her obscure message. They were under strict instructions not to write about their destination. She folded the letter with a smile.

'Good news?' Erika said.

'Very.' She beamed. 'It's from my cousin Lilly. She has a place on the next transport.'

'That's wonderful! I'm so happy for you. And after hearing so much about Lilly, I can't wait to meet her.'

'This means our journey to Eretz will still happen, doesn't it?'

'Yes, of course it will.' Erika wagged a finger at her. 'Which is why you must build up your strength and recover. The Prague group has also started Hebrew lessons. We should join them as soon as you feel up to it.'


In mid-January, all the refugees were called to the communal room for an address by Berthold Storfer, the man responsible for the transport. Their shared sense of excitement was short-lived, however.

'You will leave here soon,' Herr Storfer said in a confident voice. He stood before them in a three-piece suit, his white hair and dark moustache neatly groomed. His demeanour was less reassuring. He fiddled with his tie and his walking stick. His eyes were bloodshot and sunken in their sockets. 'We must remain true to ourselves and Vienna.'

He was met with laughter. 'What a load of *scheisse*!' shouted one man, stunning Berthold Storfer into silence. 'We're from Prague. What do we care about Vienna?'

The others from Prague murmured in agreement.

'Excuse me, Mr Storfer.' Isaak raised his hand. 'I was born and raised in Vienna, but the city of my birth failed me. I had to escape to Prague to avoid arrest. My father wasn't as lucky. He spent time in Dachau. Vienna has betrayed us, leaving us stranded as refugees for weeks in this broken-down, smelly hostel. There's nothing left for us to stay true to!'

Berthold Storfer cleared his throat. 'I have arranged—'

But Alexander, Janka and the rest of the Prague group were busy applauding Isaak. Many of the Viennese, including Hannah and Erika, joined in. Whatever Mr. Storfer had been saying disappeared under their rallying cries. Finally, a chance to air their discontent.

Mr Storfer waved his arms, trying to restore order, but with little success. He resorted to thumping his stick against the floor. The room fell silent. 'I have arranged for another ship to take you to British-controlled Mandatory Palestine. It has already departed from Greece and is due to arrive here any day now. You will leave here within ten days,' he said. 'Please be patient for just a short while longer.'

Herr Storfer abruptly hastened out the door before anyone had the chance to heckle him – or ask any questions. The internees converged in groups to discuss and dissect his speech. Hannah and Erika moved towards Janka, her brother, and their other friends.

'Storfer's just buying time,' Isaak said. 'I'm sure of it.'

'Exactly that!' Alexander said.

'You don't think he's sent a ship?' Janka said.

'I'll believe it when I see it.'

'Is it true that he's collaborating with the Nazis?' Erika asked.

'Well ...' Alexander tilted his head from side to side like a balance scale. 'He works with Adolf Eichmann. But he wouldn't be able to organise these transports without their permission. He probably doesn't have much choice in the matter. Does that make him a collaborator? I'm still deciding.'

'Does it bother you?'

'The way I view it, that's his problem, not mine. As long as he provides us with a ship. I just want to get out of here.'

Herr Storfer's ten days passed. Then two weeks. Three weeks. A month passed with no update about the promised ship. In the meantime, they remained trapped at the Slobodarna in a perpetual cycle of tedium and discomfort. They either wilted within its stuffy, overheated confines or shivered in the exercise yard in temperatures that hovered between -15 and -20 Celsius. It was the coldest winter anyone could remember. Worst of all was that it was impossible for them to leave; the frozen Danube would have to thaw first, and that was unlikely to happen before spring.

Somehow, Hannah endured the grim conditions at the Slobodarna for three months. The presence of her new friends fortified her. The now daily Hebrew lessons kept her occupied and gave her a sense of achievement as she practised her new conversation skills with Erika and Janka. She decided to use the opportunity to improve her Hebrew as much as she could. Keeping her mind on a future in the Holy Land helped distract her attention away from the dismal, frigid surroundings. Every few days, Gisi Fleischmann, the kind and caring woman from the local community who had appointed herself to help the refugees, visited the Slobodarna, bringing the refugees steaming pots of thick, homemade soup, words of encouragement and reassurance that they would soon be on their way. As the weeks went on, the guards even eased the restrictions a bit. From time to time, they granted a few of them exit passes from the hostel, and families from the local Jewish community of Bratislava would invite Hannah and her friends to their homes for a meal. The hospitality of the families warmed them, sitting around a table with their hosts, eating hearty good stew and schnitzel. It was a taste of home. But at the end of each visit, the Slobodarna drenched them with renewed homesickness.

The days grew longer, the weather milder, and the snow finally melted. So when a summons came for those who had arrived on convoys from Vienna, Hannah and Erika assumed, along with the others, that they would finally be leaving down the Danube.

They were wrong.

'Well?' said Janka, unable to restrain her excitement. She trailed after Hannah and Erika to their room, where, in a daze, they began gathering their belongings. 'Are you leaving?'

'No.' Hannah rolled up her blanket. 'Moving.'

Janka stopped, as if they had thrown a bucket of icy water at her. 'What do you mean you're moving?'

'They said they're sending us to another hostel in Bratislava. It's called the Patronka.' She belted the blanket to her rucksack with the bag's straps. 'We begged them and begged them not to send us away. They didn't even explain why they're moving us.'

'We all tried to get them to reconsider, but they wouldn't listen,' Erika said. 'The bus is already waiting outside.'

'I wonder what their plan is,' Janka said.

'They said something about this other hostel having more space.' Hannah covered her face with her hands. 'I don't know. I just don't know what this means.'

'We are supposed to board that boat any day now. Isn't that what they promised weeks ago? So much for ten days!' Erika slammed the lid of her suitcase. 'If they're transferring us to a different hostel, that means we're stuck here. They lied to us.'

Hannah hoisted her backpack onto her shoulders and picked up her case with a sense of dread. What lay in store for them at the unfamiliar Patronka? She stepped through the doorway and made for the staircase. But as she and Erika began carting their luggage down the stairs, a guard blocked Janka from helping them. 'They go. You stay.'

'Can't I accompany them to the bus and say goodbye?'

'You say goodbye here.'

Janka's eyes were full of sadness. 'It won't be the same without the two of you. I'm going to miss you so much.'

'We'll miss you too,' Hannah said.

'Tell Alexander and Isaak we said goodbye,' Erika said.

'I will.' Janka hugged both of them. 'I hope we meet again soon. On the boat!'

'Yes.' Hannah felt a tightness in her chest as she forced a smile. 'See you on the boat.'

Before boarding the bus, Hannah cast one last look at the Slobodarna's grim facade and experienced an unexpected wrench.

The bus took them westward, past the city limits and into the countryside, where only a few gabled cottages dotted the green hills and fields. A hostel in such an isolated area was improbable. But ten minutes later, the bus stopped on a lonely road, the air still and silent. A sudden shout to disembark startled Hannah.

She clutched her luggage and stayed close to Erika as they lumbered up the deserted road. Ahead, visible beyond a few skeletal trees, she saw the industrial buildings and chimneys of a disused factory complex. Their apparent destination.

Through the gate, beside the porter's lodge, two stern Hlinka guards waited for them. They separated the men and women and led them into the forbidding compound. This was the Patronka, a former ammunition factory.

A paved yard ran through the centre of the factory compound, lined on all sides by crumbling industrial buildings. Cutting across the compound was a small, foul-smelling stream that made even the guards cover their noses.

A guard led the women to a building at the far end of the complex and abandoned them there.

'*Schrecklich*!' Erika said, as they walked through the tall steel-plated doors into their new sleeping quarters: a cavernous and dilapidated factory hall, lined with rows of crude wooden bunks and thin straw mattresses, enough for at least a hundred people. 'These conditions are inhuman. Fit for horses.'

'What a hellhole. Why did they move us here?' Hannah said.

'I don't know what to believe anymore.' Erika cast herself down onto an empty lower bunk. 'Perhaps Janka was right and this entire plan has been a pack of lies from the start.'

'I never thought I'd say this, but I'm homesick for the Slobodarna.' Hannah pitched her unopened suitcase onto the top bunk and perched beside Erika. 'At least the hostel was dry and had proper heating.' She looked up at the sky that was visible through sections of the roof where wooden slats were missing. A stinging draft blew through the many broken panes of the steel-framed windows. The only source of heating was a tiny wood-burning stove.

Erika rose to her feet and eyed the carpet of damp, musty straw covering the floor. 'Does this place even have a lavatory?'

'Outside,' said a listless young woman lying on the opposite bunk.

'Well, isn't this marvellous?' Erika said after they located the outdoor latrine and a single tap. 'Especially when we have to stumble out at night in the cold.'

Hannah surveyed the uneven path to the primitive facilities, trailing it back to the factory hall, and pictured having to make the same trip in the pitch black. 'Do you know what I've just realised?' she said, 'I don't see any guards posted outside our sleeping quarters. That's one thing I won't miss from the Slobodarna.'

'Do you think that means we're free to roam?' Erika asked.

'Let's find out.'

As they scouted the periphery, two young men in caps emerged from the opposite building. They appeared to be refugees like them. Her attention was drawn to them as they laughed at a shared joke, appearing surprisingly at ease, despite the surroundings. One wore round, gold-rimmed spectacles, which he took off and polished on the hem of his greying button-down shirt. He examined the lenses in the light, replaced them, and then noticed Hannah and Erika.

'Oh, hello.' He crossed the yard with his friend. 'Is everything all right? Are you lost?'

'We were just checking for guards and wondering whether we're allowed to leave our building.' Hannah hoped he hadn't caught her staring.

'The guards keep to the front entrance.' He reassured her with a friendly smile. 'Don't worry, you can walk around within the complex. You must be part of the latest group.'

'We just arrived from the Slobodarna hostel,' Erika said.

'Welcome. Or should I say, "commiserations".' His friend wrinkled his freckle-dusted nose and gave a comical frown to emphasise his distaste, which made Erika laugh. 'Let's pray we all get out of here speedily.'

'Have they given you any idea when?'

'A ship is supposed to be on the way, or so they promised us two months ago, but we're still waiting.'

Erika nodded with a roll of her eyes. 'Yes, we heard that story too.'

'If we can help you with anything, we're in that building there.' He pointed. 'I'm Marcus, and this is Karl.'

'I'm Erika. Nice to meet you.'

'And I'm Hannah.'

'Nice to meet you,' Karl said.

Marcus made to head off, but Karl lingered.

'Would you ... like us to show you around?' He looked to Marcus, who shrugged, as if to say he had no objections. 'Not that there's that much to see, but it's not as if we have anywhere to rush off to.' His blue eyes lit up when he smiled.

'Why not?' Hannah turned to Erika, who nodded in assent. 'We have nowhere else to go, either.'

The four set off along the cracked cement path towards the rear of the compound. Erika walked ahead with Marcus, striking up instant conversation. Karl was more reserved, but Hannah didn't mind the companionable silence. After being holed up for months, she delighted in the freedom of a walk in the fresh air. It was the first mild day since she had arrived in Bratislava, and the early spring sun warmed her face.

After a few minutes, Karl turned to her with a shy smile. 'Where are you from?'

'Vienna,' Hannah said. 'And you?'

'Prague.'

'We were with a group from Prague at the Slobodarna. Perhaps you know them?'

'I know of the group, but I'm not sure I'm acquainted with any of them personally.'

They reached the end of the compound, turned left, and strolled through a sparsely wooded area at the edge of a freshly dug field.

'Do you work the land here?' Hannah asked.

'No. Every so often, local labourers appear to work in them. I wish we could work in the fields. At least it would give us something to do. And more experience for when we move to a kibbutz. Are you also planning to join a kibbutz?'

'I don't think so,' she said with a smile. 'I'm hoping my cousin will join me too and then we'll find a place to share together. We're both city girls. I don't think we're suited to farming life. We'll probably look to settle somewhere like Tel Aviv or Jerusalem.'

He accepted her answer with a nod. No idealistic lecture like she might have heard from Alexander. They continued in silence around the field until they returned to the path running down the centre of the compound.

'How long have you been here?' Hannah asked.

'Almost four months.'

'How have you managed all this time?'

'I've asked myself the same question many times,' Karl said. 'Conditions were tough at first. It was the beginning of winter, and so many of the windows in that building are broken that the temperature inside was almost the same as the outdoors. During the day, we tried to huddle around that one stove. Though, with a hundred men in our sleeping quarters we had to take turns. But at night, there was no way to heat such a vast space. I wore layers and layers of clothes, and I still couldn't get warm. Even my eyelashes would freeze. It was miserable.'

'That sounds awful. We had central heating in the hostel, but we didn't have bunks. We slept on dirty old mattresses on the floor.'

Karl grinned. 'Those bunks weren't here when we arrived. We built them ourselves.'

'Oh?' Hannah stopped for a moment and looked at him anew. 'That's impressive.' Karl dismissed it with a modest shrug. 'What did you sleep on before?'

'Also on mattresses, on the floor with all that matted straw. It provided some insulation from the cold, but every time it rained, the roof leaked, and then we slept on damp straw.'

'How grim.'

'That's why we built the bunks.'

'Then I'm grateful to you for improving conditions for us.'

'The building project kept us occupied for a while. We didn't expect to be here for so long, but since we had to be, it helped pass the time. We assumed it would be a day or two at most.'

'We thought the same when we first arrived in Bratislava. But here we are.'

'Yes, here we are.' Karl stopped outside their sleeping quarters. 'Can I ... invite you for another walk tomorrow?'

'I'd like that.'

A week after their arrival, Erika sat cross-legged on Hannah's bunk, swaddled in her blanket. 'Are you still missing the Slobodarna?'

'Less so,' Hannah said.

'I'd say Karl has something to do with that.' She nudged Hannah in the ribs. 'You like him, don't you?'

Hannah felt her cheeks tingle. 'How can I possibly be happy in such a hell?'

'Take it,' said Erika, with a decisive nod. 'How and wherever it comes. He's charming, and I can tell he's taken with you, too.'

'Do you think so?'

'It's obvious. Just look at the way he looks at you. And he comes to invite you to go for a walk with him every day.'

'He's so different from my last boyfriend. Gerhard was all about the superficial – dressing up, being seen at smart venues, having fun. I didn't realise it at the time, but I never had deep, meaningful conversations with him like I do with Karl. He's far more genuine. I do like him. Maybe even a lot. And what about you and Marcus?'

Hannah studied Erika's face, trying to uncover her feelings.
'You've been spending a lot of time with him, too.'

'He's sweet.'

'But?'

'I'm not sure. He's quite religious, and his upbringing ...
rather different from mine. I wasn't brought up that traditional.'

'Does Marcus think it's a problem?'

'No, not at all.'

'Then what's bothering you?'

Erika shrugged.

'It's Alexander, isn't it?'

Erika didn't respond.

'Do you still think of him?'

'Sometimes. I know it's pointless. I think he saw me as a
friend. His entire focus was on boarding a ship and becoming a
kibbutznik. It was just a silly crush on my part. It's best if I forget
about him. I may never even see him again. And Marcus is nice.
He's friendly and kind. I enjoy his company.'

'You don't have to rush into anything and there's no harm in
being friends. Take what comes. Isn't that what you told me?'

'It's good advice.' Erika pushed her hair off her face. 'Especially as we never know when things are going to change around
here.'

In early May, reports reached the Patronka internees that five
hundred young Jewish emigrants from another group had managed to depart from Bratislava on an old paddle steamer, the
*Pentcho,* down the Danube. Surely, it would only be a matter of
time until they were on their way, too.

Hannah and Karl grew closer. They spent every day in each other's company, walking and talking for hours. On rare occasions, they were able to purchase exit permits from the guards and go for a walk in the countryside as part of a small supervised group. Although they had to remain under the guard's watchful eye, it was a chance to step outside the walls of the Patronka and breathe fresh air. The cost dented Hannah and Karl's limited funds, but they treasured those rare opportunities to leave the factory compound; it helped them endure the interminable internment.

Then, one warm day in mid-May, Karl entwined his fingers with Hannah's as they strolled through woodlands alive with spring blooms: snowdrops, violets, and the fragrant purple corydalis. Hannah stopped to inhale their fragrance.

'I feel I'm like the flowers, reawakening after being frozen for the past few months.'

Karl wasn't looking at the flowers. 'I feel the same,' he said, turning her face to his and caressing her cheek.

Then he pressed his lips to hers.

June arrived, and they remained at the Patronka. With every false rumour of an imminent departure, everyone's disappointment grew, and faith in the promised boat dissipated. A sense of hopelessness overtook the refugees. Then they heard about a wave of antisemitic violence in Bratislava. In echoes of Vienna's November Pogrom, Nazi sympathisers rampaged through the city. They vandalised synagogues, smashed the windows of Jewish-owned shops, and then confiscated and Aryanised them. Jews were barred from public places. The terror from which they had escaped seemed to have followed them. It lurked in the shadows, preparing to strike.

At the Patronka, even the fields and woodland within the camp's perimeters, where Hannah and Karl had enjoyed daily walks, were declared out of bounds. No more exit permits. They were now restricted to an area within the confines of the factory buildings. Conditions at the Patronka grew steadily worse. Guards who had once acted cordial, or at worst indifferent, became malicious. They tormented the internees, shouting and hurling insults at them. The inmates were perpetually tense, fearful that the guards would turn from verbal to physical attacks.

The food, which had always been poor, deteriorated further. Too often, they ate soup that was little more than water, with a few thin slices of potatoes. Hannah would climb into bed at night with pangs of hunger.

The lack of food and the missing ship preyed on Hannah's nerves. Were it not for her friendship with Erika, and the developing relationship with Karl, she might have given in to despair. But each day, she would walk the circuit with Karl in the permitted area and he would talk about a future in Eretz, keeping their dream alive.

'One day, instead of walking between these old factories, we'll walk through the streets of Jerusalem,' he said.

'It seems so out of reach. I can't even imagine it,' Hannah said.

'Shut your eyes and try. Picture a narrow alley in the Old City of Jerusalem, paved with yellow-gold stone. A warm sun is shining on our faces.'

Hannah tilted her face to the pale sun, half obscured behind the clouds. He took her hand. 'We are walking together, heading towards the Western Wall. The atmosphere is so tranquil. We hear joyful voices, the laughter of children. We pass an old man leaning on a walking stick. He smiles at us and we greet him with a "Shalom." And then he replies—'

'You, over there!'

It was a sullen guard heading their way, shouting, 'Start packing your bags!'

'We are leaving?' Karl asked.

'She is. You're not.'

'Where are you sending us?' Hannah said.

'Back to Austria. The buses are already here. Hurry and pack. Don't keep them waiting.'

Hannah went still. 'Austria?'

'No!' Karl said. 'No. You can't do that! She can't go back. Please! Let her stay.'

The guard ignored his pleading and addressed Hannah. 'Don't make me ask you again. Return to your quarters. Now.'

Karl released Hannah's hand. She retreated and saw the terror in his eyes, the unspoken goodbye.

Hannah stumbled into the factory building. The women packing their suitcases were whimpering and sniffling. Nobody had any illusions about going back to Austria. They risked arrest – and the concentration camps, their inevitable destination.

# CHAPTER 7

Hannah kept her gaze fixed on the moss sprouting between the cracks of the path and concentrated on placing one foot in front of the other. From what she could see out of the corner of her eye, a crowd was gathering. She dared not look up in case she spotted Karl among them. She couldn't bear the goodbye.

The group trailed towards the Patronka's main gate. Ahead, a guard awaited them. Hannah propelled herself forward, blocking out every thought.

'Stop!' barked the guard.

Hannah ploughed into the person ahead who was suddenly still. Only then did she understand the guard's instruction.

'There has been a change of plan.' He folded his arms, the irritation clear in the downturn of his mouth. 'You have permission to remain. For now.' He waved his hand, as if swatting away insects. 'Return to your quarters.'

Hannah watched the inmates as they began dispersing. She heard their cries and sighs of relief. Yet she remained motionless, unable to take in the sudden fortunate turn of events.

'It's all right, Hannah.' Karl appeared by her side and placed his arms around her. 'You're safe,' he said. 'They aren't sending you back.' She felt the tremble of his body and heard the hitch in his breath.

'Are you sure?' She leaned against him, letting go of the fears that had seized her: having her place on the transport stolen from her, losing Karl, being arrested.

'You're not leaving.' He loosened the grip of her fingers from the handle of her case, eased the backpack from her shoulders, and hoisted it onto his own. 'You're staying here,' he said. 'With me.'

Karl took her hand in his and they started back on the path. She turned around to look at the main gate. The guard was gone. Her breath steadied, her heart slowed. I am safe, she thought. We are safe. At least for now. But we had better get on that boat soon.

Later, they learned the transport organisers had bribed the Slovak authorities to extend the inmates' visas, food and lodging at the last minute. For several angst-ridden weeks, Hannah and Erika couldn't bring themselves to unpack their cases. Caught in the limbo between threats and assurances, they knew their destiny hung in the balance.

In the meantime, the organisers blamed the continued delay on 'a shortage of nails'. They had heard that excuse before and were sure they were being fobbed off, but they couldn't help hoping this was the last delay, especially as rumours circulated – they always did – that the refugees were soon to depart.

At the end of August, with another autumn fast approaching, the guards called the detainees to a meeting in the factory building that served as their dining room. Herr Rottenstreich, a liaison officer, was standing in for Berthold Storfer, the convoy's organiser. 'I am pleased to announce that we have completed our arrangements for you. In four days' time, you will leave for Eretz Israel.' Herr Rottenstreich paused. The news met with a muted response. A scattering of people clapped politely. After months of setbacks, they knew better than to celebrate prematurely.

'Two Danube steamers, *Helios* and *Uranus*, are on their way to Bratislava. The Viennese groups will sail on the Helios and those from Prague on the Uranus.' Several hands shot up, including Karl's. 'Before anyone asks, there is to be no switching, no exceptions. You will sail on the boat to which we assign you. Any further questions?'

Karl turned to Hannah with a disappointed shrug. 'I had hoped we'd be able to travel together.'

'I would have preferred that too,' Hannah said.

'Perhaps we'll reunite when we board the ship in Romania?'

'And if not?'

'Then we'll meet again in Haifa. The journey should take three or four weeks, at most. It's a small price to pay. Though I'll miss you in the meantime.'

'I'll miss you too.' She held herself back from saying anything else.

Hannah couldn't stop the rush of a memory when she'd said something similar. She tensed up as she recalled her foolishness with Gerhard. But Karl was nothing like him. Everything she had seen of him so far made it clear that he was made of kinder, and more serious, stuff.

Hannah cringed in the privacy of her memory of her conversation with Gerhard when he told her he was leaving for America as they strolled through the park one evening.

'What if we were to get married?' she had said.

Gerhard stopped in his tracks. 'What? right away?'

'Well, an engagement first. Naturally,' Hannah said.

Gerhard abruptly sat on the nearest bench and motioned for Hannah to join him. Then he noticed the 'Aryans only' sign and quickly stood up again.

They continued walking. 'I ... um ... it's not that I don't want to. Of course I do. It's just ... not a good idea to rush into it right now.'

'It wouldn't be such a rush. We have already been together for several months.'

'Oh my dear sweet *Liebling,* you know how I feel about you, don't you?'

'Y-yes, I do.'

'Then why do we need a formal agreement?'

'Well ... it's just that you're leaving.'

'We'll only be apart for just a short while. Soon, you'll join me. Once I'm there, I'll be able to put all my efforts into getting visas issued much faster for you and your mother.'

'Wouldn't it help the visa process if we already had a commitment?'

'I'm not sure it would. And we shouldn't do it on the spur of the moment just for that. That's what I mean by not rushing into anything.' Gerhard stopped under a tree. 'These things take a great deal of thought and proper planning. I'd prefer to wait for the perfect moment to propose.'

'I understand,' Hannah said. But she didn't. His reaction had confused her.

'Right now, I have so much on my mind with the big move,' he said. 'Let's just enjoy this precious time together. I would like to take you out, treat you and have fun.'

She wondered where exactly he intended for them to have fun, when they were no longer allowed to frequent the theatre, cinema or cafés. 'You're probably right. Sorry I brought it up.'

'That's all right.' He patted her hand. 'You're not disappointed, are you?'

Hannah arranged her mouth into a semblance of a smile. 'No, it's fine.'

'I wouldn't like to think I've made you unhappy. You mean every-thing to me. I want to ensure I do everything right.' He flashed her a beguiling grin. 'Only the very best for my girl.'

Gerhard spent the rest of the evening plying her with reassuring platitudes, like spreading a thick layer of jam on a slice of mouldy bread.

Hannah now promised herself she would not make the same mistake twice.


The day before their departure, the group was granted permission to go into the city centre to buy essentials for their journey. Hannah and Karl purchased soap and washbowls, tinned food, and boxes of zwieback crackers, to supplement the food on board, plus a bit of dried fruit and a few chocolate bars for quick energy. Though the expense gave her pause, the thought of not having enough food once at sea – and no means to purchase anything more – was of greater worry. Thankfully, she wouldn't need additional funds until she reached Eretz, having already paid for the journey. And once there, she reminded herself, she and Lilly could stay on kibbutz with her cousin Eugen, Lilly's brother, for a few days until they found jobs and a more permanent place to live.

Completing their purchases, they wandered the narrow cobbled streets of the old town, bordered by red-roofed stone homes from the Middle Ages that held a certain fairy tale charm. The city centre was just as Lilly had once described it, after a trip to Bratislava, a lifetime ago.

The thought of her cousin prompted a wave of guilt. Hannah still hadn't told Lilly about Karl. It wasn't entirely by choice. Her mother had written, at the request of Lilly's mother, and asked her not to. They were worried Lilly might see it as a reason to give up her place on the transport. They wanted to ensure that Lilly wouldn't squander her opportunity; Vienna was just too dangerous. But that didn't make Hannah feel any better. Soon, she hoped, they would be travelling together. Then she would tell her everything.

Hannah and Karl had reached the Danube, which flowed through the heart of the city, the blue artery glistening in the summer sunshine.

'Can you believe this is our last day in Bratislava?' Karl said. 'Tomorrow, please God, this very river will lead us to the sea.'

Hannah stared at the water. Upstream lay Vienna, Hannah's past. Downstream, Romania, and an uncertain future.

Karl tilted his head and studied her with concern. 'You look worried. What's wrong?'

'It's just ...' She let out a sigh. 'We've been waiting so long and I'm afraid something will go wrong at the last minute and it might not happen. But I'm also nervous about the journey and what comes next if it does happen.'

'I know exactly what you mean. Who knows what the future holds?' He took her hands in his. 'But there is one thing I do know ... I'd like to spend it with you.'

Hannah's heartbeat quickened. Karl gazed at her steadily, his eyes matching the river behind him. 'When we reach Eretz, will you marry me?'

His question held her hopes and dreams for the future, she realised. To reach safety in the Promised Land. To be with Karl always. She had never in her entire life been as sure of anything as she was now. Hannah didn't hesitate. 'Yes,' she said. 'I will.'

He wiped the back of his hand across his eyes; she smiled through her tears. He kissed her tenderly.

With a shared deep breath, they spent their last coins to buy two stamps, and each wrote a letter home, Hannah to her mother, and Karl to his parents, telling them of their engagement. When they were done, Karl asked if he could add a few lines to her letter.

*I wish I could have asked you in person for your daughter's hand. I am honoured that Hannah has agreed to marry me. During our time at the Patronka, she has been a ray of light for me. I promise to always take care of her. I love Hannah with all my heart.*

*Signed, Karl, your future son-in-law.*

# CHAPTER 8

**27 August 1940**
**Bratislava, Slovakia**

The train lurched with a metallic screech, jolting Jenny from her seat. Silence hung over the carriage as it came to a standstill. She thought she could hear the rapid pounding of her own heart, as she clutched her clammy palms in her lap.

Her husband, Stefan, sitting next to her, pushed up his glasses and leaned over. 'Perhaps we've arrived?'

She peered out of the window, but couldn't see anything in the darkness.

The spontaneous burst of activity that followed seemed to confirm Stefan's supposition. All at once, the other passengers were out of their seats, reaching to the overhead luggage rack, and gathering their belongings.

Stefan's face relaxed. 'We've made it to Bratislava.' A small sigh of relief escaped him. 'We're safe.'

Jenny managed a smile. They still had a long way to travel, but this, their first stop out of Nazi-occupied Germany, was a victory. The twenty-seven-hour train journey from Danzig had been tense. Once known as the Free City, their hometown had become their prison. Danzig had a tumultuous history. Over the course of six hundred years, it had changed hands several times between Polish and German territory. After the Great War, under the supervision of the League of Nations, it became a city-state, the Free City of Danzig, independent of the country of Germany that surrounded it. But that freedom ended with the Nazi invasion of Poland in 1939.

Initially, when the Nazis took power in the rest of Germany, Danzig was relatively unaffected. The Free City's Senate didn't introduce any anti-Jewish laws, so business largely continued as usual, though Jenny and Stefan had become aware of a festering antisemitism in Danzig that had been politely hidden until the Nazi's rise to power.

A rampaging Nazi mob was their violent wake-up call. In October 1937, young men in Nazi uniforms smashed and looted Jewish businesses and attacked every Jew they encountered across Danzig. The brutality shocked many ordinary Danzigers, Jenny and Stefan among them, but they had hoped the incident was a one-off. Surely the citizens of their fair city would prevent a repetition, and their lives could continue much as before.

When the November Pogrom spread to Danzig the following year, however, Jenny and Stefan faced the reality that they were no longer welcome in their own city.

Theirs became a too common tale, in which they frantically tried every conventional way to emigrate, and failed. And then, in September 1939, Germany and Britain declared war and Hitler signed a law incorporating Danzig into Nazi Germany. Jenny and Stefan were trapped.

When they learned of a daring immigration scheme to Eretz Israel, they rushed to sign up. They knew it was a risky enterprise, but they believed it to be their last hope. Then, for months, they waited on tenterhooks, impatient for news of their departure.

In the interim the Nazis swept through the city, Aryanising each neighbourhood, and Jenny and Stefan lost their home. They found a spot in a cramped warehouse, which had been converted into a ghetto, and settled in, until three months later, when their situation became even more fraught. The entire Danzig Jewish community was threatened with deportation to a concentration camp. Jenny and Stefan had been living in a state of anxiety ever since. If they were not able to depart soon, they feared they never would.

They were close to despair when a community leader arrived at the warehouse early one morning with the news that the transport was to leave that very afternoon with a limit of five hundred people. Jenny and Stefan, grateful to have overcome yet another hurdle, were to meet with the rest of the group at four o'clock at the canteen on the wharf, less than ten minutes' walk from their current lodgings. Jenny could not catch her breath, so great was her relief. But they knew their departure meant leaving behind people they might never see again – family, friends, their parents most of all. The rushed goodbyes of that day were tearful and gut-wrenching, even as they received congratulations and the slightest intimations of envy.

But first, in the few hours available, Stefan dashed out to buy a few basic provisions for the journey – bread, sausages, cans of food – while Jenny packed. Some clothes had been on the line, but she'd had no time to let them finish drying. Now, as Stefan fetched their cases from the luggage rack on the train, she worried about the condition of the damp washing inside of them.

Stefan was helping Jenny to secure the straps of her backpack when a man with a cleft chin approached them. Jenny recognised his face, though she didn't know his name. They used to see him on the street, walking with his wife and young daughter, and he always tipped his hat and offered a friendly greeting.

'Excuse me,' the man said. 'Do you need any help with your luggage? A few of us have volunteered to help the other passengers in our group carrying their cases to the boat.'

'It's kind of you to offer,' Stefan said. 'I think we'll manage fine, but there's an older couple in the next carriage who I'm sure would welcome the help.'

'I'll go at once to ask them,' he said, continuing his way down the aisle.

'Thank you again.'

The man paused and touched the brim of his hat. 'It's a pleasure. See you on the boat.'

'What a thoughtful person,' Jenny said, picking up her case.

'Isn't he?' Stefan held his hand out to her. 'Are you sure you're all right carrying that suitcase? I can carry both if it's too heavy for you.'

'I'm fine. Remember, I made it to the train station.'

Stefan's face clouded over, but he didn't reply. The bitterness of their departure from Danzig was still raw.

It had begun at the designated meeting point with an official inspection. The Gestapo rummaged through everyone's luggage, confiscating – or rather, stealing – their possessions at whim. From Stefan's suitcase, they expropriated the watch Jenny had given him as a gift on their wedding day ten years earlier.

Afterwards, officers separated the men and women and subdivided them into smaller groups. Jenny and fifty other women were then paraded through the city of her birth to reach the station, with dense crowds lining the streets to jeer their farewells. They waved and cursed the women the whole route to the railway station.

'*Saujude!*'

'Good riddance, Jews!'

'Go back to Palestine where you belong!'

Jenny kept her head up and continued walking, but it was hard to ignore the insults. One woman spat at her, just missing her shoes. 'Filthy Jew,' hissed the woman, who owned a grocery where Jenny had shopped on occasion. Jenny shuddered and focused on increasing the distance between herself and the bystanders.

She found Stefan on the station platform. He studied her face but didn't ask any questions. He nodded in understanding and took her hand. They boarded their third-class carriage, noting that the adjoining second-class carriage held the commander and other members of the Gestapo who were accompanying them to Bratislava. The presence of the Third Reich looming so close made Jenny unbearably fearful that something would go wrong – that they would be sent back to Danzig, or redirected elsewhere – but the journey passed without incident, and she relaxed the tension in her jaw.

Even before the train had come to a complete halt, the gentlemen in the next carriage were on their feet. As Jenny and Stefan navigated the congested aisle towards the exit she warily watched them alight.

'I don't think they'll give us any trouble now,' Stefan said. 'No doubt they are happy to be rid of us.'

Jenny stepped off the train onto the quay and into a thick blanket of darkness. The enforced wartime blackout meant there wasn't a single light to mark their way. Still the passengers poured from the carriages. Jenny found herself swept along with the crowd and panicked. 'Stefan!'

She felt the reassuring clasp of his hand. 'I'm right here beside you, my darling.'

After being cooped up in a stagnant carriage for so long, she found the night air refreshing. Its scent reminded her of the night-time walks she and Stefan took along the bank of the Mottlau River in Danzig back when they were courting. Her eyes adjusted, and in the pale light of the quarter moon, she discerned the outline of a paddle steamer straight ahead. She had not expected the river to be so close by. Instead of a proper station, they had stopped at a siding that ran parallel to the river by the port.

'I wonder if that's our boat, the Helios?' Stefan said.

Their fellow Danzigers streamed across the quay, the wooden gangplank reverberating with their footsteps. They spoke quietly, but their voices were calmer, more joyful than they had been on the train. The closer they got to the boat, the more Jenny felt her nervousness ebb.

The organisers had told them they would spend the first night berthed at the quayside, on the paddle steamer, Helios. Tomorrow, another Jewish group – apparently stranded in Bratislava since the winter – would join them on board. Then they would be ready to set off down the Danube.

A dull splash broke the steady patter of footsteps. A scream followed.

'David has fallen in!' shouted one man.

Several people began running along the quayside, following the river, calling his name.

Before Jenny realised what was happening, Stefan had dropped his case. 'Watch the luggage, Jenny! I'm going to help.'

'Please, be careful!' Jenny called after him, but Stefan was already gone. She stayed in that spot so he could find her again, minding the two suitcases, and feeling a little helpless.

'My husband!' a woman yelled. 'I must find him!'

Two women had their arms around a woman who was surely David's wife, struggling to keep her away from the river. 'Where is he?' She could barely get the words out.

A small girl held tight to the woman's hand. Her daughter. The child looked frightened and confused, and sought shelter in her mother's skirt.

A chill ran the length of Jenny's spine as she recognised them. This was the wife and daughter of the man who had just offered to help her and Stefan with their luggage.

'Do something. Please find him!' The wife tried to pull away from the hands restraining her.

'The men are looking for him,' said one woman, attempting to calm her. 'They are doing everything they can to find him.'

Several more women gathered, wanting to bring her some comfort, but by then, she was on the verge of hysterics.

At some remove, Jenny overheard one woman say to another, 'I saw it happen. I was right there. He was carrying someone's luggage from the train to the boat when he suddenly lost his footing. He didn't see the edge in the dark and slipped into the river.'

'Poor man,' her companion said. 'And how terrible for his wife and daughter. I hope they find him.'

The men continued their search, beside the river, shouting David's name into the darkness. Jenny's stomach turned with dread.

'Where's my husband?' his wife shrieked, again and again.

Half an hour later, the search party approached her with heads bowed.

'We tried our best, but we could not find David,' one man said. 'The current is rapid here ...' He paused. 'He's gone. I'm so sorry.'

'No.' His wife collapsed onto the ground. 'No. No!'

The women at her side helped her to her feet. They hugged her and then, pushing and pulling, supporting her as they went, they guided her, sobbing, onto the boat. Another woman followed behind, carrying the daughter.

Stefan returned to Jenny, his shoulders hunched, seeming older than his thirty-seven years. He removed his glasses and rubbed his eyes. 'Do you know who it was?' He sighed.

'Yes. I can't imagine ...' Jenny couldn't finish the sentence; she could still hear the woman's screams in her ears. 'How will she cope? And they have a little girl!'

'I don't know.' Stefan said quietly.

The mood remained sombre as those still on the quay formed a queue and cautiously crossed the gangplank .

From the upper deck of the paddle steamer, Jenny peered into the gloom of the mist-shrouded river. She pictured the man touching the brim of his hat, saying, 'See you on the boat.'

Stefan handed her his handkerchief, and she leaned against him, burying her head in his chest.

# CHAPTER 9

**28 August 1940**
**Bratislava, Slovakia**

Hannah took one last look around the dilapidated warehouse that had been their sleeping quarters. Empty of its former occupants, all that remained were the wooden bunks and clumps of musty straw scattered about the concrete floor.

Erika came up behind her. 'Don't tell me you're feeling sentimental about leaving the Patronka.'

'No, it isn't that. It was awful. But I also found my greatest happiness here.'

'Your greatest happiness is coming with you.'

'Not on the same boat.' Hannah didn't want to admit she was nervous, dreading the goodbye to Karl, afraid of the uncertainties that lay ahead of them.

'It's only for a few weeks, and then you get to spend your whole lives together.' Erika linked her arm with Hannah's. 'In the meantime, Karl and Marcus are waiting outside. So let's hurry before we miss them – and our bus. I, for one, won't miss anything about this dump and don't wish to stay here even one minute longer than necessary.'

Hannah and Erika joined their young men and the crowd of soon-to-be ex-detainees who were making their way through the factory yard, hurrying towards the convoy of buses. Hannah let everyone else climb aboard before her, remaining with Karl until they could not delay their separation any longer.

'I'm going to miss you so much,' Hannah said.

'I'll miss you too,' Karl said. 'But we'll reunite in another few days in Tulcea, or else in about three weeks in Haifa.' He gave her a rushed hug as the irritable bus driver sounded his horn. 'I can't wait to spend the rest of my life with you. Shall we get married as soon as we arrive?' Karl stood at the door of the bus as Hannah mounted the steps. 'Will you think about it and tell me when we next meet?'

'I will.' Hannah turned and waved one last time, then noticed Erika hadn't boarded yet either. She was still saying goodbye to Marcus. He whispered something, and Erika's smile radiated happiness. Hannah read her lips in reply: I love you too. Another impatient blare of the horn pulled them apart and Erika leapt up the stairs. Grinning, she slid into the seat beside Hannah.

A fifteen-minute drive through the bustling heart of Bratislava brought them to the Danube, which shimmered in the late afternoon sunshine. Set against the grassy verge and thicket of trees of the opposite bank, the river presented a deceptively peaceful scene. The river here was broad, and before the war had been a busy waterway; pleasure boats filled with tourists had plied back and forth between the cities bordering the Danube. Now, two of them were moored alongside the quay, waiting to transport the refugees to the Black Sea: the Helios, a three-tiered, white paddle steamer, and, a few metres ahead of it, the Uranus, another riverboat of similar design. Hannah recalled having seen such boats while walking with Gerhard beside the narrower Danube Canal which ran through the Innere Stadt, Vienna's First District.

'How nice it must be to take a cruise down the river,' she had said.

'One day, my darling, I shall take you,' he had declared.

Of course, Gerhard never did anything of the kind. But that was the past and not worth dwelling on. Hannah realised that if he had sent for her to join him in America, she would never have met Karl. Had destiny taken a different course, Hannah might have had no reason to forgive Gerhard. She forgave him now and it gave her peace of mind to do so.

They passed a brusque and brief customs inspection by the Hlinka Guard and lined up to board the Helios. The boat looked crowded already, and Hannah wondered how they would all fit. These paddle steamers were designed to carry three hundred tourists, not a thousand refugees.

'Can you believe this is finally happening?' Erika's eyes were wide, as they stepped onto the gangway. 'Are you ready?'

Hannah looked ahead at Karl's boat, the Uranus. Its proximity reassured her. Their two boats would sail together. She adjusted her rucksack, lifted her chin and felt a surge of determination. 'Readier than ever.'

In a moment, they were on the deck of the Helios, and at once overwhelmed by the confusion and disorganisation they found there. With no one in charge to provide guidance to the refugees, hundreds of them scattered in every direction, scrambling to find an unclaimed spot. Hannah and Erika were jostled through jammed passageways as they looked for a vacant cabin. Most were already occupied, or over-occupied. They saw that as many as six people were in each two-berth cabin: two shared each bunk tier and another one or two on the floor.

Erika raised her eyebrows. 'What now?'

'I suppose we'll make do like we did at the Slobodarna hostel and sleep in a communal room,' Hannah said.

They edged their way back along the wood-panelled passageway and up the curved stairs, pressing against its spindled bannister to let others pass. They exchanged confused looks with a group of four women they knew from the Patronka, who were heading in the opposite direction, similarly bewildered.

The middle deck, if anything, was worse. As they navigated the passageway, they tripped over several suitcases. Some passengers seemed to have given up searching further and settled down to camp in the passageway.

When they reached the low-ceilinged dining room, Hannah understood why the others had turned away. Men and women, the elderly, families and children already occupied the entire space, their blankets spread across the carpeted floor to mark their territory.

A rash of heated arguments about the space allocation broke out between the first arrivals from Danzig and the Patronka newcomers.

'This is mayhem.' Erika shouted to make herself heard. 'Where are we supposed to sleep?'

'How about the upper deck?' Hannah was already backing down the passageway. 'Anything is better than this.'

They squeezed through the crowds, ascended the narrow companionway and reached the upper deck to find that too was filling fast. Erika flung her luggage, and then herself, onto the first empty bench they came upon, and Hannah followed. An auburn-haired woman sitting opposite flinched, and her porcelain complexion turned even paler. She clutched the arm of a smart-suited, bespectacled man beside her.

'Sorry,' Erika said. 'Is this place taken?'

'Not yet.' The woman's voice trembled, barely audible.

You are welcome to join us,' said the man sitting beside her, patting the woman's hand, as if to reassure her.

'I'm Stefan Mayer and this is my wife, Jenny. We're from Danzig.'

'Nice to meet you. I'm Erika Bauer and this is my friend, Hannah Rosen. We're both from Vienna.'

'Thanks for letting us share the space,' Hannah said. 'It's pandemonium below.'

'I heard a lot of shouting.' Jenny's worried gaze darted about. 'What happened?'

'Only a load of furious arguments because of the lack of space.' Hannah said. She stood up, made her way to the railing, and leaned over it for a glimpse of the Uranus. All she could see were hordes of people moving to and fro on deck, much like their boat. She wondered how Karl was faring.

Jenny pressed a palm to her heart and let out a breath. 'I'm most relieved to hear that.'

Erika leaned forward on the bench towards Jenny. 'Why? What else did you think it might be?'

'Last night, we boarded in darkness because of the blackout and a man from our group, who was helping to carry luggage across for other passengers, he ... he ... slipped and fell ... into the river.' Her face contorted with sorrow. The rest of the men organised a search party, but they never found him. He left behind a wife and five-year-old daughter.'

Hannah's arms prickled with goosebumps. '*Ach du lieber Gott!*'

'Hearing all that shouting now reminded me of last night. I'm a little shaken.'

'I can imagine,' Erika said. 'How is his wife?'

Jenny shook her head. 'Inconsolable. I can't stop remembering how she broke down when the men came to tell her. She and her daughter are in a cabin and they have good friends taking care of them. He was so close to freedom. He'd been waiting so long. We all were. I don't have to tell you. And now this.' Jenny placed a hand over her mouth in renewed dismay. 'A fatality before we've even left the port.'

Hannah struggled to sleep that first night. The Patronka may have been dismal, but at least there they had mattresses and a roof over their heads. Sleeping on a hard bench in the open air would take getting used to. And she couldn't stop thinking about the story Jenny had told them. Eventually, she dozed off, only to awaken at first light.

The sky was a masterpiece of colours from soft pink to bright orange, the rosy shades blending one into the next, like a watercolour painting. The sun's reflection gleamed off the river's surface, creating a raft of golden ripples. Erika slept on, but Jenny and Stefan were awake, and they greeted Hannah when she arose from her bench.

Hannah headed to the bow and gazed towards the stern of the Uranus where a solitary figure stood at the railings. She couldn't make out his features, but the outline was familiar. A wiry frame and that tilt of his head – she was sure it was Karl. The man straightened up. He had noticed her, too. Hannah lifted her hand in a hesitant wave. The man responded with an enthusiastic one. He cupped his hands over his mouth and called to her.

'What?' she shouted.

He tried again. She shook her head. Karl's words reached her as a faint garble. He brought his hand to his mouth and then, with a swift motion, flung it in her direction as if he were throwing her something. Hannah pretended to catch his kiss, and she blew him one in return.

Any expectations that their boats might set sail that day sank with the setting sun. At dusk, both remained lashed to their moorings. Rumours abounded that yet another group was to come aboard. How they would fit into the already tight living arrangements was anyone's guess.

The atmosphere had calmed somewhat, but trying to reach the washrooms or fetch a glass of water was like negotiating an obstacle course, and the rush at mealtimes was pure chaos.

On their third morning, as Hannah and Erika sat on their bench eating rolls with tea for breakfast, a fresh commotion announced the embarkation of a new group.

Erika's mouth fell open. 'I don't believe it!'

Before Hannah had a chance to ask what she had seen, her friend set down her cup of tea and was weaving her way through the crowd. Then Hannah spotted her approaching three familiar faces making their way through the door to the deck. She put her own cup of tea next to Erika's and followed her.

'... good to see you all again!' Hannah heard Erika's voice bubbling with excitement as she moved closer to the group, and joined them, just in time to exchange hugs with Janka, Alexander, and Isaak. 'We missed you.'

'We missed you too. The Slobodarna wasn't the same after you left,' Janka said. 'I'm really happy we're travelling together.'

'What was the Patronka like?' Alexander said.

'Worse than the Slobodarna,' Hannah said. 'We slept in an old factory building with a leaky roof and straw-covered floor with an outdoor latrine.'

Janka wrinkled her nose in disgust. 'That sounds awful. How did you cope?'

'We got used to it. The one good thing was that we were free to roam around within the complex,' Erika said. 'And I met someone.' She grinned.

'You have a boyfriend?' Janka leaned closer to Erika and lowered her voice. 'I want to hear everything.'

Hannah sensed Alexander stiffening, an almost imperceptible change before he regained his composure and his nonchalant expression.

'Let's first get you settled and then I'll fill you in,' Erika said.

'What about you?' Janka said to Hannah, who couldn't hide her smile. 'Did you also find a boyfriend?'

Erika nudged her. 'Are you going to tell them?'

'His name is Karl,' Hannah said. 'And ... well ... we're engaged.'

Janka squealed and threw her arms around Hannah. 'Mazel tov!'

Alexander and Isaak followed with congratulations and another round of hugs.

'No one else knows apart from Erika. I've written to my mother but I can't be sure she's received my letter, so please keep it to yourselves for the time being,' Hannah said.

'Of course,' Janka said. 'Where is your fiance? Can we meet him?'

Hannah waved in the direction of the Uranus. 'He's on the other boat.'

'What a shame.'

'It is. I'm disappointed we couldn't travel together, but thankful our journey is about to start. Apparently, we have been waiting for your arrival.' Her nod included the whole group of new arrivals. 'So we should be ready to set sail today.'

Isaak scanned the crowded deck. 'Where can we sleep and store our luggage?'

'There isn't much room,' Erika said. 'All the cabins were already taken when we arrived. Even the dining room is full. You can share our space here on deck.' Erika led them to their bench. 'Let me introduce you to our roommates. This is Jenny and Stefan Mayer from Danzig.'

Alexander and Isaak shook hands with Stefan, and Janka with Jenny. Then, with his arm crossed over his chest, Alexander nodded to Jenny. 'A pleasure to meet you, Frau Mayer. I'm Alexander Heller from Prague.'

'Please call me Jenny.' She fussed about, tucking first her suitcase and rucksack under their bench, and then Stefan's, to make room for the newcomers in the limited space between the two benches. 'I'm sorry about all the mess everywhere.'

'Don't worry. Conditions weren't any better in the hostel where we were staying,' Alexander said. 'But the situation is about to improve. To help maintain order on board, senior members of our Prague group have established our own *Haganah*.' He straightened his back and raised his chin at the mention of the defence organisation of the *Yishuv*, the Jewish population in Eretz Israel. 'Isaak and I have volunteered as part of the team. And we will help to maintain order on board.'

As Alexander had predicted, the arrival of their group from the Slobodarna brought positive change. A new queuing system meant no more scrambles for the washroom, meals, or water taps. But much as the new system improved their moods, it didn't lead to their departure. Two days later, both paddle steamers were still in the harbour and none of them had found anyone who could explain why that was.

At twilight, Hannah stood at the bow again, attempting to signal to Karl. She wanted to ask him if he had more information. But before she succeeded, Alexander appeared at her side.

'What are you doing?' he asked, watching Hannah and Karl gesticulate wildly, amused at their emphatic gestures.

'I'm trying to ask my fiance about our delay.' Hannah said. 'Alexander, meet Karl. Karl, meet Alexander.'

Alexander extended his arm over the railing in jest, as if to shake hands. Karl stretched his arm and did likewise. 'I look forward to a proper introduction soon,' Alexander said. 'Also, good news. I found out the reason for our delay.'

'Why is that good news?' asked Hannah.

'Because we're waiting for two more boats to catch up with our convoy.' He paused and smiled. 'From Vienna.'

'Does that mean my cousin, too?' Hannah had not dared hope Lilly would join them. In Lilly's last letter, she had written that there had been no word about another transport and she had all but given up hope of it ever happening.

'There's a strong chance she's on one of them.'

'That is the best news!' Hannah suppressed an urge to jump up and down. 'Thank you.'

Alexander nodded towards Karl, who was raising his palms as if to ask, *what is it?*

'I'll leave you to figure out how to explain that to him with your sign language.' He winked.

As Hannah attempted to explain the reason for the delay to Karl, a larger question occupied her thoughts: how would she explain to Lilly why she hadn't told her about Karl in her letters.

# CHAPTER 10

**3 September 1940**
**Vienna, Austria**

Four long hours had passed. Lilly was still sitting on her suitcase when the crowded school basement fell silent. Berthold Storfer, the transport organiser, had arrived. Dressed in a tailored three-piece suit and adorned with a gold pocket watch, he stood at the foot of the stairs, his right hand gripping a silver-handled cane. Herr Storfer's bloodshot eyes darted about the room as he offered a curt greeting and a brief explanation of the departure process to follow. Lilly could not tell if he was shifty or simply worn out. And she still was not sure whether the escape route he had provided was a trap – one for which she had paid dearly.

Hannah had thought her stay in Bratislava would be a short stopover to board a boat, after all. According to her letters, the bleak hostel where she had been confined instead seemed more like a prison. And her more recent stay in that warehouse in a crumbling factory complex sounded even worse. More troubling, Hannah's letters had become ever more vague. Either the authorities were preventing her from writing frankly, or she was censoring herself to protect Lilly from awful truths. Truths which Lilly might be about to experience herself.

Despite her unease, Lilly ascended the basement steps with the rest of the group and boarded a bus from the waiting fleet on the street outside. What alternative did she really have?

A short ride delivered them to the landing pier of the DDSG shipping line, beside the Reichsbrücke bridge and across from the railway platform where she had said goodbye to Hannah. Two white paddle steamers moored to the pier awaited, as did the Gestapo.

Three officious Gestapo officers had set up tables to process the refugees. They barked for the refugees to approach and open their suitcases for inspection in turn. A second's hesitation was met with an impatient shout: '*Schneller*!' The unsmiling officers did a thorough job of rummaging through the luggage in their search for forbidden items to confiscate: money, jewellery, gold fountain pens, and any other pieces deemed of value.

Sweat trickled down Lilly's back as she thought of her wedding ring, which she had sewn into the seam of her dress. Although wedding rings were on the list of permitted items, Lilly couldn't bear the risk of losing it.

An officer rifled through the suitcase of a grey-haired woman standing just ahead of Lilly in line. Lilly's heart pounded as he tossed the woman's neatly folded clothes and underwear into a messy heap. It brought her back to the Brownshirts tearing through her parents' home, the slap to her cheek, the punch that knocked Salo to the floor, and the push that had sent her tumbling down the stairs. She clenched and unclenched her fingers, trying to calm herself.

'Next!'

The flinty-eyed Gestapo officer glared at Lilly. She lifted her suitcase onto the table in front of him, and fumbled with the clasps, her hands trembling.

'Give it to me!' He grabbed the case, poked around her clothing and lifted out a pile of underwear, examining them one by one.

Heat crept up her neck. She wanted to turn away and hide her face, but she knew she couldn't. And then he was done. He crushed her underthings into a ball, flung them back into her case, and slammed the lid closed.

The officer handed Lilly her passport and a sum of ten Reichsmark, the only money she was allowed to take out of the country.

Ten Reichsmark wasn't a lot. Many Viennese made more than that in one day's work. Lilly had worried how much it would buy her in British-controlled Mandatory Palestine. She would need enough to cover her portion of the first month's rent, sharing with Hannah, until they found work. And what about food?

The next line was passport control. When Lilly's turn came, the officer inspected her document, and then, with a flick of his wrist, confiscated it. Lilly, Austrian by birth, citizen of the Third Reich, legal emigrant to Mandatory Palestine, was now a stateless illegal immigrant with a bogus visa for Panama. Losing her citizenship was a small price to pay, she thought, but felt bereft nonetheless. There was no turning back.

Another flick of the wrist, and he sent her onto a two-deck paddle steamer called *DDSG Schönbrunn*. Ironic that it shared the name of the magnificent Viennese palace where Emperor Franz Josef had lived with his beautiful wife, Empress Elizabeth, the iconic Sisi.

Franz Joseph had died in 1916, two years before Lilly was born, but she knew of him through her father's stories. Life under the emperor had been a golden age for the Jews of Austria. He had been benevolent towards the Jewish community and granted them full and equal rights of citizens within the Austro-Hungarian Empire. Her father and most of his contemporaries had fought for their beloved emperor in the Great War. No wonder so many of them felt betrayed and had a hard time accepting the new regime.

The other paddle steamer, *DDSG Melk*, peeked out from behind the Schönbrunn, already teeming with passengers. They crammed against the railings and watched the Viennese group stream across the gangway. Lilly heard someone say the Melk passengers were Jews from Prague and Brno.

The Schönbrunn was a small pleasure boat usually used for tourist excursions up and down short stretches of the Danube. It wasn't designed to carry eight hundred refugees, on several days' journey, down to the port of Tulcea, Romania, and therefore had no passenger cabins. Chaos reigned, as passengers competed to find seats or a patch of deck to bed down and store their luggage.

Lilly scouted the lower deck. All taken. She edged her way along the congested passageway, eyes to the floor, taking care not to trip over limbs or luggage. The black and white diamond-chequered linoleum reminded her of the foyer of her parents' apartment building. She swept aside the sudden pang of homesickness and ascended the spiral staircase.

The upper deck was slightly less congested. She wandered between two rows of wooden benches to search for a pocket of space when a grey-haired woman sitting further along waved her over.

'There's a bit of room here.' She gestured towards the opposite bench. 'You are welcome to join me. Sorry I can't offer you the luxury suite.' Her hooded blue eyes crinkled at the corners.

Lilly managed a weak smile. 'Then this will have to do. Thank you.' She offloaded her luggage and settled across from the older woman. Something about her looked familiar to Lilly, but she couldn't quite place her.

'I'm Gisela Klein.'

'Nice to meet you, Frau Klein. I'm Lilly Simon.'

'Pleasure to meet you too, Lilly. But please, call me Gisela.'

'I feel like we have met before.'

'You also look familiar.' She studied Lilly's face. 'Where do I know you from?'

'Perhaps you're a friend of my mother, Amalia Aarons?'

Gisela took a moment to think, her fingers fidgeting with the peacock-patterned scarf she wore around her neck. She shook her head. 'No, I can't say I recognise the name.'

Lilly's gaze returned to the scarf. It was striking. Then it came to her. 'You reassured me and helped me stay calm outside the Central Office for Jewish Emigration after a Nazi thug punched that poor man.'

'Ah, yes.' Gisela gave a solemn nod. 'I remember.'

'I never had a proper chance to thank you that day.'

'I did nothing. And I'm glad we are meeting again under better circumstances. Are you travelling on your own?'

'Yes.' Lilly stared down at her folded hands on her lap, dreading further questions.

'So am I,' came the reply, and Lilly looked up again to find an understanding smile. Gisela reached out to pat her hand, and then quickly withdrew to allow a couple to pass. 'Oh, excuse me.'

The couple clung to each other and Lilly wasn't sure who was supporting who. The black-haired woman appeared to be in the advanced stages of pregnancy and her husband had the shaved head, gaunt face and haunted expression that meant Dachau to Lilly. They wavered before sitting, glancing nervously around the deck. Gisela began at once to remove her luggage and placed it underneath the bench. 'There's a bit more space here,' she said, glancing at Lilly for approval. Lilly gathered her belongings and moved next to Gisela.

'We're most grateful.' The woman looked relieved to take the weight from her feet as she settled opposite. 'Your daughter?'

'No. This is my new roommate, Lilly. We're just becoming acquainted.'

The woman gave them a wan smile. 'I'm Alma Freud and this is my husband, Max.'

Her husband gave a slight nod, before dropping his gaze to his feet.

'A pleasure to meet you both.' Gisela spoke in a cheery voice, as if she were the hostess of a party.

Alma stroked Max's trembling hand and they whispered together.

Gisela turned back to Lilly, attempting to offer the couple a semblance of privacy, where none could really expect to be found. 'I have two sons who live in Eretz Israel – one on a kibbutz in the Galilee, and the other in Tel Aviv. He's married.' She found a photograph in her bag and passed it to Lilly. 'He has two wonderful children - my grandson is four, and my granddaughter is only eighteen months old. I haven't met them yet — nor my daughter-in-law, so I'm very excited to see them all for the first time.' Lilly studied the formal portrait of the young man and woman, sitting, each with a child on their lap. 'What a sweet-looking family.'

Gisela's eyes sparkled at the compliment. 'And how about you, Lilly? Do you have family there?'

'My brother. He lives on a kibbutz in the north like your son.'

'And you'll be joining him?'

'It's a little complicated. He's newly married, so I don't feel I can impose on them. Apart from that, the kibbutz is quite secular. My brother is no longer that religious. But I'm unsure whether that lifestyle would suit me, or if I'm even the pioneering type.'

Gisela gave a small tilt of her head, as if to say she understood. 'I have a similar situation with my son on the kibbutz. Everyone must find their own way, *richtig?* But if you aren't going to be staying with your brother, what do you plan to do?'

'My cousin and I are going to find an apartment together and find jobs so we can support ourselves. She left for Bratislava with an earlier transport group and I'm hoping we reunite on the journey. I'm hoping it won't be too difficult for us to get on our feet.'

'You're young. I'm sure it will be easy for you to settle.'

'I don't feel young.'

'The past few years have taken a toll on us all, robbed us of our innocence and left us feeling older than our years. But you still have a lifetime of possibilities ahead of you.' Gisela delved into her case and offered Lilly a tin full of crescent-shaped biscuits. 'Try one. I made them myself yesterday.'

The buttery vanilla biscuit melted in Lilly's mouth. *Vanillekipferl*: a taste from her childhood. Her mother used to bake them.

'Mmm,' Gisela said, between bites. 'They came out well, if I do say so myself. Have another.'

Afternoon turned to evening, and they queued for their first meal on board, an adequate bowl of soup and a roll. In the fading light, passengers continued their relentless shuffle between decks, looking for more space. Alma and Max, however, had not moved since they had parked themselves near Lilly and Gisela earlier in the day. She dozed, her head on his shoulder; his head drooped. And each time someone passed by, his eyelids fluttered and his whole body tensed up. Then, realising it was just a fellow passenger, he relaxed again. Until the next passenger passed by.

The sun dipped behind the rooftops, and the sky turned from pink to purple. Lilly was reminded of the setting sun in the Prater park, so close to where she sat on the boat, though it could have been thousands of miles away for all that she could go there. The spring after she and Salo had started seeing one another, they often went for walks through the park's tree-lined avenues. It was there that they concealed themselves in the shadows of the grand chestnut trees to kiss, away from prying eyes.

And it had been at the pinnacle of the *Wiener Riesenrad*, Vienna's giant Ferris wheel, in the same park, at sunset, with the city spread beneath them, that Salo had taken Lilly's hands and proposed to her. Of course, she had said yes, and they had both cried tears of joy. Those were beautiful days filled with love.

Lilly knew she was leaving a part of herself behind. In an alternate life, Salo and she would wander forever through the streets of a peaceful Vienna and kiss in the Prater. The loss of that reality was still hard to assimilate.

Though he was gone, Salo's presence remained with her like a guardian angel. He had paved the way for her to flee. His foresight in hiding her jewellery had provided the funds to pay for this transport. The money he had stowed away would now support her parents for the foreseeable future. An uncertain future.

Her parents' home was so close, but their separation was already real. Her mother and aunt were probably sitting down for supper and looking towards the empty seat at the table. Which of them felt the most lonely tonight? Lilly looked towards the city, lost in her thoughts.

Gisela also watched the light fading over Vienna and hummed a tune to herself, the famous song by Rudolf Sieczyński.

*Vienna, Vienna, only you alone*
*Should always be the city of my dreams ...*
*I know the city very well*
*Yes, I am at home there*
*By day and even more so by night ...*
*If I had to leave this beautiful place one day*
*My longing would have no end.*

# CHAPTER 11

L illy opened her eyes to the soft morning light. The boat's engine had come to life, shuddering and chugging as it started up.

The last thing she remembered was lying on the hard bench, staring up at the stars, lost in her memories. At some point, she must have dozed off. Now, blinking in the sun, she looked around to find most passengers crowded around the railings, Gisela included. Lilly swung her legs off the bench and rose to join her.

A plume of smoke billowed from the funnel. The paddles started to rotate, churning the water beneath. With a series of sharp hisses, the Schönbrunn released a cloud of vapour. A crew member tooted the horn. The Melk did the same. Then the two paddle steamers set off, gliding down the Danube.

Gisela dabbed her eyes and nose with a dainty, embroidered handkerchief. Vienna. What sorrow that they had to depart like this. A reluctant farewell.

Lilly watched Vienna disappear out of sight as they sailed downstream towards Bratislava. Salo's birthplace.

She turned to stare into the depths of the river, remembering another time and place. The chatter of the passengers became her memory of the hum of commuters in the Nordbahnhof. Sitting in the station's café, a few weeks after they had secretly started seeing each other, Lilly asked Salo what had made him leave his parents in Bratislava and move to Vienna.

He hitched his shoulders with a rueful smile. 'I'm an orphan. I never knew my parents,' he said. 'My father lost his life in the Great War five months before I was born. Then, when I was six months old, my mother died from the Spanish flu.'

'Oh, I'm so sorry,' Lilly said, feeling awful for having asked.

He reached across the table and took her hand. 'Don't be,' he said. 'I never knew the difference, and I had a happy childhood.'

He told her how he was raised by his doting grandmother and how they had lived next door to his uncle and aunt. Their four sons were more like brothers to him than cousins. He played in the cobbled alleys of Bratislava's Jewish quarter with those boys and other neighbourhood children, always belonging and he had never felt for one instant that his childhood was deprived.

At seventeen, Salo's life was turned upside down. His beloved grandmother fell on an icy street, hit her head, and subsequently died from the injury. He moved next door to his uncle's home and worked in the family's grocery store – an opportunity for him, as his eldest cousin had emigrated to Canada. But a few months later, Salo's uncle decided that the rest of the family would cross the ocean too, in search of the same opportunities the eldest son had found. Salo had been invited to accompany them, but he felt that he would be an additional burden to his uncle. Instead, he decided to move to Vienna, his father's birthplace, and where his great-uncle Gustav, a successful businessman, still lived.

Before leaving, Salo wrote to his Onkel Gustav to ask for assistance to find work to support himself. Gustav's reply was non-committal. He suggested only that Salo pay him a visit once he arrived in the city.

When Salo appeared on the doorstep of his great-uncle's elegant home in Vienna's First District dressed in his threadbare suit, Onkel Gustav looked at him askance. Gustav struggled to hide his disapproval when Salo politely declined the pork sausages he offered for supper. And he had no more than vague assurances that he would look into a few possibilities to comfort Salo before he departed after the tense meal.

When a week passed with no word, Salo returned to Oncle Gustav's home. The older man mumbled excuses about his business commitments and promised half-heartedly that he would try to help in the coming weeks. Salo was determined to make his living in Vienna, yet he did not want to admit his desperation: he had only enough money to cover food and rent at his cheap lodgings for one more week. He realised he could not rely on his great-uncle, so he thanked him for his time and left. He would have to make his own way.

The next two days, Salo combed the commercial streets of the Second District and inquired in every shop whether they might have a job for him.

That was the first time Lilly heard of Salo. Her papa returned from the shop that evening and they were sitting down for supper when he announced he had hired a new employee, a very polite young Jewish man called Salo, who had recently moved from Bratislava. He had approached Papa as he was raising the shutter and asked if he had any jobs available. It was an opportune moment. Two days earlier, Papa's unreliable assistant, Hans, who made a habit of showing up late, or worse, calling in sick, had handed in his notice without warning. Papa had been looking for a replacement to work alongside him and her brother, Eugen, and offered Salo a month's trial on the spot.

Before long, Papa was singing Salo's praises. How hard-working and diligent he was. How well he served the customers. His month's trial became a permanent position.

Soon, Eugen was talking about him too. They had become friendly at work and Eugen often invited Salo to join him at the Zionist youth movement meetings he attended. Eugen was intent on moving to a kibbutz and becoming a pioneer. His parents treated the idea with a degree of amusement. They couldn't imagine their city boy emigrating to become a farmer, and suspected he was participating in order to meet girls.

One night at supper, Lilly's father again mentioned Salo: 'He's the best employee I've ever hired.'

This time, Lilly's mother interjected. 'I'd like to meet this Salo I've heard so much about,' she said. 'Why don't you invite him to eat with us on Friday night?'

'I'll ask him tomorrow.'

Lilly was startled by the doorbell two hours before Shabbos. She opened the door to a tall young man with dark hair and sincere eyes, bearing a bouquet and a bottle of wine.

This was Salo? Lilly couldn't help staring at him, as she lifted her hand to straighten her hair. She had been helping her mother in the kitchen, and she was dusted all over with flour.

'I ... I am ... invited ... I'm ... Salo,' he stumbled over his words. 'Your father invited me for supper tonight ... these are for your parents.' He offered her the wine and flowers with a shaky hand.

'Thank you.'

'Good Shabbos.' His lips twitched in a subtle smile, a hint of colour rising in his cheeks. 'See you later.'

She closed the door and sucked in a breath.

'Who was that?' her mother called from the kitchen.

Lilly composed herself. 'Just Papa's assistant. He brought some flowers and wine for you.'

'That's nice.'

Hannah and Tante Rebecca arrived minutes later. Lilly practically dragged Hannah up to her bedroom and slammed the door shut.

'What's wrong?' Hannah said.

'Papa's assistant from the shop is coming for Friday night supper.'

'So I heard. And?'

'He's ... he's ...'

'Lilly?' Hannah poked her in the ribs. 'Why are you blushing?'

All that evening, Lilly stole glances at him. Every so often, he looked in her direction too. Noticing the exchange, Hannah kicked Lilly under the table. It took all Lilly's willpower to keep her composure.

'You like him, don't you?' Hannah said later as she lay in the twin bed across from Lilly.

Lilly smiled in the darkness but didn't reply. A pillow landed on her head.

'Ow! What was that for?'

Lilly took aim and threw it back. Hannah laughed, climbed out of bed, and swung her pillow. Lilly rolled out of the way as the pillow hit her mattress. She jumped onto the floor and aimed hers at Hannah. Their pillows collided with a muffled, feathery thud. Soon they were in hysterics, chasing each other around the room and wacking each other with their pillows.

'Girls, what's going on in there?' Mama called along the hallway. 'We're all trying to get some sleep.'

'Sorry!' Lilly said. 'We'll try to be quieter.'

Panting for breath, she collapsed on her bed, failing to suppress her laughter.

'Shhh.' Hannah flopped onto the bed beside her 'That was fun. We haven't had a pillow fight in years.'

'Not since we were about twelve and split a pillow.'

Hannah giggled. 'I'll never forget the horrified expression on our mothers' faces when they walked in and saw the state of your room. Feathers were flying everywhere.'

Lilly propped herself on her elbow. 'In answer to your question. Yes.'

'What do you mean?'

'I do like him.'

Hannah sat up with a soft clap of her hands. 'I knew it! He's interested in you, too.'

'Do you think so?'

'I'm certain. He couldn't keep his eyes off you.'

'How can I see him again?'

'Easy. Stop by the shop.'

'That would look too obvious. What excuse do I give if my Papa asks the reason for my visit? I never usually go there after school.'

'We'll have to figure out a good excuse.'

They sat until the early hours plotting and planning, but Lilly never got the chance to put their ideas into action. The following Monday, after her parents left for their regular night out at the cinema, Salo appeared at their door.

'Sorry,' she said. 'My father's not in.'

'I actually came for Eugen. I think we were supposed to be going to a meeting tonight, but I can't remember if he said to meet him here or there.'

'He already left. Almost half an hour ago.'

'Oh.' He didn't show any signs of disappointment, instead he seemed to have expected the answer.

'You've probably missed most of the meeting now.'

'I probably have.' He lingered in the doorway.

'Since you're already here, would you like to come in for a few minutes and have a hot drink?'

Salo entered without hesitation.

That was the start of their secret courtship.

On Mondays, when her parents went to the cinema and Eugen to his meetings, Salo would come over to visit. Other evenings, she would slip out with the excuse of seeing Hannah or another of her friends, and they would meet at the Nordbahnhof. During those icy winter nights when Salo could not yet afford to take her out, the heated train station became their haven. She would sink into his arms for endless hellos and goodbyes and furtive kisses. When spring arrived, they would take long walks through the avenues of the Prater park.

On Friday nights, Salo became a regular visitor to their home. In public, they maintained an air of civility: Lilly, the boss's daughter; Salo, her father's employee. But beneath the table, their feet would meet, and if seated beside each other, so would their hands.

They had been seeing each other in secret for six months and Lilly felt increasingly guilty for their deception.

'I ought to tell my parents,' she said as they strolled through the Prater, under a canopy of trees, on a spring evening filled with birdsong.

'What if they are against it? There could be serious consequences.'

'My father likes you.'

'Yes, as his employee.'

'He doesn't mind that you and Eugen are friendly.'

'It's not the same. We're work colleagues. I have tremendous respect for your father. I don't want him to think I've betrayed his trust or risk losing my job.'

'If I ask you a question, will you give me an honest answer?'

'Always.'

'How do you feel about me?'

'I love you. You know I do.'

'Is your love for me a short-term diversion or do you consider it something more?'

Salo stopped walking, gently cupped her face and kissed her. 'You mean the world to me. I always want to be with you.'

'Then my parents will have to find out sometime, won't they?'

'I suppose so,' he said, but his eyes betrayed his anxiety.

At the entrance to her apartment, he hesitated once more.

'Won't you come with me?' Lilly said.

'I'm worried about facing your father. What if your parents decide I'm not good enough for you and won't let me see you anymore? What will I do if your father ends my employment? I can't afford to lose this job.'

'Salo, I love you. You are the best thing in my life. I won't let that happen.'

Lilly's father was in the study, poring over supplier catalogues and order forms.

He looked up with a smile as she entered and put down his pen. 'Hello, *mein Schatz*.'

'I hope I'm not disturbing, you look rather busy. Do you have a spare moment to talk?'

'Of course I have time for you. I'm working on next month's order. Sales in the shop have increased, so I'm planning to add several new lines.'

Lilly leaned against his desk. 'That's good news. What has led to the increase in sales?'

'I believe it's down to several factors,' said her father, launching into one of his favourite subjects. 'In the spring, people plan their summer holidays and the suitcases they'll need. It is also thanks to

Salo. He's such an asset. Apart from Eugen, I've never had such an excellent assistant. He is wonderful with the customers. So helpful and patient.'

'You've taken a great liking to him, haven't you?'

'I have indeed.'

'What if I told you I liked Salo too?'

'I'd be happy to hear that.'

'I do like him,' Lilly said. 'More than like him.'

He studied her face, a faint smile playing on his lips. 'Are you saying what I think you're trying to say?'

'Yes. I am.' She nervously nibbled her lip. 'We have been seeing each other for a while. I'm sorry I kept it from you. I should have told you earlier.'

Papa's smile widened. 'We had wondered. Mama had her suspicions.'

'You don't mind?'

'Why should I mind?'

'It doesn't bother you that he's not from an established family within the Viennese Jewish community and isn't well off?'

'Lilly, you should know by now that those are not the values we brought you up with. He's a wonderful boy. Kind, sincere, caring. That matters far more than coming from a monied family.' He chuckled. 'I have to admit, Mama and I both considered him for you in the future. We didn't suggest it yet as we didn't feel you'd be ready and he is also still quite young, not yet twenty. But since it's happened of its own accord, let me offer you a piece of advice. Don't rush in. Take a little time to make sure this is what you both want. And if you do, you have our blessing.'

'Thank you!' Lilly flung her arms around her father. 'I'll tell him at once.'

'Where is he?'

'He's waiting outside. He was worried you might be angry and he would lose his job.'

'*Ach*! Poor thing. Bring him up right away. I'd like to speak to him.'

Lilly found him pacing the pavement, head bent, hands clenched by his side. Lilly took his hands. His eyes searched her face.

'You haven't lost your job,' she said.

'He's not angry with me?'

'No.' She shook her head with a reassuring smile. 'He wants to talk to you.'

Salo's face remained taut as he entered her father's study. Papa rose from his chair and put a hand on Salo's shoulder. 'I want you to know, you're always welcome in our home. And we have no objections to you and Lilly seeing each other.'

Salo looked overcome with emotion, but he clenched his jaw to contain himself and shook Papa's hand.

When Lilly accepted his proposal eighteen months later, her parents couldn't have been happier. Salo had become like a second son to them, and he had grown to love them as the parents he never had. So much so that when they knew they had to flee Vienna, Salo gave Lilly his word they wouldn't leave her parents behind.

'Bratislava!'

'Pressburg!'

Lilly was jolted out of her recollections. Some called the city by its Slovak name, others by its older German name.

The paddle steamer rounded a bend and the city came into view. Lilly recognised the red rooftops, the gothic spire of the cathedral, and the castle on the hill.

She had visited Bratislava once before, with Salo, just before their marriage. He showed her the old cobblestone streets where he played as a child. Then he brought her to the graves of his parents and grandmother where he prayed and, in keeping with the Jewish custom, symbolically invited them to attend their wedding.

Three years later, the day before she left Vienna, also in keeping with Jewish custom, Lilly had visited Salo's grave. She had gone there to say goodbye. The cemetery was crowded with people like herself, taking leave of their deceased loved ones, not knowing whether they would ever return.

Loss and guilt hit her anew like a crashing wave.

Salo had promised they wouldn't leave without her parents, but here she was. No Salo. Parents left behind after all.

Their boat neared the landing pier and two more white paddle steamers came into view. Hundreds of people crowded their decks, waving and cheering. Lilly could not see Hannah among the throng, but knew she must be there. The lingering sense of loss mixed with newly found relief became too much, and the tears streamed down her face. Without a word, Gisela hugged her tight, patted her back, and let her cry.

From the deck of the Helios, Hannah watched the two paddle steamers from Vienna draw closer. She couldn't see Lilly in the crowd, but was sure her cousin was there. The river sparkled in the sunlight, and they were on the brink of their freedom. Bratislava had never appeared as magnificent as it did that morning.

At that moment, without anyone knowing who started it, across all four boats, the air suddenly reverberated with stirring harmonies, as thousands of voices rose together, singing Hatikva, the song of hope.

*As long as deep in the heart,*

*The soul of a Jew yearns,*
*And forward to the East,*
*To Zion, an eye looks,*
*Our hope will not be lost,*
*The ancient hope,*
*To return to the land of our fathers,*
*The city where David encamped.*

Hannah was not ashamed of the tears that rolled down her cheeks. After months of delays and difficulties, they were leaving at last. On the boat ahead was her fiance, Karl, and on one of those following after, her cousin Lilly. It was nothing short of a miracle.

With a blast of their horns, the four boats set off in convoy down the Danube.

A Swastika fluttered from every mast.

# THE DANUBE JOURNEY

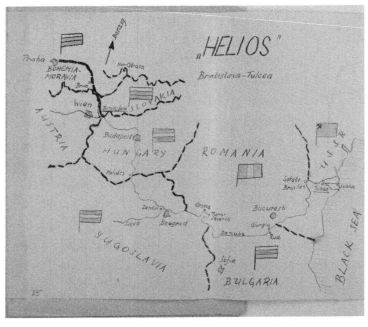

Drawn by passenger Franci-Jehudith Lederer-Berger-Schlesinger
Courtesy of the Ghetto Fighters' House Archives, Israel

# CHAPTER 12

Hannah strained to catch sight of Karl's boat, but the distance between them had grown too great as the Uranus surged forward. They had left Bratislava behind and were sailing through the Danube's floodplain forest. A canopy of mature, emerald-green trees blanketed both sides of the river, which glistened like diamonds in the sun. After the drab Patronka, the brilliant jewel-like colours were a feast for her eyes.

Hannah tilted her head, gazed at the feathery clouds drifting across an azure sky, and let the sun warm her face. She inhaled the clear, woodsy air and grew heady with exhilaration. She felt alive. Free.

As the Helios continued down the river, Hannah watched the forest give way in turn to pebbly shores, grass verges, and lastly, dense thickets. On the left bank was Slovakia, but looking to the right bank, she understood that they had crossed over into Hungary.

By mid-afternoon, they passed the Hungarian city of Esztergom. Perched on a hilltop, at a river bend, a centuries-old stone castle watched over the city, overshadowed only by the grand turquoise dome of the Esztergom Basilica.

Rolling hills gave way to flat plains, and at sunset, the skyline of a metropolis came into view. The boats passed under a series of bridges and, at the golden hour, they entered the capital, Budapest. The setting sun bathed the city's domes and spires in a radiance. But for all the city's splendour, what made Hannah's heart swell was the paddle boat docked just ahead, with Karl waiting for her at the stern.

He cupped his hands to his mouth and called, 'How are you, my love?'

'All the better for seeing you,' she replied 'And you?'

'Everything is fine, but I miss you.' He placed his hand on his heart. 'I can't wait until we're together again.'

Erika eased her way next to Hannah and waved at Marcus who had joined Karl.

'This is a bit like a pleasure cruise, isn't it?' she said, turning to Hannah. 'Apart from the overcrowding and basic food, that is.'

'Other than not travelling with Karl, it's quite an enjoyable journey. I never realised Budapest is such a beautiful city.'

'It's magnificent. I'd take this over the Patronka any day. But I miss Marcus and the deep conversations we had. I've never been able to share my thoughts and feelings with anyone else the way I can with him.'

'Do you think you have a future together?'

Erika glanced across to Marcus, waving back at her from the Uranus, and her face softened into a dreamy expression. 'I think we might.'


In the purple twilight, Budapest transformed into an enchanted city, lit by thousands of lights, and the illuminated parliament building was reflected on the Danube's glassy surface. Lilly was amazed by the contrast between this brightly twinkling city and the nightly blackouts in Vienna.

The boats had stopped to load supplies of food, water, and coal. A crowd of onlookers had gathered on the quayside to stare at the curious convoy and a police presence had arrived to ensure the peace. A pointed reminder that they were not ordinary tourists cruising down the Danube and were still subject to restrictions.

Some of those on the shore had relatives on board, and they began shouting passengers' names. The ship-bound crowd responded to the call, echoing the names until the relatives were found and rushed to the port side to greet their family.

Lilly watched the broad smiles and heard the excited cries as passengers spotted their loved ones on the quayside. She scanned the crowded deck of the paddle steamer ahead, eager for her own reunion. 'I wonder which boat my cousin is on?'

'Why not shout across and ask?' Gisela said.

Lily's eyes darted between her boat and the one just ahead, unable to bring herself to yell in public.

'I can't do that.'

'Of course you can. Go on. Don't be shy.'

Lilly took a deep breath, determined to overcome her modesty.

'Lilly!' She pricked up at the sound of a passenger calling her name. 'Is there a Lilly Simon here?'

She leapt to her feet. 'Yes.'

'There's someone on the next boat asking for you.'

Lilly navigated her way to the bow and found Hannah standing not quite near enough to touch, on the stern of the Helios. She waved both arms above her head in her cousin's direction. 'Lilly!' Hannah called, her voice joyous. 'I'm so happy to see you.'

Hannah was thinner than Lilly remembered, her cheekbones more pronounced, but she looked well despite the months of incarceration. Better than Lilly had prepared herself for.

Lilly shook her head in wonder, scarcely able to take in the reality of seeing her cousin once more. 'We're together again,' she said, struggling to make herself heard over the commotion of dozens of other conversations. 'Just like you said we'd be. How are you?'

'I'm doing well. I'm so pleased we're on our way at last and relieved you are here with me.' Hannah smiled. 'Well, almost here.'

Lilly realised Hannah seemed different somehow. Possibly more content? It was difficult to tell.

There was an awkward pause. Lilly had dreamed of this day. The thought of what she would say to Hannah when they reunited was what kept her going through the tense months of waiting. But now, in this public setting, when they had to shout across to one another, she struggled to say anything at all. 'Your mama sends her love,' Lilly managed.

'Thank you. How is she?'

'She's keeping well.'

'And your parents?'

Lilly shrugged. She wanted to tell Hannah everything. But how could she share such personal details when it would mean broadcasting her news across the boats for everyone to hear?

Hannah nodded. She seemed to understand. 'Probably easier to talk when we have more privacy,' Hannah called. 'We have a lot of catching up to do. I also have some news—'

The boat horns blared, the engines released a hiss of steam, the paddles began to turn, and the chorus of goodbyes that followed drowned out the rest of Hannah's sentence. She shook her head in frustration. All Lilly could do was wave as the boats set off again. Knowing Hannah was just ahead made her feel less alone, yet Lilly felt oddly deflated. She had pictured a very different reunion – an emotional reconnecting, hugging, crying, laughing. She thought of how they usually spoke over each other with so much to share. Were they not able to have a proper conversation anymore? Of course, the hordes of people on the boats didn't help.

The convoy passed beneath the Chain Bridge, twinkling with lights, and sailed out of Budapest. Soon, Hannah's boat, the Helios, raced into the distance. Lilly kept her focus on the little dot of light shining like a beacon.

The convoy had already established its formation for travelling: the Uranus took the lead, followed by the Helios, the Schonbrunn, and finally, the Melk. Sometimes they sailed close together, sometimes the distance grew between them.

By dawn, the boats had crossed the border into Yugoslavia. Lilly exchanged good mornings with Alma and Max. The couple still kept to themselves, but as the miles increased between them and Vienna, Max seemed less anxious.

They glided on and, intermittently, the shrub-covered banks gave way to thickets of trees, small towns, and villages. The scene was largely monotonous and flat, but the wide open spaces conveyed their own kind of magnificence.

Lilly and Gisela watched the changing landscape as they sipped cups of tea. Lilly offered her friend a piece of her mother's Gugelhupf cake. A taste of home amid all the unfamiliar.

'Your mother's cake is delicious,' Gisela said, in between bites. 'Tastier than anything shop-bought.'

'My mama's an excellent baker. Her Gugelhupf is my favourite. She specially made it for me.'

'I hope you have the recipe?'

A morsel of cake lodged in Lilly's throat as the reality of her departure struck her anew. 'I didn't think to ask.'

'Never mind. When you write, you can ask her for it,' Gisela said in her calm and reassuring way as she glanced up at the cloudless sky. 'Isn't this wonderful? Sitting here with you on this fine day eating your mama's tasty cake. The next best thing to being in a Kaffeehaus.' She heaved a sigh. 'How I miss those days. I used to love sitting with my late husband over a coffee topped with a generous layer of cream and a slice of apple strudel. He told the best stories and could always make me laugh. We would talk for hours. He was the kindest, most patient man I ever knew. Then came the November Pogrom and life was never the same.'

'How did you carry on?'

'I had no choice.' Gisela's eyes seemed to search Lilly's. 'We've all had our share of suffering over the past couple of years, haven't we?'

Lilly nodded slowly.

'Some days it is hard, really too much to bear, but I try to be grateful and count my blessings. I have two lovely sons and gorgeous grandchildren whom I'll meet soon. We are so lucky to have secured places on this transport.' Gisela swept her arm at the Danube's expanse. A faint smudge of a vessel and its steam funnel revealed the Helios ahead. 'Even though it's heartbreaking to leave our homes and loved ones, this opportunity for a fresh start, away from the fear and terror is a gift. We mustn't take it for granted.'

'A fresh start.' Lilly turned the words over in her mouth like an unfamiliar flavour.

'Meanwhile, this is turning into a rather pleasant excursion, even if the sleeping accommodation is not the Hotel Sacher.' She patted Lilly's hand. 'And lovely to have made a new friend.'

'I am grateful to have met you too.'

'Once we're settled in Eretz Israel, and you have your mother's Gugelhupf recipe, please bake one for me. Then you'll come and visit me in my new home and we'll sit in the garden under the shade of a tree to drink coffee and eat your cake.'

Lilly raised her cup of tea in toast to what Gisela had said. 'That's a deal.'

It was after nightfall when the Schönbrunn sailed past the lights that were Belgrade, the capital of Yugoslavia. This time, they continued without stopping. Their journey was going to plan. They were making steady progress and closing the distance towards their destination. They had left the Nazi-controlled countries, and hopefully also the war, behind them. Still, Lilly couldn't shake a growing sense of unease as she settled in for the night.

# CHAPTER 13

Daybreak of the third day on board the Helios revealed a change of scenery. Gauzy, rose-coloured clouds brushed the peaks of dove grey hills that fringed the river on either side and dipped into the water's edge. The Danube here again served as the boundary between two countries: Yugoslavia on the right and Romania on the left.

As the light grew brighter, the viridescent shades of the landscape shifted from sage to forest green, and the river narrowed. Hannah and Erika had positioned themselves with their friends on the starboard side of the boat in order to best take in the views. Hannah gazed in awe as the hills gave way to majestic, steep-sided mountains, famously known as the Iron Gates, where the fast-flowing Danube wound its way through a string of gorges between the southern Carpathian Mountain range. On the Yugoslavian bank, an engraved stone plaque set into a hollow caught Hannah's eye. 'Tabula Traiana,' she read the carved sign on the lip of an overhanging rock. 'I wonder what it means.'

'I think it's Latin,' Erika said. 'It looks ancient. Perhaps it's from Roman times.'

'IMP. CAESAR. DIVI. NERVAE. F.' Hannah tried to decipher the first line. 'You may be right. It says "Caesar."'

'You're both correct,' Stefan interjected, having heard their musings. 'It is a memorial plaque written in Latin to commemorate the victories of the Roman Empire over the Kingdom of Dacia and their completion of Emperor Trajan's military road. The full inscription means: "Emperor Caesar, son of the divine Nerva, Nerva Trajan, the Augustus, Germanicus, Pontifex Maximus, invested for the fourth time as Tribune, Father of the Fatherland, Consul for the third time, excavating mountain rocks and using wood beams, has made this road.'"

'*Unglaublich*!' Erika regarded him in amazement. 'How do you know that?'

'I used to be a history teacher.' He looked wistful.

Used to be, Hannah thought, until they dismissed him from his post because he was a Jew.

'A good teacher, it would seem,' she said.

'And an excellent tour guide,' Erika added.

Jenny laughed. 'The best.' She leaned her head on her husband's shoulder. Stefan smiled at her praise.

The rest of their companions gathered around to ply him with more questions.

'Where's the Kingdom of Dacia?' Alexander said.

'It has ceased to exist. But once,' Stefan tilted his head towards the opposite bank. 'It occupied part of the territory of what is today Romania. Until the Romans conquered it.'

'What happened to the Dacian people?'

'The Romans killed many. They put others into slavery. Those who managed to evade the Romans fled and survived.'

'It sounds similar to our history in ancient Judea,' Isaak said.

'Yes, there are similarities.'

'I'm guessing this military road they mention on the plaque was used to convey the troops who defeated the Dacians,' Alexander said.

'Yes, as well as other purposes like transporting supplies, slaves ...'

'Did they also transport Jewish slaves on this road?' Isaak said.

'Most probably.'

'Father of the Fatherland.' Alexander quoted the words Stefan had translated from the plaque. 'Sounds like the type of phrase the Nazis would use today.'

Stefan's mouth tightened into a straight line. 'Where do you think they got it from?'

'Do evil empires always succeed?' Janka asked.

'Only in the short term. Even the Roman Empire eventually collapsed.'

A reflective mood came over the group, until Erika broke the silence. 'Will there be any other historic sights along our route?'

'If memory serves me correctly, we'll soon be passing the town of Kladovo, and on its outskirts, there's another point of interest.'

The rock cliffs receded to gentle hills and lower plains again, and soon afterwards, Stefan drew their attention to the remains of a large stone fortress on the right bank of the river. 'That's Fetislam, a fortress from the Ottoman times when they occupied this region. They built it as a stronghold to launch further conquests into Hungary and invade Transylvania. Did you know there was a Turkish garrison that remained there until the middle of last century?'

Hannah continued to take in the landscape along the Danube's right bank. The riverbank widened on the Yugoslavian side, and in the distance, she perceived a gathering crowd. As the boat drew closer, she heard their calls and saw arms raised and waving in the air.

She pointed to the curious gathering. 'I wonder what's going on over there.'

'They are shouting something. I can't make it out,' Janka said. 'It sounds as if they're trying to attract our attention. What could they want with us? How do they even know who we are?'

A piece of white fabric fluttered above the group.

'I think they're trying to surrender,' Erika said.

Hannah eyed the swastika flapping from their boat's mast. 'I hope they haven't mistaken us for Nazis and are afraid we're about to invade or attack them.'

Alexander squinted at the crowd's flag, which the people waved from side to side in a wide arch. 'That's not a white flag.' His voice rose with excitement. 'It's a white and blue flag, with a Magen David at its centre!'

Isaak strained his eyes. 'Oh my, you're right!'

'Perhaps they're members of the local community who have come out to cheer for us.' Janka said. 'We should wave back.'

Alexander raised his hand. Then, almost at once, dropped it back to his side. 'I don't think they're cheering. They are calling to us. Listen.'

The Helios drew nearer. Close enough to discern that some were shouting names and others, the greeting 'Shalom!' Close enough to distinguish faces in the crowd.

Isaak leaned forward. His eyes widened. The blood drained from his face.

'Stop the boat!'

'Isaak,' Alexander said. 'What—'

'Papa!' Isaak shouted, and scaled the railings. 'Mama! Aron!'

'*Mein Gott!*' Alexander grabbed hold of him.

The boat was now parallel with the crowd on land. Other passengers were also calling out to their families and friends.

'We have to stop this boat at once,' Isaak said. 'We have to rescue them.'

Without loosening his grip on his cousin, Alexander turned to Janka. 'Alert the captain! Call the Haganah. Quick!'

Janka hurried down the steps. She wasn't the only one.

'Stop! Stop the boat!' a chorus of passengers shouted.

'Papa! Mama! Aron!' cried Isaak, waving his hands desperately in the air. He stumbled, almost losing his balance. Jenny screamed. Stefan rushed forward and helped Alexander support him.

'Isaak!' A man in a greying moustache, standing next to a gaunt, middle-aged woman in a kerchief, and a lanky boy of about fifteen, waved wildly. The noise drowned out the rest of his words.

'What?' he said as their boat sailed by.

They cupped their hands to their mouths. 'See you ... Eretz Israel.'

'See you in Eretz,' Isaak said, his words heavy with emotion.

As the divide between them grew, he waved and blew kisses until the faces on the bank were no longer visible.

Alexander and Stefan supported Isaak as he descended the railings and slumped to the deck. Alexander hugged him. 'I'm so sorry.'

Isaak buried his head in his hands. 'Why couldn't we rescue them?'

Stefan opened his mouth to speak, but the words failed him, and he patted Isaak on the shoulder instead.

Janka came back, panting. 'I tried. Others begged too. The Haganah said if it were up to them, they would have stopped and taken on board as many people as possible.' She nodded to the odious flag that taunted them from its mast. 'But the officials won't permit our boat to stop in Kladovo. And the Haganah can't risk doing something reckless that jeopardises all of us.'

'Thank you for trying.' Isaak could barely get the words out.

Alexander sat on his haunches. 'Try not to despair. When we almost gave up hope while we waited in the Slobodarna, you were the one who kept up our spirits and told us to have patience because our boat would come in time. And you were right. Have faith that another boat will come for them too.' Alexander leaned in close to Isaak, as he attempted to reassure him in whispered tones.

To give them more privacy, Hannah and Erika stepped away, and Janka did the same.

'I don't understand,' Hannah said. 'I'm sure I remember when we first met Isaak at the Slobodarna, he mentioned how lucky his parents were because they were already on a ship.'

'That's what he thought at the time.' Janka glanced towards Isaak and Alexander, then backed away further towards the stern to make sure they were out of earshot. A sombre mood had descended upon them all.

'His parents and younger brother left on a transport last December. Apparently, when the river began to freeze, the crew forced them off the boat and abandoned them at Kladovo.'

'What?' Hannah paused to take it all in. 'Do you mean they've been stranded here all this time, for over nine months and throughout the bitter winter?'

The grave expression on Janka's face stopped Hannah's questions.

'I don't understand,' said Erika. 'Why didn't they continue their journey once the river had thawed?'

'First, they would need a boat in order to continue down river to Tulcea and second, they would need the guarantee of a ship waiting for them in the port in Romania to transport them for the rest of the journey,' said Janka.

'Is there no boat or ship for them?' Erika said.

'It seems not.'

'What's to say this crew won't discard us like the group in Kladovo?' Hannah said.

'I doubt that will happen,' Janka said.

'What makes you so sure?'

'Because rumour has it that these boats are going to be used to repatriate Bessarabian Germans on the return journey. They needed the boats down the Danube. So, rather than send them empty, they crammed them with Jews, who were desperate enough to pay the outrageous fare, and thereby subsidise the Germans' return journey. But at least we got out – it gave us the means to leave.'

Erika's eyes widened in surprise. 'You're saying the Nazis used us?'

'Did you think they were looking out for our welfare? They figured out how to make some money and get rid of a bunch of Jews at the same time.' She laughed, but a modicum of bitterness coloured her laughter. 'Funny how the Nazis claim we're the greedy ones controlling the banks when they are the ones freezing Jewish bank accounts and bleeding us dry for every Reichsmark.'

Hannah surveyed the Helios with new eyes: an overcrowded pleasure boat filled with Jewish refugees who were not yet out of harm's way. They may have left Germany and Austria and Czechoslovakia behind, but they remained under Nazi authority. The holiday-like good cheer was like a sinister masquerade — they knew they had been lucky to get permits to leave, they appreciated the Danube's views and fresh air, but the Third Reich still held sway over them.

'How do we know there will be a ship waiting for us in Tulcea?' she asked.

'Well ... I ...' The question doused Janka's heated rhetoric. Suddenly she looked less sure of herself. 'I suppose we'll only find out when we get there.'

# CHAPTER 14

The Danube had lost its lustre. In the misty morning light, its water was a muddy brown. Gone was the dramatic scenery of gorges and soaring mountains; in their place, tree-carpeted plains. The Helios continued onwards, indifferent. On the right bank, they crossed the border from Yugoslavia into Bulgaria. On their left, they plied a steady course along Romania's border towards Tulcea and the Black Sea. The landscape was as flat as Hannah's mood. She couldn't shake off the previous day's events. Witnessing the stranded Jewish group in Kladovo had awakened a slew of fears.

The encounter at Kladovo had also left its mark on Isaak. When Hannah met him in the tea queue, she sensed his melancholy.

'I'm sorry about what happened to your family,' she said. 'It must be very hard for you.'

'It is,' he agreed. 'I feel terrible leaving them behind. But we're all in a precarious situation, aren't we? When my parents and brother left Vienna on their transport, I was stuck in Prague. Each time our group got to the railway station expecting to leave, the Gestapo just laughed and sent us home. On the third attempt, we finally boarded a train and reached Bratislava, only to be interned at the Slobodarna. Meanwhile, my family boarded a boat, but were stranded in Klado-vo. And there were times we thought we'd never get on a boat, but here we are, sailing down the Danube. So please God, I hope they will continue their journey soon too.'

'Maybe they'll catch up with us when we reach the port in Tulcea.'

'Let's hope so.' Isaak attempted a smile, but Hannah suspected it was a show for her sake.

She returned to her place on the bench and was sipping her tea when she spotted a line of river boats berthed on the Bulgarian side of the river. The Helios was approaching the port city of Ruse. She rose to get a better view.

Ahead, anchored in the centre of the river, Hannah caught sight of a decrepit, grey paddle steamer with a rusting smokestack that listed starboard. The peculiar vessel appeared to have been abandoned there for quite some time and looked on the verge of sinking. But as the Helios drew parallel with the dilapidated boat, Hannah got a closer look and went cold. The boat wasn't empty; gaunt, emaciated people crowded its deck, desperately waving their arms to attract attention.

'Help us!' the wasted figures called. 'We are hungry.'

'*Mein Gott*!' Janka drew in a sharp breath. 'It's the Pentcho.'

'The group that left Bratislava in May?' Hannah said in disbelief.

Janka nodded, her eyes fixed on the sunken faces.

Hannah remembered the news reaching the Patronka about a group of five hundred Jewish refugees who had successfully boarded a boat from Bratislava. Back then, the report had given her hope for her own chances of leaving. What had happened?

'We're hungry! Please help us!' Their cries were pitiful.

'We must do something,' Erika said as they sailed past. 'We can't leave them in this state.'

No sooner had Erika finished speaking than their boat slowed down and came to a sudden stop beside another paddle boat docked at the quay. The Uranus. Karl's boat.

Passengers from both sides hurried to the railings to greet each other. But they only had words for the Pentcho, still in view. Hannah searched for Karl in the jostling crowd, edging closer to the railing to do so. Then, to her surprise, the crew laid a gangplank between the boats and allowed the passengers to cross. Hannah and Erika waited in a long queue, and then shuffled carefully along the gangplank to board the Uranus.

Karl was already waiting for Hannah. She rushed to hug him. 'How I've missed you,' he said.

'I've missed you too.' Relief washed over Hannah as Karl's arms enveloped her, followed by a rush of passion.

He felt it too. 'Let's try to find somewhere more private.'

It was difficult to find any vacant space, let alone a private one. The open deck, communal rooms and corridors heaved with people. They sought refuge behind the curved staircase on the lower deck. He pulled her close and their lips met in a deep, lingering kiss. For a few moments, the world outside disappeared. Hannah melted into his embrace until her head felt light and her legs unsteady. Soon, they came to rest on the floor, their backs against the wall, their breath coming in short gasps. Hannah leaned on Karl's shoulder, intertwined her fingers with his, and felt the tensions of the past few days fade away.

Karl's breathing slowed. 'How has your journey been?' he asked.

'Overloaded. Like your boat.' Hannah thought for a moment. 'But really everything was fine until yesterday when we passed Kladovo. Isaak, whom we know from the Slobodarna, spotted his family among those stranded there. And just now,' she shuddered. 'The Pentcho ... so awful.'

'It's a terrible situation.' His face creased with concern. She could tell the sight had affected him as much as it had her. She appreciated him more because of it.

'Do you know how they got stuck?'

'From what we've heard, the Pentcho left Bratislava without a transit visa and was forbidden to continue the journey. The boat is such a wreck that neither Romania nor Bulgaria is willing to supply it with a certificate of seaworthiness.' He shook his head in frustration. 'On top of that, it's flying a yellow quarantine flag because there are sick people on board, so neither country will allow it to dock. That's why the Pentcho's stuck on the river – it's no-man's-land between the Bulgarian port of Ruse and the Romanian port of Giurgiu. But they seem to have used up all their food supplies.'

'Can we help them?'

'Our organisers are trying to figure that out, but apparently we're not allowed to approach the boat or even attempt to communicate.'

'Then why have we stopped here?'

'What we heard is that our sea-going ships aren't ready yet.'

Hannah looked into Karl's eyes, searching for reassurance. 'Are you sure? That sounds odd. Do you think it's true?'

'I don't know. But let's try not to worry,' he said, looking worried.

Hannah decided to let it go for now. Better to focus on this unexpected time they had together.

Rapid footsteps clattered down the steps. Erika and Marcus peered around the staircase, hand in hand. 'So this is where you've been hiding.' Erika grinned. 'I thought you'd want to know, the Schönbrunn docked beside us a short while ago and they're about to lay a gangplank between their boat and ours.'

Hannah scrambled to her feet. 'I should go to Lilly.'

'Go.' Erika's smile widened. 'You've waited a long time.'

Hannah rushed along the passageway with Karl in tow to join the queue to board the Helios. But by the time it was her turn to cross, her excitement had given way to nerves.

'Perhaps,' she said, feeling uncomfortable, 'I should first speak to Lilly alone.'

'Of course.' Karl nodded. 'I understand.'

'I won't be long.'

'Take as long as you need,' he said. 'I'll be here waiting for you after your reunion.'

As Hannah shouldered her way through the crowd, she spotted Lilly already making her way across the gangplank to the Helios. She wore a navy blue summer dress, fresh and pristine from Vienna. But she looked fragile. Lost.

'Lilly!' The din drowned out her voice, but Lilly's face lit up when she noticed Hannah waving. She reached the other side and a moment later, they were hugging each other tightly. This was the reunion Hannah had waited for all these long months and feared might never happen. Lilly smelled of fresh laundry and soap.

'I can't believe you're here,' Hannah said.

'Nor I.' Lilly breathed.

Hannah pulled away to take her in. 'How are you?'

'I'm doing well.' Lilly nodded vigorously, but her troubled eyes hinted at the inner turmoil she was trying to hide. 'It's finally happening, just like you said, isn't it? Soon we'll reach Eretz Israel and start our new lives together.'

'Uh-huh.' Hannah couldn't meet her gaze. 'How is your papa?'

She heaved a sorrowful sigh and her shoulders sagged. 'The doctor says there's nothing else that can be done. It's only a matter of time.'

'I'm so sorry.'

'It was difficult to say goodbye.' The words caught in Lilly's throat. 'To be honest ... I nearly changed my mind. I was ready to cancel my place, but my mama and yours convinced me not to.'

'I understand how hard it was for you to leave, but they were right to encourage you. I'm relieved you're here and you know they are too. How are they?'

Lilly fidgeted with a letter she held in her hands. 'They are keeping as well as they can, under the circumstances.' She handed the letter to Hannah. 'From your mama.'

'Thank you.' Hannah took it and stuffed it into the pocket of her dress, one that Lilly had made for her before she left. It had once been emerald green, but now it was faded to a muted olive.

'Don't you want to open it?'

Hannah wanted nothing more. 'I want to enjoy this time with you. I'll read it later.'

'Has it been a terrible ordeal for you these past few months in Bratislava?' She examined Hannah with a furrowed brow. 'Did they censor your letters?'

'The conditions were uncomfortable,' Hannah began slowly, preparing herself to break the news to Lilly. 'We had many restrictions. But it wasn't all bad.' She guided Lilly up the companionway back to her place on the upper deck. 'Let's sit. I have a lot to tell you—' Before they even reached the bench, they were surrounded by Janka, Alexander, and Isaak. 'You must be Hannah's cousin.' Janka said to Lilly. 'I'm Janka and this is my brother Alexander and my cousin Isaak. He's also from Vienna.'

'And I'm Erika.' she said, appearing alongside them. 'I've heard so much about you. I'm really happy to meet you at last.'

Lilly glanced around the circle, pausing at one face and another. 'H-hello,' was all she could manage.

Suddenly, Hannah realised that while she had been living in close quarters with many others, her cousin had remained isolated at home. The once-vivacious Lilly was no longer used to being around so many people at one time.

'You look alike,' Janka chattered on. 'Apart from your hair colouring, you have such similar features, you could pass for siblings.'

Lilly acknowledged her comment with a slight nod.

'We grew up together, almost like sisters,' Hannah said, filling the silence.

'Nice to grow up with a sister.' Janka gave Alexander a playful jab in the ribs. 'Better than a brother.'

'Hey! Excuse me,' Alexander said.

Janka laughed and draped her arm across his shoulders. 'Only joking. I love you really.'

'And what about me?' Isaak said.

'You too.' Janka placed her other arm around him.

Lilly's mouth turned up slightly at the corners, amused by the good-natured banter.

'I ... have a brother, too,' she ventured in a soft voice. 'He moved to Eretz Israel two years ago. He lives on a kibbutz.'

'He does?' Alexander said. She had his full attention. 'I'd be very interested to hear more.' He gestured towards the closest bench. 'Would you care to sit down?'

After a moment's hesitation, Lilly joined him.

'Here we go,' Erika whispered in Hannah's ear. 'The lecture.'

They shared a grin and focused on the conversation.

'Actually,' Erika said, after several minutes had passed. 'Maybe not.'

Instead of his usual kibbutz recruitment speech, Alexander was asking Lilly questions. He listened closely to her answers too, nodding every so often. Lilly's initial nervousness had dissipated; Alexander had managed to make her feel at ease. Erika watched them in amazement. 'He's hanging on her every word.'

'Are you a touch envious?' Hannah said.

'No. Not at all.' Erika broke off her attention and she gazed over to the Uranus. A look of contentment washed over her face. 'Speaking of which, I should head back. Marcus is waiting for me. I only meant to come over for a few minutes, to introduce myself, but it looks like Alexander might keep this conversation going for a while yet.'

Hannah then felt her own twinge of envy. She was eager to return to Karl. Who knew if they would have another opportunity to spend time together on this journey?

'Have you told Lilly yet?' Erika asked.

'I didn't get a chance,' Hannah said. 'To be honest, I'm a little nervous about telling her.'

'You have to. As soon as possible. You don't want her finding out from someone else.'

'I know. I'll pull her aside as soon as they stop talking.'

Erika turned back to study Alexander once more. 'Ah!' she said with a sense of satisfaction. 'There it is. Now he's trying to recruit her to move to the kibbutz.'

Lilly was shaking her head in response to a question. Alexander persisted, to be met with an amused smile and another shake of the head. At that, he shrugged and smiled in return.

'Good luck.' Erika patted Hannah on the shoulder. 'I'll see you later.'

But as she was about to leave, a Haganah member appeared on the bridge with a megaphone.

'Can I please have your attention?' he said. 'As you know, our fellow Jewish brothers and sisters on the Pentcho have become stranded and their food has run out. For the past few days, they have been surviving on nothing but scraps of potato peelings. We believe it is our duty to help. Which is why we want to ask whether any of you would be prepared to forgo a meal, so we can send them some food. Please raise a hand if you are willing.'

Without hesitation, every hand waved in the air.

'Thanks to you all. In addition, if anyone has other foodstuffs they can donate, we'll be grateful to collect them.'

Lilly rose from the bench and returned to Hannah. 'I have a few spare cans in my luggage,' she said. 'Would you like to come over to the Schönbrunn with me to fetch them? There's someone I'd like you to meet.'

Hannah found the conditions on Lilly's boat similar to her own. Every square metre was occupied. Lilly introduced Hannah to a grey-haired woman with a rounded face and kind eyes. 'Gisela, this is my cousin, Hannah.'

'A pleasure to meet you. I've heard so much about you,' Gisela said. 'Lilly has been telling me about your plans for the future.'

Hannah forced a smile and tried to suppress her guilt at forsaking the plans she'd made with Lilly to be with Karl.

Gisela pulled out a tin of homemade *Vanillekipferl* biscuits and offered her one. Then another. Hannah thought it only polite to sit with her for a few minutes.

Despite her impatience to take Lilly aside, Hannah rather enjoyed her chat with her cousin and Gisela. It reminded her of the cosy conversations she used to have in the kitchen with Lilly and both their mothers. There was nurturing in the older woman's presence, and Hannah realised how much she missed her mother.

As for Lilly, she was talking about the future for the first time since losing Salo. She looked happier than Hannah had seen her since that dreadful day.

It was early evening by the time they returned to the Helios, with Lilly bearing three cans of food for the Pentcho. Just as she was about to ascend the stairs, Hannah touched her arm.

'Wait,' she said. 'There's something I want to tell you.'

Lilly turned to face her with a look of anticipation. 'Tell me everything. We have so much to catch up on.'

'We do. I'm not quite sure where to even begin.' Hannah took a deep breath. 'Do you remember back at the end of March, I wrote to you to tell you they had transferred us to an old factory complex called Patronka?'

'I do. I was so worried about you after I read that letter. The place sounded horrible, and you seemed quite upset at being separated from the friends you had made at the Slobodarna.'

'It was a horrible place. And I was upset at first. But ... on that first day, as Erika and I were exploring our new surroundings, I made a new friend ... Eventually, we became very close.'

Lilly tilted her head, eyebrows raised, as if trying to recall the details. 'I don't think I remember you mentioning that.'

'No.' Hannah's stomach churned with nerves. 'I didn't.'

'Were you worried about the censor?'

Hannah shook her head. 'It's because I wanted to tell you myself. In person.' She swallowed. Her mouth felt as dry as if it were stuffed with straw. 'His name is Karl, and he's from Prague. In time, we became more than friends. We fell in love. Before we left Bratislava, he asked me to marry him. And I said yes.'

Lilly stared at Hannah, waiting, as if she expected her to say something else.

'We're engaged,' Hannah added.

'Oh.'

Silence hung in the air. Hannah couldn't tell what Lilly was thinking. Then Lilly's face broke into a shaky smile. 'What an unexpected surprise. Mazel tov.'

'Thank you.' Hannah felt a sense of relief at her reaction. She seemed to have taken the news well.

'I'm so happy for you.' Lilly leaned over and gave Hannah a perfunctory hug, barely making contact before pulling away.

'Would you like to meet him, perhaps?'

'Maybe later.' She started up the stairs. 'First, I need to hand in these cans of food.'

'Lilly,' Hannah called, following her. 'Is everything all right?'

She turned around, the smile still fixed on her face. 'Of course. I'm so happy for you.'

As Lilly handed over her donation, they ran into Jenny and Stefan.

'This must be your cousin who you've told us so much about,' Jenny said.

Hannah smiled but groaned inwardly as she made the introductions. Although she was fond of Jenny and Stefan, all she wanted to do was have a few minutes alone with Lilly to talk further. But she needed to remain courteous while Jenny chatted about this and that.

Half an hour had passed when Jenny said, 'I don't wish to send you away so soon, but it's already twilight, and once it's dark, it might be dangerous to cross the gangplank. When we first boarded the Helios, there was a terrible accident. A member of our group fell into the Danube in the pitch black. The currents swept him away, and he drowned. His wife and daughter are still on the boat, though.'

Lilly gasped. 'That's awful .'

'I shiver whenever I think of it.'

'I suppose I should go back to my boat.' Lilly offered Jenny a polite smile. 'Lovely to meet you.'

'Likewise. I enjoyed talking to you. I hope we'll have another chance soon,' Jenny said. 'Please be careful and watch your step.'

'Do you have to leave so soon?' Hannah hurried to catch up with Lilly who seemed eager to get back to her boat and was already making her way down the companionway.

'Jenny is probably right. I don't want to risk it.'

Hannah stood beside her in the queue. 'We still haven't had a proper chance to talk.'

'We can continue tomorrow.' Lilly's eyes remained focused on her boat ahead.

Hannah took a step closer to make Lilly meet her gaze. 'Shall I come over to your boat first thing in the morning?'

'Yes.' Lilly wore a fixed smile, but her tense shoulders hinted at deeper emotions. Let's talk again in the morning.' She stepped onto the gangplank. 'It's been lovely spending time with you today. Have a good night.'

A quick wave from the other side reassured Hannah that Lilly had crossed safely. Hannah was left alone to ponder her cousin's reaction, confused and unsure of what to make of it. She debated following Lilly to try to talk to her, then reconsidered. Perhaps Lilly just needed time to digest the news.

Hannah's thoughts returned to Karl. After all this time, he was probably wondering what had happened to her. She wanted to talk to him about the conversation with Lilly and didn't want to wait for the next morning. The convoy might have resumed its journey by then. Hannah ignored the possible risks and crossed the gangplank in the fading light. Karl was sitting on the upper deck with a group of friends. As soon as he saw her, he broke away from them and came over to her.

'I'm sorry I took so long,' Hannah said.

'There's no need to apologise. You haven't seen your cousin for months. I can imagine you had lots to discuss.'

'We kept getting sidelined by friends wanting to meet Lilly.'

'Did you tell her about us?'

'I did.'

'And?' He looked eager. 'What did she say?'

'She wished me mazel tov. She said she was happy for me.'

'That's good.' He studied her uncertain expression. 'Isn't it?'

Hannah still felt unsettled. 'I think she and I still need to talk.'

Karl took her hands in his. 'I know you'll find the right words to smooth things over,' he said.

'I think, perhaps, first you and I need to talk further about our future together ...?'

Before they knew it, night had fallen. In the inky darkness, only the faint outlines of the boats were visible.

'Why don't you stay on board for tonight?' Karl said.

'Won't we get in trouble?'

'We aren't going anywhere this evening. It should be fine.'

They reclined against the port side railings. Karl stretched his blanket across them both, and placed his arm around her. Hannah rested her head on his shoulder. Before long, Karl was fast asleep. Hannah remained awake, tense, her stomach in knots. It wasn't from hunger – despite skipping supper for the Pentcho passengers. She would have to steer through a course through her love for Karl and her commitment to Lilly. Tomorrow she would make sure she spoke to her cousin.

Hannah finally closed her eyes, but lights from the Pentcho kept her awake. It flashed a distress signal at regular intervals, and she couldn't help but worry that they were all fated for distress too.

# CHAPTER 15

Lilly woke up to a magnificent rose-gold sky and its duplicate reflected in the shimmering water. She felt the same heaviness that had kept her up most of the night and had a tangle of emotions she couldn't unravel. Hannah was due to arrive any time now. Lilly hoped she would feel better after they had spoken further, but since Hannah didn't realise Lilly was upset, she didn't see how they could clear it up.

She folded her blanket, careful not to disturb Gisela, who slept on. Then, picking her way between sleeping passengers, she hurried to the bathroom before the long queue began. Lilly found the boat's shared facilities, the communal living, and lack of personal space to be more of a challenge than she had realised they would be. She reminded herself that it was only for another few days. Hopefully, conditions would be better on the larger, sea-going ship in Tulcea.

Returning to the upper deck, Lilly looked for Hannah, and then retraced her steps back down to wait for her cousin beside the gangplank, her unease growing. The sun's rays cast an aurulent sheen on the ripples of the river, not far from where the tragic Pentcho remained. The other four boats had collected a substantial food donation, but the authorities still refused to let them contact the Pentcho's passengers, even though they were starving.

A flock of white birds flew in formation overhead, heading east, following the river towards the Black Sea. Lilly envied their freedom of flight. She spotted several figures moving about the deck of the Helios, and wondered whether Hannah was awake. Would Hannah be coming to Lilly's boat first thing in the morning? Had Lilly misheard her? Maybe she had meant for Lilly to meet her on the Helios. After a moment's deliberation, Lilly crossed the gangplank to Hannah's boat, and made her way to the upper deck.

Alexander, standing by the railings while looking out over the river, was the first to notice her. 'Good morning, Lilly.' His face broke into a wide, friendly smile. 'How did you sleep?'

Lilly couldn't help but offer a smile a little in response. 'I suppose I slept as well as one can on a hard bench. And you?'

'The parts when I slept were good.'

She gave him a quizzical glance. 'Because you were also on a hard bench?'

'I slept on the deck, actually. I'm not sure if that's more or less comfortable than the bench. But no, it's because I'm a Haganah volunteer and I had a night shift keeping watch.'

'Oh, I see.' As she processed what he'd said, she asked, 'Did you perhaps hear anything further from the Haganah about when we'll be able to deliver the food to the Pentcho?'

'Not much. The Romanian authorities refuse to allow us to contact the Pentcho or pass anything to them. So we petitioned the authorities to deliver the food donations on our behalf. We are waiting for their response.'

'I hope they agree. Those poor people . How much longer can they hold out, on nothing but potato peels? Do you think they'll allow them to continue their journey?'

Alexander shrugged. 'Who knows? Romania is in such turmoil. Let's hope they let us continue on ourselves.'

Lilly tensed. 'What do you mean? I thought we were just waiting here until our ships were ready.'

'It's possible, but I think it's more likely a lousy excuse. The main problem is the political situation in Romania. The day before yesterday, the fascist Iron Guard took power and forced the king to abdicate. Now this new government refuses to recognise our transit visas and so we're waiting here on the Bulgarian side.'

'Do you mean we're stuck?' She tried to hold back the alarm in her question.

'Well, yes,' Alexander said, adding quickly, 'But only for a short while. The convoy organisers are trying to resolve it all.'

Her attention shifted back to the pitiful boat listing in the river. 'And if they can't?'

'They'll have to.' He maintained a positive, determined attitude.

Isaak joined Alexander against the railing, stretching and yawning. 'No need to panic. We've endured and overcome many crises since departing from Prague. We got stuck at the Slobodarna, our first ship sunk, and then they threatened to return all the Viennese refugees. But against the odds, we've made it this far. Try not to worry.'

'All right,' said Lilly, but she couldn't match their level of confidence.

She searched the deck. Erika and Janka, wrapped in their blankets, were on a bench, propped up on their elbows and talking to each other, but there was no sign of her cousin. 'Do you know where Hannah is?'

'Not sure. I haven't seen her since yesterday evening.' Isaak gave Alexander a questioning look.

'Maybe she went over to the Uranus, to visit Karl.' Alexander pointed to the boat moored on the opposite side. 'You'll probably find her there.'

'Oh.' Her heart dropped and her discomfort grew, but she didn't want to appear weak in front of Hannah's friends. 'Th-thanks. I suppose I should go and look for her.'

'See you later!' Alexander called after her as she headed towards the stairs. She responded with a slight nod.

Upon reaching the Uranus, Lilly found herself in a sea of strangers. She began on the upper deck. wading through the crowd from bow to stern and back again. Then she tried the middle deck, but Hannah was nowhere to be found. She descended the winding stairs to the lower deck, even though all she wanted to do was give up and retreat to the safety of her place on the bench next to Gisela. No, she realised, that's not what she wanted.

She longed to return home. To be with her family.

Lilly looked up and down the passageway, trying to decide which direction to go first. It was then that she heard whispers and noticed a couple wedged in the confined space behind the companionway, arms wrapped around one another. With a sense of dread, she noted the woman's hair was caramel-coloured, with light tips, where the blonde dye was growing out. Somehow, the couple must have sensed her presence because they broke apart at once.

'Lilly—' A small gasp escaped Hannah's lips. She flushed and avoided her cousin's eyes. 'I was about to come over to your boat.'

Lilly shrank back. Conscious of the two pairs of eyes on her, she wasn't sure how to comport herself. 'I can see you're busy. I'll come back later.'

'Please wait.'

Lilly tore along the passageway, ignoring Hannah's call.

Hannah caught up with her just as she reached the gangplank. 'Don't go,' she said. 'We need to speak.'

'Do we?' Lilly's reply came out harder than she intended.

'I promise I was about to come over to you. I hadn't forgotten.'

Lilly shook her head, finding an unexpected anger beginning to brew inside her. 'Is that what you think is bothering me?'

'Then please tell me what's wrong.' Hannah's voice remained steady. She seemed to have no idea why Lilly was upset.

'Why didn't you tell me about your engagement?' Lilly blurted out.

'I did. I told you yesterday at the first opportunity we had to talk alone.'

'I mean before I left home!' Lilly steadied her shaking hands by gripping one with the other.

Hannah blinked rapidly, seemingly at a loss for words. 'I couldn't.'

'Why not?'

'Because ... because ...' Her eyes flicked back and forth, as if searching for an answer, becoming increasingly agitated. 'Does it matter?'

'Yes, it matters. We had a plan. I wasn't expecting this. What am I supposed to do now?'

'I understand how you must be feeling.' Hannah paused and took a deep, long breath. 'Nothing quite worked to plan. I didn't expect that I would be detained for nine months. Or that I would meet someone. The conditions we endured in Bratislava were hellish at times. Finding Karl ...' She shrugged with an apologetic smile. 'It was like a ray of light in such a dark and anxious time.'

'Do you think it's been a picnic for me?' Lilly threw up her hands. 'My husband is dead. My father is bedridden. I had to become a parent to my parents. I know you got stuck in terrible conditions, but every time I went outside, I risked another encounter with Nazi thugs. Every knock at the door made me hold my breath.'

For the first time, Hannah sounded strained. 'I never stopped worrying about you. I know how much you've suffered. I wish I could take away your pain. But can't you be happy for me? That I found some happiness?'

'Yes. I can. I am. But I'm not sure where this situation leaves me. We were meant to start off in Eretz Israel together. You begged me to come with you. You encouraged your mama and mine to pressure me, to convince me to join you. Now what will I do?'

'Oh Lilly,' Hannah was silent for a moment. 'Don't you realise how very fortunate you were to secure a place on this transport? Thousands of Jews still trapped in Vienna would do anything to trade places with you. I know it won't be exactly as we planned, but it's still a wonderful chance for you. You can make a fresh start for yourself in Eretz.'

'Where? With who? You'll be with Karl. Eugen has Allegra. Salo is dead!' she cried.

Hannah paused. 'I know, Lilly. I know. If I could bring him back … But you're here. And you still have me. I spoke to—'

'I left my Papa dying! I doubt I'll ever see him again.' Lilly was too upset to pay attention to Hannah's reasoning. 'If only you had warned me earlier. I could have delayed my journey, stayed with him until the end, and been there for Mama.'

'No, you couldn't.' Hannah pursed her lips and let out a heavy sigh. 'That's why they didn't want me to tell you.'

'Who is "they"?'

'Your Mama and mine.'

'You're lying.'

'It's the truth.'

'Why? It should have been my choice! I could have left later.' Lilly became aware they were attracting a growing audience who watched their heated exchange with unreserved fascination. Once, she would have been horrified by the idea of making a public spectacle of herself. But she was past the point of caring.

'Don't you understand?' Hannah's voice grew firmer. 'There probably won't be a later. And if this was our last opportunity to flee, our mothers didn't want to risk you giving up your place. They wrote and urged me not to say a word until you were already on the boat.'

'You deceived me. All of you deceived me!'

'No. We love you and we were worried that you'd do exactly what you just said and refuse to leave.'

Lilly stepped back, unable to handle the weight of these new revelations.

'You are such a loyal daughter. Our mothers realised that had you known about Karl and me, you might have cancelled your place. They couldn't let that happen. You had to go,' Hannah faltered. 'Do you think it was easy for my mama to let me go? For her and your mama to keep this news from you? To encourage you to leave? They wouldn't let you see how much they were hurting. But they had to do it. They wanted you to get out of Vienna and make a new life.'

'What life? Tell me!' Lilly couldn't hold back. 'Even if what you say is true about our mamas, I abandoned my family. You're with Karl. Eugen is married. I have no one. What will I do all on my own? That is, if we ever get there. Chances are, we're trapped here. Like the group we saw in Kladovo and the passengers on the Pentcho.'

'What are you talking about? We're just waiting here for a short while until our ships are ready in Tulcea.'

'No, we're not. Haven't you heard? The king of Romania has abdicated and the new government won't recognise our transit visas. If they don't let us pass, we can't reach our ships in Tulcea. That's why we're stuck here, on the Bulgarian side.'

'That can't be true. Who told you this?'

'Your friend, Alexander. Ask him yourself,' Lilly said. 'I've come all this way only to die here, on this damned river. I might as well have stayed in Vienna.'

Lilly turned her back on Hannah and crossed the gangplank to the Helios. She heard Hannah call her name, but she ignored her, looking straight ahead while furiously wiping her eyes as she traversed the boat to get back to the Schönbrunn.

'Did you find Hannah?' Alexander called down to her from the upper deck.

Lilly forced a smile. 'I did, thanks.'

'Is everything all right?'

'Yes, all fine. I just need to return to my boat for something.'

Her vision blurred, she lost her footing and slipped. Somewhere above, Lilly heard a woman scream. She grabbed onto the side rail for support and heaved herself up before anyone could add to her indignity by running down to help her. She kept her chin held high and continued onwards until she reached the safety of her bench and sank down beside Gisela.

'You seem upset,' Gisela said. 'Is something the matter?'

Lilly's shoulders lifted in a quick, dismissive shrug. 'Hannah met someone in Bratislava and is engaged to him.'

'Did you only just find out?'

'She told me yesterday.'

Gisela nodded sagely. 'So that's what's been on your mind since you came back last night.'

Lilly sighed. 'My aunt knew. My mother knew. Before I left Vienna. They hid it from me.' She couldn't hide her resentment. 'What am I supposed to do now?'

'You'll go to Eretz Israel just the same.'

'But we were planning to live together.'

'Don't worry, things will work themselves out. You're still young and have so many other options. With a bit of luck, you may also meet someone along the journey and fall in love yourself.'

'I had someone. He was the love of my life. Now I'm a widow and my life is over.'

Gisela was startled into silence. 'I didn't realise,' she said, after a moment. 'I'm sorry. I shouldn't have made such a thoughtless comment.'

'You weren't to know.'

'Did it happen recently?'

'During the November Pogrom.'

'I understand.' Gisela's fingers brushed against the smooth silk of her peacock scarf. 'That's when I lost my husband too. Was yours also arrested?'

Lilly shook her head slowly as the memory sparked shock all over again.

'We were at my parents' home. We were all about to leave. Escape in my father's car for somewhere safer.' She had never before spoken about that day. She and her family bore the pain daily. There had been no reason to discuss it. And she hadn't wanted to speak about it to anyone else. Yet she found herself opening up to Gisela. 'Before we had a chance, four Brownshirts burst in and ransacked the apartment. One of them slapped me hard, and when my husband begged him not to hurt me, the Brownshirt punched him. He fell and hit his head but managed to stand up again. Then they threw me and my mother out of the apartment and one of them pushed me ... down the stairs. They arrested my father, but not Salo ...' She let out a sob. 'I ran back upstairs to the apartment, but when I got there, I found him lying on the floor ... not how I left him ... They had beaten him so badly ... I hardly recognised him. Salo looked at me and opened his mouth to talk, but he couldn't even speak.' Her words came out as a choked whisper. She covered her face with her hands. 'He ... he ... he died in my arms.'

'Poor darling.' Gisela held her tight as she shook with sobs and finally released the sorrow and anger she had kept inside for so long. 'So hard.' Gisela soothed. 'So, so hard. It's all right to cry.'

'Not a day that goes by when I don't think of him and replay the events over and over in my mind.' Tears streamed down Lilly's cheeks. 'I ask myself, if I had done something different, would he still be alive? If I hadn't slowed him down when we ran to my parents' home. If I hadn't sat down for a cup of tea. If only we had left five minutes earlier. Then maybe the Brownshirts wouldn't have found us.'

'Don't.' She clasped Lilly's shoulders. 'You musn't torture yourself like that. It will destroy you. You could not have predicted the outcome, and there is nothing you can do to change it. It's natural to miss Salo and cry for him, but he would not want you to live in the past. He would want you to move on and to continue living.' She spoke with a fierce intensity, as if she were trying to infuse Lilly with her own strength.

Lilly drew in a deep breath and steadied herself.

Gisela continued, absentmindedly stroking her silk peacock feather scarf. 'I too miss my husband, Moses. More than I can say. But I know I can't blame myself or dwell on the what-ifs.'

'What happened ...' Lilly said in a halting voice. 'What happened to your husband?'

Gisela let out a sad sigh and nodded. She had been waiting for the question. 'On the morning of the November Pogrom, Moses was returning home from morning prayers when they arrested him on our street. I heard a police van. I looked outside our apartment window and saw them grab him. I came running downstairs but by the time I reached the street they had already driven off. I went straight to the police station hoping to find out where they had taken him. There were at least a hundred other Jewish women already waiting for information about their husbands, sons, fathers ... loved ones. The police wouldn't tell any of us anything. I came back the following day, then the next, then the one after. Five days later, a police officer said to me, "He is here. Wait a moment and I'll fetch him." I breathed a sigh of relief. I couldn't wait to see Moses again. In almost forty years of marriage, we had never spent a night apart.' Gisela dabbed her eyes and nose with a lace handkerchief. 'The policeman returned, but he was alone. I didn't understand. "Here's your husband," he said with a sneer. Then he handed me an urn. I opened it to find ... it was filled with his ashes.'

Lilly sucked in a breath. 'Oh Gisela. I'm so sorry.' It was her turn to embrace the older woman.

'I miss Moses every day.' A sniffle escaped her. 'I cherish the memories of the good times we had. For him, I carry on. I was afraid I would be left on my own and never be able to leave Vienna. I couldn't get a visa for any country and the *Hechalutz* were only giving places to youngsters. But then Berthold Storfer organised this new transport and was also willing to accept seniors. It's a dream come true for me. Soon I'll be with my sons, my daughter-in-law, my grandchildren, the family reunited once more. There will always be a space where Moses should have been, but I'm certain he'll be looking down and smiling on us.' Her smile was bittersweet as she wiped her eyes. 'Please God, you too will start a new life. Isn't that what Salo would wish for you?'

'Yes.' Lilly knew Gisela was right. 'That is what he would want.'

'At this moment, you think your situation looks bleak. But I promise, it won't always appear so. Perhaps Salo has become your angel and is helping to guide your path.'

Lilly remembered the preparations he made: the hiding place he had constructed, the money he had saved to support her parents, the hidden jewellery that had paid for her passage. Was it a premonition or fear that caused him to do it? Either way, he had provided her with the means to escape and start over.

'I feel terrible about the way I spoke to Hannah. It was selfish of me. She has also been through a lot and I am glad that she has found happiness at last. She deserves to have love and stability in her life. I don't resent her for that. I'm just scared of what will happen to me. I don't know how I'll cope on my own.'

'The security you were resting on has been pulled out from beneath your feet. It's not surprising that Hannah's announcement has unsettled you. But other opportunities will present themselves. Things will work out. You'll see. And you are welcome to stay with me if you need a place when we arrive. You won't be alone.'

'I appreciate the offer, but I don't want to be a burden.'

'Not at all. I'd welcome your company. The invitation is open if you ever need it.'

'What do I say to Hannah? We've never had words between us in that way. What if things are never the same between us?'

'Talk to her. Explain.'

'I'm sure she's angry.' Lilly wondered if Hannah would even listen to her if she sought her out again. 'She might not even want to speak to me.'

Gisela gazed upwards. 'I think you'll find she will.'

Lilly followed Gisela's gaze. Hannah hovered beside them. Her eyes were red and puffy. 'I'm sorry.'

'So am I,' Lilly said.

'Go on,' Gisela patted her on the arm. 'The two of you need to have a long talk.'

Lilly and Hannah walked in silence, searching for a quiet corner before hunkering down behind the curved stairs on the lower deck.

'I didn't mean to hide Karl from you,' Hannah began. 'We only did what we did because we were worried about you. We all wanted to ensure you wouldn't lose your place. All the same, I feel terrible that I didn't tell you sooner.'

'And I apologise for how I reacted. I shouldn't have shouted at you the way I did.'

'No, you had every right to be upset. I think I'd have reacted the same way, if not worse, if I'd been in your place. Please forgive me.'

'Of course I do.'

Hannah pulled her into a tight embrace. 'I had a long talk last night with Karl, and we continued this morning. That's the real reason I was delayed coming to see you.' Hannah paused, abashed. 'Even if that's not what it looked like. We've agreed to delay our wedding plans for a few months. First, you and I will get settled, find work and we'll live together, just as we planned. I'm not going to abandon you. Karl is very understanding and also said you are welcome to come live with us after our marriage.'

'That's kind of him, but I wouldn't impose. The two of you will need your space and privacy once you're married. Gisela offered me a place to stay if ever I should need, so perhaps I could move in with her, short-term.'

A fleeting expression flashed across Hannah's face. Lilly recognised it as relief.

'I am pleased for you. Really, I am,' Lilly said. 'You deserve this happiness. I can't wait to dance at your wedding.'

'He's wonderful.' Hannah's face was quick to take on a dreamy expression. 'You know, my experience with Karl made me realise how foolish I was about Gerhard. Gerhard and I really had no future. But Karl ... we haven't done any of the "dating" that Gerhard liked so much. No evenings out on the town. Instead, we went for walks around the Patronka, and a few times, in the nearby countryside. But we talked and talked about anything and everything: our backgrounds, childhoods, families, plans and dreams. We have very similar outlooks. And I feel comfortable with him. I regret all the time I wasted waiting for Gerhard. If I hadn't been stuck in my mind waiting for him, we'd have applied for a visa to England earlier. We'd already be there.'

'But then you never would have met Karl.' Gisela's admonition to not get lost in the 'what-ifs' rang strong in Lilly's mind.

'That's true. But Mama wouldn't be trapped in Vienna either. I still can't believe my naivety – and how wrongly I steered us all.'

'You believed you were doing your best. Deep down, I wonder if you hung onto that relationship for the promise of a visa,' Lilly said. Hannah gave a sad nod. 'You knew it was strange he left without committing to you. And your mama isn't angry with you. She knows you were doing everything you could.'

Hannah dabbed at the corners of her eyes. 'Mama is such an incredible, selfless woman. She persuaded me to book a place on this transport and used almost all her savings to help pay for it.'

'How did you break it to her that you're engaged?'

'I wrote to her after Karl proposed. In the letter you brought me, she said she was so happy and gave us her blessing. I just wish ...' Hannah shut her eyes for a moment, and then stared into the distance, trying to compose herself. Lilly considered comforting Hannah by saying that the war would end soon, but she knew that wasn't likely. Instead, she squeezed her cousin's hand, and Hannah squeezed hers back.

'Karl would very much like to get acquainted with his new "sister-in-law." Can I make a proper introduction?'

'There's nothing I'd like more.'

# CHAPTER 16

'L'chaim!'

The group of friends raised cups of black tea in a toast to the happy couple, their cheers filling the air. The party had been Lilly's idea. As they continued their uncertain wait in Ruse Port, they needed something to lift their spirits, and what better way than to celebrate Hannah and Karl's engagement?

All the friends from their new circle had gathered on the Helios: Janka, Alexander and Isaak; Jenny and Stefan; Erika, with Markus beside her, holding her hand and gazing at her adoringly. Lilly wondered if he would be the next to propose. Seven of Karl's friends, *chaverim*, from his *Hechalutz* group had come over from the Uranus to wish 'mazal tov' to their dear friend and his bride. Even Gisela had crossed over from the Schönbrunn for the event and seemed in her element among the young crowd.

With limited supplies, the friends had set up a modest spread on the bench that Hannah and Erika had claimed as their own. They rejoiced with the leftovers of Lilly's Gugelhupf cake cut into thin slithers, the last of Gisela's *Vanillekipferl* biscuits, two tins of fruit donated by Janka and Alexander, a bar of chocolate from Erika, and a bunch of grapes that Jenny and Stefan purchased from the boat's canteen.

Hannah and Karl wouldn't have been happier in an elegant hotel with uniformed waiters and a string quartet.

Traditionally, at this point in the celebration, the mothers of both bride and groom would have broken a china plate together – a symbolic act to temper the joyous occasion with remembrance of the destruction of the Holy Temple in Jerusalem. It was the beginning of an exile lasting more than two millennia for the Jewish people, removed from their homeland, and subject to countless tragedies over the centuries. But with no mothers present, no spare plate, and no need for reminders of tragedies befalling their people, Hannah and Karl were willing to forgo the tradition.

'Speech! Speech!' Karl's friends chanted until he stepped forward reluctantly, spurred on by Hannah's encouragement.

'I'm not one for speeches,' Karl said. 'But we would like to thank you all for coming together and contributing to this joyous celebration. It's a blessing to be able to celebrate with you even in these difficult times. Both Hannah and I are so touched. We especially want to thank Hannah's cousin, Lilly – our cousin – for arranging this magnificent party.'

Applause echoed across the deck. Alexander, standing on Lilly's left, leaned over to speak in her ear, trying to make himself heard above the din, even as he himself clapped loudly. 'Your idea was truly inspired.'

Lilly blushed until the ovation ended and the spotlight shifted away from her.

'As most of you are aware, Hannah and I met under unusual circumstances,' Karl continued. 'We didn't exactly have a glamorous courtship. But we have a lot of love and respect for each other.' Karl turned towards Hannah. Their eyes connected. 'I can't wait to spend the rest of my life with you,' he said. Then Karl returned his attention to the group and gestured towards Pentcho. 'Please God, may we all arrive safely in Eretz, including our brothers and sisters over there, and also the group we passed in Kladovo, and the loved ones we had to leave behind. Let's hope they will be able to follow us soon.'

'Amen!' came the heartfelt response.

'And we look forward to celebrating our wedding with you all in Eretz Israel.'

Karl's friends broke into a chorus of the traditional song, *Siman tov, u'mazal tov*, clapping and tapping and stomping their feet to the rhythm, for there was no room to dance.

Erika, to Lilly's right, gave her a gentle nudge. 'Doesn't Hannah look beautiful?'

Hannah wore a navy blue cotton dress borrowed from her cousin – one of the new dresses Lilly had sewn from fabric given to her by her old neighbour, Helga. Erika had styled Hannah's hair in an elegant pin curl updo and a dab of Lilly's burgundy lipstick completed her look.

'Radiant,' Lilly said.

'You and I make a good team.' Erika's smile conveyed her genuine warmth. 'I'm glad you're here with us. And I know it's made Hannah so happy. In all these months, she has never stopped worrying about you.'

'Thank you for making me feel so welcome.'

Giving Lilly another smile, Erika disappeared into the crowd with Marcus.

Lilly remained, watching the way Hannah interacted with Karl, a look of contentment on her face that Lilly had never seen before. She was happy for her cousin, even if she was still concerned about her own future. She felt relieved that they had reconciled after their harsh words.

Lilly couldn't help thinking about the last time she and Hannah had celebrated together. It was Serena's wedding, and Hannah was still with Gerhard. Salo and Lilly had been newly married and blissfully happy. Lilly felt an aching void where Salo should have been. How was it possible to feel at once both joy and overwhelming sadness?

'I imagine it's still painful, but arranging this party was such a thoughtful gesture,' said Gisela, appearing in front of Lilly. 'I'm proud of you.'

Lilly allowed herself to relax her smile for a few minutes, but tried to sound resolute. 'As you said, it's time to start a new life.'

Gisela's eyes conveyed a deep empathy. 'Yes,' she said.

The singing ended, and the guests parted for Hannah and Karl, who walked among them and headed straight for Lilly. 'Thank you for this evening.' Hannah embraced her, then lowered her voice to speak in confidence. 'We will always be here for you, no matter what.'

Then Karl leaned in as if he meant to hug her, but seemed to reconsider and quickly pulled back. 'Thank you for accepting me. It means a lot. I want to echo everything Hannah said. And—'

A splash.

Then a shriek.

'*Ach du lieber Gott*!' Jenny cried. 'Someone on the Pentcho has fallen overboard.'

All heads turned to the river in time to see a second person plunge into the river.

'They didn't fall,' Alexander said. 'Look. They are jumping and trying to escape!'

The two swam from the Pentcho with broad, desperate strokes. In the gloaming, a third figure, a woman, climbed over the Pentcho's railings, dove in and followed. Then a fourth. He flailed about for several seconds, righted himself and trailed behind.

The party rushed to the starboard railing. They stood silent, not daring to speak, as they watched the swimmers' progress.

They weren't the only ones who noticed the escape. Three river patrol police boats were circling around the Pentcho like sharks on the hunt.

Alexander grabbed a lifebelt from its mounting. 'If those swimmers get close enough, I'll hoist them up before the police get them.' He didn't need to add, 'and just let the authorities try to come after me.'

A hand pressed to her mouth, Lilly strained her eyes to follow their progress in the fading light. Please make it to safety, she prayed.

'Come on,' Isaak urged in an undertone. 'You can do it.'

A crack of gunfire punctured the air.

Lilly flinched. They all did.

From the water came wild flailing and yelling.

The first swimmer reached the Bulgarian coast where the police were waiting to haul him out. When the next two reached the coast, they arrested them along with the first man and began to lead them away. The three Pentcho escapees dragged their feet and turned their heads towards the Danube, shouting in panic for the woman who had dived in. But the water was still. She didn't emerge.

The lifebelt slipped from Alexander's hands and rolled a short way along the deck before hitting the bench. Jenny broke down into uncontrollable sobs and Stefan folded her into his arms. Karl hugged Hannah. Marcus comforted Erika.

Lilly remained by the railing, staring unfocused at the Pentcho's flashing distress signals.

'I'm not sure if you heard, but on the night Jenny and Stefan boarded there was a tragic drowning,' Isaak said to her.

'Yes, Jenny told me,' Lilly said.

'That may be why she's so upset.'

Lilly shivered, despite the mild weather. She wrapped her arms around herself.

'You're cold.'

Lilly wasn't sure whether Isaak's words were meant as a question or a statement. But before she could reply, he was gone.

A small group clustered around Jenny trying to calm her. Janka kneeled in front of her, trying to coax her to drink some water.

Something heavy and comforting settled across Lilly's shoulders. A woollen blanket.

'Maybe this will help,' Isaak said.

'Thank you. That's very kind.'

Alexander joined them, and his gaze fixed on Lilly with a look of concern. 'Are you all right?'

'Are any of us?' Lilly said.

His nod of understanding was accompanied by a resigned shrug of his shoulders.

'Do you think they shot her?' she asked.

'Either that or the current swept her away, and she drowned.'

'What will happen to the others on the Pentcho?'

'That's hard to know.'

'And what about us? Will the Romanian authorities recognise our transit visas?'

'There is a rumour that they are about to.' Alexander didn't sound convinced. 'I'm not sure what to believe anymore.'

'Let's try to stay hopeful. For them and for us,' Isaak said. 'We've made it this far. There's a good chance we'll continue.'

'How do you stay so optimistic?' Alexander said.

Isaak thought for a moment. 'I suppose it's because faith is all I have. It is the only thing I have a choice over.'

Alexander's expression reflected his admiration. 'I wish I could summon your outlook.'

Lilly moved to be nearer to Hannah and Karl. 'I'm sorry your party ended on this sad note,' she said.

'Oh no,' Hannah said. 'It was a wonderful evening until ...' A heavy sigh escaped her. 'What have we all been reduced to?'


Lilly and Gisela declined Alexander's chivalrous offer to escort them back to their boat, preferring to spend the night on the Helios with the rest of their group. Lilly curled up on the edge of Hannah's bench, wrapped in Isaak's blanket, but sleep eluded her. The sky was already paling to a grey-blue when she finally drifted off, vivid images of the Pentcho filling her mind. The desperate swimming of the desperate refugees fighting against the current. The impact as they landed in the river. The police, offering no compassion at all.

'They are trying again.' She heard Isaak say.

Another splash.

Lilly opened her eyes. It was already light. And she wasn't dreaming.

Alexander and Isaak stood against the railings watching the Pentcho. After the third splash, she scrambled to her feet. 'What's going on?'

'Three more people have jumped overboard,' Alexander said.

Lilly spotted them in the water. Their strokes were fast and frenzied.

'Come on, keep going,' Isaak said.

Lilly clutched the railings and braced herself for the sound of gunshot.

The first man heaved himself onto the bank, then reached out to his companions. As they bent over trying to catch their breath, four Bulgarian policemen closed in on them. The escapees bore haggard faces, sunken eyes, and their sodden clothes hung heavy from their bodies. They couldn't summon the strength to run. An officer spoke to them and they sat down without protest. He hurried to a nearby building and returned a few minutes later, his arms laden with food. The men snatched the hunks of bread he offered, and ate them ravenously. He handed them each an additional food package before two other policemen loaded them onto a small patrol boat and returned them to the Pentcho.

'So much for that,' Alexander said.

'At least they got something to eat for their efforts,' Isaak said.

The Bulgarian officer who had fed the escapees noticed Lilly, Alexander and Isaak looking on from the Helios. He studied them intently for a brief moment before hurling an object in their direction. 'What on earth?' Alexander said, as the three of them quickly ducked out of the way. A few small missiles soared through the air and thudded onto the deck.

Isaak began to laugh. 'Don't complain.' He crouched to scoop up the offerings: two bars of chocolate and a packet of cigarettes, and then stood to wave his thanks. The officer touched his hat in acknowledgment.

'Whatever prompted him to do that?'

'Perhaps there are still a few decent people in this world.'

'The chocolate is welcome. What shall we do with the cigarettes, give them to the smokers on the boat?'

Isaak wagged his finger. 'No, no, no. We'll keep them.'

'But we don't smoke.'

'They'll come in useful.'

'In case you decide to take up smoking?' Lilly said.

'No,' Isaak said. 'For bartering.'

Alexander clapped him on the back. 'You're something else, cousin.'

Isaak opened a chocolate bar, broke it into pieces and presented them to the others in the group who had all since awoken, apart from Jenny, who was now curled up in a blanket, fast asleep on the bench. Gisela, sitting beside her, looked exhausted.

Isaak presented her with the unopened bar. 'This will give you some energy.'

'*Ach*!' Gisela pinched his cheek. 'You are so sweet.'

The gesture amused Isaak. 'My *oma* used to do the same thing.'

The public address system squawked to life. 'Can I have your attention? Those who are visiting from different boats must now disembark. In the next few minutes, we'll be lifting the gangplanks and continuing our journey.'

The announcement prompted an immediate flurry of activity, the passengers scurrying to the gangplanks, and traversing them back to their own boats.

'We ought to leave too,' Gisela said.

'You can go ahead. I'll catch up with you in a moment,' Lilly said.

Lilly frantically searched the deck for Hannah. In all the excitement, she had lost sight of her. But there was no sign of her cousin. Lilly reluctantly joined the end of the queue, most of the passengers having already returned to their boats, including Gisela who waved to her from the other side. Lilly was swallowing her disappointment when felt a tap on her shoulder.

'I hope you weren't intending to take off without saying goodbye?' Hannah asked with a raised eyebrow.

'I certainly didn't want to. I've been looking for you.'

'I was doing the same. We must have missed each other.' Hannah paused, facing Lilly. 'Let's not say goodbye, but see you soon. I'm grateful we had these few days together. And I'm sorry for ...'

'Let's put it behind us and not speak of it again.'

'Lilly! Hurry!' Gisela beckoned her frantically. She would be the last to cross.

'You had better go.' Hannah gave her a quick hug and Lilly quickly made her way across the gangplank right before the crew removed it.

Smoke billowed from the Schönbrunn's funnels, the paddles rotated, and the boat pulled away from the quay. But rather than continuing downstream, it turned and headed directly towards the Romanian port of Giurgiu on the opposite bank.

A minute later, the Schönbrunn slowed. Their boat eased up to the dock, behind the Helios. The anchor chain rattled down to the river bed, leaving them and the rest of the convoy at a complete standstill once more.

# CHAPTER 17

Hannah watched Lilly on the Schönbrunn from the Helios' stern and shook her head in disbelief. 'I was sure we would travel longer than this before meeting again,'

The convoy had docked end to end in a straight line, with the Helios wedged between Karl's boat in front and Lilly's at the back.

'Any idea why we have stopped again?' Lilly said.

'Your guess is as good as mine.'

Hannah noticed a Romanian police officer approaching the Helios from the quayside. A Haganah representative descended the gangway to meet him. The representative handed the police officer the sacks of food donated by the passengers on the transport. The officer loaded them onto a waiting patrol boat, and set out to deliver them to the Pentcho. A measure of kindness in an otherwise bleak situation. If nothing else, its passengers would receive some sustenance and reassurance that their fellow Jews cared about them.

The four boats of the convoy, and their impatient passengers, continued to wait.

Hannah moved to the bow of the Helios to find Karl waiting for her at the stern of the Uranus. 'We're back to this,' he said.

'So it seems.'

'Well, I'm glad I didn't have to wait too long to see you again. And we don't have to yell and involve half the boat in our conversation. That's a good thing.'

'Are there any updates from your side about what this means?'

'Nothing yet.'

Morning turned to afternoon.

Hannah alternated between the stern and bow, talking to Lilly and Karl. No one had heard any word why they had stopped. There were no announcements of any kind from the crew, or even the Haganah representatives.

Hannah and Karl watched three Haganah men standing on the quay with the four German boat captains, who passed paperwork over to a Romanian officer. Then the men smoked while they stood around and waited.

'What if they leave us behind?' Hannah said.

'Doubtful,' Karl said. 'Apparently, they need to ferry these boats to Bessarabia in order to repatriate the local German population.'

'That may be true, but do they need us? They've already taken our money. There's nothing to prevent them from dumping us here, just like the group before us at Kladovo.' Hannah was haunted by the image of Isaak shouting to his family as their boat sailed past.

Karl, however, was not perturbed. 'None of our men appears concerned. Bored yes. Worried no.'

Hannah looked down at them. 'They don't seem calm to me. Dov hasn't stopped chain-smoking.'

The sun was setting again on the tranquil Danube. So far, the weather had been kind to them. Clear and mild every day without a drop of rain.

'Hello!' Karl noted the sudden flare of activity on the quayside. Dov stubbed out his cigarette, and the captains returned to their respective boats. 'I think we're about to continue.'

Moments later, the horns sounded in confirmation.

'See you in Tulcea, my love,' he said.

The four boats turned in a circle, passing the Pentcho at close quarters. They watched as the boat sent out a last distress signal in Morse Code, as if saying, 'Take us with you.'

The gaunt-faced passengers watched their departure, grief-stricken.

Isaak dared to shout out to them, 'Shalom!'

Hannah, Janka, and Erika joined the call.

'Shalom. Be patient,' Alexander said.

'Don't give up,' Isaak said.

Melancholy clouded Hannah's relief. Their convoy would continue on, while the Pentcho's fate looked bleak.

'I wonder what persuaded the authorities to let us pass?' Hannah contemplated aloud.

Alexander nodded to the swastikas fluttering from the masts of their boats. 'This might be the only time those despicable flags provided some protection.'

At noon the next day, they arrived in the Romanian port of Braila. A melange of old and new. Tall, modern apartment blocks dwarfed ramshackle houses with crooked timber windows. Trams, horse-drawn carriages, and smart motor cars shared a narrow thoroughfare. On the pavement, women wearing headscarves, farmers dressed in work clothes, and merchants in suits vied for space, as did squawking geese and grunting pigs.

Their destination was near. Hannah could see several ocean-going ships ahead of them that had sailed upriver from the Black Sea.

Then, twenty kilometres farther downstream, approaching the port town of Galati, they encountered the ominous signs of war: barbed wire, cannons, fortifications and soldiers. This area was under Russian control.

Hannah could see the tension in every passenger's face, as a German officer on a military patrol boat approached their convoy. It seemed that no arrangements to allow the boats to pass had been made with the Russian authorities, but Alexander's assumption proved correct. Almost at once, the German officer came to an understanding with the Helios' captain and allowed the Nazi flag-bearing flotilla, overloaded with Jewish refugees, to pass without hindrance.

That night, Hannah found herself unable to sleep. She knew from previous experience that you could never tell which direction the wind would blow. She wondered whether they were in for more unwelcome surprises. But at the pink light of dawn, the convoy entered Tulcea's inner harbour and dropped anchor in the middle of the river, close to the jetty.

It was exactly a week since they had left Bratislava.

The architecture of the sleepy yet picturesque harbour town seemed different from the other Romanian ports they had passed on their route. Stefan, their resident history teacher and tour guide, explained that this region had been the Turks' last bastion on the Danube. 'Less than seventy years ago, it was still under Ottoman rule.'

The architecture reflected the Ottomans' influence. White stucco, houses with arched windows and terracotta roofs nestled in the green hills. Rising between the towering church domes, mosques and minarets peppered the skyline, providing a hint of the east.

Tulcea. Their portal out of Europe. Their gateway to the Black Sea.

The harbour was all but deserted. Three dilapidated ships bobbed at the dock, devoid of names or flags.

'Please don't tell me those are our ships,' Hannah said.

'I shouldn't think so,' Erika said. 'I overheard someone say that the ships are due to arrive tonight.'

'I'll believe that when I see it,' said Alexander.

A pounding of hammers broke the silence of the somnolent harbour, and a crew of carpenters emerged, hauling large sheets of timber onto the deck of the largest ship.

Alexander's eyes widened. 'They might be ours.'

'No way,' Erika said. 'They look like ancient relics.'

His lips curved into a playful smirk. 'Did you expect they would lay on the luxury for us?'

'I'd much prefer it. But at this stage, I'll settle for any vessel that can stay afloat in the sea. Those wouldn't make it out of the port without falling over.'

Erika wasn't wrong. The smallest of the three had an obvious starboard list.

'Just our luck, and they'll turn out to be ours,' Isaak said.

'And then they will expect us to row them, like a galley ship,' Jenny said.

Her comment sparked a wave of chuckles. Only Janka remained straight-faced. Hannah had noticed that her friend was becoming withdrawn. She tapped Janka on the shoulder. 'Let's talk.'

Leaving the others to their dark joking about the rickety ships, Hannah and Janka went below deck. 'What's troubling you?' Hannah said, as she settled herself in the niche behind the stairs. 'Are you worried about those ships?'

'Perhaps. A bit.' Janka let out a quiet sigh. 'I don't know. Once, this all seemed such an exciting idea. But I'm not sure anymore.'

Two young men talking animatedly clattered down the stairs. Janka waited until they passed.

'Alexander is an idealist. He was seventeen when he first became enamoured with the idea of becoming a kibbutznik. At first, our parents thought it was a passing phase, but they humoured him. He'd go to the youth group meetings and come back fired up with enthusiasm. I was fifteen. I looked up to him, of course, and I got swept up in his excitement. The stories he told about the pioneers sounded like heroes out of a book. I wanted to share in the adventure. Then, as time went on and the situation in Europe changed, our parents urged us to move to Eretz.'

'Are you sorry you came?'

'I regret leaving our parents. Alexander tried to persuade them to join us, but my mother wouldn't leave my grandmother, and she's too frail for such an arduous journey. Our father reassured us they would be fine, but ...' Janka's voice trailed off. 'Prague is occupied by the Nazis. There's a war. Who knows what will happen?'

'I understand how you feel only too well. I also left my mother behind. I still feel guilty.'

'It's so hard, isn't it? I can't stop worrying about them. I know they want me to be here. I know I'm better off here. But are we really better off? Look at what we've been through. There are no guarantees we'll even reach Haifa. Maybe it was a mistake to leave Prague.'

'You didn't make a mistake. We're all having mixed emotions. These are unsettling days, and for good reason. But when the ships arrive, you'll remember why you're here. And, I hope, you'll feel better.'

Janka shrugged, unconvinced. 'Once I had this romantic image of being a pioneer. I imagined picking oranges by day and gathering around a campfire in the evening to sing and dance with the other kibbutzniks. I thought how wonderful it would be to belong to such a close-knit community.' Janka's laugh sounded hollow. 'After nine months in the Slobodarna, and a week crammed on this boat, I'm tired of communal living. I crave privacy. A plush armchair and reading lamp in a quiet, cosy corner where I can read a book in peace. A comfortable bed. A proper bath.'

'Oh, for a long soak in a deep bath.' Hannah said. 'Especially after the single tap at the Patronka. And I wouldn't say no to sleeping in a proper bed with a feather pillow and a fluffy duvet either.' She paused to think about what Janka had said. 'The funny thing is, I'm the opposite. A city girl who never considered herself the pioneering type. Then, after my cousin Eugen moved to a kibbutz and he wrote to us describing his new life, I began to understand the appeal. And now I'm engaged to Karl who is keen to settle on a kibbutz with his group.'

'Do you want to?'

'I'm open to the idea. Maybe the lifestyle would actually suit me. But before I commit, I want to visit a kibbutz and experience it for myself. Karl says if I don't like it, he will respect my decision and he won't pressure me. But first of all, until we marry, I'll live with Lilly and help her get settled too.'

'You have a real plan. At least you are deciding for yourself.'

'If you don't feel you're suited to kibbutz life, you're also allowed to change your mind.'

'I'd be letting down so many people. Alexander especially. He'd be disappointed in me.'

'Listen to me.' Hannah caught Janka's eye. 'Remember, he decided his own direction in life. If that's your direction too, that's wonderful, but if it's not, you can choose your own the same way he did.'

'Perhaps.' Janka pursed her lips together and pondered the idea. 'I've never considered an alternative. What would I do? Where would I live?'

'You could move in with us, if you like. We could all share a place together.'

'That's a very kind offer. Do you think Lilly would mind?'

'I'll ask her first, but I don't think she would mind. It would also make things easier when I move out.'

'Well ... thank you, I'll give it some thought. In the meantime, please don't tell anyone else.'

'Of course not!' Hannah was quick to reassure Janka.

Janka hoisted herself up from the floor. 'I missed you and Erika when you left the Slobodarna. Even though conditions were worse at the Patronka, at least you moved on and found someone. I hoped that when I became part of this group I would find a boyfriend, but it hasn't happened yet. I think most of the boys see me as Alexander's younger sister, nothing more. I've wondered how many of the girls are only my friends in order to get closer to him.'

'Don't worry. You'll have plenty more opportunities to meet boys in Eretz. Your turn will come.' Hannah paused at the top of the stairs. Their group stood in the same spot, still making jokes. 'Did you ever know that Erika once had an eye for Alexander?'

'I did wonder. If something had developed between them I wouldn't have minded. She is genuine and caring and always nice to me. You can't help but like her. I'll never forget how she nursed you back to health when you fell ill. Day and night, she sat by your side. It's for the best that she didn't hold out for him though. At the moment, the only thing he's in love with is the promise of Haifa and then a kibbutz. Erika and Marcus seem good together though – do you think they'll end up marrying?'

'I wouldn't be surprised if they do. He adores her, and she cares a great deal for him. If he proposes, I think Erika will say yes.'

Hannah stared up at the velvet sky studded with sequin stars, trying to ignore the usual discord of snores, coughs, and grunts of hundreds of people sleeping in close quarters. To her right, Erika lay on the bench, with her limbs sprawled and her mouth twitched into a smile. Janka lay to her left, burrowed under her blanket, her form rising and falling with her slow breathing.

Their conversation earlier had reopened the scab of her conscience. If Janka was having second-thoughts, what about Lilly? Hannah had allied with her mother and aunt to persuade Lilly to join her. Lilly wouldn't have left home of her own accord. But Lilly had trusted Hannah and her assurances. Who could blame Lilly for her initial reaction after learning about her engagement to Karl?

Hannah renewed her vow to herself to put Lilly's welfare before her own. She would do all she could to insulate her cousin from further pain and help her rebuild her life.

Hannah flung off her blanket and navigated her way around the sleeping people. The layers of darkness fell away to reveal the outlines of the same three ships from the day before. The only thing that had changed was their position. But the harbour was awakening from its slumber and a crew was painting names onto the ship's hulls. *Atlantic* was the largest, *Pacific* the smallest, and *Milos,* the one with the starboard list. Then they raised an unfamiliar red, white and blue flag on the mast of each ship.

Alexander was also awake and watching the activity. 'I'm now certain they're our ships.'

'What makes you so sure?'

'First of all, no others have arrived. Second, they've just hoisted the flag of Panama. That is the fictional destination on our visas.'

'How can they be? They don't look large enough to accommodate us all.' Two of them were smaller than their boat and even the biggest one, a narrow steamship with a high bow, wasn't much larger. 'How will four boatloads of people fit onto three ships when we're already short of space?'

'Perhaps they're bigger than they appear. I suppose they'll merge two boats.'

'Do you think we might merge with Karl's?'

Alexander shrugged his shoulders noncommittally.

'Perhaps you could ask your Haganah friend, Dov? Maybe he has more answers.'

Alexander sauntered off to find Dov, as the team of carpenters reappeared on the Atlantic. By the time he returned, they had begun to erect the frame of a curious superstructure on the upper deck's stern.

'I've got good news, bad news, good news, bad news, and finally good news.'

Hannah couldn't tell whether or not he was joking. 'Let's start with the bad news.'

'I have confirmation that those are our ships.'

'And the good news?'

'Those are our ships.'

She shook her head in mock exasperation. 'And the bad news?'

'We will board the ships in our existing blocks. No choice of ship or travel partners. They have allocated us to the Atlantic and Karl's boat to the Pacific.'

'Oh.' She felt a prick of disappointment, though she had expected as much.

'But the good news is the Schönbrunn passengers will be joining us.'

Hannah smiled. 'That's some consolation. At least I'll be with Lilly.'

'And the last bit of good news ...' He drummed his fingers on the top of the rail. 'We transfer to the ships the day after tomorrow.'

# CHAPTER 18

Hannah waved a last goodbye to Karl. Too far to shout, Karl resorted to communicating with the sign language they had developed over the past few days. He held up ten fingers, pointed to the awaiting ships, mimed a rippling motion, then placed his hand to his heart. She understood: after ten days at sea, they would be together again. As the announcement came through the megaphone that the transfer to the ships was about to begin, Hannah blew Karl one last kiss. She wouldn't see him again until they reached the Promised Land.

The ship Hannah and Lilly were to travel on, the Atlantic, had manoeuvred itself between the Helios and Schönbrunn, and they were to board straight from their respective boats. Hannah hurried down the stairs with Erika, who had been saying goodbye to Marcus, and they quickly found Janka, who had held their place in line and watched their rucksacks. To ensure a smooth embarkation, the Haganah had organised a strict order for boarding. First, women with children, followed by the elderly, then younger women, middle-aged men, and finally young men. Each passenger was to carry only his or her hand luggage, and a team of volunteers, which included Alexander and Isaak, would transfer the suitcases later.

'As soon as we board, let's find Lilly, then a place to sleep,' Hannah said. 'No matter what, I want to stay together.'

'Agreed,' Janka said.

The line of passengers shuffled along the aisle in line towards the exit. At last it was the turn of the three friends to walk up the steep gangway.

'This is it. Next stop, Eretz!' Erika's beaming face revealed her dimples.

'As long as this thing gets us there,' Janka said, sending a sceptical glance towards the rusting ship's hull.

Hannah gazed at the sky. Pale sunlight struggled to break through a thick cover of grey clouds. In a few days, the ships would sail through the Mediterranean under clear blue skies. Away from Europe. Away from the war.

Please let this ship carry us safely across the sea, Hannah prayed. Then the three of them stepped onto the upper deck of the SS Atlantic.

Janka gaped at the scene before them. 'This. Is. A. Disaster.'

Hannah lipread her words. It was impossible to hear her above the commotion. The ship heaved with people and luggage, even though half a boatload of passengers were still waiting to board. The Schönbrunn passengers had boarded first – and it was clear that they had done so with little organisation. The earliest arrivals had staked out generous areas for themselves and were sprawled among their suitcases, forcing everyone else to step around them and between them, like climbers grappling to find a foothold. The passengers' raised voices and heated disputes created bedlam, which was further compounded by the shouts of family members trying to locate each other in the crush of people.

Hannah stood on her tiptoes to search for Lilly among the hundreds on deck. She stepped aside for a woman balancing two backpacks and a child in each hand. From behind, the crowd surged, pushing her forward as they continued to board. She bumped into a middle-aged woman dressed in a silky salmon-pink dress, blonde hair piled high on her head, as if she were headed for a night at the opera. Her glossy scarlet lips twisted into a sneer and she jabbed Hannah under her collarbone.

'Out of my way!'

Hannah took a step backwards, tripped on a suitcase and lost her balance. Her arms flailed as she reached to steady herself, but she landed on her rear, accidentally jostling the arm of a man wearing round silver-framed glasses. He had been sitting on his case, writing in a notebook. When Hannah bumped him, the pencil flew out of his hand and rolled away.

'My pencil!' The man shot Hannah an angry look.

'I'm very sorry,' she said, attempting to rise with the dignity her fall did not afford.

'You clumsy girl. That's the only pencil I have. Go and find it!'

Hannah scrambled on all fours, crawling through a forest of limbs. The pencil had settled in a groove between two weathered boards a couple of metres away. She stretched to reach it and yelped as a sturdy, knee-length boot stamped on her hand. Its mortified owner helped her to her feet. 'I'm so sorry. I apologise. I didn't see you there,' he said.

Erika rushed to Hannah's aid, giving her hand a quick examination. She shouted in her ear to overcome the din, 'I don't think you've broken anything.'

Hannah rubbed the black tread imprint from her stinging hand and through a blur of tears saw Janka admonish the bespectacled man as she returned his precious pencil. Erika grabbed Hannah's arm and steered her out of the path of two elderly women, Janka took her other arm and, keeping their backs pressed against the railings, they edged their way forward. It was slow going; each step a protracted effort against the oncoming tide of shouting, shoving, elbowing passengers. The Atlantic didn't measure much longer than the Helios, but it took them at least thirty minutes to advance from one end to the other. It occurred to Hannah that there was a real danger of people being crushed to death before they even left port.

'This is chaos!' Janka shouted. She watched her every step, careful not to collide with any other passengers. 'It makes the Helios look spacious.'

Hannah searched the crowd. 'How will we ever find Lilly?'

'I think our priority is to find somewhere to sleep and grab it. Then I'll guard it with Erika, and you can go search for Lilly.'

They navigated the stairs in single file, Janka leading the way, then Hannah, with one hand gripping the rail, the other on Janka's shoulder, and Erika behind, holding onto Hannah's arm.

Passengers and luggage clogged the lower deck too, but they found a few cabins on both sides of the passageway.

Janka tried a handle. 'They're probably all taken, but worth checking.' As expected, the door was locked fast.

Erika checked the cabins on the opposite side, and Hannah started on the doors to Janka's left. The first door didn't give, but to her surprise, the next one swung open. A woman in a peach silk dressing gown appeared in the doorway and blocked her entry. With her blonde updo and glossy red lips, Hannah recognised her from their unpleasant contact earlier that morning. A round-faced man with a florid complexion and unusually greasy hair appeared behind her.

'Get out!' the woman yelled. 'This cabin is occupied.' She slammed the door, and Hannah jumped at the bang.

'What a rude woman,' Janka said. 'Don't let her upset you.'

'Let's forget the cabins and investigate below,' Erika said.

With each step down the steep, narrow ladder, the air grew mustier with the smell of damp until they reached the hold below the waterline. Hannah peered into the gloom to see dozens of passengers scurrying around trying to search for a spare place to sleep while manoeuvring their luggage through tight aisles. The cargo hold had been converted into what looked like a catacomb, but was clearly supposed to be sleeping quarters, judging from the people lying on what appeared to be shelving. The only natural light and ventilation came from a shaft above. The rough wooden bunks, such as they were, extended from floor to ceiling. In some places, there were nine tiers.

The floor, covered in gravel chips to serve as ballast, crunched beneath their feet as they investigated their options. A few spare bunks remained at the bottom level, just over the gravel, and a few more were several tiers above, reachable by rickety ladders. The men and women who had claimed the best spots lay on their pallets in the semi-darkness. The gap between the bunks was so small, however, that there was no room to sit up. Hannah's gaze darted between Janka and Erika. They shook their heads in unison, eyes wide with dismay.

'The Slobodarna was bad, the Patronka, terrible,' Erika said. 'I didn't think it could get any worse. I was wrong.'

They backed away, climbed the ladder to the next deck, and squeezed past the tide of passengers heading for the catacombs.

'I wonder how many will decide to stay once they've seen the bunks?' Janka said.

'I couldn't imagine sleeping there for ten days. I'd prefer to sleep outside,' Erika said. 'Standing up, if I have to.'

'Why don't we search the rest of the lower deck?' Hannah said. 'Lilly has to be around here somewhere. Maybe she's already found a place and is saving it for us.'

They climbed over sprawled limbs and luggage and stumbled upon the rudimentary sanitary facilities: three toilets for women and two for men. Since the engines were not yet running, there was no electricity to work the water pumps and the toilets did not flush. It had only been a few hours, but the stench of the lavatories was already too much to bear. Hannah held her nose and retreated. How would eighteen hundred people cope in these facilities?

Further down the passageway, they found the dining room. It too was crowded, mainly with passengers in their sixties or seventies, though some looked well over eighty. Exhausted and overwhelmed, they huddled wherever they found space: sitting on suitcases, lying under the room's curved mahogany chairs and tables. Some even bedded down on top of the tables.

Hannah exited as fast as she had entered, embarrassed to see the older passengers in such a pitiful state. Ashamed of the degrading conditions they were subjected to. The elderly should have been given priority for the cabins, instead of them being seized in a free-for-all by people like that rude woman in the peach dressing gown.

'Let's go back to the upper deck,' Erika said.

'Hannah!'

She thought she heard someone call her name, but with all the noise and commotion she couldn't be sure.

'Hannah, wait!'

Hannah turned. Lilly was stumbling and tripping down the aisle after them. Hannah held open her arms and caught her cousin in a tight hug. 'Am I glad to see you. We've been searching the whole ship trying to find you.'

'I was with Gisela. It was tiring for her to walk through the squash and I didn't want to leave her,' Lilly said. 'And I thought we might end up missing each other, so best to not to move. I've been keeping a look out for you. Have you found anywhere to sleep?'

'Not yet. We were about to try the main deck again.'

'I'll just tell Gisela where I'm going and then I'll join you.'

Gisela sat on her suitcase, leaning against the wood-panelled wall. 'Hello, my dears.' She looked weary, but greeted them with a warm smile.

'How are you keeping?' Hannah said.

'Mustn't grumble. Under the circumstances, I'm more fortunate than many others. I don't know what I would have done without your wonderful cousin. She carried both her suitcase and mine through the ship until we found a corner to sit.'

Lilly shrugged off the compliment. 'It's what anyone would have done,' she said. 'I'm going to go with Hannah to see if we can find more room on the upper deck. Perhaps everyone has boarded by now, and we'll be able to find some space. Will you be all right on your own for a while?'

'Don't worry about me.' Gisela heaved herself to her feet. 'I have just spotted an old friend I've not seen in years. I am going to go over to her to say hello.'

The situation above had not improved. If anything, it was worse. Some people crouched, others, hemmed in on all sides, could only stand. One man in a tailored suit and fedora leaned against a post, asleep on his feet.

'What are those strange wooden shacks?' Lilly said, spotting the superstructure they had watched under construction from the Helios. 'Do you think they're additional cabins?'

They pushed along the deck, and slowly made their way to the top of the stairs to investigate. At the front of the structure, they noted a painted sign for a hospital. Erika considered it with particular interest. 'I wonder if they'll need volunteers?'

'With this many people on board, I bet they'll be grateful for all the help they can get,' Hannah said.

To its side was a bench and a long line of people winding their way around it. She spotted Jenny in the queue. 'What are you waiting for?'

'To go to Panama.' Her blue eyes crinkled, amused by her own joke.

'Panama?'

'The lavatories,' said Jenny. 'We heard these unofficial ones overhanging the stern are more hygienic than those down below.'

'That's good to know. Because I saw those other ones.' Hannah wrinkled her nose. 'Why do you call them Panama?'

'The Panamanian flag is painted on the roof. Someone made a joke earlier and the name seems to be sticking.'

Erika giggled.

'We were wondering where you'd all got to,' Jenny said. 'Have you found a place to sleep yet?'

'No. We're still looking. Apart from the dark, airless catacombs, there's nothing to be had – and those spots are probably gone by now too. But I didn't want to spend ten days down there. How about you?'

'We have.' Jenny gave a conspiratorial wink. 'And there's space for you as well.'

'You got a cabin?'

'Not quite. Wait for me and I'll show you.'

'Since we're already waiting, I might as well take a trip to Panama, too.'


'This is genius,' Hannah said when Jenny showed them the empty lifeboat she and Stefan had discovered on the upper deck.

'It's a bit of a squeeze, but we should be able to fit six in here. And another two or three on the deck beside it.'

Hannah noticed Stefan and Jenny had draped clothes and bags around the boat to reserve the space. 'Do you think they will let us stay here?' Hannah asked.

'Unless someone tells us otherwise, we'll stay put,' Stefan said. 'We must never leave the boat unoccupied, or someone else will surely take it.'

'Thank you for sharing your space with us.' Lilly dropped her backpack under one of the benches. 'I'll go down to tell Gisela. She can have my space in the boat. I don't mind sleeping on the deck.'

Hannah stowed her luggage beside Lilly's. 'I'll come with you.'

When they reached the dining room half an hour later they found Gisela chatting to three older ladies. 'Hello, my darlings. How are you getting on?'

'Jenny has found places for us in a lifeboat,' Lilly said. 'Would you like to join us?'

'Lilly, dear, thank you. I do think it may be too much for me to move again right now, though. And I don't fancy climbing in and out of a boat.' Gisela gave a wry smile. 'I think I'd prefer to remain down here.'

'Would you like me to stay with you?'

She raised an eyebrow. 'No. You go and join the young people.'

Lilly did not move. 'I don't think I should leave you here on your own.'

Gisela brushed away her concerns. 'I'll be fine. Besides, I'm not on my own. I am with these new friends.' She waved her hand again, encouraging Lilly. 'You go.'

Lilly kissed Gisela on the cheek. 'I'll come back and visit you often.'

By the time they returned to the upper deck, Hannah's legs felt stiff from hours of shuffling around. She wondered how Karl was getting on. His ship, the Pacific, had docked at too great a distance for her to distinguish him from the other passengers.

Alexander passed them, sinking under the weight of two large suitcases. Droplets of sweat trickled from his forehead and wet patches had appeared under the arms of his shirt, his chest and on his back.

'You must be exhausted,' Hannah said.

'We're almost done.' He managed a brief smile. 'Have you got somewhere to sleep?' he asked.

'Yes, in a lifeboat.'

'A lifeboat?' He nodded, impressed. 'That's a clever find.'

'All thanks to Jenny and Stefan who discovered it.'

'Is Janka with you?'

'Yes, we're all there together.'

'Any room for me and Isaak?'

'Stefan saved space on the deck beside it. There's room for you both.'

'Wonderful. I'll come and join you when I've finished.'

'Where's Isaak?'

'I think he returned to the Helios to bring the last of the luggage. I'll tell him when I see him.'

Daylight was fading when Alexander climbed into the lifeboat, his clothes soaked through, and droplets dripping from his hair.

'You're drenched with sweat,' Janka said.

'It's water. I just showered myself with a bucket from the river.'

He sat on a bench and shut his eyes just as a loud voice came through the megaphone announcing that they could line up for supper.

'Do you want me to fetch you something?' Janka said.

Alexander groaned. 'I'll get up.'

The overcrowding, luggage-clogged pathways, and hungry, exhausted passengers added up to the perfect combination for tempers to flare. A woman's voice rose in heated debate with an older man in silver-rimmed glasses. It was the man with the pencil Hannah had encountered earlier. She ducked behind Alexander before he could notice her.

'It's been a long day and my boys are tired and hungry,' the woman said, keeping a firm grip on four-year-old twin boys to make sure they wouldn't stray.

'Aren't we all?' Pencil Man said. 'But we're not making an infernal noise like your whining brats. Can't you keep them quiet?'

'Listen here. You pushed your way into the queue ahead of me and I didn't make a fuss. So you can just keep quiet yourself.'

Dov from the Haganah group wove his way through to Alexander. 'This is impossible. The deck is so packed people will have to take turns sleeping or sleep standing up. We are setting up a left luggage in the hold to stow everyone's suitcases and free up more space. Are you able to help us?'

'Yes, sure, all right,' Alexander sighed. 'Let me quickly get something to eat and I'll come help.'

Supper was a piece of bread and a cup of tea. Hannah bit into her slice. It was stale. She nibbled at it, taking sips of tea in between to soften it and make it easier to swallow. Lilly also appeared to be struggling but stoically forced it down. Alexander, meanwhile, devoured his piece as if it were a delectable slice of apple strudel.

By the light of flickering kerosene lamps, the Haganah team and other volunteers from among the passengers cleared the deck of luggage. Curled between two benches in the lifeboat, Hannah dozed and woke, hearing the men's laboured breathing and the dull thud of suitcases as they were passed from person to person down into the hold. When the job was finally completed, late into the night, Alexander collapsed, exhausted, beside the lifeboat.

Janka was still awake. She leaned over to him. 'Where's Isaak?'

'Isn't he back yet?' Alexander said.

'I haven't seen him all day. I thought he was working alongside you. Did you tell him where to find us?'

But there was no reply. Alexander was asleep.

# CHAPTER 19

It was after midnight when Isaak finally emerged from the hold. His joints ached. He had been ferrying luggage for most of the day. First from the Helios to the Atlantic, then labelling, stacking, and stowing the suitcases in the ship's hold, or as they called it, 'left luggage.'

The initial commotion had subsided and the passengers were attempting to settle down for the night. Isaak stretched his arm out into the blackness. Without the ship's engine running, there was no electricity and therefore no lighting. He felt for the wall, slid his hand along its smooth wooden surface and used it to guide himself down the passageway.

Isaak hadn't seen Alexander since early afternoon and didn't know where to find him or any of the others. He held onto a vague assumption that he would find them on the upper deck, as they had made a place for themselves there on the Helios. At the moment, however, he was so fatigued that he would have lain down to sleep just about anywhere.

In the darkness, he tripped over an obstacle. It shouted in a booming voice, 'Watch where you're going!'

'Sorry.' Isaak took a step back.

'Ouch!' said another man, his voice more of a squeak. 'Get off. That's my hand.'

'So sorry.'

'Be quiet,' said a third.

'Shall I step on you and see if you remain silent?' said the man on whose hand Isaak had trodden.

Isaak cringed.

'Enough!' shouted a voice further along the passageway.

A lock rattled, a door opened, and a blonde woman in a silky dressing gown appeared in the doorway holding a kerosene lamp. She shined it in Isaak's face.

'What's going on?' she said.

'Sorry if I disturbed you,' Isaak said in a low voice. 'I'm on my way to the upper deck. I'm trying to find somewhere to sleep.'

'Oh.' She offered him a little smile, and then beckoned to him with her finger. 'We have a little space left on the floor. Why don't you come in?'

Isaak couldn't believe his luck. 'Much appreciated.'

The two-tier berths on either side were already occupied and another two sleeping figures lay wrapped in blankets on the floor between them. Isaak removed his rucksack from his stiff shoulders, set it at his feet, then unstrapped and unfurled his blanket.

The woman dropped her dressing gown onto the floor, extinguished the kerosene lamp, and slipped under the covers of the lower bunk. 'Good night.'

Isaak covered himself with the blanket, vaguely aware he hadn't removed his shoes, and knowing he was too tired to reach for his feet. 'Good night,' he mumbled.

When he awoke, he found himself on the floor of a dimly lit cabin. His head was spinning. He couldn't remember where he was or how he had arrived there. He looked to the bunk on his right, then his left and the recollection came to him in snatches. He had tripped, stepped over a passenger and the cabin door opened ...

A blonde woman sat up in the top bunk. She wore a strappy pink nightdress that had slipped off one shoulder. She smiled lazily at Isaak. 'Good morning.'

His cheeks burned, and he lowered his gaze, keeping his focus on the bunk below where a red-faced man with greasy hair opened his eyes. He gave Isaak a disinterested glance, pulled the cover over himself, and turned over.

'Did you sleep well?'

'Y-yes, th-thanks.'

His cousins would be frantic, wondering where he was. Isaak scrambled to his feet. 'I have to go.'

'See you later, *Schätzchen*.' She blew him a kiss.

Isaak stumbled out into the passageway. His legs felt like rubber. His throat was dry and his tongue tasted grit in the hold. He pressed his forehead to the wall to steady himself.

'Isaak, are you all right?'

Isaak turned to see Hannah's cousin, Lilly, escorting Gisela, shuffling along a queue. He experienced an odd sense of relief. Lilly held a bucket of water, and the sloshing was making his mouth water. 'Can I please have a sip?'

Lilly looked confused. He pointed to the water.

'This?' she asked, still uncertain.

He nodded. The effort made his head hurt.

Lilly looked at the bucket, then at Gisela. They both chortled. 'You wouldn't want to drink this, Isaak. It comes from the river. It is for the ... the ...' Lilly hesitated. 'For the lavatory.'

Isaak attempted a smile. He placed a hand on his forehead.

Lilly observed him more closely. 'You're looking rather pale. Do you need a drink?'

He mouthed the word, 'Yes.'

She set down the bucket. 'I'll be right back.'

His field of vision was shrinking and fading to black when she pressed a cup into his hand and guided it to his mouth. He gulped the water.

'More?' she said.

'Please.'

She darted, sure-footed, between sprawling limbs and returned with another cup. He downed it at once. 'Thank you.'

'You looked as if you were about to faint.'

'I think I was dehydrated. I suppose I must have been if I considered drinking from your bucket.'

'I'm just accompanying Gisela to the—' Lilly gave a sheepish smile.

'Understood. I'll wait for you and have some more water in the meantime.'

He found the drinking water tap and drank another three cups in quick succession. When he returned, Lilly was waiting outside the conveniences for Gisela.

'Where are the others?' he said.

'We are together in a lifeboat on the upper deck. I'll show you where it is if you don't mind waiting a few more minutes.'

'Not at all. I'd appreciate that.' He breathed more easily, comforted by the prospect of rejoining his family and friends.

Gisela emerged and Lilly accompanied her to her spot in the dining room. 'Is there anything else you need?' she said, crouching beside her.

'I'm fine, my darling. Thanks for your help.' She turned to Isaak. 'And how are you, dear? Feeling better?'

'Much. It seems I didn't drink enough yesterday when I was carrying all the suitcases.'

'You must be careful, especially when you are doing hard physical work.'

'I realise that now.'

Gisela's attention was distracted by Lilly, who was making her way to the other side of the room.

'How are you and Lilly related?' Isaak said.

'We're not related. We met on board the Schönbrunn and in this short time she has become as dear to me as family. She's a wonderful girl.'

A tinkle of musical notes floated through the air. 'Now what has she found over there?' Gisela got to her feet and went over to investigate, Isaak following.

Lilly was standing at an dilapidated upright piano and sampling the keys. Not surprisingly, a few notes were off-key.

'Do you know how to play?' Isaak said.

'A little. How can I not?' she shrugged. 'I'm from Vienna, the city of music.'

'I'm also from Vienna, but I can't even play the triangle,' he said. 'Will you give us a song?'

Lilly glanced around at the dining room filled with passengers. 'I'm not sure.'

'Yes, please do,' Gisela said.

Despite the piano's poor state, Lilly teased out a tune. After the first few bars, Gisela recognised it, and, in a low voice, began to sing along. '*Wein, Wein, nur du allein.*'

Soon, three other ladies joined her, then two men. Before long, Lilly's playing had attracted an audience of thirty people or so. One white-haired woman had a faraway look in her eyes – surely she was remembering another time and place. An elderly man in a hat wiped a tear from the corner of his eye. A frail woman supporting herself with a walking stick sang along, even as her mouth quivered.

*Vienna, Vienna, you alone*

*Should always be the city of my dreams!*
*Where I am happy and overjoyed ...*
*And it leaves nobody cold*
*No matter if they are young or old ...*
*If I had to leave this beautiful place one day*
*My longing would have no end.*


As the last note faded, Isaak and Gisela started to clap. The others quickly joined in, a rapturous round of applause.

Lilly whirled to face the audience and her eyes widened. She hadn't known how many people had circled round.

'Take a bow,' said Isaak.

Lilly bobbed a shy curtsy.

Isaak put two fingers between his lips to whistle, then clapped again.

Then Lilly and Isaak left the dining room, with promises that she would return to play sometime soon.

On the upper deck, Isaak rubbed his arms against the unexpected brisk wind and rolled down his shirt sleeves. The sky hung heavy, and when they reached the lifeboat, they found Alexander, Janka and the others immersed in a serious discussion.

Lilly climbed in. 'Look who I found.'

'Hello, stranger,' said Alexander. 'We were wondering where you had got to.'

Isaak settled himself on the opposite bench. 'Has something happened?'

'It is what hasn't happened that is the problem,' he said. 'For the meantime, we're stuck here.'

'What do you mean? Why?'

'They are still waiting for the crew to arrive.'

'When were they supposed to come?' Isaak said.

'No one seems to know,' Alexander said. 'I wonder if they even have a crew.'

'When did you hear this?' Lilly said.

'After you went to Gisela.' Hannah looked glum. 'So much for arriving in Eretz in ten days.'

'Don't worry,' Isaak said. 'We've already boarded the ship. They can't keep us here for too long. And like we said on the Helios, we'll row there if we have to.'

'That's the spirit.' Alexander patted his back. 'So, tell me, where were you last night? I couldn't find you anywhere.'

'I was down in the hold until after midnight helping to organise the left luggage.'

'Did you sleep in the hold?'

'No, I found a place on the floor.'

'Where?'

Isaak squirmed in his seat. The question was innocent, but he suddenly felt awkward, recalling the woman in her strappy night-dress. 'In a cabin.'

Hannah's mouth gaped. 'How did you manage that?'

'I tripped over a few people in the dark. They complained, of course, and the noise of their complaints woke up the people inside one of the cabins. Someone came out and offered me a place on the floor. So that's where I slept.'

'Lucky you. When we tried the cabins, a rude woman slammed the door in my face.'

'You can have my place, if you want,' he said, half hoping Hannah would agree.

'Oh no, it's fine.' Hannah flapped her hands, brushing off his offer. 'I'm glad you got a good spot. I'm just frustrated that every time we make a bit of progress, we face another setback.'

'I understand. It is endlessly frustrating. But I meant it – take my place.'

'No, don't worry. I'll be fine here with Lilly, Janka, and Erika . You made the lucky find, and since we're going to be here longer than expected, you might as well enjoy it.'


Isaak didn't consider himself lucky when he reluctantly left the company of his cousins and friends later that night. If anything, he felt homesick, leaving them. But their enthusiasm for his good fortune pushed him to return to the cabin.

It was late when he crept back into the cabin and he was relieved to determine that the others were already in bed and asleep, as evidenced by the snoring. But amid the normal sounds of slumber, there was a rustling of sheets and low moans coming from the top bunk. Isaak burrowed himself under his blanket and pretended he was sleeping. He placed his hands over his ears to block out the noise until exhaustion overtook him.

In the darkness, he awoke with a start. Something, someone, was pressed against his back.

'Shhh. It's only me,' a female voice whispered.

The touch of her arm on his shoulder rendered Isaak numb; his body frozen, his mind blank.

'There aren't many pleasures on this miserable excuse for a ship.' She kissed his ear. 'Shall we make our own?'

The woman's husband – at least Isaak presumed that's who he was – lay snoring in the right-hand bottom bunk.

This wasn't happening to Isaak.

It couldn't be.

He remained stock-still and squeezed his eyes shut, willing her to go away.

Her hand slid across his shoulder and fumbled with the top button of his shirt. His heart pounded and, like an alarm, jolted him from his paralysis.

Isaak pulled himself to his feet, staggered a step or two, and groped for the door handle.

'Where are you going?' Her voice trailed after him, dripping with disappointment.

He ignored her and fled the cabin – stumbling into a man who had been resting against the door.

The man cried out in pain.

'Sorry.' Isaak hastily stepped away, his eyes adjusting to the dimness. 'I didn't see you there.'

'Every. Single. Night.'

'Will you be quiet!' The sound of a loud, braying voice reverberated down the passageway. 'It's hard enough to get some sleep as it is.'

'I also want to sleep, but he stepped on me. Again!'

'My apologies, it was an accident,' Isaak said.

'What are you doing wandering around in the dark in the middle of the night?' said a man slumped against the opposite wall.

'I was only—'

'Quiet already!' the braying man said.

'Why are you shouting?' said the first man. 'You're making more noise than everyone else.'

'Maybe because you woke us all with your squealing. And when you're not squealing, you're snoring like a pig.'

'How dare you call me a pig!'

'Will you all be quiet!' shouted a new voice.

'I didn't call you a pig. I said you snore like one. You snort, and you disturb everyone with your snorting.'

'At least I don't have a voice like a braying donkey.'

Along the passageway, people laughed.

'Do you want to say that again?' A menacing tone crept into his voice.

'You sound like an annoyed, braying donkey.'

More laughter.

'I've had about enough of you. Let's see if you laugh when I punch your snout.'

'You just try.' The man stood, his muscles tense.

'Stop this right now.' Someone grabbed hold of him.

In the gloom, Isaak saw several other men restrain the braying man, as others shouted and traded insults. It was all they needed to let off their pent-up steam. Isaak had been forgotten. He was just as glad to make his way to the stairs, avoiding two men leaning against the railing, asleep. Dov and another Haganah man passed him, blowing furiously on their whistles to restore order among the brawling passengers.

When Isaak reached the upper deck, he ran into Alexander, who was on his way after Dov. 'Sounds like trouble down there. Any idea what happened?'

Isaak looked down. 'It's sort of my fault.'

'What?' Alexander gave a soft chuckle. 'Why? How?'

'I stepped on a passenger by accident and when he shouted at me, he woke other people who shouted at him, and it just became a huge screaming match.'

Alexander gestured dismissively. 'Oh, don't take it to heart. Everyone is irritable. The slightest spark sets anyone off like a tinder-box. Do you want me to walk you back down to make sure there's no more trouble?'

'No!' Isaak blurted out. 'I ... I'd rather not return.'

'Isaak, what's the matter?'

'It's nothing. I'd just prefer to stay here. Do you have any room for me?'

'It's clearly not nothing ...' Alexander waited for Isaak to explain.

'The cabin ... well, let's just say it was too good to be true.'

'What do you mean?'

'There are weird things going on in there.'

Alexander studied Isaak intently. 'What kind of weird things?'

'Last night, the woman who offered me a place ... I think ... no, I'm sure she was sleeping on the bottom bunk. But when I awoke, she was in a different bed. I thought I must have been confused because of the dehydration and all, but this evening ...'

'Go on.'

Isaak shook his head. 'I can't.'

'Of course you can.'

'I woke up to find that woman pressed against me. She put her arm around me. She was trying to ... you know ... And her husband was snoring on another bunk.'

'*Mein Gott*! Did she ...? Did you ...?'

'I was so shocked that at first I couldn't move. Then I came to my senses and got out of there as fast as I could. But I'd forgotten about the passengers sleeping outside.' Isaak shook his head at the recollection. 'I should have realised ... the situation ... sooner. Nothing happened, but I feel ... I don't know.' He threw up his hands. 'But it's a bad feeling.'

'Listen to me.' Alexander grasped his shoulders. 'There are a few strange types on this ship. I'm not sure where Storfer dragged them from. Perhaps I ought to warn Dov. But you had the sense to extract yourself from a compromising situation, and none of that was your fault.'

Isaak nodded. 'I know you're right, but even so, please don't tell the others.'

'I won't. This stays between us. We'll find a spot for you.'

Isaak tapped his hand against his forehead. 'My backpack and blanket are still down there. I don't want to see her again if I can help it.'

'You won't have to. I'll fetch them for you tomorrow. You can use my blanket tonight.'

Though a young man of nineteen, Isaak allowed his cousin to settle him on the deck beside the lifeboat and cover him with a blanket, the way his parents had done when he was a small boy.

'Try and get some rest,' Alexander said, settling down himself. Within minutes, he was asleep, while Isaak remained alert, the events of the night replaying in his mind.

The wind picked up. Isaak pulled the blanket tighter around himself and burrowed inside. He heard a steady pitter-patter against the deck and peeked out. Heavy drops landed in front of him and a blue flash streaked across the sky. In minutes, the shower became a torrent, making puddles on the deck and soaking the blanket through.

A clap of thunder brought the crowd on deck to their feet. Moaning, cursing, and grabbing what they could carry, they converged at the stairs, trying to reach shelter on the lower deck, only to be met by protests from those in the passageway below. Alexander had awakened with a groan from his spot on the deck as well. He yanked on his backpack as another flash lit up the night. 'Let's find some shelter below,' he called to Isaak through the rain.

Isaak shook his head. Better the storm outside, he thought to himself.

'Then we'll go down to the catacombs.'

The occupants down below tried to make room on their bunks and in the narrow aisles for the new arrivals, but it was so crammed that Alexander and Isaak squatted on the stairs. The air reeked of damp clothing and stale sweat; it was hard to breathe.

'This is hell,' Alexander said.

'At least it's dry,' Isaak replied.

Without warning, the people on the stairs above them began to shriek. Then they shoved and jostled each other, desperate to get out of the rain, as a rush of water cascaded down the staircase, dousing them all.

'As you were saying, Isaak?' Alexander gave a grim smile.

Isaak burst out laughing. It was all there was left to do.

# CHAPTER 20

'Don't eat the mouldy parts,' Erika cautioned her friends, sitting in the lifeboat.

Lilly examined her piece of bread and picked off two green patches before biting into her slice. The food she was eating with appetite, if not quite verve, would have disgusted her old self. But she was hungry, and this was all there was to eat. She had almost run out of her stock of food and wanted to preserve what she had left. Hannah, sitting opposite Lilly, grimaced as she chewed.

'This is the third day with no decent food. If they don't give us some soon, we'll starve before we ever leave Tulcea,' Janka said.

The morning air, following the previous night's deluge, was fresh and breezy. They were finally sitting down for something to eat after having returned to the deck, where they spent an hour bailing out the water that had pooled in the lifeboat. The wet clothing and blankets they had abandoned in their rush for shelter were now hanging on makeshift washing lines.

The night before, while Alexander and Isaak had run for the catacombs, the rest of them had made their way to the dining room, where they waited out the storm crouched on the floor beside Gisela. Lilly had caught a glimpse of Max and Alma from the Schönbrunn among the throngs of people. Alma, in the late stages of pregnancy, looked particularly uncomfortable, sitting cramped in a corner.

Jenny and Stefan had also joined them in the dining room until Jenny started heaving from the stench. She fled with a hand clamped over her nose and mouth, Stefan close behind her.

Lilly had already learned to endure the smell. She had made a point to visit Gisela twice a day with a bucket of river water, so Gisela could use the facilities with a semblance of dignity. For most of the elderly passengers, the effort of navigating the crowds to reach the upper deck, fetching the water, and lugging the heavy bucket back downstairs was simply too hard. Some had difficulty waiting in the queue for an hour or more and had become incontinent. The situation was pitiful and the foul odour unbearable.

As Lilly sat beside Gisela, fully experiencing conditions in the dining room, she decided that she would have a word with Alexander. Since he was a Haganah member, he should be able to raise the issue with the leadership who could help improve the situation.

Later that morning, as she and Hannah carried buckets of river water for Gisela and a companion of hers, Lilly spotted Alexander navigating the passageway with a sense of urgency. She initially hoped it would be a good chance to speak with him, but he seemed preoccupied at that moment and he strode by without noticing them. He marched up to the entrance of a cabin and rapped on the door. A simpering blonde in a pink dressing gown opened it.

Hannah nudged Lilly, then leaned closer to whisper, 'That's the horrible woman I told you about. The one who jabbed me when I bumped into her on deck by accident and then later slammed the cabin door in my face. I wonder what he wants with her?'

'Do you think they could be involved?' Lilly said.

'For his sake, I hope not.'

The silk gown had slid suggestively off her shoulder, but far from expressing pleasure, Alexander's posture remained rigid with his hands clenched by his sides. Her suggestive smile faded as he spoke.

She shrugged and stood aside to let him pass. Seconds later, he reemerged, carrying a rucksack and blanket, not giving the woman a second glance.

Her cat-like eyes followed him. Then she noticed Lilly and Hannah, and her pursed scarlet lips became a sneer filled with such ugliness that Lilly felt compelled to turn away. The woman slammed the door with a sharp bang.

Now, as Lilly forced down her last mouthful of bread, she thought again of the peculiar encounter she had witnessed earlier. 'I wonder what happened between Alexander and that woman in the cabin?'

'I can't make it out.' Hannah glanced back to ensure Erika and Janka hadn't overheard them. 'Her behaviour was rather suggestive when she first opened the door.'

'He didn't look interested, though. More angry if anything.' Lilly couldn't understand why it bothered her and why she was grateful for Hannah's reassurance.

Hannah, on the other hand, seemed to find the situation amusing and grinned. 'Perhaps he was jealous she'd found another man.'

'Do you think she's his type?'

Hannah stiffened. 'Shhh ...'

Lilly looked up to see Alexander and Isaak quickly heading towards them, no longer encumbered by the many passengers clogging every walkway. As of that morning, the Haganah had established pedestrian traffic regulations – a one-way system around the deck meant that one could walk from one end of the ship to the other without being impeded by people walking in the opposite direction, blocking their path.

'Isaak has decided he misses us so will be joining us on the upper deck.' Alexander said, leaning into the boat to address his sister, Lilly, Hannah and Erika. Isaak stood awkwardly behind him, moving his backpack and blanket from one shoulder to the other. Lilly recognised the backpack and blanket as the ones Alexander had retrieved from the cabin.

'Now why would you want to do that?' Janka said, oblivious to all the commotion that had taken place below. 'Wouldn't you prefer to sleep in your luxurious, dry cabin?'

Janka winked in her attempt to cajole her cousin to join her in their usual playful banter, but Isaak stared at the floor, shuffling his feet.

'It's far better we all stay together as a group on this voyage, in any case,' Lilly said, filling the awkward silence. 'I'm glad to stay near my cousin too.'

Isaak's smile at Lilly was grateful.

'Yes, I'm also glad we'll be together again,' Janka said. 'Don't mind my teasing.'

'Can I have your attention, please?' said a Haganah member, speaking into the megaphone. 'Herr Storfer will come onto the ship in a moment to say a few words.'

Even appreciation for the efficient traffic rules didn't prevent the immediate squall of passengers shouting protests. They directed their pent up anger at Berthold Storfer: architect of their flight to freedom, source of their misery. Herr Storfer boarded the ship surrounded by a ring of Haganah men for protection. From the fury his presence had provoked, perhaps that wasn't an overreaction.

Berthold Storfer stood on the bridge and seemed wary as he faced the passengers. His suit was immaculate as always, but his ashen face was more haggard than Lilly remembered, having last seen him in Vienna less than two weeks before. He shakily brought the megaphone to his lips, 'I understand your frustration—'

His words were drowned out by a torrent of complaints about the lack of space, the lack of food, the quality of the food, the dreadful lavatories, and poor sanitation.

Storfer flapped his arms. 'Please allow me to speak.'

The Haganah ordered the crowd to hush.

'Although conditions on this ship are somewhat cramped, it is only temporary. I have arranged for a fourth ship to ease the crowding. It is now on its way from Greece. In a few days, the Rosita will arrive, along with your crew, coal and additional provisions. We will transfer five hundred passengers to the new ship. You'll all have more space and then you can depart.'

'We were supposed to have left already!' shouted one man.

Isaak whispered to Alexander something about braying like a donkey. Alexander smiled knowingly.

'And you will. Soon. When the new ship arrives. The wait is almost over and the journey will only take between six to ten days.'

'What about proper food?' It was Pencil Man with the spectacles. 'What we are eating isn't fit for a dog.'

'I believe several kitchens will open tomorrow for the assorted groups, including a kosher kitchen. We are trying to get more food. But as you are no doubt aware, there is a war on. It's not so easy to procure supplies.'

'What about the state of the sanitation facilities?' asked the mother of the twin boys.

'Your organisers here have to take responsibility for the rest. From first impressions, their organisation leaves much to be desired.' His gaze swept across the Haganah men who surrounded him. 'You need to be more responsible. Sort things out. Make some order.'

Their jaws hardened at his admonition.

'He's got a nerve,' Alexander muttered.

'Why don't you have a proper look around the ship and see the poor conditions for yourself?' shouted Ignatz, a friend of Alexander's from the Prague group. 'Then tell us how you suggest we sort things out.'

'Thank you.' Berthold Storfer waved his stick in a forward motion, signalling that he wished to leave. The Haganah escort ushered him from the vessel, thwarting any further angry confrontations, and leaving a trail of blazing arguments behind.

Alexander slumped onto a bench in the lifeboat. 'Well, then.'

'That was a pointless exercise,' Janka said.

'Surely some of it is positive news?' Lilly said. 'He mentioned there's only a brief delay until the fourth ship arrives.'

'We've had assurances like this before,' Alexander said. 'When we first arrived at the Slobodarna, they told us that a ship was on the way. That ship apparently sank. Then winter set in and it was almost nine months until we finally left there.'

'Lack of nails!' Isaak said, mimicking Berthold Storfer's clipped inflection. His comment elicited chuckles from the Slobodarna internees.

'Yes! I'd forgotten that.' Alexander turned to Lilly. 'They told us the mysterious delay was because of a lack of nails.'

'Nails?' she said.

'Exactly.'

'He's a Nazi spy!' A man with a shock of white hair, shaking his fist in the air, shouted at no one in particular as he walked past the lifeboat.

'Really?' Lilly looked at Alexander for reassurance. 'Is that true?'

'We've all heard that rumour, but I doubt it,' he said. 'If he was a spy, he wouldn't have waited to hand us over to the Nazis. He wouldn't go to the trouble of arranging boats down the Danube and make further arrangements for these ships. They may be near-wrecks, but he made good on his promise. Despite his harsh words and apparent indifference, I think he's trying to get us out of here. Though it's true, he answers to the Nazi authorities. Without their permission, we don't leave.'

'Also, it must be a real headache to put together a crew,' Stefan broke in. 'Who in their right mind wants to risk sailing a shipload of Jews to Mandatory Palestine, when the British threaten they will arrest and jail any crew who do so?'

Alexander nodded. 'And it's almost impossible to find more ships when there's a war on.'

'Realistically, how long might we still have to wait?' Lilly said.

'Who knows?' Alexander looked grim. 'Days. Weeks. Months?'

'How long does it take for a ship to sail here from Greece?' Erika said.

'About five days,' Stefan said.

'That is, if it has left already,' Alexander said. 'More likely it hasn't.'

'If Storfer says it's on the way, that probably means it will leave in about a week and then five more days to reach Tulcea,' Isaak said.

Hannah remained silent during the discussion, her eyes on the bow of the Pacific. Karl's ship was too far to recognise any individuals on board. Her longing was evident. Lilly reached across and took her hand.

'I miss him so much,' Hannah said, as the others continued their calculations.

'You'll see him soon.'

'If Alexander is right, it could be weeks, or even months. And who knows what will happen in the meantime?' She stared at the surrounding port. New gun emplacements with coiled barbed wire seemed to have sprung up overnight. The war was fast approaching and they all knew that endangered their chances of leaving. 'What happens if we don't get out in time?'

Lilly felt the hairs on her arm stand up on end. 'We've come this far. Surely, we'll leave before it's too late.' Her tone sounded like she was trying to convince herself too.

'Ahh, Lilly, we all want to believe that, but in the meantime, since we aren't going anywhere anyway right now, I wish they would let us go ashore or cross to the other ships. It's really hard to be so close to Karl, and yet impossible to see him.'

A burly, moustached man in a tatty fedora approached the lifeboat, carrying a shallow wooden crate filled with delicacies: sweets, apples, biscuits. They all took note of him, and Lilly's stomach rumbled.

He swept his tobacco-stained fingers over his crate. 'You want to buy something?' he asked in broken German.

Isaak studied him and his offerings. 'Where have you come from?'

'From here. Tulcea.'

'How did you reach our ship?'

'My rowing boat.'

'Do you visit every ship?'

'Yes.' He puffed up his chest, 'And I can get you anything you like.'

Isaak paused to consider. 'How do we pay you for your service?'

'I can take Romanian lei, German Reichsmark, British pound, Swiss francs, American dollar, gold, silver.'

Isaak pointed to the shiny red apples. 'Would you also take payment in cigarettes?'

'Yes.'

Isaak entered a bout of intense bartering. Though slighter in build than the hawker, Isaak was relentless as he held his own, and the hawker couldn't keep a hint of his admiration from the slight curl of his lips. He gave Isaak five apples for two of his cigarettes.

'Excuse me,' Hannah stopped the hawker and pointed to the Pacific. 'Are you going to that ship too?'

'All the ships.'

'Are you able to deliver a letter for me?'

'I can,' he said. 'Forty pfennigs.'

'Oh.' In that moment, she shed the brief glimmer of her hope. 'Never mind. I don't have the money.'

'I do.' Lilly hastily reached for her rucksack.

'No. I wouldn't ask that of you.'

'But I'm offering.' Lilly fished out the money from her purse and extended payment to the hawker, ignoring Hannah's protests.

'Thank you.' Hannah could not disguise her joy. 'Thank you so much.'

As the hawker reached to take the money, Isaak stepped in and blocked his way. 'No, no, no.'

'Why ever not?' Lilly was startled by his intervention.

Isaak addressed the hawker, 'You said so yourself that you're heading to that ship anyway. She'll pay twenty pfennigs.'

'But I have to find passenger,' the man tried. 'Will take time. Thirty.'

'Twenty-five.' Isaak said, with finality. 'And that includes a reply letter from the other ship. Once you finish your rounds of our ship, come back here to fetch the letter and payment. Then tomorrow, you will return with a letter. Yes?'

The man nodded, turning to continue his peddling. 'Agreed.'

Hannah was already rummaging through her bag for a pencil and paper. Using the bench as a makeshift desk, she began to scribble furiously.

Lilly turned to Isaak, her impatience with him for taking over her transaction forgotten. 'You were brilliant!' she said.

Isaak shrugged off the compliment. 'It was nothing.' He pulled out a penknife, sliced three of the apples, gave her a piece, then passed the others around. It had been a long time since any of them had eaten a fresh apple, and their sighs of delight were audible. Lilly shut her eyes, savouring the sweet, tart flavour.

True to his word, the hawker returned twenty minutes later to retrieve Hannah's letter and his payment.

Hannah impulsively threw her arms around Lilly and Isaak. 'Thank you.'

'Any time.' Isaak grinned. Then he swung his legs out of the lifeboat, stood, stretched, and sauntered off down the deck, still holding his slice of apple.

Lilly watched, fascinated, as Isaak paused to talk to two men who were playing cards and smoking. Isaak threw the apple into the air and caught it. Crunching into his apple slice, he greeted the men and appeared to be asking them about their game. One of the men eyed the whole apple. It was short work for Isaak: in a moment, he handed over the apple and received a cigarette in return.

Alexander grinned with pride.

'He's smart,' Lilly said.

'He has had to be,' Alexander agreed. 'When he was sixteen, he fled his home in Vienna and came to ours in Prague with only one Reichsmark in his pocket.'

# CHAPTER 21

Lilly awoke the following morning to an unfamiliar sound: children's laughter.

She peered out of the lifeboat. Eight youngsters and their parents had huddled in a tight circle, transfixed by a magician who squatted in the centre performing tricks for them.

Isaak.

He was using odds and ends to make magic. A black button disappeared from his hands, then reappeared behind a boy's ear. A scrap of paper blossomed into a rose, which he handed to a three-year-old girl sitting on her mother's lap. He turned a frayed length of string into two pieces then made it whole again.

The scene warmed Lilly's heart. Within the tight confines of the ship, it wasn't easy for the harassed parents to keep their children amused. For a short while, he had conjured happiness, entertaining the children and giving their parents a break.

'Isaak!' A man with a greying beard wrapped in a *tallis* and *tefillin* called from the other side of the deck. 'You're the tenth man. We need you.'

'I have to go,' Isaak said. 'But I'll make more magic for you soon.'

To a round of applause from the children and their parents, Isaak hurried to fetch his *tefillin* from his rucksack and joined the *minyan*.

Breakfast brought the same stale bread and Erika's consistent reminder to check their pieces before eating and break off any green patches of mould. But the sun-filled morning brought renewed optimism.

Erika announced she would start work that morning as an assistant nurse in the infirmary. She had spoken to one of the volunteer doctors who said he would be more than happy for the additional help.

Alexander and Isaak had signed up for daily traffic shifts. The new one-way system of pedestrian traffic had proved effective and brought a dose of order to the ship.

By lunchtime, the ship's kitchens began operating. They received their first hot meal, consisting of a watery soup in which floated a few pieces of potato and pearl barley. The 'lifeboat chevra,' Alexander's coined name for their group, wasn't impressed by the food, but it was hot, at least. A start.

Soon after lunch, the hawker returned bearing a letter from Karl. Hannah devoured the words on the page like a starving person at a feast and immediately penned another note back to him.

That afternoon, they took advantage of the mild weather to catch up on their laundry, using river water. Lilly hadn't thought to pack a bowl, so she shared with Hannah, whose sojourn in Bratislava had schooled her in what she might need.

'How many times have you read that letter already?' Lilly asked, as she wrung out her blue dress. Hannah was dipping her green dress into the bowl, her movements slow, a dreamy expression on her face.

Hannah flushed. 'He was so surprised and happy to receive my letter. He says he misses me terribly.'

Janka batted her eyelids. 'She's in love!'

Hannah scooped up a handful of water and playfully tried to splash her but Janka laughed and dodged out of the way. She was still chuckling to herself as she hung her blouse on the temporary washing line they had rigged between the poles that supported the canvas tarpaulin shading the deck.

Lilly joined her to hang up her washing.

'What about you?' Janka said. 'Do you have a special someone?'

Lilly shook her head and focused on straightening her dress on the line.

'Has no one caught your eye yet on the ship?'

'Not looking.' She cleared her throat. 'I ... I already had the love of my life.'

Janka put a hand to her mouth. 'Oh, I'm sorry. I didn't mean to pry or make you uncomfortable.'

'It's all right. It's in the past.' Lilly reassured her with a little smile. 'How about you.'

'Still looking,' Janka said.

'Is there no one from your group that you have taken a liking to?'

'There was someone.' Janka shrugged. 'But he never noticed me.'

'Why not drop him some hints?'

'He's since got together with another girl. They may get engaged soon.'

'I'm sorry.'

'It was a silly crush. Nothing more.' Janka waved it away. Then she scanned the deck and winked mischievously. 'So I've since decided to set my sights higher.'

Intrigued, Lilly followed her gaze, searching for the tall, handsome, charismatic young man she imagined Janka might have taken a liking to, but couldn't find anyone who fitted that description. All she could see was a group of middle-aged men engaged in a heated political discussion. 'Who is it?'

Janka nodded to one of the men in the group. Emil – the one Hannah had nicknamed Pencil Man. He was wearing a white cotton vest, waving his scrawny arms for emphasis as he made his point.

'Him?'

Janka nodded with a deadpan expression.

Lilly stared at Janka. 'Emil?'

'Uh-huh.'

'Are you serious?'

Her lips quirked. 'No!' She could no longer suppress her grin. 'I may be better off staying single for the time being.'

Emil must have sensed their attention because he broke off his conversation and glanced up at them. They quickly looked away and occupied themselves with the laundry. A snort escaped Janka and Lilly's shoulders shook as she tried to suppress her laughter.

'*Ach*, my darlings are doing the laundry,' said a familiar voice.

Lilly turned in surprise. 'Gisela!'

'I thought I would visit you for a change. These new traffic regulations make it far easier to move about. Besides, I need some air.' She wafted her hand in front of her nose. 'Sometimes it gets a bit much down there.'

'Why not join us on deck?'

'I appreciate the invitation,' Gisela said. 'But the lifeboat is a place for young people. I'd struggle to get in and out each time.'

'Then what about on the deck? I'm sure Alexander and Isaak can make some space for you.'

'It's getting too cool at night and I'd rather not get caught in a rainstorm like you did the other evening. Don't worry, I'll be fine.'

'Hello, Gisela,' said Alexander, back from his shift. 'What a pleasure to see you up here.'

'I decided to pay you all a visit.'

'You're always welcome.'

She patted his cheek. 'Thank you *mein Schatz*.'

Alexander paused. 'Can I ask you a slightly embarrassing question?'

Gisela studied his face. 'This sounds intriguing. Yes, of course.'

Then he showed her the bottom of his shirt. 'The button fell off and I don't know how to sew it back on. Can you teach me how to do it?'

'And there I was thinking it was going to be a juicy question.' She gave him a gentle nudge. 'Have you got a sewing kit?'

Janka threw a kit over to Alexander in reply. He handed Gisela a needle and thread. She took off her glasses, licked the thread, and squinted at the eye of the needle. After three attempts, she threaded it.

'Soon, you'll find yourself a wife and then she'll be able to do this for you.'

Alexander gave a half smile, his eyes twinkling with amusement. 'I'd rather learn to do it by myself so that I can choose someone for more than her button-sewing skills.'

'Good answer!' She nodded in approval and handed him the needle. 'Now follow my instructions.'


Later that evening, Alexander accompanied Lilly when she walked Gisela back to the dining room. 'I see why you are fond of Gisela,' he said, after they had left the older woman. 'She reminds me a lot of my grandmother.'

'Gisela was so kind to me when we first boarded the Schönbrunn. She has become almost like family,' Lilly said. 'But I'm worried about her. You saw the conditions in the dining room?'

Alexander shuddered. 'They are awful.'

'I wish we could find a better solution for everyone. But since that's not possible ... if only we could at least find an alternative place for Gisela. I invited her to join us on the upper deck, but that isn't suitable either.'

Alexander stopped and turned around. 'There may be somewhere.' His brow furrowed as he surveyed the line of cabins. 'These were supposed to be for women with children and other vulnerable passengers. But when we boarded, the organisation broke down. The situation descended into chaos. Many of the people who most needed the cabins didn't get one. The Haganah have reallocated some, but there is at least one they haven't.' He nodded, his face taking on a determined expression. 'It might be possible to arrange for the current occupants to be turfed out.'

'The cabin Isaak was in?'

His eyes widened. 'You know? Did he tell you?'

'No, I guessed,' she said. 'Yesterday, after bringing a bucket for Gisela, Hannah and I saw you enter a cabin and retrieve a rucksack. Hannah recognised the blonde woman. It was the same rude passenger who had slammed the door in her face when they were first looking for a place to sleep. Then, when Isaak returned to the deck, he was carrying the same rucksack. I figured the rest from his expression.'

'Please don't think badly of him. Nothing happened!' Alexander was emphatic. Then he became uneasy. 'From the little Isaak would tell me ... I gather she ... well, she tried. But Isaak fled in fright. He got out of there as fast as he could.'

'*Schrecklich*! Is he all right?'

'It left him shaken at first, but I think he'll get over it and put it behind him.'

'She's bad news. You can see it.'

'Isaak didn't. He's young. Inexperienced in such matters. He was exhausted and just glad for her invitation for a place to sleep.' Alexander beckoned Lilly away from the cabins and spoke in an undertone. 'There are weird goings-on in there. Her husband was fast asleep in one of the bunks when she tried it with Isaak.'

'No!' She examined his face and found it deadly serious. 'What if he would have woken up and seen his wife?'

'Not sure if he would have been that bothered. I think they're all in on it. Playing musical beds.'

'*Mein Gott*!' She placed a hand over her mouth. 'It's like Sodom and Gomorrah. Where do these people come from?'

'God knows. Or perhaps, Storfer knows.' They walked in silence to the stairs. Alexander paused again. 'I'll have a quiet word with Dov at the first opportunity to find out if he can free up that cabin.'

'If it is possible, there is another woman who could do with a place in a cabin. She and her husband travelled on the Schönbrunn with us. She's heavily pregnant. They are sleeping in a crushed corner of the dining room and she doesn't look at all comfortable.'

'I'll keep you informed. If the cabin becomes available, you are welcome to speak to her. But please don't let our conversation go further. Isaak would be mortified.'

'Not a word. I promise.'


'Oh, my!' Hannah nudged Lilly in the ribs as they headed back to the stairs with their empty buckets. 'Take a look at that.'

Two days had passed since Lilly's conversation with Alexander. He had not mentioned anything further to her, but he seemed to have kept his word and spoken to Dov.

Two Haganah men stood guard outside the blonde woman's cabin. The door was wide open and someone was flinging blankets and bags into the corridor. A pink silk nightgown sailed through the air like a parachute, chased after by a hapless, red-faced man with a greasy comb-over flopping into his eyes.

A man in a tailored suit, his black hair slicked with pomade, crept out of the door holding hands with a woman in an elegant green tea dress, and they slunk away.

'You promised me a luxurious cabin,' a woman shouted from inside. 'You call this luxury? And now where are we supposed to sleep?'

The man didn't respond. He was busy picking up broken glass from a smashed bottle of powerful cologne.

The blonde woman stomped out of the cabin together with a brunette whose painted scarlet lips matched her own. A bald-headed man followed, weighed down with pieces of luggage.

'I want my old life back. My beautiful home. The parties, evenings at the opera, summers by the lake,' she wailed. 'I don't even want to go to British-controlled Mandatory Palestine.'

'There, there, my *schatzi.*' The red-faced man stroked her shoulder. 'The war will be over in a few months' time and then we can go home.'

'Don't you *schatzi* me.' She flicked his hand away and linked arms with the brunette woman.

Then the blonde noticed Lilly and Hannah. Lilly lowered her gaze, pretending she hadn't been watching, but it was too late.

She marched up to Hannah. 'I suppose this is all thanks to you and your sister here.' She jabbed Lilly's clavicle with a sharp lacquered finger. 'And that tall boy you both fawn over who thinks he's some bigshot in the Haganah.'

Hannah eyebrows shot up. 'What are you talking about?'

'I know you're responsible for my eviction. You've coveted this cabin since the first day we arrived.'

'What are you talking about?' Hannah repeated. 'I had nothing to do with it.'

'Don't pretend to be so innocent. Jealous aren't you? You and your ugly sister can't get a man between you.' She nodded toward the facilities. 'You spend your time hanging around with ancient grandmothers.'

Hannah gasped. 'You are so rude. I'm not sure who evicted you, but I'm glad they did.'

The woman raised her hand and slapped Hannah's cheek. Hannah staggered backwards.

'Don't touch her!' Lilly placed herself between her and Hannah. Her vision clouded and suddenly, she was no longer on the ship, but back in her parents' apartment. 'Leave her alone!'

'Your sister is crazy. Now I understand why you need the cabin. You want to have her locked up.'

'She is not crazy.' Hannah said in a low voice, straining to control her anger. 'And the only ugly person here is you. Both inside and out.'

A Haganah man grasped the woman by her elbow. 'If you don't want further trouble, you need to leave at once.'

She shook him off. 'I'm going.'

She gave Hannah a final, menacing stare. 'I won't forget,' she said, and turned on her heels.

Hannah rubbed at the red finger imprints on her cheek.

'I ... so ... sorry.' Lilly's voice shook. 'This is all my fault.'

'None of this is your fault. Do you hear me?'

'But—' Lilly stopped herself. She couldn't say a word. She had promised Alexander.

'Don't blame yourself. She's just a nasty piece of work.' Hannah shook her head at the woman's vulgarity. 'I hope she enjoys sleeping in the catacombs tonight.'

# CHAPTER 22

Lilly's hand hovered at the cabin door, about to knock, when Max called her name.

'Thank you for thinking of Alma,' he said. 'It was so kind of you. And thank you for your help in getting her a bunk in the cabin. She found it difficult in the dining room. Especially now.'

It was the most she had ever heard Max speak. 'I'm glad I could help. I hope she'll be more comfortable. But I am sorry you're now forced to camp out in the passageway.'

'I'm content that conditions will be easier for Alma and she will get a better night's sleep.' He ran a hand over the stubble sprouting from his shaven scalp. 'I'll be fine. I've slept in far worse places.'

Lilly understood he meant Dachau. Like her father.

She swallowed the lump in her throat. Best not to dwell. It hurt too much. Lilly could not know how her parents were faring in the three weeks since she had left, and she was worried. Although she had given the hawker a letter to post to them, she had no return address for them to get word back to her.

Peels of laughter suddenly resounded from within the cabin.

'What's going on?' Lilly said.

Max shrugged. Then, at the sound of hysterical screeching, his lips turned up at the corners. It was the first time she'd ever seen him smile.

Lilly knocked. The noise from the cabin halted as Gisela peered out and pulled Lilly inside. As soon as she closed the door, the laughter rose once more.

'What's so funny?' Lilly set down her bucket and searched the faces of the new cabin occupants: Gisela and Alma; two older women Gisela had befriended in the dining room, a young woman with a three-year-old girl, and another with a baby not much older than six months.

Gisela was laughing so hard she couldn't get a word out. She pointed to a black piece of fabric on the floor next to her bunk.

'Good heavens! What is that?' Lilly stepped forward to examine it more closely: it was the frilliest, sheerest pair of women's unmentionables she had ever laid eyes on. They left little to the imagination. 'Are they yours?'

Gisela patted her ample thighs and cackled. 'Couldn't ... even get ... one leg through!' She waved a pair of her white, knee-length bloomers like a flag of surrender and collapsed on the lower bunk, heaving with laughter.

Their mood was infectious. Lilly began to giggle too.

Alma stroked her rounded stomach and wagged her finger in mock disapproval, wiping away tears of laughter.

'Perhaps ... they belonged to ... one of the crew,' said of the young mothers, clutching her sides.

It took Gisela several more minutes to regain her composure. She sighed and chuckled once more before catching her breath. 'We found them underneath the bunk while we were stowing our bags. Who would think of wearing something as ridiculous as that on a journey like this?'

'Someone ridiculous.' Lilly smiled. 'How is the cabin?'

'*Ach*, it's wonderful! Such luxury. I can't remember the last time I slept so well. My roommates are lovely. We have a room with a view.'

She waved at the tiny porthole between the bunks, then looked at the bucket. 'And there's even room service. What more could I ask?' Gisela lifted herself up from the mattress. 'Let's go. I shouldn't delay you.'

'As if I have anywhere else to be,' Lilly said as they left the cabin and began to slowly negotiate the passageway. 'Today, as every day, I will mainly spend my time standing in queues, for lunch, supper, the Panama, and the left luggage to fetch another dress from my suitcase.'

'I'm going to an *Ivrit* lesson later.' Gisela smiled proudly. 'They are beginning new classes. By the time we arrive, I want to have the skills to communicate with my grandchildren in Hebrew.'

'That sounds like a great idea. What time do the classes start?'

'Eleven. Come and join me.'

'I might—' They stopped at the end of the unusually long queue that had formed for the toilets. Many of those who waited in line clutched their stomachs and groaned in agony. 'What is happening?'

'Hurry!' called a man called close to the front. 'I can't wait much longer.'

Gisela shook her head. 'They must have eaten something bad.'

Isaak sauntered up to them, holding a cup of water. 'Good morning!' he said, raising it to show Gisela. 'See. I'm remembering to drink.'

'Good lad,' Gisela said. 'How was your shift?'

'There were no arguments, so it was a good night. I'm having another drink, then I'll catch up on sleep.'

'Any idea why all these people are groaning?'

'No idea. Maybe they didn't follow Erika's advice to pick off the green mould from the bread.'

Lilly smiled. Erika repeated these instructions every time bread was served.

Isaak brought the cup to his lips, then paused. 'What a coincidence. Here she is now.'

Erika was pushing her way toward them through the crowded passageway, frantically waving her arms.

'No!' she shouted.

'I wonder what she's so panicked about?' he said.

Erika lunged at Isaak and knocked the cup from his hand.

'Hey!' He flapped his soaked shirt. 'What was that for?'

'Don't ... drink ... the water.' Erika said, catching her breath. 'The fresh water supply ran out yesterday evening and they replaced it with river water. It's contaminated. You must boil it before drinking.' She turned to Gisela. 'Have you drunk any water since last night?'

'Only tea.'

'Lilly?'

'Also just hot tea.'

'Sorry about your shirt,' she said to Isaak.

'It's fine.' Isaak winced. 'But I'm already on my second cup this morning.'

'Oh no!' Erika looked horrified. 'It seems it has caused an outbreak of stomach upsets. The doctors suspect dysentery. If you get any symptoms, come straight to me. I can arrange a pass so you can go to the front of the line. Wash your hands often and well, especially after using the toilet and before you eat.'

'Have you told Alma?' Lilly said. 'She's pregnant.'

'Not yet. I have to sort out this queue. Please warn her. Quickly!'

After Alma had assured Lilly that, on Max's advice, she had only ever drunk boiled water since the start of their journey, Lilly left her to warn the others. She headed up the stairs, and attempted to force her way through the human tide. The Haganah guard on traffic duty blew his whistle. 'Right towards the bow, left towards the stern,' he ordered.

She switched course, took the long route, trying to attract Hannah's attention all the while. Finally, Hannah noticed her and, with a big smile, waved a piece of paper. Another letter from Karl, Lilly assumed.

The megaphone crackled. 'Your attention, please. Do not drink the water without boiling it first. We have been advised of possible contamination. I repeat, you must boil the water before drinking.'

As if in response, three passengers barged past Lilly, making a dash for Panama.

'I was just coming to tell you about the water,' Lilly said when she reached the lifeboat.

'Don't worry, we heard,' Hannah said. 'Erika was running around in a frenzy warning everyone.' She handed an envelope to Lilly. 'Post.'

'What did Karl say?'

'This one's for you. From your mama. They delivered a sack of post while you were on the lower deck.'

Lilly glanced at the address on the envelope. It had been sent 'in care of' Berthold Storfer's office, Vienna. Much to her surprise, he had managed to forward their letters to the ship in Tulcea. Lilly opened the envelope with trembling fingers. She noted the date at the top, 6 September, two days after she had sailed from Vienna. The day they passed Kladovo.

*Dearest, darling Lilly,*

*By the time you receive this letter, I imagine you will have already arrived in Eretz Israel. I hope your journey was a safe and pleasant one. Please write to us when you can to tell us how you are doing and how you are settling in.*

*How are Eugen and Allegra? How was it to reunite after so long? Send them our love and kisses.*

*I miss you. The place seems empty without you, but Tante Rebecca keeps me from getting lonely. Papa misses you too. I can see it. I placed a picture of you on his bedside table. His eyes turn to it often, and then he looks back at me. I know he wants to send you his love. Try not to be sad. Look towards the future. Build a new life for yourself. May we reunite one day soon.*

*All my love.*

*Mama*


The letter was over two weeks old. By now, they should have landed in the Holy Land, or at the very least, be nearing its shores. And yet, they remained in Tulcea, lingering in the harbour with no fixed date for departure.

'What's news from your mama?' Hannah hesitated. 'How is your papa?'

Lilly shrugged. 'She doesn't say much. Mama misses me. Papa seems the same.' But that was two weeks ago, she thought. Had there been any changes since?

'Mama assumed we were already in Eretz.'

'My mama too. She said she wishes she could be there for our wedding, but that we should go ahead and not delay until her arrival.' Hannah released a long exhale. Lilly squeezed her hand in place of words. 'They also gave us franked cards so we can send a reply,' Hannah said.

When the hawker arrived with another letter for Hannah, Lilly was still composing her letter – in her tiniest handwriting so she could fit more on the postcard. Hannah lived for Karl's letters and eagerly tore through the envelope. A second page, folded tightly into quarters, fell onto her lap. Hannah turned it over to read the message in precise script: 'Please pass to Erika.'

'It must be from Marcus,' Hannah said. She glanced at the line of groaning, writhing passengers extending down the stairs. 'I won't be able to squeeze through that. I'll have to give it to her when she returns for lunch.'

There was no sign of Erika when the lifeboat chevra met for their midday meal.

Meanwhile, Isaak was struggling to eat the thin broth with slivers of potatoes and carrots. The colour had drained from his face. He set down his bowl, doubled over and clutched his stomach.

'Go straight to the infirmary,' Lilly said. 'Erika will give you a pass to go to the front of the queue.'

Heaving and panting, he clambered out of the lifeboat.

'Do you want me to come with you?' Alexander said.

'I'll manage,' Isaak said through gritted teeth.

A four-year-old boy with a head of black curls dashed up to him and tugged at his trouser leg. 'Isaak, make magic for us.'

Isaak's attempted reply came out as a groan.

Alexander leapt out of the boat after him and grabbed Isaak, who was about to retch. Lilly was about to follow when Stefan got there first. 'I've got him,' he said, and the two men helped Isaak to the infirmary.

The little boy remained beside the lifeboat, pouting. 'Why won't he make magic?'

'He isn't feeling too well.' Lilly ruffled his hair. 'He'll make more magic for you when he's better, all right *Schätzchen*?'

The boy nodded and scampered back to his mother.

By early evening, neither Isaak nor Erika had returned. Bands of violet and amber painted the sky above the harbour. If not for the coils of barbed wire, guns, and bunkers dotting the hillside, it might have been a beautiful scene. But Tulcea had already lost its appeal. Lilly longed for a different view, though there had been no sight or any word about the promised fourth ship.

Before it got too late, Lilly decided to pay a visit to Panama. She hated fumbling her way across the deck and up the steps in the dark. When she reached the back of the queue she found Isaak still standing there.

'Have you been waiting all this time?'

'No, I've had a season ticket to Panama.' Isaak winked. 'If Erika's pass was a passport, I'd have a stamp on every page.'

Lilly snickered. 'How are you feeling?'

'Like a washed-out rag, but at least no longer in pain. Erika has me drinking plenty of boiled water so I don't dehydrate.'

'I'm relieved to hear. You looked as if you were in agony earlier.'

'It wasn't pleasant.'

A flash of white stretched across the bench behind Isaak caught Lilly's attention.

She tried to peer over Isaak's shoulder, but he moved from side to side as if he meant to block her view. 'How are things in the lifeboat?'

'The usual. Queuing, washing, repairing,' Lilly said. 'But there's an exciting surprise waiting for Erika. Marcus sent her a letter. Though, not one of us has seen her since this morning to tell her.'

Lilly stepped to the side. Isaak did likewise. 'She's had a busy day.'

Lilly attempted to angle herself to view past him. Isaak drew her attention to the view of Tulcea. 'Isn't the sunset beautiful tonight?'

'Yes,' she said. 'But Isaak, what's on the bench behind you?'

He closed his eyes for a brief moment, then looked at her with sadness.

'What are you hiding?'

'Try not to be alarmed.' He spoke in a gentle voice. 'It's a body. Wrapped in a shroud. Unfortunately ... a passenger has died.'

A heaviness settled in her core. 'Who was it?'

'An older woman. In her eighties.'

'Was it because of the contaminated water?'

'I don't know.' He shook his head. 'Maybe she was already ill or conditions were too much for her. We're young and finding the situation a challenge. How much harder for the older people?'

'Why were you trying to hide it? I would have found out soon enough.'

'I wanted to break it to you gently. I didn't want you to get a shock.'

'Did she stay in the dining room?'

'I'm not sure.'

'She may have been part of the audience when I played the piano.'

'It's possible.'

'Oh.' Lilly took in the outline of the shrouded body. 'She never even got to see Eretz. She might have had children or grandchildren waiting for her. Now they will never meet again.'

'I know.' He lightly touched her arm. 'It's very sad.'


That night, Lilly, Hannah, and Janka waited up for Erika. Most nights they went to sleep soon after dark. As long as the ship remained stationary and without electric lighting, they tried to preserve their limited fuel for the kerosene lamps.

It was after eleven when Erika shuffled down the steps, shoulders hunched. They waited for her at the bottom, Hannah holding a lantern to help guide her path.

'It's been a hard day,' Erika said when she reached them.

'We heard,' Hannah said.

'I saved you some supper. Tomatoes, slices of pepper and a piece of cheese,' Janka said.

'I appreciate it. I didn't have time to eat anything.'

'And some post came for you,' Hannah said.

'Post?'

'We had a delivery today, and you got a letter from Vienna. And Marcus tucked in a note for you together with mine from Karl.'

The news seemed to comfort her somewhat. She settled onto a bench, and read them by the lamplight. Then she hugged them to her chest. 'My mama thought I'd already be in Eretz. She asked me what it's like.' Erika stared into the distance. She still clings to the hope that Papa will return soon, and they can join me.'

'And Marcus?'

'He says that he misses me even more than he expected. Being apart has given him a lot of time to think, and he can't imagine his life without me. When we next meet he would like to talk about a future together. But only if I feel the same and when I am ready. He will be patient.'

'What do you think your answer will be?' Hannah asked.

'Yes.' Erika paused, choking up. 'If we ever leave and if we ever meet again.'

'Of course we'll leave, and you'll see him soon.' Hannah hugged her. 'Do you want to send Marcus a reply? I can slip it in with my letter to Karl.'

'Thank you. I would like that. Very much.'


Lilly had spent a disturbed night listening to the passenger's groans, the scraping of their feet as they shuffled back and forth from Panama. And Isaak had been right – she was haunted by the sight of the body on the bench. There was also something else to worry about: a sickness had struck Jenny. At intervals, Stefan escorted her to vomit over the side of the ship.

When morning finally came, Lilly tried to sleep in. She cocooned herself in her blanket to block out the daylight, until Isaak's animated whoops made her raise her head. He was shouting something incoherent and gesturing at the river. Several passengers surged to the starboard railings. The ship rocked and tilted with their shifting weight.

Alexander leapt into the lifeboat and stood on the bench for a better view. 'I don't believe it! *Unglaublich*!'

'What on earth?' Janka said, jumping up beside him. 'How did they manage to travel this far?'

Lilly scrambled to her feet and stared, unable to believe her eyes. Heading towards them was a rusting, rickety paddle boat, listing starboard but making steady progress.

The Pentcho.

The Atlantic passengers pulled out handkerchiefs, and waved and cheered.The Pentcho sailed past without stopping and continued down a river branch, heading for the open sea.

'It's a miracle,' Isaak said. 'They made it!'

'Not yet,' Alexander said. 'They still have a long journey ahead. This is only the beginning.'

'May God be with them and protect them.'

'Amen,' they replied.

Lilly fixed her gaze on the puff of smoke the Pentcho had left in its wake.

Perhaps there was still hope for the Atlantic?

# CHAPTER 23

Three days after they had waved goodbye to the Pentcho, Berthold Storfer stood on the Atlantic's bridge in the fading daylight, wearing his signature grey suit and looking slightly worse for wear. He cleared his throat. 'The Rosita will arrive tomorrow morning.'

Did anyone still believe him? He waved his arms to calm the agitated passengers.

Standing on the deck, Lilly overheard Alexander behind her, muttering to Isaak, 'I'm not holding my breath.'

'Does that mean we are leaving tomorrow?' a voice shouted from the crowd.

'The ship isn't quite ready yet,' Berthold Storfer said.

'You wait,' Isaak said. 'I bet he'll blame it on a lack of nails.'

'Several days ago, you told us the ship was already on its way and that we would leave as soon as it arrived,' said Emil, the pencil man. 'What is causing the delay?'

'The ship needs further modification. The slight delay is due to ... to ...' Berthold Storfer's eyes shifted from side to side. 'A lack of nails.'

'There you go!' Isaak said. 'What did I tell you?' Lilly stifled a laugh. Passengers all around the ship erupted in fury. No amount of arm flapping by Storfer would calm them. He appealed to the ring of Haganah members surrounding him. Their piercing whistles restored order.

The following evening when the lifeboat chevra sat down together for a supper of reduced rations, the conversation centred on the latest development: the formation of a new Transport Committee made up of leaders of the different factions from Vienna, Prague, and Danzig, with twenty-seven-year-old Dr Horetzky from the Prague group at the helm. Their job would be to represent the passengers and present a list of requests to Herr Storfer. They hoped a united committee might have greater success in extracting answers and finding solutions to their problems. But the lifeboat chevra doubted their chances of success. Patience was wearing thin, food was running short, and medical supplies were dwindling.

Erika confided that the doctors of the infirmary had resorted to making improvised mixtures of whatever they had available, with varying degrees of success. And the mild epidemic that the passengers had named 'Atlantitis' continued to spread.

Despite every precaution, Lilly had succumbed the day before, and needed to avail herself of a medical pass from Erika to jump the queue to Panama. Jenny too continued to struggle with her bout of sickness.

And still no sign of the promised fourth ship.

'Just as well you didn't hold your breath,' Isaak said. 'You'd be in the infirmary by now.'

Alexander rolled his eyes. 'More likely on the bench of the dead.'

'Lack of nails,' Isaak said, in his best impression of Berthold Storfer. 'It's the perfect excuse for everything. What a shame I never thought of it before. When I was in school and the teacher asked, where's your homework? I could have said, Sorry, I was unable to complete the assignment because of a lack of nails.'

His quip raised a round of laughter.

'When patients come to the infirmary and ask why we have no more medicine?'

'Lack of nails,' they chorused.

Alexander waved the limp slices of pepper and cup of sweet tea that passed for their evening meal. 'Why is this all we're getting to eat?'

'Lack of nails!'

'What's causing the ship crew's delay?' Stefan said.

Even as Lilly joined the standard refrain, she marvelled at their ability to joke about their situation. Perhaps it was a means to cope with circumstances that were unimaginable.

Like the bench of the dead. At first, Lilly had felt uncomfortable whenever she needed to pass the shrouded corpse as she walked to and from Panama. Especially at night when it was illuminated by a flickering lantern. In time, though, like everything else, she acclimatised to its presence.

But two days after Storfer's visit, she was shocked anew, when she noticed a second body there.

As she stared, she felt an arm link through hers. Erika stood next to her. 'I've finished my shift. Let's walk back together.'

Erika seemed unsteady on her feet and she held onto Lilly for support.

'Who was it?' Lilly asked.

'Not someone we knew.'

'What happened?'

'An overdose of medicine.' Erika's face held a pained expression. 'It was deliberate. By the time someone discovered him, it was too late.'

'How terrible.'

'I feel awful.'

'But it's not your fault.'

'I still can't help thinking, if only we had found him sooner. If only someone had noticed and stopped him. If only he hadn't decided he had no other resort. So many "if only"s.'

'I understand that,' Lilly said, 'Only too well.'

Bathed in the burnt orange light of the setting sun, the Atlantic was its usual hive of activity. Some people had lined up for their evening meal, others were hanging laundry, playing cards, reading, or praying. The regular debaters were gathered together to discuss politics, the war, and most of all, their current predicament. But when Lilly and Erika reached the lifeboat, their chevra seemed more subdued than usual. No one mentioned the incident, but it was obvious they had heard. Alexander's gaze rested on Erika, conveying his sympathy.

Janka handed Erika her bowl. 'I fetched your rations.'

'Thank you. That's very kind of you,' said Erika.

'I'd better fetch mine,' Lilly said.

'No need. I already got yours,' Hannah said.

They tried to pretend everything was normal by performing their regular ritual of comparing meals from the Prague, Danzig and kosher kitchens. But the customary jokes were missing tonight, and their stilted conversation dissolved into silence.

A series of shouts and a stampede of footsteps reverberating up the wooden steps broke the silence.

'What is it now?' Erika snapped with uncharacteristic ire.

They had almost grown accustomed to the sound of bickering. Arguments broke out almost every night. Who would have thought that throwing together 1,800 people in crowded, unsanitary conditions, with a shortage of food, poor sleep and nerves frayed from endless waiting, uncertainty and a rash of broken promises, could be such an explosive combination?

This time, though, was different. At least twenty-five men piled onto the upper deck in a panic with their clothes dripping. Something was very wrong. Moving as a unit, they hurried to the bridge. Immediately, two Haganah men were dispatched down to the hold, only to emerge less than five minutes later, their clothes as soaked as the group of men who had come to alert them.

'Alexander! Isaak!' Dov called across the deck as he hurried to the lifeboat. 'We need your help. A water pipe has burst. It's gushing into the hold and has flooded the sleeping quarters.'

Isaak got to his feet. 'Never a dull moment, is there?'

Alexander tossed aside his half-eaten supper with a groan. Usually the most enthusiastic volunteer, even he had reached the end of his tether. 'Anything that can go wrong on this damned ship will go wrong.'

'Have you managed to turn off the water?' Stefan said.

'Yes,' Dov said. 'Now we need to bail out the hold.'

'I'd be happy to help. Do you need any more volunteers?' Stefan asked.

'We'd be grateful for any extra help we can get,' Dov said, already descending the ladder into the catacombs.

Erika watched the other men follow him and her shoulders drooped. 'I'm beginning to doubt that we'll ever reach Haifa.'

'To be honest, I'm also losing hope,' Hannah said. 'Sometimes I feel as if I'm slowly going crazy with all this uncertainty.'

'Same,' Janka said. 'All we get from Storfer are vague promises which turn out to be lies.'

Their words churned up Lilly's darkest fears. She felt as if she were once again teetering on the edge of a steep staircase. She didn't know whether she would survive another fall.

'What if they transfer us somewhere like the Slobodarna or the Patronka?' Erika said. 'I don't think I could go through that again.'

The colour drained from Hannah's face. 'What if they return us to Vienna?'

'We can't go back.' Jenny's hands shook on her lap. 'That man today who ... I knew him. He was part of our group from Danzig. What if he did what he did because he knew we'd never leave?'

The words struck Lilly like a blow. Her stomach lurched.

'What if they don't send us anywhere, but leave us here to die of starvation?' Janka said. 'Maybe that man was right to choose the quick way out.'

'No! I will not fall again!' Lilly grappled for a handhold. She found the boat's side, grabbed onto it, and hauled herself up. 'We will go to Eretz Israel!'

Stunned into silence by Lilly's uncharacteristic outburst, four faces turned to stare up at her. Lilly was surprised to realise that she was standing on the bench.

Hannah reached for her arm, encouraging her to sit. 'We have to face reality. It may not happen.'

Lilly stepped down from the bench but remained standing. 'We will go to Eretz Israel.' She repeated her words like a mantra. 'We will go to Eretz Israel.' All four women looked at her with concern. There was pity in their eyes.

Hannah shook her head sadly. 'It may be that your reservations were correct from the start, and we have been deceived after all. I'm sorry I persuaded you to come.'

'I'm not sorry.' Lilly's voice was firm and unwavering. 'You were right. We will get there.'

Hannah shrugged, unconvinced. 'What makes you so sure?'

Lilly looked at her cousin. 'When we said goodbye in Vienna, you assumed you would board the boat straight away, but something went wrong and you got delayed in Bratislava for nine months. Nevertheless, Berthold Storfer and the Central Office for Jewish Emigration still planned for the next group to leave. My group. If they intended for you to return, why send us after you? Why go to the trouble of arranging boats to transport us down the Danube all the way to Tulcea?'

Hannah looked troubled, but she inclined her head, accepting Lilly's point.

Lilly pressed on. 'When I sat in the school basement before my departure, I was filled with all kinds of doubts. What if the entire scheme was a deception and the moment we landed in Bratislava they ordered us off the boat and imprisoned us alongside you? Instead, you were already waiting on the Helios and we followed behind. We almost got trapped at Ruse. Then we were stopped by that Nazi officer. On either of those occasions, they could have arrested us. They didn't. We made it to Tulcea and, as decrepit as our ships may be, they were here, as promised.'

Erika gave a little nod.

'Then why all the deception and the manufactured delays?' Janka asked. 'Our hopes are raised only to have them dashed each and every time. What if the Nazis and Storfer are playing mind games before they arrest us?'

'I don't have the answers, but I don't think so,' Lilly said. 'Look at the Pentcho, trapped on the river for three months, its passengers surviving on potato peels. But they made it out to sea and now they are sailing towards Eretz. If Berthold Storfer's intentions were malicious, why does he keep coming onto the Atlantic to speak to us? He must be under tremendous strain. Each time he visits, he looks as if he's aged another ten years. The Nazis may pull his strings, but if they wanted to arrest us, they would have done so already. They wouldn't bother to wait.'

Janka narrowed her eyes. 'How do you know that?'

'Because I watched them arrest my father in a round up.' Lilly swallowed hard. 'They sent him to Dachau concentration camp. He came back a broken man. And now he's ... dying. I'll probably never see him again ...'

Lilly took a deep breath and steadied herself before continuing. 'In a single day I lost everything. The November Pogrom destroyed my life. Salo and I had been married for less than a year.' Her lips quivered, but Lilly pressed on. She finally needed to say it out loud. She needed them to hear. 'We were looking forward to becoming a family. I was four months pregnant.' Her eyes prickled. 'The Nazis burst into my parents' apartment. They pushed me down the stairs. Arrested my father. They beat my husband until he was barely recognisable.' Her breath hitched. 'Salo died in my arms.' Lilly's voice was halting as she choked on her words. 'And then I miscarried our baby ...'

Hannah rose from her place and put her arms around Lilly. Lilly ran the back of her hand over her eyes but couldn't stem the flow of tears. 'I didn't know ... how I'd carry on ... living,' she said between sobs. Then she steadied herself and turned to Hannah. 'You were the one who helped me through. You gave me hope. Something to live for. The chance of a new future. This newfound hope is all that I have.'

Lilly faced her friends. Their faces were etched with visible emotion. 'We've all left lives behind. Families. Friends. But we have this one chance. Each of you has a dream for when you reach Eretz Israel. You know you do. Please don't give up. Not until we're down to the last scrap of potato peel like the Pentcho. And even then we must carry on. They have stolen too much from us already.'

Hannah nodded, tears rolling down her cheeks. 'We still have so much to live for. We can't let them win.'

Erika stood up and moved to Lilly's other side. 'You're right. We must not give up hope.'

'We won't give up.' Janka stood. 'We must stay strong'.

Jenny followed. 'We'll support and strengthen each other.'

They formed a circle, wrapped their arms around each other, and together, they cried.

The following morning, as Lilly floated in that hazy space between slumber and consciousness, she thought she was still dreaming when she heard Hannah say, 'You were right, Lilly! You were right.' But the hand that shook her shoulder was real.

'Wake up!'

Lilly peeled open her eyes to be met with a beaming smile. The light in Hannah's blue eyes sparkled like sunlight dancing on the rippling surface of the river.

'Come and look at this—' A wave of cheers drowned out her words.

Lilly tossed aside her damp blanket, the scent of rain from the overnight drizzle still hanging in the air. Hannah extended a hand to her and Lilly clambered up to a bench alongside the rest of the lifeboat chevra. There she discovered the cause of the excitement: a ship had entered the port.

It was smaller than the Atlantic, but at first glance, seemed in better condition.

Alexander flashed Lilly a broad smile.

'The fourth ship?' she said.

He nodded. 'It has to be the Rosita.'

The ship dropped anchor, surrounded by a flotilla of dinghies. All were too far away to see what they contained – except for one which accommodated eight men. The passengers' exuberant cheers continued to rise. 'They must be our crew,' Alexander said, as the men began rowing towards them.

The dinghies drew closer.

Lilly adjusted her gaze as the men came into focus. The roar of the crowd died in a collective gasp. Whispers punctuated the awkward silence.

'*They* are going to sail this ship?' Isaak said.

'I don't think they're sailors,' Hannah said. 'They look more like pirates.'

The slovenly and dishevelled men were the shiftiest-looking bunch Lilly had ever seen. 'What if they intend to attack or rob us?'

'Maybe we should alert the Haganah to set up a line of defence?' Erika said.

'I think they have already been alerted,' Alexander replied.

A Haganah representative greeted the first man to board the Atlantic. He wore a tatty peaked cap low over his sunken, blood-shot eyes and had the girth of a wine barrel. The lurch in his step and the red veins on his nose suggested it was possible he had recently ingested the contents of one.

Alexander raised an eyebrow. 'No. I think they really are our crew.'

'They resemble a band of criminals,' Isaak said. 'Storfer must have plucked them from prisons around the Mediterranean.'

'Are you surprised? Who else would risk sailing a group of illegal immigrants to Mandatory Palestine and attempt to break through the British blockade?'

Dr Horetzky, head of the Transport Committee, stepped forward and introduced himself. For a moment, the man in the peaked cap stared at the outstretched arm. 'Oh ... right,' he slurred, shaking hands. 'I'm ... Spiro. Captain Spiro.'

'God help us,' Alexander said under his breath.

The rest of the crew followed, swaggering around the deck, inspecting their new ship and its passengers.

Lilly averted her eyes and fixated on a scuff on her shoe to avoid the overt leers of a colossal man with bushy eyebrows that met in the centre, sporting a rumpled shirt that strained at the seams. She wasn't the only one. Every woman appeared to be trying to avoid attracting his attention.

'What a bunch of ruffians,' Jenny said. 'We'd best stay out of their way as much as possible.'

'They are creepy. Can we trust them to sail the ship?' Janka said. 'And what does that one want with Isaak?'

A crew member with unkempt, greasy hair and a bristly chin had drawn Isaak aside and slipped open a suitcase. Isaak peered in, questioned him and with a shake of his head, returned to the boat. The man shrugged and approached someone else.

'What was that all about?' Janka said.

'He was trying to sell me some chocolate and tinned food,' Isaak said. 'He's even more of a crook than our regular hawker. Speaking of which ...'

Hannah looked relieved at the arrival of her postman. Spiro, the Captain, didn't seem as pleased. He sized up the hawker circulating the deck, selling and distributing items. He was heading for the lifeboat when Spiro blocked his path. 'What do you want on this ship?'

'I come to sell.'

'No one sells on my ship.' Spiro prodded his shoulder. 'Now clear off and don't let me see you again.'

The hawker retreated without protest, exiting the Atlantic as fast as he could.

'My letter,' Hannah whimpered.

# CHAPTER 24

A blanket of calm enveloped the passengers of the Atlantic, as they stood in the fading golden light of an unexplored port whose view they had long tired. For tonight, at least, they set aside their troubles and arguments. It was Rosh Hashana, the solemn Jewish new year, and everyone was reflecting on the past year and pondering what the coming year might bring. Heads bowed, united in prayer, the passengers faced in the direction of Jerusalem, singing the traditional synagogue melodies.

Lilly stood on the deck lined up with Gisela, Hannah, Erika, Janka and Jenny, taking part in one of the many prayer services organised throughout the ship's cramped confines. They concluded their prayers with a heartfelt utterance of the traditional invocation: '*L'shana haba'a b'Yerushalayim!*' Next year in Jerusalem.

Those words had never felt as relevant. Especially since Captain Spiro's arrival the day before, and the course of events that followed, when their optimism had risen and fallen like the tide.

On seeing the state of the Atlantic and the severe overcrowding, Spiro had declared it unseaworthy. He refused to set sail unless they transferred five hundred passengers to the Rosita.

The head of the Transport Committee, Dr Horetzky, speaking on the passengers' behalf, agreed to comply. Additional space would benefit them all.

They summoned Berthold Storfer.

Herr Storfer refused to transfer anyone. He insisted the Rosita was not yet ready for passengers. Instead, he suggested they could ease overcrowding by transferring all the luggage to the Rosita. The passengers protested and refused to comply. They feared that if they sailed without their luggage, they would never see it again. Those meagre possessions were all they had left.

Dr Horetzky was caught in a difficult situation, torn between pacifying passengers, negotiating with a stubborn Storfer, and appeasing a capricious captain ready to abandon ship.

Berthold Storfer suggested a solution: he would invite a Romanian official from Tulcea's port authority to inspect the ship.

The official declared the Atlantic seaworthy and issued a certificate of navigability. Whether he was paid to do so, none of them could be sure, but that ruling satisfied Captain Spiro, who finally agreed to take the helm. Whether he himself had been paid off, no one was certain.

Their situation looked promising when the crew loaded food, water, and fuel for the voyage – until Berthold Storfer informed them that he could only provide half of the food and coal they needed because of war shortages. They would stop at another port along the way to load more, he explained.

'Perhaps Istanbul,' he suggested vaguely.

The unfolding drama had led to a lively discussion the night before amongst the lifeboat chevra.

'I believe Storfer took the right course of action,' Alexander said.

'Are you crazy?' Janka said. 'We're about to embark on a risky journey in an overcrowded ship, which even our drunk captain thinks is unseaworthy, and we don't have enough coal or food to reach our destination!'

Alexander threw up his hands. 'What choice did he have?'

Stefan tilted his head towards the Rosita. 'The extra ship, for a start, so we wouldn't have to travel like a tin of sardines.'

'We don't know what conditions are like inside,' Alexander said. 'What if Storfer is telling the truth and it still needs modifications.'

'Lack of nails,' Isaak suggested, raising a chuckle.

'Yes, that too.' Alexander tried to keep a straight face. 'But let's be serious for a moment. What if the Rosita can't yet accommodate that many people using the facilities?'

'As if our current facilities were sufficient,' Janka snorted.

'Would you be willing to put up with worse conditions?' her brother asked.

Janka tilted her head one way and then the other as she considered the question.

Alexander's brow furrowed as he thought about worse conditions. 'What if the ship were infested with rats?'

'Eeek!' Erika flinched and wrinkled her nose in disgust. 'I couldn't deal with that.'

Lilly also shuddered at the thought.

'See what's happening over there?' Alexander swept his arm towards Tulcea, where each day more signs of war – bunkers, coils of barbed wire and gun emplacements – were popping up like mushrooms on the hillside surrounding the town. 'Storfer knows the war is snapping at our heels. If he delays us further by waiting to transfer five hundred people, we might not escape its reach.'

'Couldn't we leave straight away and the Rosita follow later?' Hannah said.

'And what if we were the ones they selected for transfer?' Alexander asked. 'Would you be happy to wait and risk getting stuck in Tulcea while the other ships, including your fiance, sail off to Eretz?'

Hannah's shoulders slumped. 'You're right,' she said. 'Seaworthy or not.'

'We leave no one behind,' Alexander said. 'I'll give Storfer credit for realising that. So he was ready to make the choice to leave the luggage, but the passengers wouldn't agree. What was he supposed to do at that point? He needs us moving, so he did what it took to help us leave, including – possibly – paying people off.'

'If the option is to travel as sardines, or not travel at all, I'll pick the sardine tin,' Isaak said.

'*Shana tova*, Gisela! Happy New Year!' Alexander called as he and Isaak made their way across the deck after prayers to join the women. Gisela opened her arms to embrace him, then gave Isaak a grandmotherly pinch on the cheek, which he accepted in good humour.

Alexander hugged his sister, then Erika and Hannah in turn, but he hesitated when he reached Lilly. 'May I?'

'You may,' she said, smiling as his arms wrapped around her.

Alexander reminded her so much of Eugen – his idealism and his charisma. They would get on so well. She would have to introduce them after they landed in Haifa.

Isaak followed his cousin's lead, giving Lilly a shy, awkward hug, lasting just as long as it took him to say, '*Shana tova.*'

Hannah and Lilly left Alexander talking to Stefan and Jenny, and arranged a pile of blankets as a comfortable seat for Gisela. The group then sat close together in a circle, given the limited space on deck.

'What is this?' Gisela said, as she settled on the blankets. 'I'm the queen?'

'Indeed, you are,' Alexander said. 'Our queen.'

'*Ach*!' She brushed his declaration away, but the flush of pink on her cheeks said she enjoyed the compliment. 'I hope no one objects that I invited Alma and Max. They had no one else to eat with and I didn't want them to be on their own for the holiday.'

'Not at all. We'd be delighted for them to join us,' Lilly said.

Gisela scanned the deck. 'They should have been here by now. I wonder if they remember where to find us.'

Lilly spotted them caught in a tangle of passengers. They hung back, however, clutching their ration bowls, exchanging uncertain glances.

Alexander noticed them too. Without a word, he went to meet them. He shook Max's hand and gave a slight bow of his head to Alma, but Max still appeared hesitant. Lilly came over and joined Alexander. '*Shana tova*!' she said, hugging Alma.

Alexander nodded his appreciation to Lilly. He placed an encouraging hand on Max's shoulder and led them to the gathering where the lifeboat chevra gave Max and Alma an enthusiastic welcome.

'We appreciate your kind invitation,' Max said, his voice faltering.

'It's a pleasure to have you join us for this festive meal.' Gisela swept her arms over their paltry ration bowls. 'As you can see, I have spent all day in the kitchen cooking up a feast.'

During the laughter that followed, the tension on Max's face began to fall away. He joined the circle, as Alexander and Isaak quickly improvised their rucksacks into a seat for Alma. Max supported her as she eased herself down and settled in.

'How is that?' Alexander said. 'Comfortable?'

She gave him a grateful smile and rested a hand on her extended belly. 'Yes, thank you.'

Lilly's eyes travelled around the circle, from Alexander, on her left, to Isaak, Janka, Erika, Gisela, Alma, Max, Stefan, Jenny. The chevra. People who had been strangers just a short time ago had become an adopted family.

Her gaze stopped at her cousin. Hannah and Tante Rebecca had been a consistent presence at her family's festive Rosh Hashana meals for as far back as she could remember. Throughout her childhood, their grandparents were also present, and later, Salo.

The family would sit around her parents' extended table, laid with a white starched linen cloth, sparkling silverware, crystal glasses, and their best dinner service, the heirloom Meissen porcelain with blue painted flowers, passed down from Lilly's grandmother. Papa, standing tall and proud, would recite *kiddush* over the wine in his deep, melodic voice, before reciting the blessing over Mama's homemade honey-glazed challa filled with plump and juicy raisins. Next came the highlight: a blessing for a sweet new year and eating crisp apple slices dipped in thick honey.

Was Mama sitting with Tante Rebecca tonight dipping apples in honey, staring at the empty chairs, while Papa lay in his bed unaware of the night's significance? That is, if he was even still—

'I miss them too,' Hannah said, mirroring her thoughts.

'I'm so grateful that at least we're together,' Lilly said.

Their first Rosh Hashana away from home, and they were sitting on the rough wooden deck of this crowded, stationary ship, eating rations from their bowls. No table. No festive meal. Never mind apples and honey.

Then, as if by magic, Isaak conjured up two shiny red apples.

Janka's eyes widened. 'Where did you find those?'

'I bought them from the crew's canteen,' Isaak said. 'Daylight robbery. Far more than the hawker ever charged. But how could I let Rosh Hashana go by without at least an apple or two? Unfortunately they didn't have honey.' He shrugged.

'This is more than we could have hoped for.' Alexander patted him on the back.

'I have something sweet we can have instead.' Gisela rummaged in her bag and presented a bar of chocolate like a trophy. 'Also thanks to you, Isaak. You gave this to me when we were stuck in Ruse Port and the Romanian Police threw chocolate and cigarettes onto the deck. I'm so glad I saved it.'

'Oh, Gisela! You remind me of my mama.' Isaak got up and walked around the group to plant a peck on her cheek.

Gisela broke up the chocolate bar into small squares while Isaak cut the apples into thin slices with his penknife. They each held up their piece of apple and chocolate as Isaak led them in reciting a blessing for the apple and the traditional prayer: 'May it be your will, Lord our God and God of our fathers, to renew us for a good and sweet new year.'

'And next year, may we all celebrate together in Eretz Israel,' Alexander added.

'Amen!' they said in unison.

The apple was crunchy and juicy. The cube of chocolate, sweet and delicious. Lilly sucked on it slowly to make it last as long as possible.

'Next Rosh Hashana, God willing, I invite you all to join me. You'll meet my children and grandchildren,' Gisela said. 'It will be my pleasure to spend a day in the kitchen.'

'We can help with the cooking,' Alma said.

'I think you'll be too busy chasing this little one all over the place,' Gisela said, addressing her bump.

Alma beamed and stroked her stomach.

Lilly turned to Hannah. 'Can you imagine, when we all meet next Rosh Hashana, you and Karl will be married!'

Uncertainty flickered in Hannah's eyes as she smiled. 'I really hope so.'

And what about me? Lilly wondered. Where will I be next year?

# CHAPTER 25

Clouds of smoke billowed from the chimney of the Atlantic, as the crew and passengers prepared for departure. On the bridge, a Haganah guard blew his whistle, then shouted into the megaphone, '*Alle nach rechts*. Starboard.'

Lilly shuffled to the right across the deck with the other passengers, trying to balance the ship and compensate for its listing to the far side. Captain Spiro, standing beside the guard, examined their progress and shook his head. The guard sounded his whistle again and gestured for them to divide in half. 'This side, *nach links*. Port.'

Lilly moved to the left with half of the passengers.

Captain Spiro wasn't satisfied. Yet a third time, the guard blew his whistle. 'That quarter, *nach rechts*. Starboard.' He pointed.

Alexander bent his head to Lilly. 'This is rather like a dance.'

'But even they don't know the steps,' Lilly chuckled, as they crossed the deck again.

An engineer ran up to the bridge, spoke to Spiro, and ran back down to the catacombs. He reappeared moments later to confer with the captain and guard.

'We require several men to redistribute the ballast and luggage,' said the guard. 'Any volunteers?' Hands shot up, and he picked them out as they did: 'One, two, three, four, five. Please go down to the hold.'

'To be continued.' Alexander winked and headed down to the catacombs with a spring in his step.

Now that they had a confirmed departure date for the seventh of October, the day after tomorrow, nothing proved too much trouble – not for Alexander, nor for anyone else. All of them were ready to help with enthusiasm and a renewed sense of purpose.

One day to go and the Atlantic was a hive of activity. The Haganah and crew were engaged in last-minute preparations. An electrician rigged up a system of bells connecting the bridge to the engine room so they could communicate without the need to send crew members to convey messages. The Atlantic had no wireless equipment, few nautical instruments, and only 900 life jackets available for the 1,800 people on board. To make up for the shortfall, the life jackets were cut in two. They determined it was better for everyone to have half a life jacket than to leave half the passengers with none. They estimated that the coal supply would last for the expected ten-day crossing – although Captain Spiro strutted about the bridge boasting he could make the crossing in five or six.

And then it was their final evening in Tulcea.

A crescent moon cast a faint silvery light across water and outlined the buildings of the town they recognised only from a distance. They had not walked its streets and were unlikely to do so.

Yet the lifeboat chevra were in a celebratory mood when they gathered for supper.

'Can you imagine, by the end of this week we'll be in Eretz Israel?' Hannah said.

By the end of the week, Hannah thought, she and Karl would be reunited.

'I'll be happy to be off this ship,' said Jenny. Her cheeks looked pallid. Dark circles rimmed her eyes. Sickness, lack of sleep, and the worsening weather was taking its toll.

'Spiro's claims may be too ambitious,' Alexander cautioned. 'When we were redistributing the ballast in the catacombs earlier, Dov said the journey would probably take about ten days, including a brief stop in Istanbul to load additional fuel. So with a bit of luck, we'll arrive by the middle of next week.'

The windlass creaked, the anchor rose, and the ship's horn gave such a powerful blast that Hannah felt it in the pit of her stomach. The Atlantic's engine thumped, raring to go. Yet, the ship held back as if waiting for a signal. The crowd crackled with anticipation. Then the horn on one of the other ships, the Pacific, sounded in response, setting course towards them amidst cheering.

Hannah and Erika pushed through the throng and pressed themselves against the railing. Hannah's stomach flip-flopped as she spotted Karl. His cheeks were more gaunt than she remembered, but that hadn't diminished his beautiful smile. For a fleeting moment, they waved and blew kisses before the Pacific sailed on, and Hannah lost sight of Karl in the crowd.

Karl. Her future husband. Hannah was eager to spend the rest of her life with him. She hoped she wouldn't have to wait too long. In his last letter, before Captain Spiro had put an end to their delivery system, Karl had said much the same.

*I can't wait to marry you. Let's not delay longer than necessary. I'm so happy to hear you are willing to give kibbutz life a try. I think you might like it. We will have work. They'll provide us with a home.*

*(Well, perhaps a tent to begin with.) But at least we'll have a roof over our heads and we'll be together. Far better than separated and packed into the confines of the Atlantic and Pacific. After all this time apart, and on these crowded ships, the idea of a kibbutz with wide open spaces, and you by my side, is the closest thing to paradise I can think of.*

*But I don't mean to pressure you. I understand the situation with Lilly and I never want to come between you and your cousin. I know she is like a sister to you. We will make sure she gets settled first, and I will help in any way I can. And if we need to wait to marry, then we will. You are worth the wait.*

Hannah had read Karl's words over and over again. If only they could marry straight away. But she wouldn't abandon Lilly. Not until her cousin was settled or, better yet, if she met someone. Hannah wondered, not for the first time, whether Alexander might suit.

Lilly seemed oblivious to the shift in Alexander's demeanour when he was around her, but Hannah had noticed. The way he always expressed concern for her welfare. How on Rosh Hashanah, he seemed to hug Lilly for a fraction of a moment longer than he had hugged the others, and maybe a little closer too. He sat next to her during meals, though whether that was strategy, habit, or happenstance, Hannah couldn't be sure.

There he was now, coming to stand beside Lilly as they all embarked on their momentous journey. What did Lilly think of Alexander, though? She certainly seemed fond enough of him, but whether she harboured deeper feelings or not, Hannah couldn't decide. Nor was she going to broach the subject. It would be an awkward conversation, and what if she had misread Alexander's signals, and Lilly were disappointed? Maybe she should discreetly suggest to Alexander that he be more direct in his conversations with Lilly.

All at once, the passengers buzzed in excitement. With a gentle sway beneath their feet, the Atlantic began to move. They were leaving at last.

Alexander beamed at Lilly as their ship departed the Port of Tulcea – after nearly a month – to follow in the Pacific's wake.

Hannah's heart was full. She deftly wedged herself into the narrow gap on Lilly's right, and embraced her cousin in a tight hug. At that moment, anything seemed possible.

The ship turned onto the exit canal, the crowd cheering. But before they reached the branch of the Danube that would ultimately lead them to the open sea, the ship came to an abrupt halt.

The crowd's enthusiasm faded into silence. Hannah watched Karl's ship disappear into the distance, while the Atlantic's bow floundered and ran aground.

'What is Spiro doing?' Alexander asked. 'Is he drunk?'

The Atlantic juddered with the full force of the engine, boiling water dripping onto the deck, as the captain tried to release their ship from the bank.

'Everyone to the stern!' Spiro yelled into the megaphone.

They hurried en masse to the rear.

The ship blasted its horn, the bell system rang frantically, and communications broke down between the bridge and the engine room. The crew resorted to shouting a relay of commands from person to person.

A motor launch carrying Herr Storfer had arrived to observe, and on the tree-lined bank opposite, a growing crowd of onlookers gawked at the unfolding drama.

Hannah could barely breathe while she watched the captain conduct a series of reverse manoeuvres.

One long hour later, the captain finally extricated the ship from the muddy verge and repositioned it in the centre of the river. Hannah breathed a sigh of relief when they set off without difficulty.

But they hadn't travelled more than a few metres when the ship lurched and headed straight for the other bank. The crowd of spectators screamed and fled in panic for fear of being mowed down by this uncontrollable, rusty monster. The Atlantic stopped only just in time; but not before its keel scraped the bottom. Hannah winced. This could not be happening.

The ship wobbled its way back to the middle of the river and dropped anchor, listing starboard. A hush descended on the ship like fog, until Spiro broke the silence, 'Everyone move to port.'

They shuffled left to steady the vessel, just in time to see Milos, the third ship of their convoy, sail by. The vessel still had a noticeable list, but, unlike them, it was moving in a straight line.

Alexander put his head in his hands. 'Well, this is just fantastic.'

Hannah could only look on in envy as the Milos sailed out to the sea.

By nightfall, they still hadn't moved. A tugboat was supposed to ferry them to the Black Sea port of Sulina for repairs, but it hadn't yet arrived, and they faced another night on the river. Supper was stodgy rice with a hint of cinnamon, which the lifeboat chevra ate in silence. No one was in the mood for conversion or jokes, not even Isaak. It was more than just nails they were lacking.

Erika returned from her shift, her eyes downcast.

Lilly was almost afraid to ask. 'More bad news?'

'Do you remember that elderly lady with the sweet smile who shared the cabin with Gisela and Alma?' Erika said. 'I'm sorry to say she passed away.'

'Oh no!' Lilly placed a hand over her mouth. 'Does Gisela know?'

'I'm not sure. Perhaps you ought to break it to her?'

Below deck, Lilly passed the crew quarters. The smell of succulent roast chicken wafted into the corridor and taunted her hungry stomach. While the passengers faced food shortages and rationing, the crew apparently enjoyed an ample food supply.

From the opposite end of the passageway came the sound of female laughter, loud and unnaturally enthusiastic. The tall crewman they had nicknamed The Giant, who had initially intimidated Lilly with his stare, was returning to the crew quarters with his arm around a woman. Lilly slipped into the line for the facilities and lowered her head to avoid being seen. The Giant opened the door and, with a swish of pink silk, his blonde companion sashayed after him.

Lilly found Gisela sitting on the edge of her bunk, dabbing her eyes with a handkerchief. Lilly settled beside her. 'Erika told me the sad news.'

'She was a lovely lady. I used to enjoy talking to her until she took ill and was transferred to the sickbay.' Gisela twisted the cotton handkerchief in her hands. 'She was looking forward to being reunited with her children and grandchildren. Now she'll never get the chance. She won't have a proper burial or even a grave for her family to visit.' She heaved a sigh loaded with despair. 'I've lost my husband, my home, and my security. My only wish in life is to reach Eretz Israel and be with my family.' She faced Lilly with the unmistakable look of fear. 'So many people are succumbing to illness. What if it happens to me?'

'I'll look after you. All of us will. Hannah, Erika, Isaak ...' Lilly put an arm around her shoulder. In the five weeks since they'd left Vienna, Gisela had lost her roundness. Her bones jutted out. She looked and felt fragile. 'And in just a few more days, you'll see your sons again and meet your grandchildren,' Lilly said in an attempt to reassure her.

'I hope so. I truly hope so.' Gisela reached for her hand. 'I'm so grateful for your care and concern. If I had a daughter, I don't think she could be any kinder to me than you have been.'

Lilly sat with Gisela until the older woman said she was tired. Once Gisela had settled in for the night, Lilly returned to the upper deck where she found Hannah and Erika huddled by the railings, engrossed in conversation. The moment they noticed Lilly, they stopped talking.

'How is Gisela?' Erika asked.

'She's upset,' Lilly said. 'And quite scared.'

'That's understandable.'

'How did it happen? Why did she pass away?'

'The hard conditions were a strain on her.' Erika shook her head sadly. 'I suppose it became too much to bear. She was already quite elderly and had some health issues.'

'And what about all the other cases? Why are so many people falling ill?'

'Upset stomachs from rotten food. Contaminated water. Poor sanitary conditions.' A glance passed from Erika to Hannah. She lowered her voice. 'This mustn't go any further ... The doctors suspect there are a few cases of typhoid.'

'*Ach du lieber Gott*!' Lilly said. 'Is there even medicine for that?'

'There is no medicine available, only a preventative vaccination.' Erika paused. 'Which we don't have.'

'Isn't there something you can do?' Lilly pleaded

Erika kept her composure. 'We'll try to isolate cases when we find them and take care of the patients as best as we can. And we'll have to maintain hygiene on the ship. It's important to keep washing your hands, especially before you eat and after using the toilet.'

'And if someone contracts it … what are their chances?' Lilly asked. She knew people whispered 'typhoid' like it was an automatic death sentence, but she hoped Erika would give her reason to hope.

'The young and strong have a decent chance of pulling through, if they contract it. Unfortunately, not everyone will overcome it. We'll need to be especially careful with those who are vulnerable. But please, not a word to anyone. We don't want to cause additional panic.'

A tugboat appeared soon after daybreak and towed their stalled vessel on a slow journey through the Danube Delta. Five hours later, they reached the sleepy port town of Sulina, punctuated by low houses with pitched red-tiled roofs, a distinct church with multiple turrets and domes, and an old, abandoned lighthouse. They continued a short distance farther out to sea, and found cause for cautious optimism, when they dropped anchor there to await repairs. The quayside was still in sight, with its modest taverns and hotels. Hannah hoped they wouldn't have to face the view for too long. She scanned the horizon for any sign of Karl's ship, but it was long gone and far out to sea.

At sunset, when the lifeboat chevra sat down to eat, a stiff wind stirred the waves, causing the ship to rock and creak. Supper was a repeat of the previous night's clumpy rice; Jenny managed only a few mouthfuls of the slop before she scrambled out of the lifeboat with a hand over her mouth, running to heave over the side of the ship.

When she was quite done, Stefan carried her back to the lifeboat. She hadn't had the energy to climb back in under her own power. She sat there lethargically and, when she couldn't stop her teeth from chattering, Stefan wrapped his blanket around Jenny in addition to her own.

Lilly quietly left them without explanation. When she returned some ten minutes later, she drew Alexander aside. He listened intently to her, nodding in agreement and together they approached Jenny who was shivering under her two blankets.

'These chilly nights aren't helping you get well,' Lilly said. 'There's a spare bed in the cabin. I've spoken to Gisela, Alma, and the others and they would be happy for you to join them.'

'But that bed belonged to the woman who ...' The expression on Jenny's face revealed her thoughts.

'They have switched beds. Someone else preferred the bottom bunk.'

'You'll be warmer and have a more comfortable night's sleep,' Alexander said.

'It's a very kind offer, but what about Haganah rules? Won't I get in trouble for moving into a cabin?' Jenny said.

'It will be fine, he said. 'I'll have a word with Dov for you.'

Jenny glanced from one face to another. 'I'd rather not leave you all.'

'You can rejoin us whenever you want,' Lilly encouraged. 'But you have to build up your strength again.'

'Lilly and Alexander are right,' Stefan said. 'You should take the bunk. You haven't had a proper night's sleep in weeks.'

'But what about you?'

'I'll move to the lower deck and find a space in the corridor next to Max. I'll be right outside. Take the bed – please.'

Jenny gave a reluctant nod. 'All right.'

Stefan gathered their belongings and helped Jenny out of the lifeboat. As they started for the cabin, he turned around to Lilly and mouthed, 'Thank you.'

As the night progressed, the wind intensified. The ship bobbed like a cork and all around them people groaned and retched. Hannah didn't know whether it was the ship's movement or the noise of the passengers that made her feel queasy. Soon she and her friends were all reaching for paper bags.

'If these are the conditions when we're near the coast, what is the journey going to be like out at sea?' she said.

'I hope it doesn't get any worse. I have nothing left inside me,' Janka said, already on her second paper bag. She studied Isaak, sprawled out on his blanket, sound asleep. 'How does he manage that?'

In the early hours of the morning, the waves lost some of their wildness and Hannah was finally able to sleep.

At the break of dawn, Hannah opened her eyes, feeling groggy, to find that a small tug boat had brought a group of mechanics to the Atlantic. They assessed the ship's damage and headed back to Sulina to get the parts and tools they needed to fix it.

Isaak joined the *minyan* on deck as he did every morning but, on this occasion, he prayed with greater fervour than usual, his motivation clear as he turned periodically to look at the mechanics making repairs. When he returned to the lifeboat, Alexander held out his arm. 'Show me how to put on the tefillin. The only time I ever wore a pair was for my bar mitzva and I can't remember how to wind them.'

Janka, sitting cross-legged on the opposite bench looked on, bemused. 'I thought you're an atheist.'

'Agnostic,' Alexander said. 'Not atheist.'

'Same thing.'

'Big difference.' He rolled up his sleeve for Isaak, who began wrapping the leather strap around Alexander's arm. 'And right now, we need every prayer we can get.'

By mid-morning, the mechanics had completed their repairs, and returned to their own boat to observe the results of their work.

The sun's rays touched the inky water of the Black Sea; its choppy waves had become gentle ripples.

Hannah squeezed Lilly's and Erika's hands. Gisela, standing beside Lilly, began to whisper a quiet prayer.

The tension was palpable.

The engine started.

The anchor lifted.

Slowly, the ship began to glide forwards.

None of them dared to say it aloud: they were moving.

The ship was sailing.

The tug hooted, the Atlantic replied with a mighty blow of its horn and, with a last wave, the mechanics returned to port. The ship was on its own.

The ship increased its speed, its engine chugging in a steady rhythm, and Romania's coastline faded into the distance. Ahead stretched only the vast expanse of the Black Sea.

Hannah and Lilly locked eyes and dared a smile. In an instant, the entire chevra came together, their embraces accompanied by a chorus of sighs, laughter, and cries of happiness. It sounded, to Hannah, as beautiful as the opening bars of a symphony.

Nine months detained in Bratislava.

A precarious week on the Danube.

A month trapped in Tulcea.

Finally, the voyage to Haifa was underway.

# THE SS ATLANTIC VOYAGE

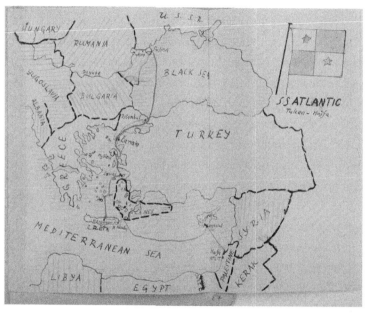

Drawn by passenger  Franci-Jehudith Lederer-Berger-Schlesinger
Courtesy of the Ghetto Fighters' House Archives, Israel

Lilly stood at the Atlantic's stern and watched the waters of the Black Sea froth in the ship's wake. The slipstream marked the growing distance between her and the escalating war in Europe, as well as the increasing separation between Lilly, her parents, and the place she used to call home. Surrounded by the vast expanse of the blue sea, she felt suspended between her past and future.

Caught up in emotions that fluctuated between fear and cautious optimism, Lilly closed her eyes for a moment, breathing in the salty mist and tasting its briny tang on her lips. When she again looked out to sea, she couldn't help but smile: two dolphins had appeared and were swimming alongside the Atlantic. Lilly had never seen the gentle sea creatures in person, but she recognised them from a book she had read as a child, and their presence calmed her. The graceful animals escorted them for a few nautical miles, alternately leaping into the air and diving back into the shimmering water.

The joy brought by the pair of dolphins was short-lived. Later, as the sun dipped below the horizon, sorrow seemed to descend on the ship, casting a shadow over the crowd on the deck. The passengers fell silent as they parted to create a path for the pall-bearers, a mournful procession of four men shouldering a wooden board. They carried the body of the first woman who had died on board, wrapped in a white shroud. As the passengers gathered at the railings, a rabbi gave a short eulogy, and then recited the Kaddish prayer. At the appropriate moments during the prayer, the crowd responded in low voices and the occasional sniffle.

After the final 'Amen,' the men rested the board on the railings and angled it towards the sea. The shrouded body slipped into the water with a dull splash, and vanished into the depths.

'I knew her from the dining room,' Gisela whispered. 'She too was travelling to Eretz Israel to join her family. But she didn't make it and never had the chance to see her children again.' Gisela wiped her eyes with a damp handkerchief. 'Her children don't even know she passed and that they need to sit shiva for her. There is no grave for them to visit.'

Lilly placed her arm around Gisela. 'At least we were here to honour her and say Kaddish.'

Gisela appeared not to hear. She was watching the four pallbearers carrying the board back up the steps, preparing to collect the next body for the second of four funeral services that day.

Lilly's thoughts drifted to Salo. Would she ever visit his grave again? Night was falling. Lilly, aware of the darkness that threatened to pull her down and break her spirit, once again promised an absent Salo that she would keep looking towards the future.

The next afternoon, the crew spotted land and raised the Turkish flag. Perhaps Captain Spiro hadn't been exaggerating when he'd claimed he could make the crossing to British-controlled Mandatory Palestine in six days.

The Atlantic slowed and entered the Bosphorus Strait, with Europe to their right and Asia on the left – the crossroads of two continents. The waterway was the narrow dividing line, with a promontory from each side flanking the ship.

Lilly squeezed in at the bow of the ship for a better view. Old castles, grand palaces, and elegant hotels lined the shore, backlit gloriously by a golden sunset.

Hannah let out a sigh. 'Would you look at that? It's as if we've entered another world.'

'Not that long ago, we would have thought all this was normal too,' Erika said. 'We took so much for granted, never realising that the freedom we had was such a blessing.'

'You could almost forget the war.' Alexander moved his head in accompaniment to the strains of jazz music drifting across from one of the beachside restaurants.

Janka refused to be moved by the scene, gesturing towards the restaurant's patrons with a jut of her chin. 'They eat, drink, and dance, utterly unaware that a wretched bunch of Jewish refugees fleeing Europe are sailing past them on this packed, filthy ship.' She rolled her eyes.

'You're right,' Isaak said, causing Janka to straighten upon hearing his unexpected agreement.

'To them, we're just another passenger ship,' Isaac continued. 'And for tonight, that's exactly what we are. Ordinary passengers enjoying a beautiful evening cruise.' He held his arms wide. 'Look at the buildings. No swastika flags draped from buildings. No Nazis to terrorise us.'

'I can hardly remember that,' Lilly said. 'Imagine being able to walk the street without fear of being attacked. To enter a shop with no signs forbidding you to enter. To sit in a café, walk in the park or visit the cinema.'

'Isn't that why you're on this ship, taking risks and accepting the difficulties?' Alexander asked. 'I want a chance to live like a normal person in our own land. To never have to feel afraid just because I'm Jewish.' He nodded toward the carefree crowd dancing, drinking, and laughing on a terrace decorated with light bulb garlands. 'Soon, that will be us in Eretz Israel.'

The Atlantic glided into Istanbul at nightfall. Domes and minarets were illuminated against the purple sky. Usually the chevra turned in early to conserve their limited supply of lamp oil, but tonight they would stay up late. They couldn't tear themselves away from the enchanting views.

When Lilly finally turned in, she slept peacefully, and, for the first time in almost two years, unencumbered by nightmares.

Opening her eyes, Lilly sat up and marvelled at the white, blue, and gold architectural grandeur that was Istanbul by the light of day. She noted the grand, stone-clad buildings of the modern financial district lining the opposite bank, but much preferred the eastern style. The neoclassical and Ottoman blend reminded her of the Nordbahnhof in Vienna.

'I have to admit, it is impressive,' Janka nodded at the view. She had just returned from fetching her breakfast: weak tea and a single, sugar-dusted biscuit that bore resemblance to a ginger Lebkuchen.

'Now I understand why Istanbul is said to be one of the most beautiful cities in the world,' Lilly said.

Janka sipped her tea and stared wistfully at a sleek white ferry crossing the strait from one side of the city to the other; from one continent to another. 'If only we'd been stuck here for a month instead of boring Tulcea. I'll almost be sorry to leave this evening.'

Janka's comment left Lilly perplexed. 'Don't you want to continue to Eretz?' she asked.

'I do. It's only ...' Janka fiddled with her biscuit. 'Has Hannah spoken to you yet about the possibility of me moving in with the two of you?'

'Yes. And we'd be more than happy for you to join us.' Lilly smiled at Janka.

Janka smiled back, the relief apparent in her eyes. 'I appreciate that.'

'Do you mind me asking, though, why don't you want to live with Alexander, or near him, anyway? Hannah didn't explain. Did you two have a falling out?'

'Oh, no. Nothing like that. It's just ...' she shrugged . 'To tell you the truth, I'm not sure I'm suited to kibbutz life. We're going to land in Haifa in a few days and I don't know what to do.'

Lilly could relate to her dilemma only too well. 'Have you spoken to your brother about it?'

'No!' Janka's eyes widened. 'Please don't tell him. He'll be so disappointed in me.'

'Why would he be disappointed?'

'Oh, you know ... He's such an idealist. He's really set on the idea of living on a kibbutz. He believes it's what every young person should aspire to. His enthusiasm won me over. That, and our parents who persuaded me to leave Prague and join him. But I suppose I imagined something a little more romantic than our current reality.' She shook her head ruefully.

'The conditions will be far better when we reach Eretz.'

'Possibly,' Janka agreed. 'Or maybe not. Hence my quandary.'

'You should talk it over with Alexander.'

Janka sighed. 'I suppose I'm putting off the inevitable. I'd rather we didn't have a falling-out.'

'Your brother is more reasonable than you give him credit for,' Lilly said. 'Talk to him.'

'I'll have to pick the right moment.'

'Here he is now.' Lilly nodded to Alexander, who was heading back from the ship's galley with Isaak, both of them balancing tea and biscuits. 'No time like the present.'

'Maybe later,' Janka muttered so Alexander wouldn't overhear. 'First, breakfast.' She took a bite of her biscuit, and immediately spluttered. '*Pfui*!' She examined it closer. 'What is this repulsive thing?'

'Isn't it a Lebkuchen?' Lilly said.

'You wish. They told me it's a sea biscuit.' She scraped off the coating. 'It's as hard as stone and this pretty coating is mould masquerading as sugar! Apparently, this is all the food we have left until we load up new supplies today.'

'Try dipping it in the tea,' Lilly said. Maybe that will help – or at the very least make it softer.'

'Go fetch yours and we'll try together.' She cackled, sending Lilly off with a wave of her hand. 'If I am to be poisoned, I'm not doing it alone.'

As Lilly queued for the meagre breakfast, a sudden flurry of activity on deck caught her attention. Two men dressed in fine shirts and waistcoats boarded the ship and were lugging hessian sacks almost as tall as they were. After setting them down on the deck they shook hands with members of the Transport Committee and patted several of the Haganah men on the back. Then they turned their attention to the passengers.

'*Shalom aleichem*, brothers and sisters!' said the older of the two, with a head of thick salt-and-pepper hair and eyes that crinkled when he smiled. He addressed them in English. 'We represent the Turkish Jewish community and we've brought you our members' donation of food supplies for your journey.'

A murmur spread through the crowd as his words were translated from English to German and passed from one passenger to another.

'In addition, if you wish to send letters to your families, we will be happy to collect them and take care of the postage for you. We will be here for the next couple of hours to collect your correspondence.'

Lilly relinquished her place in the food queue and hurried to the lifeboat for her writing paper. Janka, Hannah and Erika were already hunched over the lifeboat benches, feverishly composing letters home. As Lilly penned a letter to her mother, the mouth-watering aroma of freshly baked bread filled the deck, making her stomach growl. Having gone to inspect the delivery, Alexander and Isaak returned with their report: 'They have 1,500 loaves of fresh white bread.' Isaak could barely contain his excitement. 'Grapes and cognac for the sick.'

'And,' Alexander said, stressing every syllable, 'cho-co-late.'

Lilly looked up from her letter and laughed. 'Stop it. I'll faint from hunger. I haven't even had breakfast yet.'

'You must make sure you eat today.' Isaak cast her a concerned glance. You're fasting tomorrow. Have you at least been drinking?'

'Not yet. I'll fetch a cup of tea after I finish this letter.'

Alexander leaned over Janka's shoulder. 'Are you writing to Mama and Papa?'

'Yes,' she said 'Are you going to write too?'

'I'm sure you've already told them everything there is to say. I'll add a few lines to the bottom of yours.'

'Send Onkle and Tante my love too,' Isaak said.

Lilly wondered why he wasn't writing his own letter, but he wandered off before she could ask. She turned to Hannah instead. 'Doesn't Isaak want to write to his parents?' she whispered.

'He can't,' Hannah replied. 'His parents and brother are stranded in Kladovo, with that group waiting for a boat.'

Lilly covered her mouth with her hand to stifle her gasp. 'I didn't realise.'

Within moments, Isaak had returned. 'Here you go.' He handed Lilly a cup of tea. 'You can drink this while you write.'

'Thank you. That's very kind.' Lilly hesitated. 'I'm sorry.' She fiddled with the pen in her hands. 'About your parents. I hope a boat reaches them soon, and they'll join you in Eretz before you know it.'

Isaak flinched. A tinge of pain clouded his face. 'I hope so too. Thank you, Lilly.' His smile was a brave one, she thought.

She was refreshed by the tea, which she sipped as she started a second letter to Eugen. She could hear the murmur of a heated conversation between the Haganah and Transport Committee members and Captain Spiro, but she dismissed it; disagreements between them were a frequent occurrence. She quickly wrote a few sentences and joined the winding line of passengers waiting to hand over their envelopes, shake hands with the men, and offer their thanks.

Thirty minutes later, Lilly reached the front of the queue.

'Thank you for helping us and for taking our post,' she said to the older gentleman in halting English. 'We were delayed for so long, I appreciate it even more. My mother will be very glad to get the letter.' She wished she could express her gratitude at being able to put her mother's mind at ease more fully, but she couldn't find the appropriate words.

'It is our pleasure.' His words were filled with warmth. 'We are always honoured to help our fellow Jews on their journey to Eretz Israel.'

'Do you help a lot of ships like this?' she asked.

'Yes, every time a ship of Jewish refugees stops in Istanbul. Though ever since war broke out there haven't been many. Our community has a special fund to assist Jews on their way to Eretz Israel.'

'Your community is so very kind. We have already faced many challenges and sometimes feel alone and helpless. It's comforting to know that the Jews of Istanbul care for us.'

'Well, we're all one family, aren't we?'

'We are.' Someone in the queue behind her impatiently cleared his or her throat, but Lilly wasn't ready to step away from this man who had shown such concern for their welfare. 'In Vienna, where I'm from,' she blurted out, 'we used to have a Turkish synagogue. I prayed there often because my best friend's family belonged to the community. Her sister is married to my brother.'

'Oh?' The man gave her the full focus of his attention. 'What is the family name?'

'Elias.'

'That was the maiden name of my maternal grandmother.' His smile had taken on the benevolence of a kind uncle. 'Perhaps you and I are actually related by marriage.' He patted her arm. 'Go well, my dear, and may the rest of your journey be safe and without incident.'


Before the Yom Kippur fast, the lifeboat chevra feasted on the donated bread. Lilly inhaled its yeasty scent and bit into the golden crust that gave way to fluffy comfort.

Later, in the light of the setting sun, Lilly joined the passengers who had assembled on deck for *Kol Nidrei*, the opening prayer of Yom Kippur. Behind them, Istanbul's skyline glinted like burnished gold.

Lilly remembered the days when she used to attend the magnificent Türkischer Tempel with Serena. Now, all that remained of it was a pile of rubble. The same fate had befallen the Schiffschul, where she and Salo had married, and the synagogue close to her parents' home where they had been members. The Nazis had destroyed one hundred of Vienna's synagogues during the November Pogrom.

Only the Stadttempel in the First District remained standing, and it too had been ransacked and desecrated.

The buildings may have been lost, Lilly thought, but not their prayers.

Tonight, they didn't pray inside a synagogue, but on a dilapidated ship, under an indigo sky, in exotic Turkey. But they were returning with their heritage to its birthplace: their ancient homeland.

At eight o'clock, when the service ended, it was time for the Atlantic to leave. Their twenty-four-hour permit to stay in port had expired.

The mood on board should have been one of relief as they departed Istanbul and continued their journey into the Sea of Marmara, but the anxious looks on their faces said otherwise. The Atlantic hadn't accomplished its main purpose for stopping in Istanbul. It had not loaded the most important commodity of all: the coal needed to fuel the engines.

# CHAPTER 27

I saak's warning proved correct: Lilly should have drunk more before the fast. She felt the pulsing of an impending headache while the chazzan led the *Musaf* prayer. Gisela, standing to Lilly's right, hummed along to the traditional melodies. On Lilly's left, Hannah swayed gently, her face hidden within the pages of her *machzor*, the special prayer book for the high holidays. Lilly herself struggled to concentrate, however. No matter how hard she tried, her attention kept shifting to the passing view.

At sunrise that morning, they had reached the entrance to the Dardanelles, a narrow strait connecting the Sea of Marmara to the Aegean Sea. Little towns and villages nestled along the coast, their sugar cube white houses topped with red-tiled roofs. Amid the tranquil backdrop, reminders of the Turkish military presence were ever-present, with older fortifications from the Great War standing alongside more recent additions. Meanwhile, the usually bustling shipping channel was eerily quiet; only a few other vessels passed them by. The tentacles of war were spreading.

Before the Atlantic left Istanbul, the passengers learned from the Jewish community representatives that Romania had fallen into the hands of the Nazis. German troops had crossed into the country on the 8th of October, the day after their ship ran aground in Tulcea. Their ships had left just in time.

Lilly glanced over at Isaak who was standing with the rest of the men and praying with fervour. She suspected that uppermost in his mind was the fate of his family, still trapped in Romania. Standing next to him, Alexander shifted restlessly from one foot to the other. The expanding war was one worry, their precarious situation on board, another.

It wasn't until they had left Istanbul the night before that Alexander learned from Dov what Captain Spiro had done. Afterwards he stormed back to the chevra.

'The crew are a bunch of crooks!' he ranted. 'The main reason, the only reason, for our twenty-four-hour stay in Istanbul was to reload essential supplies.' He held up three fingers and tapped them in turn. 'Food, water, and coal. The organisers knew they'd have to restock along the way, and they even budgeted for that from the extortionate fares we all paid. But once in Istanbul, the captain refused to load anything until we paid even more money.'

'What did the Transport Committee say?' Janka asked.

'As you can imagine, they were furious. But what choice did they have? If we don't have food and water, we won't survive the trip. And without coal, we can't sail much further. So the committee had to hand over the extra payment. The crew did buy food and water with the additional money, but then Spiro decided that the coal was too expensive. So we left the port without loading any fuel.' Alexander glared at the bridge where Spiro loitered. 'He also confiscated the cognac and cigarettes that the Istanbul Jewish community donated to us as a gift. The crew is storing them in their canteen – to sell back to us! Can you believe it? Spiro says he needs additional funds to pay for the fuel. Additional funds? The Transport already paid him extra.' Alexander glanced up at Spiro once more and muttered an expletive under his breath.

Isaak's jaw dropped in disbelief. 'We're being held hostage by a gang of pirates.'

'What on earth was Storfer thinking when he handed us over to this crew?' Janka said.

'Probably happy to be rid of us and pass the problem over to someone else,' Alexander said.

'We need to watch the crew at all times,' Isaak said. 'I'm not sure what their intentions are, but I think they are up to no good.'

'But what will they do about the coal shortage?' Erika asked.

What indeed? Lilly wondered as she pressed her hands on her throbbing forehead. She left the prayer gathering to join Janka and Erika in the lifeboat. Janka was sprawled out on the back bench, engrossed in a book. She had recently teamed up with a group of fellow bibliophiles on board; they pooled their books to create a lending library. Erika was curled up asleep after a night shift at the infirmary. Earlier that morning, another passenger had succumbed to the bench of the dead.

Lilly drew up her knees and rested her head on them.

'What's wrong?'

Lilly glanced up as Alexander climbed into the lifeboat and took a seat opposite. 'My head hurts.'

'You should drink something,' he said.

'I can't. I'm fasting.'

'This year, I'm also fasting. So, you can drink and I'll fast in your place.'

'I don't think it quite works like that.' Amused by his logic and touched by his thoughtfulness, Lilly managed a slight smile. 'But thank you for offering.' She released a sigh. 'I also can't stop worrying about our coal situation.'

'I know,' he said. His brow furrowed in solidarity. 'I think it's weighing on all of us.'

The tension was palpable on deck. Some passengers were praying with fervour, others huddled in groups, talking among themselves in hushed tones. Three members of Alexander's Prague group stood together beside the lifeboat, all looking drained, the hope nearly gone from their eyes. One lit a cigarette with jittery fingers and took a desperate drag.

'But in the meantime, we're still moving,' Alexander observed.

Lilly hacked and coughed as the smoke drifted in her direction, irritating her dry throat.

'What's wrong?' he said.

'S-smoke,' she wheezed.

Alexander immediately swung himself onto the deck to confront the smoker. 'What do you think you're doing, lighting up a cigarette?' he snapped. 'It's Yom Kippur.'

'Who made you the rabbi?' The smoker glared at him. 'It's my choice. I'll do what I like and I'm not keeping Yom Kippur.'

'You can do or not do as you please, but it wouldn't hurt to have a little respect for others.'

'Likewise. Don't tell me what to do.'

'Can't you abstain for a single day?' He cast a glance at Lilly. 'Your smoking is bothering others who are fasting.'

He responded with a dismissive shrug. 'Then that's their problem.'

'In case you haven't noticed, we are all in this ship together, fleeing the antisemites from all our various countries just because we're Jewish. Is there no room for tolerance? Do we have to hate each other on this ship too?'

The cigarette dangled from the smoker's fingers, and he fell silent.

'If you don't want to keep Yom Kippur, that's your choice, but, at the very least, have some respect for those who are observing the traditions.'

'You're right.' With care, he stubbed out his cigarette. 'I'm sorry. I just needed to calm my nerves.'

'I understand. We're all worried about the situation. But if we're going to get through this journey, we have to be united.' Alexander extended his hand, and his friend shook it.

'We'll make it.' Alexander placed his other hand on top. 'Don't give up hope.'

Alexander returned to the boat. 'Apologies for that,' he said.

'Do you really believe we will be all right?' Lilly said.

'I do.' His sincere expression remained steady and unwavering. 'We're not out of coal yet. I was speaking to Dov earlier and he says we'll stop for coal at one of the Greek Islands. Being Greek, perhaps that is Spiro's preference.'

'Do you trust the captain?'

'No. Isaak is right. We should keep a careful watch on him. But we still have a small amount in reserves,' Alexander continued. 'And I'm sure ... Haganah will ... the Transport Committee.' His voice faded away as Lilly fought to keep her eyes open.

'Sorry,' Lilly said. 'What was that?'

'Sleep,' he said with a patient smile. 'You'll feel better afterwards. We can talk more later.'

When Lilly next opened her eyes, it was with a sense of disorientation. Someone had thoughtfully draped a blanket over her, but she was all alone in the lifeboat. And something felt different. She realised she was missing the familiar rocking movement of the ship. They were no longer moving.

Lilly flung off the blanket and stood from the bench. The chevra were gathered by the railings. She hurried over to stand beside them. The ship had docked beside a small port. Further ahead she sighted an old Ottoman fortress. Then she noticed Turkish police officers on the quayside preparing to board their ship.

'What's wrong?' Lilly said, panic seeping into her voice. 'Why have we stopped?'

Alexander quickly turned to her with a reassuring smile. 'Nothing to worry about. 'We've only made a quick stop in Çanakkale for the authorities to check that our transit visas are in order. We'll soon be leaving Turkey and entering Greek maritime territory. Another step closer.'

'That's a relief.'

Hannah shifted along to make some room for Lilly. 'How are you feeling?'

'A lot better. My headache is almost gone. Was I asleep for long?'

'Not that long. Maybe an hour.'

'How are you fasting?'

'Not too bad. But what a strange Yom Kippur it is.'

'Isn't it peculiar?' Isaak said. 'Here we are sailing on a ship and later this afternoon at *Mincha* we read about Jonah and the whale.'

Janka playfully rolled her eyes. 'Let's hope we don't replicate the story and find ourselves swallowed by a whale,' Janka said.

As if on cue, all six of them leaned over the railings and peered down into the depths of the Dardanelles. The gentle water was clear enough to spot small fish swimming below the surface.

Isaak chuckled. 'We may have many problems, but I doubt a giant whale is one of them.'

With the police inspection complete, the ship continued its journey and sailed into the Aegean Sea. The light was clear, and the water a vivid turquoise as the ship passed several tiny uninhabited islands. Lilly tuned out the habitual rants and heated debates that had resumed on deck. Instead, she lost herself in the beauty before her until the afternoon light faded and prayers resumed.

As the chazzan read the Book of Jonah, the wind whipped up and the ship's rocking became more pronounced. The parallels between their own precarious voyage and Jonah's tale were not lost on Lilly. The Bible's account also started with a storm at sea, which didn't calm until the sailors cast Jonah overboard. Isaak caught Lilly's eye. He tilted his head in the sea's direction and mouthed, 'No whales.'

The ship's movement was not wholly predictable, and it was not long before Gisela lost her balance and dropped her *machzor*. Lilly held onto the older woman to prevent her from falling and noticed that Gisela had turned quite pale.

'Maybe I should take you back to the cabin?' Lilly said.

'It might be better,' Gisela said. 'I would like to stay to the end but I am rather dizzy. I'm finding it difficult to follow along.'

Lilly and Hannah helped Gisela down the steps and along the passageway, supporting her on either side. They paused several times to lean against the wall for balance. 'We look like we are drunk.' Gisela gave a smile, despite the diminishing colour in her cheeks. Then she added quickly, 'Not that I ever drink.'

Inside the cabin, Alma and Jenny were also suffering from the turbulence. Both held their paper bags at their mouths; Jenny was filling hers.

Lilly and Hannah eased Gisela into her bunk. 'Ah! That's better.'

'Are you still fasting?' Lilly whispered. 'Maybe you should eat something?'

'No, I'm not fasting. I spoke to the rabbi before Yom Kippur. I've forgotten his name. You know, the young friendly one with a dark beard who wears a long black coat. He said that under the circumstances, it wasn't advisable for me to fast.'

'I'm so glad he gave you good advice.' Lilly handed Gisela a paper bag. 'Just in case.'

'Is there anything else we can do for you?' Hannah said.

'Thank you my darlings, but I'm fine for now, just a little tired. I'm going to try and take a short nap.'

Lilly shut the door to the cabin and lurched forward as the ship jolted to the left. She held onto the door handle to steady herself.

'It's getting worse,' Hannah said.

Lilly and Hannah staggered down the passageway to make their way back to the upper deck.

'Doesn't this remind you of the *Hochschaubahn* that time on my birthday?' Lilly asked, calling to mind the wild, high-speed roller coaster ride they had taken together in Vienna's Prater park when she had turned thirteen.

'Yes, and as I recall we both screamed throughout and were sick as soon the ride was over.' Hannah laughed.

When they reached the upper deck, the sun was setting on the horizon, and the chazzan had begun *Neila*, the service that concluded Yom Kippur. The ship bounced in the waves and Lilly fought to stay upright. Several passengers rushed to lean over the side. Their frequent groans and retching disturbed the prayers and made Lilly feel increasingly queasy.

Captain Spiro appeared on the bridge and handed the megaphone to a Haganah member. 'Move to starboard!' he ordered

The passengers stumbled across the deck, colliding in the fading light, while the tenacious chazzan kept leading the prayers.

'Portside.'

'*Ovinu malkenu* ....' The chazzan competed with the crashing waves, the howling wind and moans of the seasick passengers. 'Our Father, our King, remember your compassion and suppress your anger, end all pestilence and war, famine and plundering, destruction and iniquity, bloodshed and plague, affliction and disease, offence and strive, all types of calamities, every evil decree and groundless hatred ...'

'Starboard.'

'*Shema Yisroel* ....' intoned the chazzan.

'Hear o Israel, the Lord is our God, the Lord is One,' the passengers shouted in response.

'Next year in Jerusalem!' Alexander said, invoking the traditional conclusion of the *Neila* service.

'Amen to that,' Lilly said. A moment later, she leaned over the railing and heaved.

At the unexpected sound of a man crying pitifully she glanced up to find a white-haired elderly gentleman, his shoulders shaking in distress.

'Sir,' Isaak addressed him. 'What's the matter?'

'My teeth! I've lost my teeth.' The man stared into the blackness where he had vomited.

'There, there!' Alexander patted the man's shoulder. 'In a few days we'll reach Eretz and you can get another pair.'

'How will I eat in the meantime?'

'It's going to be all right,' Isaak said. 'We still have some of the soft bread from Istanbul.'

Janka raised an eyebrow, but said nothing. Lilly wondered too: what would happen if they ran out of bread and had to again resort to eating sea biscuits?

Hannah trained her eyes into the distance. 'Oh, thank God for that!'

'You found the teeth?' There was a touch of surprise and anticipation in Isaak's voice.

'Not the teeth, unfortunately,' Hannah said, 'But I think we've found shelter from the storm. Look over there.'

A dot shimmered in the distance. It grew larger and larger until they could discern a cluster of lights.

Land.

# CHAPTER 28

The morning view took Lilly's breath away as she gazed out from the ship docked at Mytilene on the Greek island of Lesbos. A blue sky, scattered with small, fluffy clouds, hung above the aquamarine sea, which rippled like soft silk. Sailors in crisp, white uniforms and families in their Sunday best strolled around the promenade lined with quaint shops and tavernas. Children chased each other, playing near the small fishing boats tied up at the dock. Even from the ship, the passengers could make out the rhythmic beat of drums and the blaring brass instruments that indicated the arrival of a military band, marching along the promenade. Lilly could almost feel as if she were on a holiday, but the island was out of reach. She could only look on as a spectator.

After sipping the last of her breakfast tea, Lilly indulged in a rare shower – with a pail of sea water – taking care to shield herself from view. She no longer hesitated to use the crude washing facilities, now grateful for the relative luxury. A few minutes later, she was dressed in her blue cotton dress. The fabric, once navy, had faded to a greyish blue from the effects of salt water and sun.

Then Hannah took her turn in the so-called shower, while Lilly and Janka caught up on their laundry, glad for the mild weather. Lilly had discovered that washing clothes at sea was far more challenging than it had been on the river: she found she couldn't coax a lather from the soap in the salty water.

Even learning how to draw water from the sea had proved difficult at first, though she eventually mastered the technique. Lilly recalled how she had lowered her bucket into the water, only for it to bob on the surface until she drew it up empty. It was the same for Hannah and Janka, despite their best efforts.

'Girls, why aren't you able to draw water?' asked Emil, Pencil Man, who had been observing their efforts. 'It's simple enough to do.' He set aside his pencil and notebook and fetched his own bucket. 'Allow me to teach you.'

'That's quite all right,' Lilly said. 'You don't have to trouble yourself. We'll figure it out.' Ignoring Lilly, Emil manoeuvred his way between them to stand at the railings. 'Watch me and learn.'

Emil made a grand show of tying a rope to the handle with an elaborate knot.

'After you tie a nautical knot, lift the bucket with both hands. Then you take aim and throw it like this.'

Emil's demonstration had attracted a crowd of onlookers. They watched as Emil lobbed his bucket in an arc towards the sea. It soared through the air, hit the water, and disappeared below the surface. He addressed his audience, wearing a smug grin. 'And now you draw your filled bucket of water.' With theatrical flourish, he started hoisting the rope.

'See how easy it is? A child could do it.'

Lilly stared at the end of his rope, and covered her mouth to stifle her exclamation. The bucket was gone.

Janka let out a snort – which freed the frozen spectators, and sparked a chain reaction of laughter.

Red-faced, Emil glared at the frayed end. 'Faulty rope,' he muttered, moving away from them.

Now, days later, Lilly laughed at the memory.

'What's so funny?' Janka said.

'Emil and the bucket.' Lilly didn't have to say more.

Janka chuckled as she soaked her blouse in the bowl. 'It makes me laugh every time I think about that. He's so embarrassed he won't look at me when our paths cross.'

'I suppose it's good you gave up on the idea of him as a boyfriend.'

'Indeed.' Janka gave a mock sigh, her lips curling into a mischievous smile. 'I still need alternate plans for my future.'

'Speaking of which, have you spoken to your brother?'

Janka's face clouded over with worry. 'Not yet.'

'Don't you think you ought to tell him? If they load the coal today, we probably only have three or four more days left at sea.'

'Yes, you're right. I just haven't found the opportunity.'

Lilly inclined her head towards Alexander, who, not far from them, was leaning against the railings watching the activity on Mytilene's promenade. 'What about now?'

Janka focused her attention on her blouse, and scrubbed vigorously. 'I'm busy with the laundry right now.'

'I think you're nervous to raise it with him.'

Janka let her blouse sink into the water. 'Yes. I suppose I am.'

'Speak to him. You'll feel better for it.'

'Perhaps. Perhaps not.' Janka got to her feet, and wiped her wet hands on the back of her skirt. '*Jawohl*, let's do this.'

Alexander smiled at his sister's approach, but as she started talking, his expression became more serious. He nodded at intervals, listening intently, allowing her to explain herself without interrupting.

Lilly wrung out her clothes, every so often casting discreet glances in her friends' direction. Janka's shoulders had drooped. She looked up at her brother as he responded, and she appeared to be on the verge of tears. He spoke at length and didn't look angry in the slightest. As Lilly hung her clothes to dry, she peeked at her friends from between them. Janka was speaking once more. Her face and posture had relaxed. Alexander extended his arms to Janka, and the siblings hugged.

Lilly found the scene heartwarming, and it made her think about her own brother. In just another few days, she would see Eugen again. It had been so long. After all that had happened to her in the past two years, and the different path he had taken, she wondered what their reunion would be like. Would they be as close they once were, or had time and distance weakened their bond?

'You were right,' Janka interrupted Lilly's musings. She was standing on the other side of the hanging laundry. 'I told Alexander everything – all of my doubts and concerns.'

'And?' Lilly smiled.

'He listened and he was understanding. Alexander said he never realised that my main reason for joining the group was because of him. He always assumed that I shared his views. All of them.'

'Was he upset when you told him you didn't?'

'I expected he would be. But no. He said that the most important thing is that I am here with him, safely away from Europe. For Alexander, living on a kibbutz is a dream and he would love for me to join him there, but not if it makes me unhappy. He suggested I give it a trial to see how it is. And I'm willing to do that. Alexander promised that if I'm not happy, he won't pressure me to stay. He just wants us to keep in close contact and see each other often.'

'That sounds like the perfect agreement. Aren't you glad you spoke to him?'

'Very.' Lilly watched the relief change Janka's face. 'Thank you for your encouragement. You seem to read Alexander better than I do, even though I'm his sister.'

'Maybe it's easier because I'm *not* his sister. I can be more objective.'

Janka nodded, her expression turning thoughtful. 'I hope I'm not letting you or Hannah down after I asked to come and live with you.'

'Not at all. It's a good idea to start off near Alexander and to try kibbutz life. If it isn't for you, you can always move in with us later.'

'Thanks for understanding, Lilly,' Janka said. 'We'll stay in touch, though, won't we? You've become such a good friend, I wouldn't want to lose you.'

'You're not going to lose me. I'll even come to visit you on the kibbutz.'

'You will?' Alexander's voice piped up as he walked towards them. 'We may make a kibbutznik of you yet.'

Lilly laughed. 'I'm not sure about that.'

'You don't know until you try it.' He winked at her playfully before turning to Janka. 'Are you done with the washing bowl?'

'I'll just rinse out my blouse. Then it's all yours.'

Janka returned to the spot on deck where she had left her washing, but Alexander lingered. 'Janka mentioned you encouraged her to talk to me,' he said to Lilly. 'I appreciate it.' He touched her shoulder. 'I didn't realise she had been feeling such stress, and I'm happy we cleared the air.'

'Alexander!' Dov interrupted, hurrying across the deck. 'We need a few volunteers.'

'We do? What for?'

'We must leave port by five and need to get the reserve coal out of the bunkers in order to sail.'

'Sorry? I don't understand.' Alexander stiffened. Didn't we stop here to load additional coal?'

'We did.'

'Then why are we leaving without it?'

'Ask Spiro.' Dov's shoulders rose and fell in a gesture of annoyance. 'I don't speak Greek and have no clue what he said to the port officials. He has only given us vague excuses. We can't make out whether there is no coal to buy or if it's too expensive. As it is, he requested additional money from the Passenger Committee for port fees, which he claims he laid out from his own funds.'

'Don't tell me they paid him?'

Dov threw up his hands. 'What choice did they have? They had to sell some of the cigarette stocks belonging to the transport to help raise the complete amount.'

Alexander's face darkened. 'What is that pirate Spiro playing at? What a swindler.'

'Tell me something I don't know. Unfortunately, we need him to sail the ship.'

'Since he's extorted yet more money, why is he making us fetch the coal reserves ourselves? Isn't that the crew's job?'

'Ask Spiro.'

'Will our reserves be enough to get us to Haifa?'

'Unlikely.'

'Then where will we get more coal from?'

Dov shook his head. He didn't need to say anything more.

# CHAPTER 29

Another day. Another island.

This time, Samos showed off its picturesque landscapes. Fishing boats moored in the port, colourful waterfront shops and tavernas, the recognisable whitewashed houses clustered around the bay, vineyards on the rolling hillsides, and mountainous slopes rising beyond. But beautiful views were of little comfort when they could not purchase the vital resources they needed. They had rationed their drinking water, food was short, and they were running low on coal.

Later that same afternoon, the Atlantic raised anchor.

'Well, that was pointless.' Alexander's disappointment showed on his face as he slouched by the railings. 'More time lost, more precious fuel wasted and nothing to show for it.'

On the quayside, a crowd of locals had gathered to watch the decrepit ship sail away from the harbour with its cargo of desperate refugees.

'They look at us like we're like animals in a zoo,' Janka said.

What did these people see, Lilly wondered? The shopkeepers, weather-beaten fishermen, mothers and their children, the young couples, and black-clad widows, who stared at the people crammed on deck in worn clothes, gaunt with hunger. After the ship had departed and they returned to their homes, to eat at their supper tables, and to sleep in their clean beds, would the islanders give any further thought to the Atlantic passengers? Did they realise that these wretched refugees once also had good lives, homes, jobs, wore presentable clothes, sat down to proper family meals and slept in comfortable beds? They had been ordinary citizens who visited coffeehouses, theatres, and parks, free to walk the streets of their cities unhindered. They had never imagined that their ordinary lives would be so thoroughly upended.

'I wonder what they think of us,' Lilly said, voicing her thoughts.

'Not much,' Alexander said. 'Or else they would have sold us coal and food.'

'I don't think it's their fault,' Isaak said. 'Shifty Spiro is the one to blame with his list of lame excuses.'

Alexander agreed with a sad nod. 'Quick to pocket our money, but slow to help us.'

'It would seem we're being blessed,' Janka said. She pointed to a man in a white collar and black Catholic clerical attire who stood at the head of the gathering and appeared to be reciting prayers over the ship. 'Is that a good or bad sign?'

'I can't decide,' Isaak said. Does he know something we don't?'

'I pray he's praying we get more coal soon,' Alexander said. 'Our reserves won't last much longer.'

Samos soon faded from view. Steely clouds smudged the sky and veiled the sun. The ship rocked in the choppy waves. As Lilly joined the supper queue, the wind intensified. It whipped up her hair and rattled the tarpaulin stretched over the deck that served as a sunshade.

Upon Lilly's return to the lifeboat, she wrapped herself in her cardigan and dipped her spoon into her supper: a dollop of stodgy rice barely flavoured with cinnamon. Lilly ate slowly, to make it last longer, and tried to imagine it was the manna from heaven eaten by her ancient Israelite ancestors when they wandered through the desert. Then she caught a delicious whiff of roast chicken. Captain Spiro was obviously eating better than they were tonight.

'Do you think the captain is making any serious effort to buy food and coal?' Isaak said, scraping his bowl clean. 'And if not, why is he taking us on a tour of the islands?'

'I can't make it out,' Alexander said. 'He seems cagey and jumpy.'

'I wonder where we'll land next,' said Lilly.

Alexander shrugged. 'Spiro knows. Provided there's coal, I'm past caring.'

'Could it be to do with the war?' Isaak asked. 'We haven't passed a single ship since we entered the Aegean Sea.'

'This far away? We've seen no sight of any Nazi military. I suspect he's getting nervous about landing us in Haifa. Technically, we're illegal immigrants. I suppose he's risking arrest by captaining a shipful of us,' Alexander said.

A shrill wind whistled in Lilly's ears. The clouds had coalesced and covered the sky in hues of slate, soot, and melancholy. A fiery red slash brightened the horizon as the sun set. Waves crashed against the ship's hull, and raindrops stained the deck.

No one referred to the gathering storm, however. Maybe, if they were stoic, they wouldn't tempt fate.

Captain Spiro appeared on the bridge, a drumstick in his hand. He passed the megaphone to a Haganah member and kept eating. 'Everyone move starboard!'

Swept along in the crowd, Hannah's hand reached for Lilly, who clasped it tight.

The ship rose on the crest of a wave, as if taking flight, throwing them off balance. Then it dived downwards. The crash of the waves muffled their shrieks.

'To port,' the megaphone crackled.

Passengers groaned. Several retched and expelled their supper. Lilly shut her eyes as the ship scaled a towering swell, and rocked precariously before hurtling forward.

'Starboard!'

A throng of passengers streamed down the steps to shelter in the already crowded catacombs. Lilly and the chevra clustered together with everyone else on the right side of the ship.

This storm wasn't like the others. They were not just drenched and the ship was not just rocking. The crew was fighting with all they had to keep the Atlantic upright. The swollen sea tossed them about every which way. In the vast expanse of the sea, they felt as insignificant as driftwood.

'Will we even get through this?' Lilly couldn't disguise her fear.

In the twilight, Isaak reassured Lilly with a faint smile. 'This storm too will pass.' Shouting to make himself heard over the waves, he recited the Traveller's Prayer, 'Lead us towards peace, and guide our footsteps towards peace, and make us reach our desired destination for life, gladness, and peace.'

'Port!'

The wind tore through the tarpaulin, ripping away a section that took flight like a kite. The remaining shreds flapped furiously.

'Starboard!'

Waves pounded against the hull, spraying the passengers who waded across the foam-filled deck. A flash of lightning split the night sky. For an instant, it was as bright as day. The roar of the waves made it hard to hear the accompanying thunder. The Atlantic swayed violently.

Erika tapped Lilly's arm. 'I need to check ... Alma, Gisela, also ...' The rest of her words disappeared into the tempest, carried away by the howling winds.

'Wait!' Lilly yelled. 'I'll come with you.' But Erika's attention was on the slippery path, and she was unaware of Lilly following behind.

'Port!'

The passengers surged to the other side, trapping Lilly, and separating her from the chevra. She fought to free herself from the crush and catch up with Erika. With an upward jolt, the ship tilted sharply, causing most of the passengers to lose their balance on the slick surface. People collided. A flailing arm rammed into Lilly's stomach and knocked the wind out of her. She doubled over and clutched her abdomen.

Then the ship plummeted. She fell headlong. A mighty wave swept over the railings and suddenly Lilly could feel nothing solid beneath her, only water, as she was dragged by the wave. She was disoriented, unable to determine up from down, not sure she was still aboard the ship. Struggling to hold her breath, she flung her hands in search of something to grab onto. She realised she was sinking, not from grief or despair, but drowning. In that moment, Lilly's desire to live surpassed all else.

'Lilly!'

She thought she heard someone calling her name.

Lilly wrestled against the water.

*I want to live!*

She felt a firm surface beneath her, exerted all her strength, pushed her hands against it, and raised her head.

A hand took hold of hers and helped her to her feet. Lilly gasped for breath, coughing and spluttering.

'I've got you,' Isaak said. 'Don't worry.'

A lightning flash lit up the deck, and Isaak gripped her shoulders to keep her from falling as another wave hit.

'I don't want to die,' Lilly said.

'You won't. You're safe now.'

'Lilly, are you all right?' Hannah said, an urgency in her voice

Lilly swayed on her feet.

'I think she's hurt.' Alexander raised his voice to be heard.

'Where's Erika?' Janka said.

'Gisela ... Alma ...' Lilly's words came out slurred.

The ground disappeared from beneath Lilly once more, but this time firm hands supported her.

'Have you got her?' said a male voice.

'Steady, now.'

She could no longer differentiate the voices, but their presence comforted her. They carried her in their arms, down the steps, along the passageway, straining to keep their balance with every rock and sway of the ship. An arduous journey that seemed without end. The minutes felt like hours. Then everything faded to black.

# CHAPTER 30

Lilly found herself lying in a bed, covered by the comforting weight of a blanket. In the faint glow of a flickering kerosene lamp, through half-closed eyes, she made out someone sitting beside her. 'Erika?'

'I'm right here.' Erika stroked her hand, offering reassurance. 'Do you remember what happened?'

'I was ... under ... the water.' The effort to speak was exhausting.

'Rest.' Erika soothed.

Before Lilly's fatigue took over, she heard Erika say: 'It's not as bad as it looks.' But in her drowsiness, she couldn't tell if Erika's words were meant for her.

The grey light of early morning was visible through the small porthole when Lilly opened her eyes again. The tiny, crowded cabin came into focus. Two women and their sleeping children carpeted the floor. Across a narrow aisle, Max sat next to Alma, holding her hand as she tried to sleep. Jenny lay in the bunk above. Her hair hung limp, and her face was a sickly green. Stefan stood beside her, holding a paper bag and rubbing her back. The ship still roiled and creaked, but the storm had lost some of its ferocity.

Lilly brought a hand to her head to find a bandage wrapped around it.

'How are you feeling, *mein Schatz?*'

Lilly turned to find Gisela sitting at the foot of the bed, and attempted a smile. 'My head hurts, she murmured.

'You cut your forehead when you fell on the deck during the storm. Erika bandaged you up.' Gisela's smile was comforting. 'She says you are going to be fine.'

'I've taken your bunk.' Lilly was abashed.

'Sleep some more.' Gisela ignored her apology and tucked the blanket around her. 'It will do you good.'

Lilly's eyelids grew heavy. 'What about you?' But she didn't stay awake long enough to hear Gisela's reply.

At turns, Lilly thought she saw Hannah's face, followed by Isaak, Alexander, Janka, and Erika. But she didn't recall any conversation, and she couldn't be sure whether her friends were real or figments of her imagination.

When Lilly next awoke, the cabin had emptied, and the ship had stopped rocking. She realised they were no longer moving at all. She sat up in a rush, and caught sight of Hannah perched on the edge of the bed. 'What has happened?'

'It's all right.' Hannah reached out to give Lilly's blanketed legs a calming pat.

'We've stopped at an island called Ios.'

'What time is it?'

'Four o'clock.'

'In the afternoon?' Lilly was startled to realise she'd lost nearly an entire day.

'You slept for a long time. You needed it. How do you feel?'

'A little better, I think.' Lilly touched her head. It still felt tender and sore. 'Where's Gisela?'

'Asleep.' Hannah pointed to the bunk above. 'She stayed by your side for much of the night.'

'Were you there too or was I dreaming?'

'Janka, Isaak and Alexander and I have been taking turns keeping an eye on you.'

There was a light tap on the open door. 'May I come in?' Isaak peeped in and smiled at Lilly. 'I'm glad to see you're awake. Are you feeling better?'

'A little, thanks,' Lilly said. 'Am I allowed to get up?'

'I'll check with Erika,' Hannah said. 'Isaak, can you wait here with Lilly in the meantime?'

After Hannah had left, Lilly said, 'Thank you for what you did for me. I think you saved my life.'

'I didn't do that much.' Isaak replied, giving her a sheepish smile. 'I only helped you to your feet. You were very brave.'

'I don't think I was brave.'

'Believe me, you were.' He paused. 'You're stronger than you realise.'

'I was terrified. I thought the wave had swept me off the ship.'

'For a moment there ...' Isaak looked into the distance, as if he were reliving the experience, until he caught himself. 'Well, we were all afraid we were about to capsize. But, thank God, we didn't. We all survived.'

The two of them sat quietly, hushed by the enormity of what might have been. Hannah's return interrupted the reverie. 'Erika says it's fine for you to move about and get some fresh air. But we should help you at first, in case you're unsteady on your feet.'

'Should we tell Gisela we're leaving?' Lilly said.

Hannah considered for a moment. 'Let her sleep. I'll come back later to let her know how you're getting on.'

Lilly needed Hannah's arm to steady herself as she rose from the bed. It was only when she was standing that she noticed her clothes: she was clad in a voluminous brown dress she didn't recognise. 'Where did these clothes come from?'

'The woman who sleeps in the bed above Gisela. All your clothes were soaked, so she offered something dry for you to wear.'

Hannah and Isaak supported Lilly under each arm and she took some tentative steps.

'How are you doing?'

'A little light-headed.'

'That could be dehydration,' Isaak said.

When they reached the upper deck, Lilly blinked at the brightness. The Atlantic had dropped anchor a short distance from the shore. A ridge of low mountains hugged the curved bay and the typical brilliant white houses that looked like sugar cubes gleamed in the sun. The deep blue sky showed no evidence of the brutal storm that had raged hours before.

'When did we arrive?' Lilly asked.

'About an hour ago,' Isaak said.

Alexander was seated in the lifeboat, repairing a shirt that had torn during the storm. He glanced up when Lilly arrived with Isaak and Hannah and swiftly climbed out to meet them.

He placed a hand to his heart. 'It's good to see you up and about. You had me—' he hesitated, glancing around at the others. 'Us – rather worried.

'I want to fetch Lilly a drink,' Isaak said. 'Would you mind taking over for me?'

'With pleasure.' Alexander took his cousin's place. When they reached the lifeboat, he scooped Lilly up and carried her over the side of the lifeboat, where he gently helped her to a seat on the back bench. Her half-emptied backpack rested on the lifeboat's flat ridge along with five others. Janka was arranging three water-logged books so they would dry.

'All our belongings are soaked. I hope you don't mind that I hung your clothes out to dry,' Janka said.

Two of her dresses, a blanket and several pieces of underwear
fluttered on the line. 'Thank you so much,' Lilly said.

Isaak returned with a cup of tea and a rock-hard biscuit. 'I'm sorry
I have nothing else to offer you.'

She gave him an appreciative smile.

'Do you think we'll load more provisions here?' Lilly asked, di-
recting her question to everyone in the lifeboat.

'We had better,' Alexander said. 'We can't continue on our Greek
Island tour for much longer. Drinking water is now being rationed
and allocated to passengers most at risk. We're almost out of food
and burning through our last reserves of coal.'

'How long will we be at ... Ios?' She looked to Hannah for confirmation.

Alexander threw up his hands. 'Only Spiro knows!'

Even Isaak looked glum when their ship departed after nightfall.
'What was the point of that?'

Alexander, sitting beside him in the lifeboat, sighed in frustration.
'According to Dov, who heard it from someone in the Transport
Committee, Spiro claims he is worried about sailing through this
area during the daytime because the Italians are Fascist allies and we
are travelling through the Italian-held Dodecanese Islands. Apparently, that's why he sails after dark and docks during the day.'

'Do you believe him?' Lilly asked.

Alexander stared at the illuminated Panamanian flag, fluttering
from the mast. 'I don't know what to believe anymore.'

'So my hunch that his odd behaviour was because of the war was
correct,' Isaak said. 'Though I still believe he's behaving suspiciously.
Even if he thinks it's safer to sail at night, there's no reason he

couldn't have loaded provisions by day. It's very strange that not one of the three islands we've docked at has had coal, food or even fresh water for purchase.'

'I wonder if he means to starve us and then dump us on one of those islands,' Janka said. 'It's impossible to cook the remaining food we have left because the continual storms keep putting out the kitchen fires. We're reduced to eating those teeth-breaking, mouldy ship biscuits.'

Isaak wrapped his lips over his teeth. 'At this rate, we will all arrive in Eretz looking like this.' Lilly laughed with the others at Isaak's toothless impression. Then, she remembered the elderly man who had lost his teeth, and felt a measure of remorse. She hadn't seen him since and wondered how he was coping.

The ship rocked and swayed. 'Not again!' Alexander moaned.

'Perhaps we should take Lilly downstairs where it's safer,' Isaak said.

'I'd prefer to stay up here with you,' Lilly said.

'Isaak's right,' Hannah said. 'The waves are soaring again.'

'But if Gisela sees me, she'll give me her bed, and I can't let her do that,' Lilly said. 'She's exhausted.'

'So we'll go down to the catacombs,' Isaak said.

Lilly made a face. 'Must we?'

'Everyone to starboard!' came the order over the megaphone.

'It would appear we must,' Alexander said, getting to his feet. 'We'll keep you company.'

Alexander held her steady on one side, Isaak on the other, Hannah positioned herself in front and Janka behind to prevent anyone colliding with Lilly. In this formation, they made their descent into the gloom of the hold.

The five of them crouched on the gravelled floor near the steps. Lilly alternately gasped for air and placed her hand over her mouth, trying not to retch. 'This is like being trapped in the mouth of someone who hasn't cleaned his teeth for a month,' she said.

'After he'd been chewing on an old sock,' Isaak added.

'How could anyone bear to sleep down here for all these weeks?' Hannah said.

'What choice do they have?' Alexander said. 'There's not enough room on the ship. We're just damned lucky for our lifeboat and that tiny space beside it. Aside from the cabins, we have the most luxurious quarters on board.'

'Until our clothes and books get soaked,' Janka said. 'I just finished drying everything this afternoon. Now everything is getting sodden all over again.'

The restless ship thrashed and creaked in the churning storm. The perpetual motion, along with the catacomb's overpowering stench of vomit and body odour, had Lilly, Hannah, and Janka reaching for paper bags. Another hour and even Alexander and Isaak's spirits were flagging. They too reluctantly asked for paper bags.

'Maybe we could try the passageway outside the cabins?' Lilly said.

'We'll have even less space there than here,' Alexander said. 'Last night, the four of us took turns sitting and standing. And people constantly push past.'

'At least there's more air circulation,' Hannah said

'And we won't get any sleep down here either,' Isaak said.

'I'd prefer to stand all night in the passageway rather than crouch in here a moment longer,' Janka said.

Isaak nodded. 'The storm is weakening. Hopefully, we won't need to remain there for too long.'

The rocking had not stopped, but it had subsided, allowing them to carefully negotiate their way back up the stairs. They moved slowly and steadily as a group until a jarring, scraping noise reverberated through the ship, making them freeze in their tracks. It wasn't the regular creak of wooden joints, but more like a grinding sound against the ship's hull. The vessel juddered.

'What was that?' Hannah asked, alarmed.

Alexander looked annoyed. 'Whatever it was, it wasn't good.'

They hastened to the upper deck, Hannah holding Lilly close to support her and, Lilly suspected, to calm her own nerves. The crowd there was frenzied, some shouting, some running to and fro across the deck. On the bridge, the captain and crew were buckling themselves into life jackets.

Alexander spotted his chain-smoking friend from the Prague group.

'What happened?' Alexander asked him.

The smoker's deep drag looked hard won this time, his hands shaking so badly he could hardly hold onto the cigarette. 'They think a German submarine just tried to ram us.'

A crew member carried a stack of the halved life jackets up to the deck. Unsurprisingly, a crowd of passengers flocked to him from all directions. 'Who can't swim?' He raised his voice above the chaos: 'Please raise your hand.'

Hannah's hand immediately shot up. 'M-m-me!' she stuttered in a state of panic. 'I can't swim!'

# CHAPTER 31

Lilly watched the fiery orb of molten gold rise on the horizon and cast a shimmering reflection on the water as their ship neared Heraklion port in northern Crete. Nestled around the bay were traditional old stone buildings juxtaposed with newer high-rises of concrete. In the distance, Mount Ida rose towards the dusky pink sky, towering over low-lying mountains tinged with blue.

Gulls called to one another as they swooped and soared above the harbour, its array of small fishing boats and larger vessels coming to life in the early morning light. The Atlantic, however, was not permitted to enter the harbour because of the health conditions on board; instead, it dropped anchor behind a pier with direct sightlines to the docks.

Standing by the railings, Lilly exchanged smiles of relief with Alexander, Isaak, and Janka. Hannah couldn't smile. Silent and white-faced, she continued to clutch her life jacket.

'You can let go of it now,' Lilly said.

Hannah didn't respond. Ever since she had heard Captain Spiro's wild theory of an attacking German submarine, she hadn't said a word.

It turned out to be a false alarm. The captain had left it to the Haganah to calm the terrified passengers and the men of the Haganah reassured the crowd that German submarines were unlikely to be in that area. The ship had probably scraped its hull against a reef.

Lilly prised the life jacket from Hannah's grip. 'You don't need it anymore. We're safe.'

'Why did he do that?' Hannah choked back her emotions. 'I thought we were about to die.'

'Spiro is stupid and irresponsible,' Lily said. 'He made a drama out of nothing.'

'During the storm I was afraid we were going to capsize, and then I was afraid that you were seriously hurt. I don't think I could manage if something happened to you.'

Lilly patted the bandage on her head. 'I'm going to be fine.'

'I know,' Hannah wailed. 'But then I was certain our ship was about to go down, and all I could think was how, after all we've been through, I would never see Karl again. I know it sounds silly, when so much is at stake, but there it is.'

'Oh, Hannah. You don't sound silly at all.' Lilly pulled her cousin in for a crushing hug.

'I can't take any more of this.' She sagged against Lilly. 'The thought of seeing Karl again is the one thing that has helped me get through every unbearable moment. But this – I can't swim! I was sure I would drown before we even got the chance to start our lives together.'

Lilly put her hands on her cousin's shoulders and looked her straight in the eye. 'Listen. This is our final stop before Haifa. In just a few more days, you'll be with Karl. Even Spiro confirmed we landed in Crete to load up supplies for the last leg of our journey.'

Hannah held back her sniffles. 'Why did Spiro have to cause such panic?'

'I suppose, in a moment of alarm, he might have truly believed a U-Boat had hit us.' Lilly frowned. 'All the same, it was very irresponsible. He's such an ox.'

Alexander leaned over Lilly's shoulder. 'He's more than that.' Lilly turned her head to look at him. He flashed her a mischievous grin. 'But I won't say it in polite company.'

'Then I'll say it,' Janka said. 'He's an *arschloch!*'

Alexander sucked in a breath. 'Janka! You can't say that.'

She tossed back her head. 'Well, I did and I'll do it again. The captain is an *arschloch.*'

Lilly suppressed a laugh. A faint smile broke through the tension on Hannah's face.

'Now repeat after me,' Janka said, taking Lilly's place in front of Hannah and holding Hannah's hands in her own. 'The captain is ...'

'The captain is,' Hannah said.

'An *arschloch.*'

Hannah coloured and gave an embarrassed giggle.

'Say it.'

Hannah mumbled the word under her breath.

'What was that?' Janka said.

She repeated the word in a low voice, little more than a whisper.

'I still can't hear you. Louder!'

'The captain is ... an ... *arschloch!*'

'Well done!'

Hannah burst into laughter along with the others.

Alexander shook his head in disapproval, a smile on his lips. 'Stop being such a bad influence, Janka.' He turned to Lilly and Hannah. 'Please don't get the wrong impression. Our parents did not bring us up with such foul mouths. They would be appalled to hear my sister talk this way.'

'I can attest to that,' Isaak said. 'My uncle and aunt are respectable people.' He grinned. 'My cousin, however—'

Janka gave him a playful punch, then doled out another to Alexander. 'I didn't learn that word from Mama and Papa. I learnt it from you.'

Alexander winced. 'Then I must apologise for being the bad influence.'

'Don't apologise,' Hannah said. 'That was exactly what I needed.'

The port was waking to a new day. Life in Crete appeared peaceful, untouched. The islanders seemed to carry on with blithe indifference to the war. Were they aware of the turmoil raging in most of Europe?

Fishermen tended to their nets and boats. Vessels entered and exited the harbour. A few rowing boats paddled across to more closely inspect the curious ship that had landed in the early hours. One moustached rower in a peak cap with cigarette dangling from the corner of his mouth spotted the lifeboat chevra leaning at the railings and waved to them. Isaak returned the gesture.

'*Ellinika*?' the man called.

'Sorry, I don't understand,' Isaak said. 'Do you speak German?'

He tried again. '*Tourkikos*?'

Isaak shrugged.

'*Anglika*, speak?'

'English?' Isaak said. 'A little.'

The man held up a plump bunch of red grapes. 'Want buy?'

The group let out a collective groan of hunger.

'I feel like a young child looking through the window of a locked sweet shop,' Janka said.

'If only I had some money left, I'd buy some,' Lilly said. 'Especially for Gisela. She has become so weak from the lack of proper food.'

'Then we'll get some.' Isaak fished into his pocket and waved a cigarette. 'Good. Romanian. Want?'

Transfixed, they watched the bargaining between Isaak and the hawker.

'I have to hand it to him,' Alexander said, shaking his head while a smile played on his lips.

The man sidled his boat alongside the ship and tossed Isaak a basket attached to a length of rope. Isaak placed two cigarettes inside and lowered it back down. The Cretian hawker sniffed the cigarettes with the appreciation of a true connoisseur and packed the basket with three generous bunches of grapes. Using the rope, Isaak hauled it up, removed the grapes, and then returned the basket.

'Thank you!' Isaak said.

'*Efcharisto*,' he said. 'Is thank you.'

'Ef–char–isto,' Isaak repeated.

The man touched his cap in brief salute, then circumnavigated the ship to continue touting his business.

'Breakfast?' Isaak said.

They returned to the lifeboat, their noisy jubilance over their bounty rousing a sleeping Erika. They feasted on the sweet and succulent grapes. Crete tasted delicious.

'I can't express how grateful I am to you for this,' Lilly said to Isaak.

'My absolute pleasure.' His smile was accompanied by a warmth in his eyes that exuded sincere kindness. 'Anything but those hard, tasteless biscuits.' He beckoned her. 'Come, let's surprise Gisela.'

'Can we give some to Alma and Jenny too?'

'But of course.'

Isaak wrapped one bunch in a blanket and handed it to her, the other, he cradled in his arms. Before long, one of Emil's debating acquaintances stopped Isaak and offered to trade. Isaak handed over the bunch and pocketed the two cigarettes the man offered in exchange.

They found Gisela resting on her bunk. Despite the weariness etched in her skin, her eyes lit up with a smile as soon as she saw them.

'We have a surprise for you,' Isaak said.

Lilly unwrapped the grapes to the delighted exclamations of Gisela and her roommates. She and Isaak doled them out in the cabin and to Max and Stefan in the passageway. To Lilly's relief, the grapes revived Gisela.

'A million thanks my darlings. They were delicious,' the older woman said, relishing the juiciness of the final grape.

'It was Lilly's idea,' Isaak said.

'All the credit goes to Isaak,' Lilly said. 'He did the bargaining and bought them.'

Gisela rewarded her with a hug, and Isaak, with a pinch and kiss of his cheek.

'That must be why you bought them,' Lilly teased.

Isaak winked. 'How did you guess?'

Upon returning to the upper deck, Lilly and Isaak found the captain driving away the grape seller, along with other merchants trying to sell their goods to the passengers.

'As expected,' Isaak said. 'God forbid someone other than Spiro should make a profit.'

Despite the captain's interference, their stopover in Crete had started off more promising with no sign of a hasty departure before replenishing their supplies. But by day's end, there were no indications of an imminent delivery either. The Atlantic appeared to be settling in for the night, leaving Lilly ill at ease. Food supplies were running desperately low. Soon, they would have nothing. Not even the rock-like, mould-encrusted biscuits.

Lilly stirred awake to the blue morning sky and the crisp autumn air. Most passengers were asleep, but there was never complete silence on the Atlantic. Low snores, people muttering in their sleep, and intermittent cries from unspoken nightmares. She picked her way between the passengers to reach the railings and gazed at the twinkling lights of the Heraklion harbour as dawn approached.

'Beautiful view, isn't it?'

Lilly turned at the unexpected voice. 'Good morning, Alexander. You're up early. You also couldn't sleep anymore?'

'I've just finished my fire watch shift.' He settled beside her. 'We've stopped in so many places. It's a pity we only get the merest glimpse of them.'

'It would be nice if they allowed us ashore for a quick visit to stretch our legs, breathe the air, and see the sites,' Lilly agreed.

'Can you believe it has been six weeks since we last set foot on dry land?'

Lilly started. 'Unbelievable.'

Alexander looked off into the distance at something only he could see. 'Hopefully, in a few days, we'll walk on the soil of the Promised Land.'

Lilly took a breath. 'I've been thinking ... it might be nice to return and visit some of these places. In the future, sometime.'

'You would actually consider travelling on a ship again after all this?' The corner of his lips lifted.

'Not straight away. When I'm settled in Eretz and the war is over. Just for a holiday.' Lilly turned the idea over in her mind. 'Next time, I'd like to have more spacious accommodation, a private cabin.'

'That sounds far more inviting.'

'With a proper bathroom. And meals served at a table in the dining room.'

He raised an eyebrow. 'Served by waiters in uniform wearing white gloves?'

'Why not?'

'A three course meal,' he said. 'With proper soup and soft bread. A large piece of Wiener schnitzel with crispy roasted potatoes.'

'Don't!' she said. 'I'm already starving.'

His eyes twinkled with mischief.

Lilly took the bait. 'Followed by a dessert trolley. Chocolate mousse, Sachertorte with whipped cream, sugar-dusted apple strudel.'

Alexander clutched his stomach with a pretend groan. 'All right, you win.'

They shared a rare moment of laughter. 'After dinner,' he continued, 'a live four-piece band and ballroom dancing. Men in formal wear, women in ball gowns, gliding across the dance floor.'

'Ah,' she paused. 'That might be a problem. I can't dance that well.'

'Aren't you from Vienna?' he teased. 'Home of the waltz.'

'I am, but I never learned how.'

He edged closer. 'Perhaps I could teach you?'

'Perhaps.' Lilly focused on a fisherman loading his boat with a billow of netting. She hoped Alexander hadn't noticed her burning cheeks.

'Lilly,' he said. 'Since we met, I've grown to like you.' Alexander suddenly appeared less confident.

'Oh.' The sudden shift in the conversation left Lilly at a loss for words.

'I realise we have only known each other for a short while, but we've been in such close quarters and experienced a lot together. It seems much longer.'

'Yes, it does.'

He slid an arm about her waist and together they watched the first glimmer of sunrise casting an orange glow over the port. Unexpected butterflies fluttered in her stomach. Then Alexander faced Lilly, and she allowed him to draw her towards him. Lilly rested her head against his chest and closed her eyes. She could hear the beating of his heart. She felt good in his arms. No one had held her with tenderness in over two years.

Then Alexander drew back a fraction, tilted her chin, and stared into her eyes. He leaned towards her and brushed his lips against hers. Her body tensed, as she felt something freeze within her, something that would not allow her to respond. An instant later, she pulled away. 'I'm sorry.'

Alexander's hands dropped to his sides. 'Forgive me. I didn't mean to make you uncomfortable.'

'You did nothing wrong.' Lilly's head sank and a wave of sadness washed over her. 'I'm touched. I like you too. But I'm not quite ready for this. I'm not sure if you know I'm a widow?'

'Yes, I do,' Alexander said, his expression solemn. 'I, too, was in a serious relationship. Perhaps not quite the same. But we were engaged. In the end, though, she decided she couldn't leave Prague without her parents. And I couldn't stay. It was painful to say goodbye. It took time, but eventually I let go and I am able to move on.'

'I don't think I'm quite over it.' Lilly sighed. 'It would not be fair to mislead you.'

'I appreciate your honesty.' But she read the disappointment in Alexander's eyes.

'Thank you for understanding,' she said.

There was an awkward pause, and then he said, 'For now, shall we forget this conversation took place?' He hesitated. 'Can we still be friends?'

'Of course we can.'

He held out his hand and warmly shook hers. 'And if you change your mind …?'

'Yes.' Lilly stepped away from him, hoping that he could not see her discomfort. She did not want the situation to make things awkward between them. She hoped he would not let it happen either. 'Now, I think … I have to check on Gisela. See you later.'

Lilly knocked once on the cabin door and opened it on Gisela's cheery call to come in. Her smile faded to concern as soon as she saw Lilly. 'What's wrong?'

Lilly sank down on Gisela's bunk. 'Alexander tried to kiss me.'

'Did he now.' She studied Lilly. 'Is that so terrible?'

'I wish—' Lilly took several shallow breaths but couldn't restrain her tears. 'I wish I were ready.' She covered her face with her hands.

Gisela stroked Lilly's hair gently. 'You can't force these things.'

'I know I should try to move on. I know Salo is never coming back, but I miss him. Looking to the future is so … hard.'

'It is, my darling.'

'Have I made a big mistake?'

'It was only a kiss. Not a marriage proposal.' She shifted to a more practical tone. 'Will you stay on good terms?'

'Yes, we're friends.'

'Maybe you need more time. Or perhaps it is the wrong time. Or the wrong person.'

'I do like him. He's a lovely person.'

'Yes, he is.'

'He's kind, handsome, charismatic.'

'That's all true.' Gisela said. 'But it doesn't mean he's the one for you.'

'Things would be far easier if I had someone. I wouldn't have to be afraid to face a future alone in a new country and I wouldn't be holding Hannah back. She and Karl could move forward in life without the burden of worrying about me.'

'You don't decide to be with someone because it will solve your problems. You do it because you love him and wish to be with him.'

She pulled out a handkerchief and dabbed Lilly's eyes. 'You are lovely and he is lovely. But you are two very different people who have had different upbringings and live different lifestyles. Your outlook and ideologies aren't the same. Remember, he is an idealist – his dream is to become a pioneer and his plan is to move to a secular kibbutz with his group from Prague. Would you be ready to agree to that arrangement and all it will involve? Because you can't assume he would change his entire way of life for you.'

Lilly's heart sank further. 'I'm not sure I would want to. I don't know if that is the life for me.'

'It is something you need to consider. If you were my daughter, I would give you the following advice. Go in with your eyes open. Don't rush into a new relationship with the first person who gives you attention and affection. Make sure you are ready to let another person into your heart and your life. If you care about Alexander and choose a relationship with him, I won't discourage you. I'll share in your happiness.' Gisela patted her cheek. 'But give yourself time to think. You don't want to solve a short-term issue only to find you have trapped yourself in a long-term one, with a way of life that makes you miserable.'

'I'm scared,' Lilly acknowledged. 'I'm afraid of being alone. What if I never find someone?'

'You will. When the time is right. And in the meantime, you're not alone. I am here for you.'

# CHAPTER 32

'We appear to be Heraklion's Sunday afternoon attraction,' Janka said, nodding at the long line of rowing boats forming a queue to leave the harbour as she stood by the railings, an unwitting buffer between Lilly and Alexander.

Since their encounter three days ago, and despite their stated intentions to the contrary, Lilly and Alexander had stepped awkwardly around one another. Neither had mentioned the interlude, but it hung between them like a question mark. Lilly saw Alexander's interest in his eyes whenever he looked at her, but she couldn't reciprocate – at least not now. She wondered if she would ever feel ready?

Lilly remained torn between the allure of a more secure future and the familiarity of her beloved past. She was fond of Alexander and she felt attracted to him, but if he held her in his arms, would she be able to love him for who he was, or would she always imagine she was listening to the heartbeat of another? The practical differences between them were real as well. Would he even be willing to find a compromise?

The night before, during a discussion among the lifeboat chevra about their plans for the future, Lilly had braved the issue. 'Will you move to the kibbutz with your Prague group straight away on arrival?'

'Nothing is set in stone,' Alexander replied. 'Right now, I'll be relieved if we arrive there at all.'

What if they never made it? What if her only chance of happiness was here and now?

They had now been languishing outside Heraklion port for four days and their journey's fate again hung in the balance. So far, Captain Spiro's pledge to replenish supplies at Crete had proven to be nothing but empty words. They had not yet loaded fresh water, food, or coal.

The captain, when questioned, offered lame excuses for the delay and a vague plan to load enough fuel to sail to Piraeus. Why did he keep finding reasons to detour and prolong their journey? More and more passengers began to wonder whether he intended to deliver them to Haifa at all. As for the other crew members, they seemed content to remain in Crete instead of sailing into the Italian-occupied Dodecanese Islands and a potential war zone.

Out of sheer desperation, the Passenger Committee sent an urgent cable to Berthold Storfer appealing for assistance. His response was brief and to the point and wholly disappointing; he could help them no further.

They were on their own and at Spiro's mercy.

Lilly returned her attention to the line of boats leaving Heraklion harbour. Janka's assumption about them appeared correct. A small fleet, filled with curious locals and soldiers, rowed straight towards their ship and circled the vessel for a closer view.

'Have they come to watch us die a slow death from thirst and hunger?' Alexander asked, his voice laced with bitterness. For all his convictions, he was finally verging on despair.

'Maybe the captain will allow them to sell us some food,' Isaak said.

'Yes, perhaps.' Alexander glanced up at the bridge. 'Then he'll steal it, place it in the canteen, and sell it back to us.'

Another small boat sailed out of the harbour, but this one was unlike the others. It carried two middle-aged men, dressed in suits and ties, looking more prepared for a business meeting than a boat ride. They approached the Atlantic, boarded the ship, and minutes later were shaking hands with members of the Transport Committee. A Haganah representative escorted them to the bridge, where he handed the megaphone to the darker-haired of the two men. His deep-set eyes were full of compassion as he searched the faces of the passengers.

'*Shalom Aleichem*. I'm Mr Sevilla.' He extended his hand to indicate his companion. 'And this is Mr Cohen. We represent the Jewish community of Crete and we have come to offer our help.' He addressed them in English, just as the men from Istanbul had, and allowed time for his words to be translated into German by the English speakers among the passengers. 'We aren't a large community, nor a wealthy one, but we will do everything we can to help you. We are all family. The Jewish family. Currently, we are making efforts to organise a food delivery for you. We ask you please to be patient a short while longer while we make the arrangements.'

Polite clapping accompanied the men as they descended from the bridge. Many passengers stopped them to shake their hands before they left the ship.

Hannah turned hopefully to Lilly. 'Do you think they'll keep their word?'

'Yes, I do.' Lilly said, feeling optimistic for the first time in a long while. 'I believe they will come to our aid, just like the Istanbul Jewish community did.'

Isaak's face brightened. 'So do I.'

Alexander's expression didn't change. 'Don't expect too much,' he cautioned.

'You don't think those men are sincere?' Isaak asked.

'I'm sure they are, but you heard what they said.' He directed his gaze to the bridge from where Mr Sevilla had just spoken. 'They are a small community of modest means. Perhaps they can rustle up a bit of bread and fresh water, but we desperately need coal. I doubt they have the resources to buy any, no matter how good their intentions. Without coal, we aren't going anywhere. It's going to take a miracle.'

'Then maybe Mr Sevilla and Mr Cohen will be our miracle-workers,' Lilly said.

'I admire your optimism. I wish I could share it.' Alexander brooded. 'Down to the last potato peel. Isn't that what you once said?'

'I did.' Lilly stared at him. 'How did you know that?'

'Janka told me.'

'And look what happened to the Pentcho,' she said, still carried away by her enthusiasm. 'It overtook us and sailed on by.'

'Indeed.' He held up his hands in defeat. 'But we ran out of potatoes a while ago. Even those mouldy ship biscuits are gone.'

She had no response for him.

As Lilly returned to the lifeboat, she wondered whether she would be better off being more cautious and less trusting like Alexander. Then she wouldn't have to worry about setting her hopes too high, only to have them dashed, as they had already been so many times on this voyage. But she wasn't sure she had it in her to give up on hope.

As if to support that thought Lilly spotted Erika on her way back from the infirmary, her shoulders hunched and her mouth set in a tight line. Erika's disposition, so sunny at the start of the journey, had soured as the voyage progressed.

'We lost our ninth passenger,' Erika told her when they met at the foot of the stairs. 'It doesn't get any easier.'

Lilly put her arm around her friend. She wished there was a quiet area where they could sit and talk undisturbed or space to go for a walk, but privacy was a rare commodity on the Atlantic. Even with the one-way paths around the deck, you couldn't walk three paces without stepping aside to make way for someone else. Eventually, they settled by the railings, their backs to the rest of the ship. They gazed in silence at the sunset, at the water capturing the golden hue of the sky. Lilly marvelled that such awe-inspiring beauty continued to exist alongside such deep misery.

They watched together until the sun, flaming red, dipped behind the mountain range. Then Erika faced Lilly. 'When I decided to become a nurse, I knew not every patient would recover. But I pictured myself working in a sterile hospital environment, dressed in uniform, with proper procedures and medical supplies.' She looked in the direction of the ship's infirmary. 'Who would ever think of being trapped for weeks on end on a cramped, unhygienic ship with almost no supplies, trying to treat helpless, unfortunate people who dreamed of reaching the safety of Eretz Israel. Watching them fall ill and die because of the conditions. Stuck on this ship that should be helping them realise their dreams.'

'These past few weeks have been so very difficult for you.' Lilly reached out to squeeze Erika's hand. 'It won't bring them back, but just think, soon we'll be on our way and the situation will hopefully improve. Did you hear about the visit from representatives of the Crete Jewish community?'

'Yes, I heard their announcement from the infirmary.' Erika shrugged. 'Nice words.'

'It doesn't make you feel more hopeful?' Lilly had been so sure that Erika would draw comfort from the Jews of Crete, as she herself had.

'It is nice to know that someone still cares about us, but I'm not too excited. We've been disappointed too many times already.' She rubbed her tired eyes. 'It's good you still have hope. I lost much of mine along the way.'

'What else do I have? We can't go back. We have to move forward.

'*Richtig.*' Erika nodded slowly. 'We can't go back.'

Lilly looked out on the harbour and tried to push away the nightmarish thoughts of what would happen if aid didn't come soon. In the twilight, the bay sparkled with lights and gulls soared overhead, their calls echoing in their wake.

'You know, I was a very different person when I left Vienna eleven months ago and first met your cousin Hannah,' Erika said. 'Young. Naive. Twenty-one years old and travelling on my own for the first time. Though of course I was sad to say goodbye to my mama, it was an adventure of sorts. I imagined I'd be aboard a boat the day after I left my parents' home. I was counting on a fun voyage across the sea – I was looking forward to the chance to meet new people.' Erika let out a small brittle laugh. 'Even when we first arrived at the Slobodarna, as terrible as that place was, I thought we'd be there so briefly that I could handle it. Especially when I fell hopelessly in love the very next day.'

'Was Marcus there too?'

'No. I only met him later, after Hannah and I were transferred to the Patronka.'

'Who was he then?' Lilly was almost as curious about why she had never heard this story as she was about the identity of the object of Erika's affections.

'Alexander.' Erika was matter-of-fact in the utterance, but it was Lilly who tensed up.

'You didn't realise?' Erika's eyes widened. 'I just assumed Hannah told you. Though, I suppose, there was nothing much to say. I was just a silly young girl lovesick for a boy she hardly knew.'

'Did he feel the same way?'

'I don't know. He was always friendly, but nothing ever happened. Snatched moments at rushed meals and during brief exercise sessions in the freezing yard didn't provide many chances for deep conversation, never mind starting a relationship. Besides, back then, I think his sole interest was to board a ship. When we met again on the Helios, at the start of our Danube journey, he seemed pleased to see me. But then, as soon as I mentioned Marcus, his attitude changed. If it didn't seem so out of character, I'd almost say he was disappointed.' She shook her head. 'Maybe I imagined it. Anyway, it doesn't matter anymore.' Erika raised her eyes to Lilly's as she lowered her voice. 'He cares for you, I can tell. Early the other morning, I saw you together when I was coming back from my shift.'

Lilly's cheeks flushed and she turned to the open sea in order to avoid her friend's eyes.

'It's all right. I'm pleased for you. Really I am,' Erika said. 'Do you love him?'

'I like him,' Lilly said. 'But I'm not sure it's enough. I don't know whether it's because I'm not ready to be with someone new and my feelings will grow in time or maybe we're just not right for each other. I'm not sure what to think, I'm so confused.'

'Sometimes, it takes time to work out your feelings. Love can be confusing, can't it? It was similar for me with Marcus.' Erika looked out over the sea too. 'Perhaps it still is.'

'I thought you and he are serious.'

'We are.' Erika hesitated. 'Or we were.'

'What changed?'

'Oh, it's hard to explain. Maybe it's nothing. But after all this time apart ... I know it's only four weeks, but it feels like an eternity. We've been through so much since I last saw him.' Erika paused to collect her thoughts. 'Marcus and I are quite different, but when we first met I was instantly drawn to him. He is so sweet, kind and easygoing. His feelings were strong for me before I really knew how I felt, but, over time, I fell in love with him. At least, I thought I did. Now, I don't know if I was just caught up in the moment. Between his feelings ... Hannah and Karl getting together ... Of course, I wanted a boyfriend too. And Marcus was truly there for me. Before we parted, I was sure I'd say "yes" if he asked me to marry him. But now? I'm not certain.'

'When we get to Haifa and you can finally talk to him, you will be able to have a long, honest conversation. How you feel will surely become clear.'

'I know that's what I need to do.' Erika's breath hitched. 'The thing is, I've also been trying not to think about Marcus. Really, to put him out of my mind. Because I don't know what the future holds. What if we don't meet up in Haifa? What if I never see him again?'

'Of course you will.' Lilly was emphatic.

'But Lilly ...' Erika released a sorrowful sigh. 'So much has happened on board. We've lost so many passengers already.'

Lilly understood the precariousness of their situation aboard the Atlantic. But she also knew that love and life could be precarious. Or Salo would still be with her.

'Most of them were quite elderly.' She reminded Erika firmly. 'You are young and so is Marcus. Somehow, we'll make it through and you'll meet again in Eretz.'

'I hope so.' A tear dropped down Erika's cheek. 'Deep down, I haven't stopped caring for Marcus. I miss him.'

'I know you do.'

'Lilly, wake up!' Isaak said.

It was barely light. Lilly tried her best to ignore him. She and Erika had chatted until the early hours. Lilly was still tired and couldn't imagine why her sleep was being interrupted.

'Lilly, wake up,' Isaak persisted.

She looked at him through bleary eyes, with a mixture of exhaustion and curiosity.

'What is it?'

'You must see this for yourself.' Isaak said, with ill-contained exuberance. He shook his cousin's shoulder. 'Alexander, get up!'

'Let him sleep,' Lilly mumbled. 'He was on fire watch duty.'

'He'll want to be awake for this.'

Alexander stretched. 'What's going on?'

Before Isaak could reply, a curly-haired boy appeared at Isaak's side and tugged at his trouser leg. 'Make more magic.'

'I will, later. But first, let me show you something even more magical.'

To the boy's delight, Isaak lifted him into the air and hoisted him onto his shoulders. People started to cheer for something going on in the harbour. Isaak was glad to point it out to the boy before he returned the child to his mother. Lilly scrambled onto a bench so that she could catch a better view. And then she understood all the excitement. A convoy of three boats was sailing towards them, with Mr Sevilla and Mr Cohen standing at the bow of the leading vessel.

Still struggling into his boots, Alexander joined Lilly on the bench. He stared and blinked as if he couldn't believe his eyes. '*Unglaublich.*'

The two community representatives carried a pile of overflowing sacks onto the ship. The mouth-watering aroma of fresh warm bread permeated the air. The second vessel brought a tanker of fresh drinking water and from the third, hired workers unloaded vegetables, fruit, eggs, butter, and wine.

'This is unbelievable.' Alexander gulped. 'Unbelievable!'

Lilly beamed. 'They kept their word.'

Mr Sevilla mounted the bridge and took the megaphone. 'Our dear brothers and sisters, we have been in contact with the Jewish community in Athens and the Joint Distribution Committee in the United States. Both have agreed to contribute to our fundraising efforts. Today, we are here both as representatives of Crete's Jewish community and the "Joint" to deliver provisions. Negotiations are also underway to purchase coal so that you can continue your journey to Eretz Israel.' He waited as the passengers greeted his announcement with whistles and applause.

'We hope to have further news for you soon. In the meantime, we offer you some freshly baked bread for breakfast.'

Lilly and the rest of the lifeboat chevra joined the lengthy breakfast queue, amid laughter and chatter.

'Have a look at the captain's face,' Isaak said.

Lilly glanced up to see Spiro on the bridge observing the breakfast queue, his legs splayed, his arms crossed, his crimson face seething.

'He doesn't look happy,' Lilly said.

'Not at all.' Alexander laughed.

'If his face gets any redder, his head will blow off,' Isaak said.

The line inched forward. Lilly spotted Stefan and Max behind them and wished them good morning.

'Are you going to get breakfast for Gisela?' Stefan said. 'Or should I fetch it for her?'

'I'll do it. I was planning to go down and see her anyway,' Lilly said.

It took forty minutes, but finally it was their turn. Mr Sevilla handed each of them fresh slices of the rustic bread.

'Thank you for helping us,' Lilly said.

'It's our pleasure to assist in any way we can.'

'Do you know whether any other Jewish refugee ships have passed through here in the past few days?' Hannah asked.

'Not to Crete,' he said. 'But the week before last, a ship carrying Jewish refugees from Bratislava got shipwrecked off the uninhabited island of Kamilonissi, about halfway between here and Rhodes.'

Hannah blanched. 'Do you know the ship's name?'

Mr Sevilla shook his head. 'I can't remember. Maybe ... maybe, the name started with a P...'

'Was it the Pacific?' There was a hint of fear in her question.

'No, not Pacific. It was Pen-something or other.'

Hannah's relief was audible in her sigh.

'The Pentcho?' Lilly said.

'Yes!' he exclaimed. 'That's the name. Pentcho.'

'Did any of them survive?' Lilly asked.

'I believe they all did.' He smiled. 'The passengers made it off the ship before it sank. They were stranded on the island for about ten days. Some Italian soldiers rescued them and they were taken to Rhodes. They're being held in a camp set up in a sports stadium.'

'How are they being treated?' Hannah asked.

'Apparently, quite well. The Jewish community in Rhodes is providing them with food and supplies, and I understand the Italians have allowed them to send letters to their families.'

'Do you have any idea when they will be released?'

'Hard to say.' He raised his hand, palm up. 'Perhaps not until the end of the war. Whenever that may be.'

'Mr Sevilla,' Lilly said. 'Would it be at all possible for me to give you two letters to post to my family? My brother is awaiting my arrival in Eretz Israel and I need to contact him rather urgently.'

'Of course. I'll also tell your organisers to pass the message along to any other passengers who want to send letters and we'll collect them next time we come.'

'Thank you so much. How do we pay you for the stamps?'

'Don't worry about the cost of the postage. We'll take care of it. And if your letter is urgent, come back to me in a couple of hours when I've finished here and I'll see what I can do for you.'

Lilly couldn't resist taking a quick bite of her bread before she did anything else. She didn't want to keep Gisela waiting but she hadn't eaten solid food for two days. The bread was crusty on the outside, fluffy on the inside. It tasted of kindness.

'Lilly!'

She raised her head to see Gisela hurrying up the stairs towards her. A sheen of perspiration covered Gisella's face as she breathed heavily from the exertion.

'No need to rush,' Lilly said. 'I've already fetched your breakfast.'

'Thank you, my darling, but the food will have to wait.' She searched the deck in a panic. 'Where is Max? Where is Erika? I must find them at once.'

'What has happened?'

'Alma's waters just broke,' Gisela said. 'I think she is in labour.'

# CHAPTER 33

Max paced in a tight circle outside the closed cabin door.

From the inside, they heard Erika's words of encouragement. 'Keep going. You're doing well.'

'Come on, Alma, there's my good girl,' Gisela shouted. 'You can do it.'

Alma let out a protracted scream.

'My poor love.' Max's face twisted in anguish. He sank to his knees. 'Is she going to make it?'

Alexander patted him on the shoulder. 'She'll be fine.'

'It's been eighteen hours already,' Max said. 'How much more can she take?'

'This is all ... natural.' Alexander looked at Stefan for confirmation. He replied with a shrug.

'A long labour is quite normal for a first baby,' Lilly said, conscious of her own inexperience. She damped down the thought that by now she could have been a mother to an eighteen-month-old. 'Erika told me the labour can take many hours.'

'Max! I want Max!' Alma cried.

'Soon, my darling,' Gisela said.

'Push,' Erika said.

Alma screamed once more.

Max rose to his feet with unwavering resolve. 'I have to go to her.'

'You mustn't go in there,' Janka said. 'Erika instructed you to wait outside until the baby arrives.'

'I don't care.' He looked over his shoulder at Janka as he turned the door handle. 'She is my wife, and she's giving birth to our child. She needs me, and I want to support her.'

Max burst into the cabin, ignoring the unanimous protests from Erika, Gisela, and Jenny, and rushed to his wife's side. Beads of sweat glistened on Alma's contorted face. Max took her hand. 'It's all right, Alma, I'm right here with you.' She raised her gaze to meet his, and her strained expression softened.

'Now push,' Erika said.

'Let's do this together,' Max said. 'Squeeze my hand.'

Outside, Hannah grimaced. 'Shouldn't we close the door? I can't bear to watch.'

Lilly continued to peer through the open crack, unable to tear herself away. She was captivated by the terrifying, mystical, and beautiful scene of new life emerging.

Erika examined Alma's progress. 'Again.'

Alma moaned. 'It hurts.'

'Oh, my love,' Max brushed strands of damp hair away from her face with his free hand. 'You're doing so well.'

'I can see the head,' Erika said. 'Push.'

Alma screamed and writhed.

Gisela squeezed her other hand. 'That's it, keep going.'

'Come on,' Max said. 'You can do this.'

'Almost there,' Erika said.

Alma panted, moaned, and pushed.

'Yes, yes!' A tiny, slippery pink baby coated in patches of white and traces of blood slid into Erika's waiting arms.

Brief silence.

A thin wail.

Alma cried out in relief. Max wiped away a tear.

'It's a boy,' Erika said. 'Mazal tov!'

Gisela beamed like a grandmother.

Erika cut the umbilical cord and placed the tiny, swaddled bundle on Alma's chest. Alma helped him settle in to nurse, beaming at Max. He kissed the top of her head, then tentatively stroked his new son.

'We'll give the three of you some time together,' Gisela said.

Lilly stepped away from the door as Gisela and Jenny came into the passageway.

'It's a boy!' Gisela announced, as if they hadn't already heard. She couldn't stop smiling.

'Mazal tov!' the friends chorused.

'Isn't this quite something?' Isaak said, musing aloud. 'He was born on a ship, off the island of Crete, to Jewish parents from Danzig, and will grow up in Eretz Israel.'

'May he never experience fear or hatred. May he live free in our own land,' Alexander proclaimed.

'Amen!'

The lifeboat chevra trooped up the stairs. The pitter patter of rain thrummed on the deck. '*Wunderbar*,' Janka said. 'All our stuff is getting soaked again.'

They darted around the lifeboat collecting their clothes and belongings and stuffing them into their backpacks.

Then Isaak unbuttoned his shirt, pulled out a bar of soap and rubbed it across his arms and chest.

Alexander squinted at his cousin, mouth agape. 'Isaak, what are you doing?'

'Taking a shower,' Isaak answered, deadpan. 'I'm already drenched. At least the rain water lathers.'

Alexander shook his head and laughed. 'Mad boy.'


'Good morning, Max,' Lilly said. Standing in the passageway, Max cradled his three-day-old baby, gently rocking and singing to him. 'How is he doing?'

'He's wonderful.' Max's eyes sparkled with pride as he lowered his arms to show Lilly the baby wrapped in an oversized blanket, the excess draped over Max's shoulder. The baby's closed eyes flickered and his mouth suckled in his sleep. He had a tuft of brown hair, like his father, whose hair was growing back. Max was unrecognisable, so different from the person who had first boarded the Schönbrunn. 'Now he's happy all right, but he has a powerful set of lungs. He kept Alma up for most of the night, wanting to feed. I offered to take him so she could get a little sleep. I think Gisela is resting, too.'

'You seem to enjoy spending time with him,' Lilly said.

'I can't get enough of him.' He gazed at his son. 'I didn't realise I would feel this instant bond and immense love. Even his dirty nappies don't faze me. I've learned how to change him. Gisela was a bit taken aback to begin with. Apparently, it's not considered the done thing for fathers to deal with such matters, but it doesn't bother me.' He faced Lilly again, his eyes reflecting a blend of joy and torment. 'I've seen far worse, believe me. There were times I feared for my life and despaired of ever seeing Alma again or meeting my baby. I've been given another chance. I am immensely grateful.'

'You were in Dachau?'

'Yes.'

'My father too.'

His expression shifted. 'Did he ... get released?'

'After three months.' Lilly shook her head, pressing her lips together. 'But he wasn't the same.'

'I understand.'

'Can I ask you a question about what happened there?'

Suddenly vigilant, Max looked up and down the passageway, checking that they could not be overheard. 'I ... I don't know.'

'If you can't answer, or don't want to, it's all right,' Lilly said. My father never spoke a word about his experiences. We got the impression that they had forbidden him to talk. We thought he might have had to sign a document promising that he wouldn't reveal what had taken place.'

Max's nod was barely perceptible, as if even that acknowledgement might be saying too much.

'When my papa returned, he had a blank stare, unfocused somehow. He could no longer stand upright. He was stooped over with rounded shoulders, and he had scars that looked like scratch marks on his neck and under his eyes. Sometimes, when he had nightmares, he'd shout in his sleep about being tied to a tree with a monkey.'

Max again nodded slightly.

Lilly was tentative, but she needed to ask. 'Do you know what he meant?'

He regarded her silently, apparently weighing the gravity of what she had said, fear flickering in his eyes.

Lilly waited, wondering whether she had pressed too far.

'If I never talk and neither does anyone else, no one will ever find out,' he murmured. 'And then they'll get away with their crimes.' Max's eyes darted up and down the passageway. He drew his son closer towards him. 'Perhaps people need to know what they have done. What they are doing.' He whispered in her ear, barely audible,

'But they warned me if I did, they would find and arrest me once more.'

Then he examined Lilly's face carefully. 'Please promise not to tell anyone what I am about to tell you until we are safe in Eretz Israel. Just in case.'

She looked back at him, unwavering. 'I promise.'

He edged closer to avoid others overhearing. '*Baumhängen*.' Tree hanging.

'What does that mean?'

'They used to force us to do hours of exercises, such as slow knee-bends. If someone couldn't complete them, they suffered a punishment. They also punished us for many other minor reasons.' Max's words came out dully, and he stared at his feet. '*Baumhängen* was one of the punishments. They bound the prisoner's hands in chains behind him, at shoulder height. Then they made him stand on a stool with his back to a tree, or a pole. They tied his arms to it and kicked the stool from beneath him. He would hang in that way for an hour or more, trying not to cry out. Sometimes he might suffer dislocation of his shoulders and stoop from the damage, sometimes he might ...'

Lilly opened her mouth, a noise escaped, but she couldn't form a word.

'There was a rumour,' Max said, 'that in the early days, when the first Jewish prisoners arrived in Dachau after the November Pogrom, one of the SS men would put a pet monkey in the tree. The monkey would play tricks and tease the prisoners, scratch and bite them on the face. Since the victims hanging from the tree couldn't use their hands, they couldn't push the monkey away or protect themselves. I never saw it myself, but it would seem the rumour was true.'

Lilly took a step back. The passageway seemed to darken, and she had to blink several times before Max's face returned to focus. 'Thank you for telling me,' she said, as if he had given her an inconsequential update about the weather. She stared at her hands, unsure of what to say, what to do next.

Max held out the baby to her. 'Would you like to hold him for a moment?'

'Yes,' Lilly said. 'I'd like that. Very much.'

# CHAPTER 34

For two days, Hannah had barely slept. Two mornings before, they had awoken to discover that the Milos had arrived in Heraklion overnight. The Atlantic's Transport Committee immediately crossed over to the other vessel to speak with its management. The committee members returned with reports that the Milos had just loaded coal and food in Piraeus in preparation for the last leg of their voyage and that the Pacific was thought to be close to Heraklion as well.

Hannah began a vigil, watching every new vessel that approached the port, waiting for Karl's ship. But the Pacific didn't arrive that day. Nor the next, when the Milos – still listing to one side – departed for Haifa. The passengers of the Atlantic could only watch in envy and wonder when their coal would arrive, so they could leave too.

The morning after the Milos departed, Lilly was forced awake by Hannah's frantic prodding.

Lilly was at once alert and keen on Hannah's behalf. 'Has Karl's ship arrived?' She couldn't imagine what else could have prompted that kind of wake-up.

Instead, Hannah looked concerned. 'No. Something is wrong. The harbour has gone quiet.'

On an ordinary weekday, the port should have been bustling, but that Monday, the twenty-eighth of October, it had fallen silent. No shipping vessels entered or exited the port, no fishermen unloaded their catch or tended their nets. And in the harbour, two motorboats hoisted Italian flags.

'What does this mean?' Lilly said. She had hurriedly pulled on her shoes and joined Hannah at the railings.

Alexander came up behind them and studied the scene. 'I fear this means war.'

An official announcement from the Haganah soon followed: Italy had declared war on Greece.

By nightfall, a strict blackout was enforced. The chevra huddled in the lifeboat, on the deck of their rickety ship, anchored alone, outside the port.

Heavy darkness shrouded the harbour and surrounding bay. Only the waning crescent moon hinted at its faint outline.

'Do you think we can still get coal and leave?' Hannah asked.

'Unlikely,' Janka said in a dejected tone. 'The war has caught up with us. If we were struggling to buy coal in peacetime, what hope is there now?'

'Even if by some slight chance we can get fuel, we still have to sail out of Heraklion, through a danger zone, and perhaps mines.' Alexander's head was in his hands. 'There's no way Spiro will do any of that.'

'So we're trapped?' Hannah asked, her pitch rising. 'What will happen? Will the Italians take us prisoner like those from the Pentcho?'

No one had an answer.

'If only we could have left yesterday, like the Milos,' Hannah said. 'We would be out of the war zone by now.'

'Remember how we almost got trapped in Romania? Look how far we've come. Perhaps there is hope yet,' Lilly said.

'It's going to take a miracle,' Alexander said.

'Hasn't our entire journey been a miracle?' Isaak said.

When Mr Sevilla boarded the Atlantic the following morning, Lilly was there to meet him. In his arms, he balanced six large woven bags, and a Moses basket overflowing with baby clothes, blankets, towels, and a pile of nappies.

She stared at him in amazement. 'Good morning,' she said, 'We weren't expecting all of this.'

He smiled in satisfaction. 'Neither did I, but the community really rose to the occasion.'

'Do you need some help?'

'Thank you. I wouldn't mind.' He handed her three of the bags.

Lilly took them but then paused. 'Mr Sevilla,' she began. 'We are very grateful for everything you and the community are doing for us, but what is going to happen, now that Greece is at war?'

His expression didn't waver and he showed no signs of worry. 'So far, it is just a declaration. Apart from introducing nightly blackouts, not much has changed, and we don't know that much will. We're a resilient little Jewish community. One of the most ancient in the Diaspora. We've weathered many conflicts in the past. Please God, we'll withstand this one too.'

'What does it mean for us, though? Will the Italians round us up into a camp like the Pentcho passengers in Rhodes?'

He set off again towards the bow with a confidant stride, motioning for her to join him. 'I doubt it will come to that.'

'Is there still a possibility we can get coal and continue our journey?'

'Absolutely. We're continuing to work on this in partnership with the community in Athens and the Joint Distribution Committee.

We also received another telegram from Mr Storfer. Would you believe it? At long last, he has agreed to help.'

'That's some good news, at least,' Lilly frowned.

'Try not to worry. We'll do everything we can to help you reach Eretz Israel.'

'Mr Sevilla ...' Lilly took a hesitant breath. 'Did you receive a reply for me yet?'

Knitting his brows, he set down his load and withdrew a folded note from his pocket. 'I didn't want to give it to you until afterwards.' His eyes filled with compassion. He passed the paper to her and closed her hand over it. 'Read it later. First, we have a *brit mila* to celebrate.'

Alexander, Isaak and Stefan had hauled a weighty mahogany table and chair up from the lounge to the bow, where they cleared a small section.

'Mazal tov!' Mr Sevilla boomed at Max and Alma, the rabbi – a trained *mohel* who would perform the ritual circumcision and naming ceremony – and the small party of guests: Alma's roommates, Max's corridor companions, and the lifeboat chevra.

Max and Alma's eyes widened in astonishment. They exchanged a glance, unable to believe what they were seeing.

'What is all this?' Max asked.

'Gifts for the newborn. From the Jewish community of Crete. They send their love and good wishes.'

'I don't quite know what to say.' Alma's breath caught in her throat. 'Thank you. We are so grateful.'

'It's our pleasure.' He placed them on the table next to the rabbi's medical bag.

'Shall we begin?' the rabbi said. 'Mr Sevilla, if you can please take a seat?'

'It would be my honour.'

As Mr Sevilla headed towards the chair, Lilly peeked at her telegram. Then she composed herself, arranging her features into the semblance of a smile.

Alma handed her son to Jenny, following the tradition to give the honour of carrying the baby to a couple who didn't yet have a child. Jenny's mouth quivered as she transferred him to Stefan. He reassured her with a look of tenderness.

Stefan presented the baby to Mr Sevilla. Since there was no grandfather present, Alma and Max had given him the privilege of holding the baby for the ceremony.

'Our God and the God of our forefathers, preserve this child for his father and mother and may his name be called in Israel ...' The rabbi stopped to confer with Max and then announced, 'Chaim Rafael.'

'Mazal tov!' cheered the group.

Max kissed and hugged his son, before he gently passed him down the line from Stefan to Jenny, and into Alma's waiting embrace.

Max returned to his wife's side, carefully balancing the chair so she could nurse their son in comfort.

'Would you like to say a few words?' the rabbi asked.

Before Max could decline, he was guided into the centre of the gathering. He looked around nervously at the now-silent guests. 'Well ... I ...' Max's voice quavered. Then he caught Alma's eye. She nodded and smiled at him. Max replied with a hesitant smile, and his tension ebbed away. 'First,' he said, his eyes never leaving Alma. 'Thank you to my beloved wife, Alma. For everything and for all that you are. I wouldn't be here if not for you. I love you.'

Gaining confidence, his voice steadied, and he turned to face the rest of the gathering. 'Thank you Rabbi, for performing the *bris*.

Mr Sevilla, for your help, and all the generous gifts from you and the community. Erika for helping Alma to deliver our son. Gisela for being like a mother to us. And to you, our friends, who have become like family, for sharing in our celebration in these dark, uncertain times.'

He paused for a round of applause, then continued, 'We named our son Chaim Rafael. Chaim, meaning life. He is a new life who has given our lives new meaning and hope for the future. And Rafael, after my dear father who they arrested with me ...but ...' Max swallowed hard, his eyes reddening. 'He would have been ... proud ... so proud of ... his first ... grandson ...' He stopped, unable to continue.

Mr Sevilla patted Max's shoulder. 'I think we should all drink a *l'chaim* to little Chaim Rafael.' He opened one of his bags to reveal two bottles of ouzo, and two bottles of wine. From another bag, he retrieved three trays of little honey-glazed pastries he called baklava. Passing around small measures of alcohol, he led them in singing the traditional song, *Siman tov, u'mazal tov*.

Lilly slipped away and headed for the stern. On the way, she passed a distressing spectacle: the shrouded corpse of the most recent deceased passenger, suspended on ropes over the side of the ship. With the ship so close to the harbour, he could not be buried at sea. She knew Mr Sevilla had been in the process of intervening with the authorities on the passengers' behalf, advocating for a proper burial in Crete's Jewish cemetery.

Further along, she noticed a lone woman leaning against the railing. Her head was bowed and her shoulders heaved. It was Jenny.

Lilly gently touched her friend's arm. Startled, Jenny looked embarrassed at being found. She put on a brave front, and then crumbled almost immediately. Lilly put her arm around Jenny's shoulder.

Jenny sniffed. 'You know how it feels to lose a baby,' she said.

'Yes. I do.' Lilly inhaled slowly.

'I'm happy for Alma and Max. Really, I am. I only wish ... I long to hold a child of my own. Ten years we've been married, and I'm still waiting.' Jenny fought back a sob. 'Three miscarriages. '

'I'm sorry,' Lilly said. 'So very sorry.'

'I'm already thirty-six and I'm scared it might be too late for me.'

'That's not old. Did Gisela ever tell you how she had her first child when she was thirty-eight? You have time and when it happens, we will all celebrate with you.'

'I hope so,' she said in a broken voice. She wiped her eyes and focused her gaze on Lilly. 'How do you stay so strong?'

Lilly shook her head wearing a sorrowful smile. 'I'm not at all strong.'

'Yes, you are,' Jenny countered. Her voice was soft but there was a firmness to it. 'You have experienced loss too, yet you offer me, and all of us, ongoing encouragement. That's strength.' Jenny glanced at the bow where the celebrations continued. 'I suppose we'd better get back before we're missed. Are you coming?'

'You go,' Lilly said. 'I'll join you in a bit.'

'Thank you.' She squeezed Lilly's hand and headed back toward the others.

Alone, Lilly retrieved the paper Mr Sevilla had given her. A telegram from Eugen. She reread her brother's message.

SORRY TO GIVE BAD NEWS STOP PAPA DIED YOM KIP-PUR STOP AWAITING YOUR ARRIVAL MEET YOU HAIFA PORT

Lilly bowed her head and salted the sea with her tears.

# CHAPTER 35

On the surface, everything looked the same, but underneath, everything felt different. Her papa had departed this world almost three weeks ago, and Lilly hadn't realised. She hadn't supported her mother at the funeral. She hadn't sat shiva for him. Lilly longed to speak to her mother and brother but, trapped on the ship, there was no way to do so.

When Lilly left Vienna, she knew it was unlikely that she would ever see her Papa again. But the confirmation reopened old wounds. She found herself reliving the day the Brownshirts stormed into her parents' home.

For two days, Lilly barely ate or slept. At night, she lay awake staring up at the stars. Sometimes, she would nod off, only to be jolted awake by vivid dreams, which made her heart race. During the day, she retreated to the corner of a bench, staring into the distance. Or she sat in silence beside Gisela, who stroked her hand. Lilly floated in a daze, unable to separate herself from her sorrow.

When Lilly shared her news with the chevra, they hugged her and offered their sympathies. Since then, they had been unsure whether to give her space or to engage her in conversation, so they tiptoed around her, concerned.

There were moments when Lilly sensed Alexander's wish to reach out. Several times he approached her, only to abruptly retreat. It seemed that he didn't know what to say. Lilly didn't know either.

The only person Lilly really spoke to was Hannah, but the situation with her was even more complicated. Ever since Lilly had broken the news to her cousin, the conversation between them had become stilted. Hannah's father had died when she was just five and she had few memories of him. In his absence, Lilly's father had become her father figure. Though Hannah would not admit how much the loss of her uncle had affected her, Lilly could see that it had. But Hannah would not burden Lilly with her own sorrow. Lilly also suspected that Hannah was now worrying about her mother's fate, just as Lilly herself was for her own mama. Earlier that evening, Lilly had tried to broach the subject.

'Do you think my mama will sell the apartment?' Lilly asked. 'Then she and your mama could book places on the next transport.'

'I'm sure they'll try.' Hannah concealed her frown behind an encouraging smile. 'With a bit of luck, we'll see them again soon.'

Lilly realised Hannah was just comforting her. Deep down, neither of them believed there was any chance of another transport leaving Nazi-occupied Europe.

As the days passed, even their own chances at moving on were looking less likely. Despite Mr Sevilla's persistence and encouragement, there had been little progress with the long-awaited coal delivery.

It was now late, and Lilly's companions were asleep. She alone remained awake in the lifeboat, sitting on a bench while the others slept, her thoughts too tangled to rest. She watched the intermittent searchlight beams from points on the island, tracing above the night sky, and out to sea. On board, people shuffled in the darkness, en route to Panama. The deck creaked. Someone climbed into the boat and sat opposite her. A sweeping arc of light illuminated his face.

'Can't sleep either?' Isaak asked. He handed her a warm mug of tea.

'No,' she whispered.

'Why don't you tell me about your father?'

'What do you want to know?'

'Anything. What he looked like, his character, his job. Tell me stories about him.'

Lilly began to describe her father. The man he was before Dachau broke him into a shadow of his former self. A dignified man who wore a smart suit with a white handkerchief in his top pocket and ran a successful business selling luggage. Papa who, even when he was busy, always made time for her and Eugen. Papa, who taught her to play the piano, read her bedtime stories, and banished childhood nightmares.

Whenever she paused, he prompted her with another question. 'What was Friday night like in your home?' Then, 'Did you ever go on trips or holidays?'

Lilly described cosy Friday night meals, sitting around the table with her parents, Eugen, Tante Rebecca, and Hannah. Trips to the park, the zoo. Family holidays skiing in the mountains and swimming in the sea. Visits to Munich, Paris, and Rome.

She told him amusing stories that made them both laugh, such as the time her papa fell out of a rowing boat; he waded out of the pond in his dripping clothes, unaware he wore a piece of seaweed on his head like a toupee. Or when he accidentally got locked out of their apartment in his pyjamas. She shared stories that brought her to tears: the happiest day of her life, her marriage to Salo when Papa and Mama walked her down the aisle. And the last goodbye to her bedridden papa before she left home.

Isaak sat with her all night, listening to every word.

When she couldn't talk any longer, Lilly dried her eyes, gazed up at the dawning blue sky and felt a sense of calm.

'I feel a bit better,' Lilly said to Isaak. ' Thank you. It was good to talk about him.'

'I think that's what you needed.'

Lilly looked at him, curiously. 'How did you know that when I didn't know myself?'

'Because you weren't able to sit shiva for him. That's the main purpose of the shiva, to talk through, and come to terms with the loss. Also, I understand how it feels.' Isaak spoke with compassion. 'I lost my mother when I was nine.'

'I didn't realise. I thought your parents ...' She hesitated, so she could express her thoughts carefully. 'I mean, Hannah mentioned your parents were with the group stranded in Kladovo.'

'My father and stepmother. Or rather, my second mother. She became very much a parent to me when my father remarried. My birth mother died soon after giving birth to my youngest brother.'

'I'm so sorry.'

He nodded his thanks. 'I may never stop missing her, but I learnt to accept her loss. I found talking about her helped me too.'

'I appreciate you sitting up with me, and keeping me company.' Lilly felt her eyelids drooping. 'I'm sorry for keeping you up most of the night.'

'That's all right. I can sleep in tomorrow, or rather, today.' He chuckled softly. 'You look as if you could also do with some sleep.'

'I might try.'

'Sleep well,' he said as he rose. 'And whenever you need to talk, I'm here.'

He climbed out of the boat and turned around with a smile.

The sound of a distant wail echoed through the air.

Isaak froze and listened

Lilly's chest tightened. 'What is that?'

'A siren.' The colour had drained from his face.

The shrill note rose and fell. Rose and fell. A terrifying cry.

Across the deck, people jolted awake, flung off their blankets, and leapt to their feet.

Lilly scrambled out of the lifeboat. 'What do we do?' She looked about, panicked. There was nowhere to flee. A chaotic mass of pushing, shoving, shouting passengers had formed a bottleneck around the ladder to the catacombs.

The low whirr and drone of an aircraft cut through the air.

'Down!' Alexander shouted.

The noise grew louder, closer.

'Lilly, get down!' Alexander said. 'Everyone, down!'

Someone grabbed her hand. She huddled on the deck with Alexander, Isaak, Hannah, Janka and Erika.

She could hear their rapid, shallow breathing. Or maybe it was her own.

Plane engines roared overhead.

Passengers screamed. Lilly placed her hands on her head. She braced herself.

Isaak raised his head. 'Look!' He pointed.

'Isaak!' Alexander screamed. 'Stay down!'

'It's all right. Don't worry.' He calmly picked himself up. 'Notice the roundels on the tails? That's the RAF. British planes. For once, we're on the right side.'

Alexander dared to lift his head. 'Oh, thank God!' His face showed clear relief.

Lilly sat up, trembling, as the planes disappeared past the coast-line.

'It must have been a drill,' Isaak said.

Alexander shuddered. 'What an alarm clock,' he said, trying to make light of it.

'I almost had a heart attack.' Erika's teeth were still chattering.

'You're not the only one,' Hannah said. 'I feel like I'm going to throw up.'

The chevra sank back on the deck, taking a moment to catch their breath and laugh away their fear, until Isaak's face suddenly fell. 'Uh-oh,' he said. 'Now what?'

Their attention shifted to see Spiro, his jaw set and eyes bulging, storming towards them, another crew member in tow. When he reached the lifeboat, he began grabbing armfuls of their belongings, and tossing them onto the deck.

Janka's eyebrows shot up in disbelief. 'What are you doing?'

Lilly and the others rushed around the deck retrieving blankets, books, clothes, bags, toiletries.

'We're taking the boat,' Spiro said, as his crew member grabbed it at one end.

'Where are you taking it?' Alexander held fast to the boat between them. 'Isaak, fetch the Haganah. Quick!'

'Move away.' Spiro's face distorted in a menacing way.

Alexander stood resolute.

Lilly set down her belongings, and joined Alexander, grasping the boat beside him.

'Away, I said.' Spiro's face had turned its characteristic red.

Janka joined Alexander, and Hannah and Erika took hold of the other side of the boat. They glared at the captain, silently daring him to remove them.

Isaak returned with Dov.

'Captain, no one may leave the ship,' Dov said, asserting his authority. 'We're under strict instructions from the port authorities. The lifeboat has to stay here.'

Spiro frowned, motioned to his assistant to set down the lifeboat. Then he checked the skies, surveyed the sea and slunk away with the other man, muttering something incomprehensible.

'And he's supposed to be the captain,' Alexander said as they watched him leave. 'Seems he's more afraid than we are.'

When the planes swooped over the port the following day, there was no repeat of the previous morning's panic. Watching from the lifeboat, Alexander followed their course.

'Perhaps I should volunteer to join the Greek army?' He winked.

'What nonsense are you saying?' Janka said.

'I could help with the war effort while we're stuck here.'

She tilted her head with a dismissive glance. 'And what if they then allow us to leave? We'll be cultivating a kibbutz, and you'll be here in Crete on your own.'

'You make a good point.' His demeanour became more serious. 'On second thought, I'd better not.'

'Come on, let's fetch breakfast,' Isaak said. 'If there's anything left to eat.'

The chevra were on their feet at once. Their food was again running low.

'Lilly, are you coming?' Hannah said. 'You must eat and keep up your strength.'

Lilly's appetite had finally returned and she was glad enough to join what turned out to be a thirty-minute wait in the queue for a small ladleful of soup. She drank it up at once before walking back with Hannah and Isaak. Ahead, they could see Alexander, Janka, and Erika motioning frantically, and then rushing across the deck to peer over the side of the ship.

'What's got into them?' Lilly said.

They understood as soon as they got closer.

'The boat!' Isaak said.

'Yes. Gone,' Erika said. 'Along with my toiletry bag containing my last bar of soap and only lipstick.'

The space where the lifeboat had sat was strewn with their belongings.

'Where did it go?' Isaak said.

Alexander motioned towards the side of the ship. 'I'll give you one guess.'

Spiro and his assistant were rowing swiftly into the harbour. Before they could even reach the dock, a port authority motorboat moved to intercept them. From the captain's red face and furious hand movements, Lilly could tell he was shouting. Escorted by the motorboat, a humiliated Spiro reversed course and returned to the Atlantic. Some time later, the lifeboat was returned to its rightful place. Erika was delighted to find her bag still tucked under the rear bench.

Two port officials followed Spiro onto the Atlantic. 'Who's in charge of this ship?' one demanded.

Dr Horetzky, head of the Transport Committee, came forward.

'No one, and I mean absolutely no one, including your captain, may come ashore, under any circumstances.' He glared at Spiro. 'Furthermore, in light of recent war developments on the island, we demand that you set sail and leave Crete as soon as possible.

# CHAPTER 36

'Whatever possessed Spiro to take off like that?' Lilly asked, after the chevra had finally finished gathering their possessions and settled back in their lifeboat.

'He's a coward, that's why,' Alexander dismissed the captain with a wave of his hand.

'That first siren scared him more than it scared us.' Isaak chuckled. 'But now we know it's the RAF, I don't understand what his problem is.'

'Never mind Spiro,' said Alexander. 'We have a bigger problem to worry about. The authorities want us gone. Yes, we want to leave, but how can we do that without coal?'

Isaak suddenly climbed onto the bench and peered into the distance. 'Coal?' he said, surprise in his voice.

'Yes. Coal,' Alexander said, growing impatient. 'As you know, we don't have enough to get to Haifa.'

Isaak shielded his eyes, and squinted at the harbour. 'Could it be …?'

'What are you talking about? Are you even listening to me?' Then Alexander followed Isaak's gaze. 'Oh!'

Lilly turned to see what had captured their attention. A small motorboat was heading towards them and behind it came a larger cargo vessel. 'For us?'

'It must be,' Hannah said.

'Let's not raise our hopes,' Alexander cautioned. 'Just in case.'

'Isn't that Mr Sevilla?' Lilly said.

Isaak's face lit up. 'It is.'

Mr Sevilla and Mr Cohen stood at the prow of the motorboat, grandly waving their arms above their heads in greeting.

The motorboat drew alongside the Atlantic. Within minutes, the two men had boarded and proceeded to the bridge.

None of the chevra dared say another word.

Mr Sevilla picked up the megaphone, a broad smile on his face. 'I am delighted to announce that we have brought you more provisions. And, the first of two coal deliveries—'

The air filled with cheers, whistles, and rapturous applause from the passengers.

Alexander continued to stare at the cargo ship in amazement. 'Now I believe in miracles.'

Mr Sevilla handed the megaphone to a Haganah member who waited for more than a minute for the passengers to calm down.

'We extend our greatest thanks and appreciation to Mr Sevilla and Mr Cohen for their hard work and tireless efforts on our behalf.' The passengers again clapped with enthusiasm. 'And now,' he continued, 'we need volunteers to help with the loading.'

Every single one of the young men, including Alexander and Isaak, raised their hands at once.

The volunteers formed a human chain to heft the weighty sacks of coal through the ship and down into the hold. Mr Cohen directed the unloading from the cargo ship and Mr Sevilla observed the process from the stern, where Lilly joined him. 'Thank you for all you've done to supply us with coal.'

'It wasn't just me,' he said. 'Many people worked together to make it happen. But it was an honour to have played a part. For once, it seems, the war helped you. The authorities decided you were getting in the way, so they agreed to speed up the coal delivery. Another load will arrive tomorrow. Because of short supplies, it isn't the best quality, but it should get you to Haifa with no more stops.'

'All the same, without you and Mr Cohen, none of this would have happened. I'll never forget the kindness of your community and what you did for us.'

By the following afternoon, they had unloaded the second coal consignment, as well as food and fresh drinking water. Meanwhile, another group of volunteers prepared the ship by refreshing the paint of the Panamanian flag on the Atlantic's hull to display their neutrality. Then, in final preparation, the passengers took part in a safety drill.

As a parting gift, the authorities in Crete permitted the passengers to have a brief swim in the sea, as long as they stayed within one hundred metres of the ship. From the upper deck, Lilly and Hannah watched the young people diving into the turquoise water with shrieks of delight.

'Are you coming?' Erika said, poised in a halter neck red swimsuit, ready to take the plunge with Janka, Alexander, and Isaak, all stripped down to their underwear.

'No.' Hannah wagged her index finger from side to side. 'Remember, I can't swim. I'll watch from here.'

'Lilly?' Erika said.

'I'll keep Hannah company,' she said.

'Come on, Lilly, join us.' Janka tugged at her hand. 'It will be fun.'

Alexander nodded enthusiastically. 'Yes, join us.'

'Go on.' Hannah said. 'You'll enjoy it.'

'Do you have a swimsuit?' Erika asked.

Lilly shook her head. 'I never thought to pack one.'

'That's all right. You can make do without,' Janka said.

Lilly looked from Erika, in her form-fitting swimsuit, to Janka, standing unperturbed in her underwear. 'I ... uh ... am not sure ...'

'Would you like to borrow this?' Isaak shyly handed her one of his shirts. Lilly gratefully accepted the cover-up and went to change. Then, together with the others, she dived into the temperate waters of the Aegean.

Alexander stayed close to Lilly's side as they swam lengths within the permitted zone. He glided through the water like a sleek fish. The water and the exercise revived Lilly, cleansing her of the accumulated layers of grime, stress, and sadness. The call to return to the ship came too soon.

As they swam back, Erika said, 'I've never seen the Atlantic from a distance.'

'It's terrible!' Isaak said.

'Like a rusty old crate,' Alexander said.

'A rusty old crate with wooden boxes and washing lines,' Janka said.

'We're a floating laundry!' Lilly said, and they all laughed.

The final sunset off Crete was breathtaking: ribbons of gold, copper and ruby red spanned across the horizon. Their stop at the island, intended to be brief, had stretched into three weeks, raising doubts whether they would ever leave. But in a world that had turned against them and broken their trust many times over, Mr Sevilla and Mr Cohen had restored some faith in honest men who were true to their word. In the hours before the Atlantic's departure, the Transport Committee arranged a farewell party to thank the men from Crete.

Mr Sevilla took the baby from Alma for a last cuddle.

'My little godson,' He cooed to Chaim. 'He won't remember how he was born in Crete.'

'We will tell him,' Max said. 'He'll always have a connection to the community here and we will never forget your kindness. When the war is over, I hope you'll come visit us.'

'I look forward to that day.' Mr Sevilla kissed the top of the baby's head and handed him back to Alma.

'Mr Sevilla, I cannot tell you how thankful I am,' Gisela said, in the limited Hebrew she had learned during her lessons on the ship. 'Because of you I can look forward to seeing my sons again and meeting my grandchildren.'

Mr Sevilla clasped her hands. 'My dear Gisela, I wish you much *nachat* from your family. Look after yourself. I know you have many wonderful friends who will take care of you for the rest of the crossing.'

Then he turned to Lilly and placed a hand on her shoulder. 'Take care of yourself, my dear. I hope you will find happiness in Eretz Israel.'

'Thank you for everything you did. For arranging the telegram, sending the letters, and above all for helping to organise our provisions and coal. I'm relieved we can continue our journey, but I am a little sad to say goodbye.'

Lilly couldn't help but feel a pang of sentimentality. The community leaders had provided the passengers with a comforting shield. Without them, they would have been at the mercy of their bandit captain, who, smoking a cigarette on the bridge, sneered at the gathering.

'Goodbyes are always hard,' Mr Sevilla said. 'So let's rather say *lehitra'ot*. See you again.'

'*Lehitra'ot*,' she replied.

'Bless those gentlemen and the Crete Jewish community,' Gisela said to Lilly as they watched their motorboat head back to the Heraklion harbour in the fading light. 'Well, I suppose I had better return to the cabin now. I'd rather not stumble around in the blackout.'

'Shall I accompany you?' Lilly said.

'No need. Jenny and Stefan are waiting for me.' She clapped her hands together. 'I can hardly believe it. Just a couple more days and I'll see my family. And what about you, Lilly?' She gave her a gentle nudge at her side. 'You seem happier after your swim yesterday.'

Lilly's lips twitched with amusement. 'Let's talk more tomorrow.'

Gisela winked. 'I look forward to that, my darling.'

At ten o'clock, the Atlantic raised anchor. The sweet sound of the thrumming engine and the lapping of waves against the hull sang of their departure. Lilly and Erika leaned against the railings staring into the night. Under the cloak of blackout, Heraklion wasn't visible, but Lilly could imagine the twinkling lights that had given the bay its enchanted appearance.

The upcoming Italian-occupied Dodecanese Islands were likely to be a more formidable experience. The Atlantic was about to embark on the most dangerous part of the voyage. Best not to dwell on it, Lilly decided. They had no alternative. There was no other route.

'Next time we see land we'll be arriving in Haifa,' Erika said.

'You don't sound excited,' Lilly said.

'I'm not sure how to describe how I feel. I'm relieved that we didn't get trapped in Crete. Concerned about sailing through this stretch of the sea. And I'm a little nervous to see Marcus again after all this time apart. I'm not sure how things will be between us.'

'You'll feel better when you see him and have a long talk.'

'Lilly,' she began. 'If things don't work out between me and Marcus, can I move in with you and Hannah?'

'Of course you can. But speak to him first, before you decide anything.'

Erika sighed. 'I don't know what's wrong with me, but I can't imagine seeing him again. Somehow, it doesn't seem real.'

'That's understandable. This has been a difficult, uncertain journey. And you've seen the worst of it.'

'Perhaps you're right,' Erika said. 'Speaking of which, I have a late night shift.'

'How is the situation in the infirmary?'

'Not good. If anything, it's worsening. More passengers are becoming seriously ill every day. We'll need to admit several to the hospital as soon as we arrive.' She squeezed Lilly's hand 'I'd better go. Thanks for listening. See you in the morning.'

Most of the ship was asleep, but Lilly was still wide awake, thoughts racing through her head. She remained at the railings, staring at the silver pinpricks of stars in the clear night sky, lulled by the rolling waves.

Alexander tiptoed up beside her. 'You're also still awake,' he said.

'Yes.'

'So ...' he began

'So ...?'

He gave a low laugh. 'Have you thought about what you'll do after we arrive?'

'I think I'll spend the first few days with my brother and sister-in-law and get reacquainted with them. So much has happened in the years since we last saw each other. After that, I haven't decided. This voyage has given me a lot to think about.' Lilly said. 'How about you? Will you go straight to the kibbutz?'

'Yes, that's the plan.' Alexander turned to face her, though she couldn't discern his features in the dark. 'That morning ... I'm sorry. I didn't mean to make you uncomfortable.'

'It's fine.'

'Life on the ship has been intense. I realise our situation will be different once we land. But I'd like to stay in touch.'

'I would like that too,' Lilly said.

'When you know where you're staying, perhaps I could come to visit you?' he said. 'Maybe you could visit me on the kibbutz too. We don't have to make any promises or plans for the moment. Shall we take things day by day and see what happens?'

'Yes, let's do that,' she said, with a sense of relief.

He leaned in and gave her a brief hug.

'Do you think we'll make it safely through this area?' Lilly asked.

'We had better. Especially after all we've been through.' He thought for a moment. 'But if not, I'd rather not be aware of what's happening. Let it just be quick and maybe my soul will reach Eretz.'

'That's a rather morbid way to think,' she said, teasing, trying to mask her growing unease.

'I find it sort of comforting. To wander the hills, valleys, forests and desert in eternal peace. Perhaps that's paradise—'

'Shhh,' Lilly said. She paused and lowered her voice to a whisper. 'Do you hear that?'

Alexander stood listening. 'What are you hearing?'

'The engine. Does it sound a little strange to you?'

'Strange, how?'

'Slower than usual.'

Alexander listened again. 'Hard to tell,' he said. 'Maybe the captain is navigating this region more slowly because of the risk of mines.'

His reassurance did little to calm her. She kept her ears tuned. 'Something feels wrong.'

'I've gone and scared you with my talk, haven't I? I'm sorry.'

'No, it's not that. I hear noises.'

'Everything is fine.' Alexander kept his tone light. 'If something were wrong, you'd soon know from all the shouting.'

'You don't hear scraping?'

'The wooden deck and frame often make creaking sounds. I'm sure it's not a mine or anything serious. Try not to worry.'

'The waves don't sound as loud.'

'The sea might be calmer here.' He patted her arm. 'Lilly, nothing is wrong. We'll make it through this stretch.'

'It feels as if we're close to land.'

'We left Heraklion hours ago. By now, we must be far out at sea. We might even have already passed the Dodecanese Islands.'

Lilly peered into the night, straining her eyes. 'I think I see a faint outline.'

'It's the darkness playing tricks. Or else we might have passed close to a reef. That could account for the creaking noise. Do you remember the panic before we reached Crete and thought a German submarine had rammed into us?'

'You may be right.' Lilly's laugh had a nervous edge. 'I suppose I'm more tense than I realised. I must be imagining things.'

Footsteps approached them from behind.

'Isaak, is that you?' Alexander said.

'It is.'

'Have you come to join the meeting of the insomniacs' club?' Alexander asked.

Isaak didn't laugh. 'Something isn't right.'

'Not you as well. What has made all of you so jumpy?'

'I think we might be heading in the wrong direction,' he said. 'To reach Eretz, we should be travelling east, correct?'

'That's right.'

'At some point, our ship must have turned, because we're travelling west.' He hesitated. 'Back towards Crete.'

'Are you certain?' Alexander asked, his voice tinged with doubt. 'How can you tell in the dark?'

'My papa taught me how to calculate directions using the North Star. Also, our speed has slowed and I get the sense we're close to land.'

'I thought the same,' Lilly said.

'I think I can make out the outline of a mountain range to our left,' Isaak said.

Alexander stared into the grey-blue twilight with intense concentration. 'I don't know. I still think the two of you are seeing things.'

A metallic clank pierced the quiet.

Lilly gasped. 'What was that?'

A chain rattled.

'It sounds like the anchor.' Now Alexander's voice tensed with alarm. 'Why have they stopped the ship?'

# CHAPTER 37

Alexander ran to the bow. 'We need to stop them,' he called over his shoulder as the anchor chain rattled and continued to unspool. 'Fetch the Haganah!'

Isaak and Lilly chased after him, stumbling over sleeping passengers, ignoring their complaints and cries – until Lilly stopped in her tracks.

'The captain!' she shouted.

Isaak glanced up at the bridge to see Spiro wearing a life jacket. He hesitated. Time seemed to slow.

The ship was at a standstill. Alexander stood at the bow, arguing with a few members of the crew.

Isaak turned to Lilly, but she had since disappeared from his side.

'Lilly!' He looked frantically around in every direction.

Then he caught sight of Spiro and the assistant who had tried to steal their lifeboat charging down the stairs. Lilly was waiting at the bottom, ready to block their path.

Heart pounding in his chest, Isaak rushed to Lilly, reaching her side as Spiro landed on the final step.

'Out of my way!' Spiro ordered.

Lilly stood firm, rooted in place.

With a menacing glare, he leaned towards her until his forehead was almost touching hers. 'Did you hear me?' he said, in a low, threatening tone. 'I said, out of my way you stupid woman.'

Lilly glared back at him. 'No.'

Spiro grunted as he lashed out and struck her shoulder. He shoved her aside, knocking her off balance.

Isaak swiftly reached for her arm and steadied her before she could fall.

'Where do you think you're going?' he said to the captain.

The other crew member squared up to Isaak and shoved him aside. Before Isaak could regain his footing, Spiro and his assistant had barrelled their way to the side of the ship.

'Stop them!' Lilly cried out, as the two miscreants scaled the railings.

Footsteps echoed on the deck from either direction, and, just before the two men could jump overboard, six pairs of hands grabbed ahold of them. The Haganah men yanked them off the railings and twisted their arms behind their backs.

'Get off me!' Spiro struggled and bucked against the men, trying to free himself from their grip.

Dr Horetzky arrived and marched up to Spiro. 'Why were you about to abandon ship?'

'I am ... the ... captain.' Spiro's breath came in quick gasps, as he continued to writhe back and forth. 'I don't answer to you.'

'I represent all the passengers on board. I demand an explanation.'

The other crew members approached, banding together, closing in on Dr Horetzky.

'Hold them back!' Dr Horetzky ordered urgently.

Haganah members and passengers linked hands at once. Isaak found Alexander and together they joined the line that was creating a barrier between the errant captain and his crew.

Dr Horetzky faced the captain once more. 'Why are we still in Crete?'

Without releasing his grip, Isaak turned and surveyed the view. The pink light of dawn revealed they were in a bay surrounded on three sides by mountainous peaks. A scenic village bordered the little harbour and the ever present whitewashed houses dotted the mountainside above. It might have been the most beautiful harbour they had visited so far, but it was far from where they wanted to be. Isaak's and Lilly's intuition was proved correct. They had spent the night sailing around the coast. Instead of continuing eastward, Spiro had turned south, then diverted west into another bay, on the eastern side of the island.

Isaak searched the crowd that had gathered on the deck for Lilly, but he did not see her. He hoped she hadn't been hurt in the confrontation with the captain.

'Spiro was about to jump overboard, swim to shore, and abandon us,' Dov spoke up from his place a little further down the line. 'He has already got his money from us and he's probably too scared to sail through a war zone.'

'Or risk arrest by the British on arrival in Mandatory Palestine.' Dr Horetzky sized Spiro up and down. 'Am I right?'

Spiro glanced to the side and didn't respond.

Dr Horetzky continued his interrogation. 'Why did you stop the ship?'

'We had to. The coal is of poor quality.'

'Nonsense! Why are you lying? If there was a problem with the coal, you should have warned us before we left Heraklion.'

'You were so enamoured with your beloved Mr Sevilla and Mr Cohen you wouldn't have believed me.' Spiro adopted a whining, mocking voice as he spoke. 'Apart from that, there isn't enough.'

'What are you talking about?' Dr Horetzky put his hands on his hips. 'We loaded one hundred and twenty tons of coal. That should be more than enough to take us to Haifa.'

Spiro let out a cruel laugh.

'What's so funny?'

Spiro gave him a withering look.

Are you prepared to continue sailing this ship?' Dr Horetzky asked.

'I already told you, we can't travel further with this coal. Let me go ashore and I'll find out if I can buy more.'

'You are not going anywhere!' He snapped. Start the engine. At once.'

'I can't.'

'If you aren't prepared to do it, then we will.'

The captain sniggered. 'Good luck with that.'

'I will ask you one last time. Will you continue this journey without further delay?'

'First, I must go ashore—'

Dr Horetzky looked to the heavens, his patience at breaking point. 'Men, please escort the captain to his cabin.' The doctor waved him away with his hand. 'Lock him in and take care to guard the door at all times.'

The two Haganah men holding his arms began dragging him away.

'What do you think you are doing?' Spiro kicked out. Two more grabbed his legs and lifted him up. 'This is mutiny!'

'Yes,' Dr Horetzky agreed. 'It is.'

As they carried Spiro off, the captain continued bellowing, 'Get your hands off of me!'

Dr Horetzky pointed to the other would-be escapee. 'Lock him up too.' Then he addressed the rest of the crew members who were still being held at bay. 'Are any of you willing to help us?'

The men looked at each other but remained silent for a time. Then the helmsman raised a hesitant hand. The chief mechanic, standing next to him, did the same.

'Thank you.' Dr Horetzky nodded his thanks. 'Please allow them to step forward.'

The human chain separated momentarily, creating a narrow pathway for them to pass through.

'Anyone else?' Dr Horetzky waited, his eyes scanning the crew members. No one else came forward. 'Right, then the rest of you are to retire to your quarters. And if any one of you causes trouble I will lock you up like your captain.'

The men cleared the deck rapidly, and without protest.

'Can someone please inform me who you are and why you have docked in Agios Nikolaos?' All heads turned to see an official in a peak cap and navy uniform standing on the deck with arms folded. He had boarded the ship, unseen, during the unfolding drama.

Dr Horetzky made his way toward him. 'I am head of the Transport Committee, in charge of these passengers. And you are?'

'I am the harbourmaster.'

'Sir.' Dr Horetzky said, and presented him with a brief account of recent events.

'You don't have permission to dock in port,' said the harbourmaster after Dr Horetzky had concluded his report. 'And under no circumstances is anyone allowed to disembark. You must leave at once.'

'We fully intend to. Just as soon as we get the engine restarted.'

'Very well. Good morning to you and a safe journey.' He turned on his heels and returned to his boat and to his job of policing the harbour.

'Right,' said Dr Horetzky after the harbourmaster had left. He searched the faces of the passengers. His forehead creased in concern.

'We have a slight problem.' He cleared his throat. 'Is anyone here able to ... captain a ship?'

Isaak looked around at the sea of blank faces, fearing this signalled the end of their journey, when a voice suddenly said, 'I think I could manage.'

Isaak recognised the man who stepped forward as Erwin Kovac. In his mid-thirties, Erwin was among the more senior members of their group from Prague. Isaak, being among the youngest, had had little interaction with him, but they knew each other well enough to exchange greetings.

'I'm a mechanical engineer,' Erwin continued. 'And before the war, I was an officer in the Czechoslovak Air Force.'

Dr Horetzky's face flooded with relief. 'Excellent.'

'I may be able to assist.' It was Fritz Steiner, another member of their group, a year or two younger than Erwin. 'I'm also an engineer.'

'Every bit of help is welcome.' Dr Horetzky shook hands with them both. 'Perhaps the two of you would like to start by going down to inspect the engine room?' Then he smiled at the rest of the passengers. 'Let's get our ship moving again.'

The crowd applauded Erwin and Fritz as they headed for the ladder that led to the engine room. When the audience dispersed, people clustered around in groups to discuss the specifics, and Isaak, Lilly, and Alexander found each other again.

'Well, that was rather intense,' Isaak said. He examined Lilly. 'How are you? Are you hurt?'

'I'm fine,' she said. 'It was just a push. And you?'

'Oh, I'm all right.' He shrugged it off. 'What you did was very brave.'

'Or crazy.' Lilly shook her head in disbelief. 'I'm not sure what came over me.'

'You did well to stall Spiro.' Alexander regarded her with admiration. 'And I'm sorry for doubting your concerns earlier.'

'What is going on?' Janka rushed over to join them with Hannah and Erika in tow. 'We could hear lots of shouting, but we couldn't see over the heads of the crowd or make sense of the commotion.'

'You missed all the drama,' Alexander said. 'Spiro attempted to abandon ship, so the Haganah carried him off and he's being held in his cabin under guard.'

Janka studied his expression. 'Is this some kind of joke?'

'Unfortunately not.'

'What will we do without a captain?' she persisted.

'We have a new one,' Alexander explained.

'Who?'

Alexander's answer was matter-of-fact. 'Erwin.'

Janka raised an eyebrow. 'That Erwin?'

Isaak turned to see Erwin and Fritz, back from the engine room, now conferring with Dr Horetzky. Erwin's face was bright red and Fritz had loosened his collar as if it were strangling him. Dr Horetzky placed a hand over his mouth, took a step back and leaned against the railings for support.

'They don't look too happy, do they?' Isaak said.

'Not at all,' Alexander said.

The three of them stomped their way back to the engine room, which prompted Alexander to go look for Dov. When he returned twenty minutes later, his expression mirrored Erwin's.

'*Sheisse. Sheisse. Sheisse*!' Alexander said through clenched teeth.

Isaak had never seen him so angry. 'What is it?'

'Lilly was right last night when she thought we were going too slow and hearing strange noises,' he raged. And do you know why? That *arschloch* of a captain went and threw several tons of our best coal overboard.'

'Oh no!' Isaak took a few deep breaths to calm himself before he swore too.

'Oh yes.' Alexander's eyes burned with fury. 'That's why Spiro was laughing about us not having enough fuel. Because he made certain that we don't.'

'All that effort to get fuel.' Isaak put his head in his hands. 'All those weeks of waiting. All that expense and generosity.'

'And he's gone and destroyed most of the load in order to sabotage our journey.'

'Does that mean we're stuck here?' Janka said.

'Not exactly.' Alexander exhaled. 'You heard what the harbourmaster said. We must still leave. Erwin and Fritz are attempting to restart the engine. But since there isn't enough coal to reach Eretz, we'll need to make another stop.'

'Where?' asked Janka.

'It will have to be Cyprus. It's the nearest port after the Dodecanese Islands.'

'Cyprus?' Isaak said. 'But that's under British rule. What will they say when they realise we're trying to enter Mandatory Palestine?'

Alexander threw up his hands.

'They won't let us sail further,' Isaak hesitated as he spoke. 'Will they?'

'I don't know.' Alexander bowed his head. 'Thanks to Spiro, we have no choice. It's a risk we will have to take.'

# CHAPTER 38

The Atlantic left the harbour of Agios Nikolaos that evening. This time there was no party, no sentimental farewell, only despondency that Haifa would not be their next stop.

The atmosphere grew tense as the Atlantic sailed around the eastern tip of Crete into the vicinity of the Dodecanese Islands. In the darkness, Isaak and the rest of the chevra huddled in the lifeboat. Each of them wore half a life jacket. The risk of hitting a mine was considered so serious that the Haganah instructed everyone on deck to wear them at all times. They were almost afraid to speak.

The ship made slow progress, travelling at eight knots – half their previous speed – but the sea was mercifully calm. Placid waves lapped the hull. The gentle rocking had a calming effect. Erika was the first to fall asleep, then Janka. Hannah and Alexander followed. Lilly, however, stayed alert and anxious. Each creak of the ship had her straining her ears, observing her surroundings.

'Can't sleep?' Isaak said in a low voice.

'Every time I'm about to doze off, I think I hear noises and I am jolted awake. How about you?'

'I have to stay awake because ...' He paused. 'I actually have a fire watch shift in a few minutes.' Isaak flung off his blanket and stood up. 'Try to get some sleep and don't worry. I'll be watching and listening out to make sure everything is all right. If something happens, I'll warn you straight away.'

'Thank you.' Lilly wrapped herself in her blanket and curled up on the bench. Isaak wandered over to the railings. He watched the faint silvery reflection of the moon on the rippling waves. She didn't need to know he didn't have a shift that night. He waited. Soon her form under the blanket rose and fell with her breathing, and she was fast asleep.

Isaak located the North Star. They were still moving. Sailing east. He returned to the lifeboat and closed his eyes.

The rest of the night passed without incident. In the morning, Isaak donned his tefillin and took part in the subdued minyan on the deck. He gave thanks that they had made it through the night and had sailed through a war zone without encountering either mines or the enemy.

The mountain tips of eastern Crete were still visible behind them, but soft currents helped nudge their ship southwards. Soon, the island disappeared out of sight. Alone, surrounded by the Mediterranean, they held their course, heading southeast.

But their coal was already running dangerously low.

Twice that day, Alexander answered a call for volunteers to help in the stokehold. Because of the soot buildup from the low-quality coal, they needed to douse the fire in the furnace and then raise a fresh fire.

By early evening, all that remained was coal dust. Their fuel was gone. The engine ceased running.

The passengers were as silent as the Atlantic's engine when a Haganah member stepped up to the bridge. 'Can I please have your attention?' he said. 'We are asking for every able-bodied passenger to volunteer ...'

Isaak and Alexander wasted no time in joining the teams of young men able and willing. As soon as they had received their instructions and fetched the necessary tools, he and Alexander hurried down to the lower deck with the rest of their assigned team.

'I can't believe it's come to this,' Isaak said, as they proceeded down the passageway.

'We don't have any other choice,' Alexander said.

'Do you think it will work?'

Alexander frowned. 'It has to.'

They entered the dining room, ten men in all, each bearing an axe or hammer. Isaak cast a final gaze around the grand interior, its solid mahogany tables and chairs, wood-panelled walls, and parquet floor.

The men took up positions around the room. Isaak and his cousin each selected a table.

Alexander nodded gravely to him. 'Shall we begin?'

Isaak took a resolute breath and raised his axe. 'Let's do what we need to do.'

He brought the axe down with a resounding thud and embedded it into the polished surface. His muscles strained as he retrieved the axe head and he delivered another powerful blow, splitting the wood. He continued his assault on the table until he had reduced it to a pile of timber.

Isaak gathered the pieces, an armful at a time, and brought them to the man positioned at the dining room entrance, who was part of a human chain to the stokehold and the furnace. The line snaked throughout the ship, along the passageways. From person to person, they transferred the wood until it reached the stokers who fed the fuel to the furnace.

All night long, the ship resounded with the pounding of axes and the blows of hammers; a last-ditch attempt to save the ship by destroying its furniture and fixtures.

The engine turned slowly.

The Atlantic limped on.

At dawn, Lilly appeared in the dining room, balancing a tray filled with cups of water. Isaak observed her face as she paused at the now frameless, doorless entrance, her eyes widening as she absorbed the scene. Not a single chair or table remained. The team had moved on to ripping off the panelled walls and tearing up the floor planks.

The men halted their work and gathered around Lilly, each eagerly taking a cup and gulping down the water in one go.

'Thanks for that,' Alexander said as he returned his cup. He ran his arm across his forehead to wipe away the perspiration. 'Just what I needed.'

'Do you want any more volunteers?' Lilly asked.

'If others are available, we'd welcome the help. We need all the spare hands we can get.'

Lilly set down the tray on a stripped patch of floor, straightened up, and took a step forward with enthusiasm. 'Can I volunteer?'

Caught off guard, Alexander paused before shaking his head with a smile. 'Thank you for your kind offer, but I don't think so. This isn't really a job for you.'

'Why not?'

'It's very hard, dangerous work.'

'Didn't you say you need every spare pair of hands you can get?' Her face remained set in determination, but a trace of hurt had appeared in her eyes.

'Yes, but—'

'If Lilly thinks she's up for it, why not let her give it a go?' Isaak interjected.

Lilly responded with a keen nod and a grateful smile.

'I don't want to see her get hurt,' Alexander said.

'We can look after her,' Isaak said.

Alexander weighed the proposal, shifting his attention between the two of them. 'All right. I'm due to start my shift in the stokehold.' He passed his axe to Lilly. 'You can take my place.' Then he gave Isaak a look. 'Find her a job. But make sure you take care of her.'

Isaak saluted. 'Never fear.'

'What's next?' Lilly looked around, eager to start. 'You've already demolished everything in here.'

'There's one object left,' he said. 'I can't bear to do it.' He pointed to the far corner of the room.

'Then I will,' she said, and crossed the room with determination.

Isaak followed, a sweet memory in his mind: the first time he had heard Lilly play *Vienna, Vienna* on the piano to joyous applause from the roomful of elderly passengers.

'Take a bow,' he had said, and Lilly had bobbed a little curtsey to her audience. He realised with a pang that some of that audience had since succumbed to disease and the bench of the dead.

'One last song?' Isaak asked her.

Lilly shook her head. 'I'll play a new song when we reach Eretz.'

She raised her axe and brought it crashing down. The piano gasped a final discordant tune, then spluttered out its keys like loose teeth.

In a matter of minutes, she had reduced the instrument to a heap of firewood. Beside it lay the discarded cast-iron piano plate and strings, four castors and three shiny foot pedals. Isaak picked up a pedal and turned it over in his hand. Solid brass.

'What are you going to do with them?' Lilly said.

'They won't burn, but they might come in useful.' He slipped them into his rucksack together with the brass castors.

'What about the iron plate?'

'Too large to carry. We'll leave it here.' He began scooping up the piano remnants. 'Come on, let's deliver this load and continue to our next assignment.'

As Isaak and Lilly headed down the passageway, they crossed paths with Janka and Hannah, who were marching with axes over their shoulders, like mythological shield-maidens.

'The masts, rafts and spars were burned; the crew worked lustily, keeping up the fires,' Hannah quoted with enthusiasm.

'Passepartout hewed, cut and sawed away with all his might. There was a perfect rage for demolition,' Janka answered her.

Lilly looked at them, amused. 'What are you quoting?'

'It's from *Around the World in Eighty Days* by Jules Verne,' Hannah said. 'They also had to break up the ship's interior to continue their journey. What irony! It's the book you gave me as a parting gift when I left Vienna.'

'In the story, did they succeed?' Isaak asked.

'Yes, they did,' Hannah said.

Isaak grinned. 'Then perhaps there's also hope for us.'

'The book is fiction. I'm not sure if anyone has attempted it in real life.' Hannah narrowed her eyes in contemplation, then swiftly tossed back her head. 'But we have to try.'

'We're here to help.' Janka said. 'Alexander told us Lilly had volunteered. We decided if she can do it, so can we.'

'We demolished the lifeboat.' Hannah shrugged. 'Erika helped hack it to pieces. 'She's on deck, helping treat a few passengers who were overcome by exhaustion in the stokehold. They had to be carried out.'

'And would you believe it?' Janka said. 'The original crew offered to resume duties.'

'Spiro too?' Isaak asked.

'No, he's still locked up in his cabin with a guard posted outside. Apparently, having heard all the commotion he has been yelling and screaming that he wants us to take him back to Crete.'

Hannah laughed. 'As if that's even possible anymore. We even burnt the lifeboat's oars.'

'Right.' Janka spoke in a business-like manner. 'What can we do?'

'The cabins are next,' Isaak said.

Other teams had torn down several cabins, but there were still another six left to demolish. The door to Gisela's cabin was open. The roommates sat on their bunks, bags packed, waiting for their eviction.

'Time to go?' Gisela said as Isaak entered.

'I'm afraid so,' Isaak said.

'Oh well.' She rose from the mattress. 'It will be worth it if it helps us reach Eretz Israel.'

Max lifted Chaim's cradle and followed Alma out of the door, while Jenny carried Gisela's bag and blanket as well as her own.

'I'll try to find them a quieter corner,' Max said. 'Then I'll return to lend a hand.'

Gisela was the last to leave. At the door, she paused and stroked Lilly's cheek. 'I'm so proud of you.' Then she turned to Isaak, Janka, and Hannah. 'I'm proud of all of you. Good luck.'

After they had gone, Isaak surveyed the cabin. 'Right, this is what I suggest. I'll start with the demolition of the bunks and I'll hand over the large pieces. Two of you cut them into smaller chunks and one of you collect them and pass them to the chain. After ten minutes, you'll change tasks so each of you has a chance to take a break. When Max returns, I'll alternate with him. This way, we can pace ourselves, conserve energy and get the job done. What do you say?'

They agreed with alacrity.

Isaak raised his axe over the top bunk. 'Let's get started.'

By afternoon, they had started dismantling their second cabin when Jenny burst in, out of breath. 'You must all come quick!' she said, panting.

'What's the matter?' Isaak said.

'Stefan just carried Alexander to the deck.' Jenny's voice shook. 'He collapsed in the stokehold.'

# CHAPTER 39

J anka and Isaak rushed to follow Jenny, with Lilly trailing only a step behind them. They navigated past the chain of passengers who continued to transfer timber pieces from one to the next. When they reached the upper deck, it took Lilly a moment to get her bearings. The superstructure was all but gone. The bench of the dead and the infirmary had been demolished. A small area of the deck, delineated by a patchwork of blankets formed a triage area where several patients lay in various stages of consciousness. Among them was Alexander. Stripped to the waist, covered in soot and grime, and varnished in a sheen of perspiration, he was almost unrecognisable. A rucksack propped up his feet and Erika supported his head in the crook of her arm. With her free hand, she held a cup to his lips, offering him sips of water.

'*Ach du lieber Gott*!' Janka crouched beside him. 'Alexander!'

Lilly searched Erika's face for a sign of reassurance. 'Is he going to be all right?'

'I hope so. He's dehydrated and exhausted. He needs fluids and rest.' Erika shrugged and Lilly knew she could not say more.

Alexander's eyes flickered and he tried to mumble something.

'What's he saying?' Janka said.

Isaak crouched down on Alexander's other side and brought his ear close to his cousin's lips. 'I can't make it out,' he said. 'Something about a potato.'

Lilly kneeled beside Janka. Alexander's eyes momentarily settled on her.

'Down to the last potato skin?' Lilly suggested.

Alexander's attempt at a smile was feeble.

Lilly hovered between tears and laughter. 'Down to the last potato skin, and down to the last piece of wood,' she whispered and squeezed his hand. 'We'll keep going. You sleep and get your strength back.'

Within moments, he fell asleep.

'There isn't much you can do for him right now,' Erika said. 'Best thing is to let him rest. I'll be here to take care of him and Jenny is also here.' Lilly saw her assisting two nurses, moving among other patients.

'Almost every hour, they carry another volunteer from the stokehold who has collapsed from the heat and strain of the work,' Erika said. 'Jenny is doing an excellent job helping to take care of them.'

'I supposed we should return to the cabins,' Isaak said. 'Will you call us when Alexander wakes up or if there's any other change?'

'I will,' she said. 'And please, look after yourselves, too.'

By nightfall, the Atlantic resembled a hollow skeleton. The passengers had requisitioned everything combustible to use as fuel in order to keep the engine running. It had taken twenty-four hours, but they had even stripped the deck of its boards, down to the metal below.

The ship crawled onwards.

Aching and weary, Lilly, Hannah, Janka, and Isaak returned to their usual corner. It looked bare without the lifeboat. But they had reason to be thankful: Alexander was awake and sitting up.

Janka enveloped her brother in a hug. 'You gave us such a fright.'

'Sorry, I didn't mean to.' He gave them an exhausted smile.

Isaak patted his shoulder. 'How are you feeling?'

'Much better, all credit to Erika,' Alexander said, turning to her. 'She's been taking good care of me.'

Erika wagged a finger back at him. 'Don't you dare do that again.' Beneath her attempt at a stern expression was a relieved grin.

'I'll try not to.' He placed his hand on his chest. 'I promise.'

They gathered in a close-knit circle to eat a meagre supper of a small square of stale bread and a palmful of raisins apiece. Lilly divided her portion of raisins, reserving half.

'How far do you think we've travelled?' Lilly asked.

Isaak stared up at the stars for a minute. 'Hard to tell,' he said.

In the distance, over the sea, a light flickered, then disappeared. A dull thud followed.

Muted shrieks rippled through the passengers on deck.

Another flash in the sky. Then a boom.

'I don't think we've sailed far enough,' Isaak spoke with a quiver in his voice.

'What direction are they coming from?' asked Alexander.

'Northwest, I think. That'll be the Dodecanese Islands.'

'Are we still travelling southeast?'

'Barely.' Isaak pressed a hand to his forehead. 'But yes.'

'We've done everything we can, haven't we?'

Isaak exhaled. 'I suppose we have.'

'Then the rest is up to destiny.'

The sporadic flickers and thuds continued, briefly illuminating their faces in the dark. Isaak's lips moved in silent prayer.

'What are you saying?' Alexander asked. 'I hope nothing too depressing like your last *Shema*.'

'*Tehillim*.'

'Recite it aloud,' he said. 'We'll repeat the words after you.'

'*Mizmor l'Dovid,*' he paused, and they repeated the words after him. 'The Lord is my shepherd; I shall not want.' The familiar words brought Lilly a measure of comfort. 'Though I walk through the valley of the shadow of death, I will fear no evil, for You are with me ...'

In the early hours, the naval guns fell silent.

Soon after, so did the ship's engine.

At sunrise, the passengers took down two of the three masts. They chopped the wood into pieces, and fed them into the furnace. There was no more potential fuel to salvage. The engine turned. The ship slowly moved on. But the wood wouldn't last much longer. Neither would their reserves of food and water.

It had been four days since they had left Crete for the first time. Without navigational equipment, they couldn't tell precisely where they were or how much further they had to travel – and still no sight of land. Erwin, their captain, had no alternative: he sent out a distress signal.

SOS.

Lilly wondered what would happen if a British ship found them. Or worse, what if it was an Italian ship?

SOS.

Lilly went below deck. In the shell where their cabin had once stood, Gisela lay on a blanket on the floor in a weakened state. Jenny and Stefan sat to one side. Max and Alma huddled on the other, Chaim's Moses basket securely between them.

'Here, take these.' Lilly presented Gisela with the few raisins she had saved from supper.

'What about you?' Gisela said.

'I'll be fine. Take them. They will give you some energy.'

'You are so good to me,' Gisela said. Like a daughter. I don't know how I would have managed this voyage without you. And the offer remains for you to live with me when we reach Eretz Israel.'

'Thank you. I'm still giving it thought.'

'You'd better hurry. We'll be there soon.'

Lilly managed a half smile. 'From your mouth to God's ears.'

'Any further news?'

'Erwin is sending out distress calls, but no reply yet.'

Gisela patted her hand. 'We've come this far. We'll make it.'

'Yes, we will,' she agreed, for Gisela's benefit.


Hours ticked by. Afternoon dragged into evening.

SOS. SOS.

Silence.

Then, at dusk, Isaak leapt to his feet. 'I see a black outline near the horizon. I think it's a ship.' The others quickly stood to join him.

'There appears to be two of them,' Alexander said

'Have they seen us?' Lilly asked.

'They haven't responded yet,' Isaak said.

'They look like warships,' Alexander said.

'Italian, British, or German?'

Alexander strained to see. 'Not sure.'

The ships continued their approach.

'British,' Isaak said. 'I can see its flag.'

One ship flashed its signal light. Alexander concentrated on the sequence. The Atlantic sent a series of flashes in reply.

'Can you understand what they are saying?' Lilly said.

'They asked, who are you? What is your destination?' Alexander kept his focus on the exchange.

'What did we reply?' said Isaak.

'Port Said.'

'Huh?' Janka said. 'Why did Erwin tell them that?'

The Atlantic flashed another sequence.

As Alexander deciphered, Isaak whispered, 'Because they might try to stop us if they knew our actual destination.'

'We've just asked if they can help us with some fuel, food, or even water,' Alexander said.

The warship issued a reply of long and short bursts.

'They are turning!' Hannah grew alarmed. 'Why are they sailing away? Don't they understand we're sending an SOS message?'

'They said, sorry, we can't help you.' Alexander shook his head in despair. 'We will notify the next port.'

'That's it?' Isaak said.

Alexander slumped back onto the deck. 'That's it.'

Don't go, Lilly prayed, but the two ships disappeared into the night.

# Chapter 40

By daybreak, all of the wood and coal – even the dust – was gone. Since the brief exchange with the two British warships, no one had come to their aid, and they had not encountered any other vessels.

Helpless, they drifted, carried by the waves.

No land in sight.

Hannah stood at the railings and gazed around, realising how vulnerable they were: a small, powerless ship at the mercy of the sea. She remembered the elation they had felt when they had first left Romania and the coast disappeared from view. The freedom of being surrounded by the wide open sea. But that had been over a month ago, when they had expected their journey to last a matter of days. Before storms, hunger, thirst, disease, death, and betrayal had sapped them of hope.

Their situation was becoming more critical by the hour and it was no longer only the elderly suffering from disease. Erika confided to them that a seventeen-year-old girl was desperately ill, too.

Hannah stepped around the listless passengers lying on the deck. They were all thirsty and starving; even talking was becoming too much of an effort for some. She returned to the lifeboat-less chevra. Isaak opened his eyes. 'Did you spot anything?'

'Still nothing,' Hannah said.

She lay down beside Lilly who gazed up at the sky through half-closed eyes.

'Looks like rain.' Lilly's voice lacked emotion, as if she had become too disheartened to care.

Hannah studied the ominous grey clouds gathering overhead. 'Let's pray we don't get caught in another storm.'

'I wonder if those warships have already passed on our SOS message.' Lilly said.

'They must have done by now.' Hannah didn't want to express her fear that the ships had abandoned them and they would remain at the sea's mercy until they were overwhelmed by a storm or submitted to malnutrition, dehydration, or disease. Their skeleton ship would become a ghost ship. Hannah wondered if Karl had made it safely to Haifa. She despaired of ever seeing him again.

Hannah felt Lilly's hand find hers with a light squeeze, as if she knew Hannah's thoughts.

Isaak heaved himself up. 'I'll check if I can spot anything.'

A few minutes later, he was back. 'You'll never guess—'

Alexander propped himself on his elbow, anticipation stirring him from his stupor. 'Land? A ship?'

'Sorry, nothing as good as that,' Isaak said as he slumped down between Alexander and Janka. 'Spiro's back on the bridge.'

'Spiro? As in, Spiro the former captain?' Janka's eyes opened wide. 'Who let him out of his cabin?'

'According to Dov, Spiro has reconsidered his position and offered to help.'

'Help?' Alexander's laugh was bitter. 'It's his fault we're in this predicament. If not for him, we would have been in Eretz by now.'

'I hope they stripped all the furniture and fittings from his cabin for firewood,' Hannah said.

'And burned his possessions along with it.' Alexander fell back and exhaled his frustration.

Hannah closed her eyes. What was the point in wasting energy by working herself up? It wouldn't change anything. Hannah was still trying to calm herself down when Lilly said, 'I ought to check on Gisela.'

Lilly swayed on her feet as she stood up, her face pale.

Hannah lifted her head. 'Are you all right? Are you going to faint? Do you want me to come with you?'

'I'm just a little dizzy from standing too fast. I'll be fine. You rest.'

Relieved, Hannah lay down once more, too sluggish to move.

Lilly returned seconds later. She stood in front of Hannah with her hands on her knees, trying to catch her breath. 'Land.' She couldn't contain her relief. 'I think I've spotted land.'

Passengers were already flocking to the railings. The chevra summoned the energy to stand and join the assembled crowd. Lilly pointed to a smudge on the horizon.

'You may be right, Lilly.' Alexander squinted. 'Yes! You are right.'

'Where are we? What coast is that?' Lilly asked.

'Isaak?' said Alexander. 'Any idea?'

'Hard to tell without a map,' he said. 'It may be Cyprus.'

'I'm going to ask the crew,' Alexander said. Resolved, he headed to the bridge.

'Are we drifting closer?' Hannah said.

'We might be,' Janka said. 'It's starting to look a little clearer, isn't it?'

If only they could row themselves to shore, Hannah thought. There wasn't a single oar left on board.

Alexander reappeared and presented a folded map to Isaak. 'Erwin and Fritz think it's most likely Cyprus, but Spiro is insisting

we've travelled in a circle and reached the Turkish coast. He's ordering the Turkish flag to be hoisted on the mast. What do you think?'

Isaak spread the map out on the deck and traced their route with
his index finger. 'We left Crete and travelled south east. When we saw
that navel engagement at night, it was in a northeasterly direction,
perhaps near Rhodes. We travelled away from it, southwards, and
continued sailing east. If we were off the coast of Turkey, I believe
we would have reached it sooner. But we haven't seen land for days.'
He circled the stretch between Crete and Cyprus. 'Which means we
must have been travelling in this area here. That has to be Cyprus.'

'I'm sure you, Erwin, and Fritz are correct.' Alexander folded the
map. 'So much for Spiro's keen nautical mind.'

'A boat!' someone shouted.

Hannah's attention snapped back to the water. She trained her
eyes on a motor launch moving towards them. The vessel drew
closer until they could define its details and flag.

Isaak nodded at the Union Jack and smiled. 'Cyprus.'

Passengers waved at the boat and cheered. Alexander's reaction
was more subdued. 'At least it isn't Italian or German. Before we get
too excited, let's first wait and see if they are sympathetic towards
us.'

The crew lowered the Turkish flag from the mast and raised a
British one in its place.

No matter what happened next, Hannah thought, at least she
would live to see Karl.

The motor launch stopped alongside the Atlantic and several of
its crew members, dressed in navy uniforms and white caps, boarded
the ship to a round of applause.

'Are you really British?' called out Ignatz from the Prague group.

'Of course we are,' one of the sailors said.

'How do we know for sure?' someone else quizzed him.

He looked amused. 'We are flying the Union Jack and wearing the Royal Navy uniform. What more proof do you need? You want us to sing the national anthem for you?'

'Go on then,' another passenger encouraged.

The sailors turned to each other with a shrug. Then they stood to attention.

*God save our gracious King,*
*Long live our noble King,*
*God save the King!*
*Send him victorious,*
*Happy and glorious,*
*Long to reign over us,*
*God save the King!*

The passengers responded with a standing ovation and several cheered, 'God save the King!'

An officer stepped forward. 'Right then. That will be quite enough of that.' He spoke in clipped tones and had a down-turned mouth fixed in a permanent frown. He cast a critical eye over the dishevelled and emaciated passengers. 'Who is in charge here?'

Dr Horetzky approached the officer and held out his hand. 'I am head of the Transport Committee.'

The officer appeared hesitant and reluctant to shake his hand, but then quickly did so out of politeness. 'Where have you come from?'

'Tulcea in Romania,' said Dr Horetzky. 'But our most recent port was Heraklion, Crete.'

The officer examined the doctor's face to see if he was lying. 'Heraklion, you say?'

'Yes.'

'Do you mean to tell me that you have just sailed through the Italian mines, and you got here in one piece?' He shook his head in disbelief. 'Well I never!' He narrowed his eyes. 'So I take it you're not from Panama?'

'No.'

'And your destination isn't really Port Said, is it?'

Dr Horetzky paused as he considered his response, then answered, 'No.'

'What is your intended destination?'

'We fled Nazi-occupied Europe where our lives are in mortal peril and would like to go to Mandatory Palestine.'

'I see.' The officer stared down at Dr Horetzky who stood a head shorter than him. 'Then I assume you have permits and visas for all these passengers?'

'We do not.'

'So you were attempting to enter illegally?'

Dr Horetzky bowed his head in resignation. 'We had no choice.'

'Hmmm. I see.' The officer studied the passengers, looked to his men and then back at the man before him. 'Right. This is what we propose to do. We'll arrange a tug to bring you into port. Then we'll consider the matter further.'

At seven o'clock that evening, a tugboat dragged the Atlantic into Limassol Harbour. The passengers' lives were saved, but uncertainty interrupted Hannah's relief. Would the British agree to let them continue their journey? And if not, what would happen to them?

# CHAPTER 41

Lilly had a sense of déjà vu when a small rowing boat drew up beside their ship hawking oranges, radiant as the rising sun. They had been bobbing at the entrance to Limassol Harbour since the tugboat deposited them there the night before, albeit with no inkling of what would happen next. They had not received any food either. As in previous ports, Isaak bargained with a hawker and traded his last two cigarettes for six oranges.

Lilly and Isaak hurried down to the lower deck where he presented three of the oranges to Gisela, Stefan and Jenny, Max and Alma.

Alma welcomed his offering as if it was a precious gem. 'From the depths of my heart, thank you.' Her lips were dry and cracked. Dark circles had formed under her eyes. She was struggling to feed Chaim while she didn't have enough nourishment for herself.

In her weakened state, Gisela's hand shook as she tried to peel her orange. Lilly helped her, then fed her the segments one at a time. Gisela sucked thirstily on the juice and licked her lips. 'You have both been so good to me,' she said so softly that Lilly, sitting next to her, had to strain to hear her.

Gisela was fading. The orange had provided a shred of sustenance, but how much longer could she hold out? Would the British provide them with food? The alternative was unthinkable.

Lilly and Isaak returned to the chevra and Isaak divided the remaining oranges among them. Lilly savoured her first bite. Tangy juice filled her mouth. She wondered whether she would always associate fruit with the different stages of their journey. Apples in Tulcea, grapes in Crete, and now the oranges of Cyprus.

Lost in a citrusy bliss, she hadn't noticed that British officials had boarded the Atlantic until Alexander commented, 'It appears they are considering our destiny.'

The discussion between the officials and their Transport Committee appeared civil, punctuated by frequent nods, but the furrowed brows of both parties displayed the underlying tension. It was impossible to tell from their faces whether they had reached a decision in the passengers' favour. The men shook hands, the officials withdrew, and Dr Horetzky stepped up to the bridge holding the megaphone.

'Please, may I have your full attention?' He waited until the chatter ceased. 'The British authorities have just informed us that they are prepared to provide us with fuel and provisions and grant permission for us to continue our journey to Eretz Israel. But—'

The passengers erupted at once with cheers, claps, and whistles, drowning out his words. Dr Horetzky waved his hands, requesting calm, but the jubilation continued. After months of uncertainty, the passengers released their pent up tension with whoops of joy.

'Please listen,' he implored. 'Shhh. Please listen. There is more.' The cheering petered out and the deck grew quiet again. 'That was the good news. However, it comes with a condition.' His eyes roamed the deck, taking in his fellow passengers, a serious expression on his face. 'We are required to cover the cost of the coal and provisions.' He inhaled deeply. 'They are demanding the sum of four hundred and eighty pounds sterling from the ship.'

The ship echoed with hundreds of gasps of shock, including Lilly's. Four hundred and eighty pounds was a fortune. One pound was approximately ten Reichsmarks, the meagre sum the Nazis had permitted the Jews to take with them when they emigrated. And by now, most of them had already spent a substantial part, if not all, of that allowance on necessary expenses during their prolonged journey. How were they to raise such a large sum? Would money be the obstacle standing in the way of their dream to reach the Promised Land?

'I know.' Dr Horetzky's nod expressed his empathy. 'It is a huge amount. But if we want to reach Eretz, we have no choice except to pay. Therefore, the committee has decided every single adult passenger will be required to contribute the equivalent of one dollar. It can be in sterling, Reichsmark, or any other foreign currency. Those passengers who do not have any money must instead donate an item of equivalent value, such as a piece of jewellery or a watch. In the next few minutes, we will send Haganah volunteers throughout the ship to collect your contributions. I ask all of you to cooperate. Please do not make this more difficult for them than it already is.'

The Haganah tasked Alexander with collecting payments on one side of the deck. Some of the Danzig group and older passengers who had travelled on the Schönbrunn found enough money to pay. Alexander and Janka paid with two gold fountain pens that had been parting gifts from their parents. Isaak donated a gold cigarette lighter, no doubt the result of one of his barters.

Hannah handed over a silver watch, an eighteenth birthday present from her mother.

Alexander furrowed his brow. 'I'm sorry you have to give it away.'

Hannah shrugged. 'It has to be done.'

'Thank you for your contribution.'

From a tub of shoe polish, Erika retrieved a pair of dainty silver earrings concealed in wax paper.

'I'm so sorry to take them from you.' He let out a heavy sigh.

'It's all right,' Erika said, shaking off her regret at parting from them.

Then he turned to Lilly. 'Do you have anything?'

'Only this.' She removed the gold wedding ring from her finger.

Alexander pressed his lips together and hesitated. 'Do you have anything you can give instead?'

She shook her head. 'Nothing.'

Lilly closed her eyes and said a silent prayer, 'Salo, thank you for the short but happy time we shared. Thank you for your love and for your help in saving me now. I will never forget you.'

'Are you sure you are ready to do this?' His expression showed only kindness and genuine concern for her.

Lilly blinked back her tears. 'It is the price I must pay in order to survive and start a new life.'

She kissed the ring and placed it in the basket, where it clinked against several other wedding bands.

'I'm sorry, Lilly.' Alexander bowed his head. 'I am so sorry.'

Isaak patted his cousin's shoulder. 'Let me help you with the rest of your round.' He quietly murmured something in Alexander's ear as they continued on.

The Transport Committee scraped together the amount demanded of them. They handed over their money, jewellery, and other valuables to the British authorities, only to be told they would now have to wait for an answer from London and Jerusalem regarding the licence to continue their journey.

That same afternoon, members of Limassol's small Jewish community arrived with a generous food donation, a gesture of kindness that brought a modicum of comfort during their uncertain predicament. After days of deprivation, they had some wholesome food to eat.

And they waited.

The local press took an interest in the Atlantic, and the *Cyprus Post* recounted their escape from the Nazis and their subsequent journey. 'These people huddled in their little ship, sailing dangerous seas and a prey to disease and death are ... merely men, women and children seeking a home, something stable in an unstable world ... [Yet] it is quite possible that these wandering Jews ... will not be allowed to cry at the Wailing Wall. They will be forced to continue their tragic odyssey much further.'

Over the next few days, an appeal in the same paper drew locals' sympathy and many people donated food. Gisela and Alma began regaining their strength, but for some passengers it was too late. The seventeen-year-old girl succumbed to her illness, leaving Erika devastated. She was the twelfth person to perish on the Atlantic. The local community helped arrange her burial in the Jewish cemetery, as well as organising the transfer to hospital of four other seriously ill passengers.

A week after their arrival in Limassol, a rumour spread around the ship that the British were planning to disembark the passengers and intern them in Cyprus. The British were quick to deny the rumours, but still the passengers waited for their authorisation to sail to Haifa, as well as for the food and coal for which the British had demanded such a high price.

Lilly missed Mr Sevilla. If only he could help them as he had done in Heraklion. But whose words would sway the nameless and faceless bureaucrats in Jerusalem and London? The British had dismissed the suggestion of internment in Cyprus; why was it taking so long?

Still, they waited.

Ten days after landing in Limassol, on the twenty-second of November, Dr Horetzky appeared on the bridge with a megaphone. 'May I have your attention, please?' Silence descended over the passengers at once. 'The coal we purchased will arrive today ...' He looked out over the sea of faces, waiting in anticipation, and he smiled. 'And the British have given us permission to sail directly to Haifa under their escort. We leave tomorrow.'

# CHAPTER 42

In the stillness of the early morning, before the break of day, the Atlantic left Limassol for the twenty-four-hour journey to Haifa, escorted by a British officer and a platoon of soldiers, who had boarded the ship the night before. The last leg of an odyssey that had lasted almost three months.

Lilly watched a fiery sunrise emerge between grey rain clouds. The next sunrise I see will be over Eretz, she thought.

All morning and into the afternoon, she watched the sea, following the ship's progress in the blue waters of the Mediterranean. Wave after wave, they drew closer to the promise of home.

That evening, the chevra gathered for their last meal together. Their voices overlapped in their excitement, as they discussed their plans for after their arrival.

Alexander spoke with passion about fulfilling his dream to live and work on the kibbutz, helping to cultivate the land. Janka raised the idea of setting up a kibbutz library. Everyone – including Alexander – agreed that it was a marvellous suggestion. Perhaps kibbutz life would agree with Janka after all.

Erika was eager to complete her nursing studies. Despite the challenges on board, she was more determined than ever to become a nurse. Erika's thoughts also touched on Marcus, and she admitted she couldn't wait to see him again, whatever might be.

Hannah, of course, was counting down the hours, the minutes, until her reunion with Karl. She also turned to the others for advice. Which city did they think would offer the best opportunities for her and Lilly to find work and a rental apartment – Haifa, Jerusalem or Tel Aviv?

And Lilly? She remained silent, lost in her own thoughts. After tonight, everything would be different.

When the rest of the chevra lay down for a few hours' rest, Lilly stood by the railings, feeling the mist of the sea on her face, memorising the scent of the salty air.

She wasn't surprised when Isaak appeared by her side. 'Are you too excited to sleep as well?' he asked.

'I suppose so.' Lilly said. 'I can hardly believe that we'll reach Haifa in just a few hours and leave this ship.'

'It feels surreal, doesn't it?' he said. 'I'm actually glad we have this quiet moment. I have something to return to you.'

'Oh?' Lilly didn't recall having lent him anything.

He lowered his voice. 'Hold out your hand.'

When she did as he asked, he placed a small object into her palm and closed her fingers over it. 'Keep this somewhere safe. And don't let anyone see it.'

She opened her hand, felt the shape in the darkness, and ran her finger around its edge. 'My wedding ring?' A sharp gasp escaped her throat. 'I don't understand. How did you get it back?'

'When you put your ring in the basket, I noted which was yours. Just before Alexander was going to turn the collection over to Dr Horetzky, I traded the brass from the dismantled piano for your ring. You earned it. We weren't sure the brass would be enough, but they accepted it. '

'I don't know how to thank you.' Lilly placed a trembling hand over her mouth.

'Alexander helped me to retrieve it, but he recommended I not give it to you until we left Cyprus, just in case something went wrong and they made me return it. You looked heartbroken to part with the ring. Your husband must have been a very special person.'

'Yes,' she said, trying to keep her emotions in check. 'Yes, he was.'

'You don't have to forget the past,' he said. 'You can keep your memories close and still move forward.'

'Those are wise words.' Lilly smiled briefly.

'They are, though I can't take the credit. That's what my stepmother, my second mother, said to me when she came into our lives.'

Lilly put the ring in her pocket. In that moment, she realised she would always treasure Salo's ring for the precious memories it held; but she would never wear it again.

They leaned on the railings and watched the waves, iridescent in the silvery moonlight.

'Lilly, about your plans,' Isaak started, hesitating. 'To find a place with Hannah and which city to move to ... Well, I have another suggestion.'

She propped her chin on her hand and gave him her full attention. 'What is it?

'When we were on the Helios and I met Karl, he told me he and his *Hechalutz* group were planning to settle on a religious kibbutz in the Galilee. It's fairly near to where Alexander and Janka's group will be. I've decided I'd like to join Karl's group. What if you were to also start out on the kibbutz with Hannah and see how you like it? And if you do, then, when Hannah marries, you'll be close by. I'll be there. Maybe Erika too. And you'll meet so many others who have come on their own and are in a similar situation.'

Lilly pondered what he said.

What do you think?' Isaak said.

'It's a good suggestion.'

'And?'

'I want to think about it some more. It's a good suggestion,' she repeated.

Isaak nodded. 'Whatever you decide, please can we stay in touch after we reach Eretz?'

'I'd like that,' she said. 'I'm glad we have become such friends on this journey.'

'I am too.'

Isaak opened his arms for Lilly, and they hugged.


At dawn, the passengers crowded onto the upper deck to catch their first sight of the Promised Land.

In the dusky blue light, they glimpsed the outline of the mountains of Lebanon.

Lilly and Hannah stood side by side, waiting, watching, their anticipation mounting, each alone in her thoughts. As they neared their destination, Lilly's new plans began to take shape.

The Atlantic sailed south, hugging the coastline. The ship passed the chalk cliffs of Rosh Hanikra and its grottoes that looked like a giant elephant had set foot in the sea. Then, as the sky shifted to pink, they spotted the ancient, walled city of Akko.

At last, Lilly reached a decision.

'Hannah, I have something to tell you,' she said.

Her cousin turned to her, curious.

Lilly gathered her courage and took a deep breath. 'When we land in Eretz Israel, I think it would be best if we don't live together.'

Hannah went still. 'What?' She stared at Lilly, confused. 'I ... I don't understand. Have I done something to upset you?'

Lilly shook her head, and smiled at Hannah tenderly. 'I'm not upset. Not at all.'

'Then why?' Hannah was still confused.

'I don't want you to delay your happiness with Karl. We've been through too much already. You need to start your lives together.'

'But first I need to make certain you're settled. I don't mind—'

'I do.' Lilly laid her hand on Hannah's arm. 'It's time for me to stand on my own two feet. It is not fair for you to put your life on hold for me. And you want to be with Karl. I think you should move to the kibbutz right away and be close to him.'

'What about you?' Hannah said. 'Where will you go?'

'I think I would first like to spend a few nights with Eugen and Allegra, to reconnect with them after all this time apart.'

'And after that?'

'After that, I may stay with Gisela for a few weeks.'

'And then?' Hannah said. 'Have you decided yet where you'd like to settle?'

'I have.' Lilly paused. 'And I'm seriously considering the kibbutz where you and Karl are going to live.'

Hannah's eyes opened wider. 'Really?' She grinned with delight.

'Really.' Lilly smiled back. 'I'm not sure if I'm suited to kibbutz life, but I'd like to try it.'

Hannah processed what Lilly was saying, and her usual enthusiasm took over. 'Why don't you come to the kibbutz straight away and join me?'

'No.' Lilly's reply was firm.

'Why not?'

'I don't want to be in your way. I'll only come once you are married.' Lilly's voice trembled. 'So don't take too long about it.'

Hannah brushed away her tears before they could fall. 'Thank you.' She kissed Lilly on the cheek and hugged her tight.

'Be happy together,' Lilly whispered.

As the ship rounded the bay, the sight of Haifa port emerged, framed by the majestic Mount Carmel. They had stopped at many beautiful ports on their journey, but none had captured them quite like this.

Hannah strained for a view of the ships in the harbour. There was the Milos, and the Pacific, Karl's ship. They had already arrived.

Max and Alma lifted baby Chaim to show him his new home.

Gisela brought a handkerchief to her eyes. Somewhere on the dock, her sons, daughter-in-law and grandchildren would be waiting for her. Eugen would also be there to meet Lilly.

Overcome with emotion, the passengers filled the air with the sound of *Hatikva*. The hope.

*Our hope will not be lost,*
*The ancient hope,*
*To return to the land of our fathers ...*

Lilly watched the coastline. The first rays of sunlight touched the slopes of Mount Carmel.

After all of the obstacles, they had finally reached their destination. Vienna felt very far away. She had come home. To their ancient new homeland.

The chevra formed a circle, all wrapping their arms around each other in a tight embrace, laughing and crying.

'Lilly, are you sure you'll be all right on your own?' Hannah said.

Lilly's gaze lingered on the beloved faces of the friends surrounding her: Gisela, Max and Alma, Jenny and Stefan, Erika, Janka, Alexander, Isaak.

'Don't worry about me.' She smiled through her tears, and suddenly felt a wave of calm. 'I won't be alone.'

No one knew what lay ahead, but Lilly was sure of one thing: she would take the opportunity she had been given to look to the future. She would start over. One day at a time.

# Author's Note

*Wave After Wave* began with a brief, seemingly innocent conversation. One afternoon, while working at the Aden Jewish Heritage Museum, I sat down with a woman of around eighty who told me about her childhood in 1940s Tel Aviv. She related how one night her family provided assistance to Jewish refugees who had swum to shore from a ship whose passengers had been denied entry into British-controlled Mandatory Palestine.

About three years later, I included her account in my short story collection, *Passage From Aden: Stories From a Little Museum in Tel Aviv*. While doing further research on the history of Aliyah Bet (clandestine immigration before Israel's independence in 1948 ), I stumbled across the incredible, compelling and little-known story of another refugee ship, the SS Atlantic. I immediately knew that this would be the subject of my next novel. Research revealed this to be a complex, multi-layered tale. I soon realised I could not do the story justice with just one book, so *Wave After Wave* evolved to become the first book of a planned trilogy.

Writing *Wave After Wave* involved several years of intense research, reading first-hand accounts, testimonies and diaries, and visiting museum archives. I had the opportunity to speak to a few people who travelled on the Atlantic as young children and they related some of their experiences to me.

The novel is based on true historical events. Although the main characters are products of my imagination, several of the supporting characters are based on real people.

Wherever possible, I have tried to stay as close as possible to the original dates by cross-referencing a timetable of the journey, written by one of the Atlantic passengers, with a calendar for 1940. One particular date that had little relevance when I first began the novel suddenly took on a different meaning as I neared the end of the project. 7 October 1940 was the day the Atlantic was set to leave Tulcea, Romania. In 2023, however, 7 October became the largest targeted massacre of Jewish civilians since the Holocaust. The parallels between writing about historical events of 1938, such as rampant antisemitism, the Anschluss and Kristallnacht (which historians regard as the start of the Holocaust), with the rising antisemitism 85 years later, were not lost on me. As history appeared to be bent on repeating itself, I gained even greater empathy for the events and characters.

Although *Wave After Wave* isn't the story of my family, I felt a particular kinship to the refugees as some of my family originated from the same places as they did, including Vienna and Bratislava. My grandparents, however, followed different escape routes. Numerous relatives were unable to leave, despite various attempts. Tragically, many perished in the Holocaust.

As a way to honour and remember them, I chose to use some of their names for my main characters. For example, my grandfather's first cousins, sisters, were named Lilly and Erika. They were born in Bratislava and both perished in Auschwitz after contracting typhus. In a strange coincidence, I discovered that in 1942 after being rounded up, and before being sent on a train to Auschwitz, Lilly and Erika were detained in a holding camp called Patronka. This was the same Patronka that two years earlier acted as a hostel for many of the Jewish refugees who ended up on the Atlantic and Pacific.

On 4 September 1940, approximately 3,500 Jewish refugees departed from Bratislava, the capital of the Slovak Republic. This was the largest transport of Jewish refugees ever to travel down the Danube during the Second World War.

While Jews could still leave Germany and Austria at this stage, there remained the near-universal problem of procuring a visa. Most countries enforced immigration quotas and refused to accept the thousands of desperate Jews who queued outside their embassies and consulates, trying every which way to leave.

The Danube transport was arranged through the Central Office of Jewish Emigration, which was under the command of the Nazi Adolf Eichmann (the same Eichmann who would later become a senior figure in the implementation of the Final Solution). Initially, his primary aim was to rid the Nazi-controlled territories of Jews and exploit the situation to extort from them as much money and other items of value as he could.

As hinted in the novel, part of the reason the Nazis permitted this particular transport was because they needed a means of transport to repatriate ethnic Germans from Bessarabia (modern day Moldova and Ukraine) when the region was ceded by Romania to the Soviet Union. Rather than send empty boats down the river, a plan was devised to charge the optionless Jewish refugees exorbitant fares in order to help subsidise the cost of this repatriation.

Eichmann, however, wasn't interested in organising illegal transports to British-controlled Mandatory Palestine. That was left to his agent, Berthold Storfer. Sixty-year-old Storfer was an enigmatic, controversial figure. He wasn't well-known among Vienna's Jewish community, and many, including Zionist Organisations such as the *Hechalutz*, were suspicious of his motives. Nevertheless, it is estimated he facilitated the rescue of over 9,000 Jews – including those who travelled in the convoy of four DDSG paddle steamers down the Danube and then across the sea on the ships on the *SS Atlantic*, the *SS Pacific*, and the *SS Milos*.

In October 1941, when the Nazis banned Jewish immigration, Berthold Storfer went into hiding, but was caught in 1943. Despite begging Eichmann for his life, he was sent to Auschwitz. A year later, in 1944, he was shot.

Gisi Fleischmann, briefly mentioned as bringing hot food to the refugees in the Slobodarna and Patronka, was a devoted, brave woman and leader of the Bratislava Working Group who worked tirelessly, risking her own life, to help and save Slovakian Jews. She was arrested in October 1944 and sent to Auschwitz where she was murdered three days later.

Until I began my research, I had not realised that many small Jewish communities assisted Jewish refugees on their journey, including those in Istanbul, Crete, and Cyprus. The passengers of the Atlantic credited Mr Sevilla and Mr Cohen of Heraklion, Crete with enabling them to continue their voyage. I could not find out what happened to the two men after they so graciously assisted the Atlantic or if they managed to leave Crete prior to German occupation.

The Jewish community in Crete was one of the oldest in the world, existing since the 4th or 3rd century BCE. The attempted Italian invasion of Greece in October 1940 failed, but the Germans then occupied Crete from April 1941. Between 1941 and 1943, the Nazis shot several individual Jews. Finally, in May 1944, the Nazis rounded up the remaining Jews of Crete, planning to send them to Auschwitz. The Nazis loaded them onto a steamship, which was subsequently spotted by a British submarine who assumed it was a German military vessel and sank it with two torpedoes, killing everyone on board.

Captain Spiro was described and characterised in diary entries by a few of the passengers. There was also a drawing of him done by the artist Fritz Haendel who was a passenger on board the Atlantic.

I wasn't able to find details of the actual conversation that took place after Captain Spiro tried to escape with a member of crew and after the passengers discovered they had thrown the coal overboard, so I have used poetic licence based on details mentioned in various diaries.

Dr Paul Horetzky of Prague was the 27 year-old head of the Transport Committee. Erwin Kovac and Fritz Steiner really did take over the ship after Captain Spiro refused to go any further.

Many of the little anecdotes sprinkled throughout the novel are also based on actual events, which I wove into the experience of the main characters. For example, a series of cartoon drawings by Fritz Haendel inspired the humorous story about Emil and the bucket.

There really was a piano in the dining room of the Atlantic, though I don't know if any of the passengers ever played *Wien, Wien, nur du allein* (Vienna, Vienna, you alone) like Lilly did during the voyage. In their desperate attempt to yield more fuel for the ship, the passengers destroyed it along with the rest of the furniture. The brass from the piano was indeed used as part of the payment to the British in Cyprus for food and fuel to complete the crossing to Haifa. It is also true that some passengers used their jewellery and wedding rings as payment because they didn't have any other items of value left to contribute.

If you're familiar with the words of the *Hatikva* (later to become Israel's national anthem), you may have noticed that the words the passengers sing differ slightly to the current version. These were the original lyrics, from the second verse, written by Naftali Hertz Imber:

*Our hope will not be lost,*
*The ancient hope,*
*To return to the land of our fathers,*
*The city where David encamped.*

But in 1948, after Israel's independence, these lines were changed:

*Our hope is not yet lost,*
*The hope of two thousand years,*
*To be a free nation in our land,*
*The land of Zion and Jerusalem.*

As part of my research, I travelled to Vienna and Bratislava to visit some places mentioned in the novel, and even found the locations of the Slobodarna and Patronka. That is a tale of its own. If you are interested in learning more, there is a companion ebook which you can download free of charge. This also includes behind the story details with pictures of Vienna, Bratislava and rare pictures from on board the Atlantic. For more details of how to get your copy, please visit my website: **www.sarahansbacher.com**

# ACKNOWLEDGEMENTS

I would like to give heartfelt gratitude to many people and institutes who helped me with the writing and researching of this novel.

To Kitty Schrott, Oscar Langsam, and Isaac Adler for graciously sharing their childhood memories with me, and Mickey Steiner, for relating details about his father, Fritz Steiner.

Yad Vashem in Jerusalem and the Wiener Library in London provided helpful research assistance. Special thanks to Dr. Roni Mikel-Arieli who helped me from the outset and answered many questions along the way, Anat Bratman-Elhalel of the Ghetto Fighters Archive, Yael Kaufman of the Atlit Detention Camp Database, and Rav Moshe Silberhaft for all your valuable help with my research.

For your encouragement, advice, beta reading, feedback, research help, translations, and so much more: Elana Abraham, Claire Adler, Marion Adler, Tom Gross, Hadassah Sabo Milner, Yanky Schleimer, Nadine Stark, Ben Weiss, Michelle Wellins, Rachel Woolfson, and Chen Yefet.

Anne Gordon, thank you for your incredible editing work. To Lina Erez, for the beautiful cover. And special thanks to Laura Karp, from beta reader to final eyes on the manuscript (and everything between), thank you, ayuni.

To my father, Robert Schleimer, for your guidance and encouragement.

Alon, Oren, and Itamar for your enthusiasm and understanding along the way.

Finally, to Shmuel for sharing this journey with me, every step of the way, including the research trips. Thank you for believing in me, for your support and advice, your friendship and love.

# GLOSSARY

Key: G = German A = Hebrew Ashkenazi/European pronunciation
M = Hebrew Modern and Sefardi Pronunciation

**Ach du lieber Gott!** - Oh dear God! (G)

**Alle nach links/rechts** - All to the left/right (G)

**Aron hakodesh** - Torah ark (M)

**Boruch Hashem** - Thank God (A)

**Bris/Brit mila** - Ritual circumcision (A/M)

**Chazzan** - Cantor in a synagogue (M)

**Chevra** - A group of friends (M)

**Chaverim** - Friends (M)

**Eretz** - Land - Short for the land of Israel (M)

**Gott sei Dank!** - Thank God! (G)

**Hechalutz** - A Jewish youth movement that trained young people for agricultural settlement in the Land of Israel (M)

**Ivrit** - Hebrew (M)

**Jawohl** - Yes, indeed (G)

**Jude/Juden** - Jew/s (G)

**Kibbutz** - A collective agricultural community (M)

**Kibbutznik** - A member of a kibbutz (M)

**Kiddush** - A blessing over wine at Sabbath and festival meals (A & M)

**L'chaim** - To life. A drinking toast (A & M)

**Lehitra'ot** - See you again (M)

**Liebe** - Dear (G)

**Liebling** - Darling (G)

**Machzor** - Prayer book for festivals (A & M)

**Mädchen** - Girl (G)

**Mazel tov/mazal tov** - Congratulations! (A/M)

**Mein Gott** - My God (G)

**Meine Liebe** - My love (G)

**Mein Schatz** - My sweetheart (G)

**Minyan/Minyanim** (pl) - A prayer quorum (A & M)

**Mohel** - A man trained to conduct ritual circumcisions (A & M)

**Nachat** - Pride (M)

**November Pogrom** - This was the original name for Kristallnacht - the Night of Broken Glass

**Pfui!** - An expression of disgust like yuck (G)

**Richtig** - Right (G)

**Schatzi** - Honey (G)

**Schätzchen** - Baby, sweetie (G)

**Schneller** - Quicker (G)

**Shabbos** - Saturday, the Sabbath (A)

**Shalom aleichem** - A greeting. Literally: peace to you (M)

**Shema** - A cornerstone prayer said morning and night, before sleeping, and also before someone passes away (A & M)

**Shiva** - Seven days of mourning (A & M)

**Schrecklich** - Terrible (G)

**Tallis** - Prayer shawl (A)

**Tefillin** - Phylacteries worn at morning prayers (A & M)

**Um Gottes willen!** - For heaven's sake! (G)

**Unglaublich** - Unbelievable (G)

**Wunderbar** - Wonderful (G)

# ALSO BY SARAH ANSBACHER

Ayuni

Passage From Aden: Stories From a Little Museum in Tel Aviv